MW01193615

MY FRIENDS

Also by Fredrik Backman

Fiction

A Man Called Ove

My Grandmother Asked Me to Tell You She's Sorry

Britt-Marie Was Here

And Every Morning the Way Home Gets Longer and Longer

Beartown

The Deal of a Lifetime

Us Against You

Anxious People

The Winners

Nonfiction

Things My Son Needs to Know About the World

MY FRIENDS

A NOVEL

FREDRIK BACKMAN

TRANSLATED BY NEIL SMITH

ATRIA BOOKS

New York Amsterdam/Antwerp London
Toronto Sydney/Melbourne New Delhi

An Imprint of Simon & Schuster, LLC
1230 Avenue of the Americas
New York, NY 10020

Interior design by Erika R. Genova

Manufactured in the United States of America

ISBN 978-1-9821-1282-0

To anyone who is young and wants to create something.
Do it.

The world is often unkind to new talent, new creations.
The new needs friends.

—Anton Ego

MY FRIENDS

ONE

Louisa is a teenager, the best kind of human. The evidence for this is very simple: little children think teenagers are the best humans, and teenagers think teenagers are the best humans, the only people who don't think that teenagers are the best humans are adults. Which is obviously because adults are the worst kind of humans.

It's one of the last days before Easter. Very soon Louisa is going to be thrown out of an art auction for vandalizing a valuable painting. Old ladies will shriek and the police will come and it really wasn't planned. Not to brag, but Louisa did have a perfect plan, it wasn't the plan's fault that she didn't stick to it. Because sometimes Louisa is a genius, but sometimes she isn't a genius, and the problem is that the genius and the non-genius share a brain. But the plan? Perfect.

The auction is one where extremely rich people go to buy ridiculously expensive art, so teenagers aren't welcome there, especially not teenagers with backpacks full of cans of spray paint. Rich adults have seen far too much news about "activists" who break in and vandalize famous paintings, so for that reason the entrance is protected by security guards weighing three hundred pounds with zero ounces of humor. They're the sort of guards who have so much muscle that they have muscles that don't even have Latin names, because back when people spoke Latin, idiots as big as this didn't even exist yet. But that shouldn't have been a problem, because the plan was for Louisa to get in without the guards even noticing she was there. The only problem with the plan was that Louisa was the person who was going to carry it out. But it *started* well, it has to be said, because the building where the auction is being held is an old church. We know that because all the rich people at the auction keep saying to each other: "Did you know this is an old church?" Because rich people love reminding each other about how incredibly rich they are, so rich that they can buy things from God.

In a couple of days, at the start of Easter, obviously no one in the room will spare a thought for God, because then God won't have anything interesting to sell to them. But the thing that's so incredible about God is that God understands people's needs, so there are always bathrooms in churches, so Louisa broke in through one of the bathroom windows, in full accordance with the plan. Her friend Fish taught her how to do that. Fish is the best at everything. For instance, the best at losing things, and the best at breaking things, but she is the best of all at breaking into things. And Louisa? She's bad at pretty much everything, but good at being angry. Not to brag, but she's actually world-class at that. And she's particularly angry about rich people buying art, because rich people are the worst sort of adults, and the worst way to vandalize art is actually to put a damn price tag on it. That's why rich adults hate the sort of thing that Louisa paints on the walls of buildings, not because they love walls, but because they hate the fact that there are beautiful things that are free.

So Louisa got in through the window with a backpack full of cans of spray paint and a perfect plan. When she tumbled onto the floor inside the bathroom, she stopped for a while and painted a very realistic portrait of the guards on the wall. A more shallow artist might have chosen to portray them as bulls, seeing as their necks were so thick it was impossible to tell where their heads began, but Louisa would never do that. Because she can see inside people, so she painted the guards as jellyfish. Because jellyfish, like guards, have neither backbones nor brains.

Then she put on a white dress shirt and snuck into the crowd.

It has to be said that Louisa hates many things about herself, but most of all her height and her weight. She's wished for many things throughout her childhood, but perhaps none greater than to be smaller. She doesn't like her body because there's too much of it, she doesn't like her voice because it's too deep, she doesn't like her brain because it always tells her to talk when she's nervous. Most of all she doesn't like her heart because it's always nervous. Stupid, stupid heart.

Bearing all this in mind, you might of course think that someone ought to have noticed her when she stepped into the old church, but first you have to realize that rich adults hardly ever notice anything, apart from mirrors. There are expensive paintings hanging on all the walls, each masterpiece followed by an even grander one, but the room is full of people busily trying to see their hairstyles in the reflection of their Champagne glasses. One group of cheerful women are taking photographs, not of the art, but of each other. A group of serious men are talking about their favorite paintings, not as works of art, but as investments, as if they were framed banknotes. Then the men start talking about golf instead, and the women laugh loudly at something fantastic, because everything in their lives is the best, everyone is so wonderful, and isn't it amazing that this building is an old church? Obviously none of them dares to actually talk about the paintings on the walls, they're far too frightened of accidentally thinking the wrong thing, someone else needs to think something first so they can know what they're allowed to love. One of the women returns from the bathroom and looks horrified, because someone has painted "graffiti" on the walls in there, the paint smelled and now the woman has a migraine.

"Graffiti? How awful! Vandalism!" one of the women exclaims, but one of the other women whispers:

"But . . . do you think the graffiti is part of the exhibition? Do you think it's . . . art?"

Panic spreads through the group like pee in a tent. Because what if they're wrong? The women hurry over to the men who are talking about golf to ask if it's art. One of the men asks: "Is there a price tag?"

Then the women shake their heads and laugh. No price tag, no art, oh, what a relief! The men point at the walls and talk about investments again. When they talk about the very best investment in the whole church, they point at one painting and say, "*The One of the Sea*," as if that's all it is: blue and expensive.

Angry? Louisa can't understand how she could possibly be anything else.

Around the men and women, waitstaff in white shirts circulate, serving hors d'oeuvres, because rich people love tiny food. Everything else should be big, except for taxes and sandwiches. No one looks the waitstaff in the eye, staff mean so little to rich adults that they don't even react to the fact that one of them is carrying a backpack.

Louisa moves gently through the crowd, if you've always felt too big you get pretty good at not being in the way, so it isn't until she catches sight of the painting she's looking for that she suddenly starts to panic. Because it makes her so happy, she imagines everyone else there must be able to hear her stupid, stupid heart beating in her chest. But no one reacts. Not so strange, of course, because if you're an adult, you've forgotten how that sounds.

The One of the Sea was painted by the world-famous artist "C. Jat." It's the most expensive painting in the whole auction, so everyone wants it, not for what it is, but because of its story. It is said to be the very first picture that C. Jat painted, at fourteen years old, a prodigy. That was how his career started. But the men talking about golf don't care about that, they eagerly tell the women who are drinking Champagne that the picture, most of all, is such a "damn fine investment" because of other rumors altogether. Because the newspapers say that the artist is a drug addict, that he's in such bad shape that he no longer goes out at all, so if the buyer is really lucky, he might die! Imagine what the painting would be worth then!

Everyone laughs. Louisa clenches her fists.

The painting is already expensive. So expensive, in fact, that there's a velvet rope hanging in front of it. So incredibly special that if a poor person accidentally breathed too close to it, it might be offended. Next to the rope stands a small old woman draped in diamonds, looking very unhappy, which, in her defense, is probably the only way her face can look, seeing as it has had so much plastic surgery it looks like a sneaker that's been tied too tightly.

"Here's *The One of the Sea*!" she hisses unhappily to her husband, because the painting is smaller than she had imagined. Presumably the poor thing had imagined the sea being bigger.

Her husband, an old man with a watch the size of a grown turtle and pants so tight his butt looks like it has its own butt, doesn't even look at the painting, he just reads the sign next to it to see the estimated auction price. He looks happy, because not just anyone can buy paintings like this, and that means the old man isn't just anyone. The woman says it's a shame that it isn't orange, because they have a lot of orange furnishings in the summer house this year. She says this in a tone that suggests she is also irritated that ice cream isn't more like pickles, or that doorknobs aren't more like opera—as if it is rather rude of the world not to adapt to her every wish at all times.

"Perhaps we could put it in an orange frame, Charles?" she suggests, but the old man doesn't answer, because his mouth is full of tiny sandwiches.

Louisa hates them all. The men who invest and the women who photograph, and the old woman who decorates and the old man who consumes. God, how she hates them. You have to know that, because otherwise you can't understand what a painting can do to a person.

In her backpack Louisa has, apart from cans of spray paint, her passport and an old postcard which says, in very shaky handwriting: *It's so beautiful here, the sun shines every day. Miss you, see you soon. —Mom.* You need to know that too, to understand that once Louisa has crept through the crowd and is finally standing by the rope in front of the painting that everyone else there thinks is of the sea, she is no longer standing in an old church. She isn't alone. She isn't even angry, not even with her friend Fish, who was so good at breaking into places but so bad at getting out again.

Once Fish and Louisa broke into a tattoo parlor in the middle of the night and they tattooed each other. Louisa drew a heart on Fish's upper arm, and it was the most beautiful heart Fish had ever seen. Then Fish did a tattoo on Louisa's lower arm, and it really was remarkably ugly, almost incomprehensibly hideous, because Fish was the best at almost everything, but terrible at drawing. It was a tattoo of a one-armed man in a tree, and Louisa has never loved any picture more. The first time she and Fish met, in a group foster home where no one dared to sleep, Fish had whispered jokes to her all night. Her favorite was: "How do you get a one-armed man down from a tree? You wave at him!"

No one could laugh at their own jokes the way Fish did, Louisa had never heard a better sound, or met a bigger person. Sometimes Fish broke into ice cream parlors at night, because there weren't many things she liked more than ice cream, but more often she broke into paint shops, because Louisa needed cans of spray paint. One time she broke into a hardware shop because they needed screwdrivers, but a hundred times she broke into the back doors of movie theaters so they could sneak into late-night screenings, because there weren't many things Louisa loved more than movies.

As seventeen-year-olds they would sleep next to each other almost every night in the foster home, with ice cream stains on their clothes and each other's laughter in their lungs, a chest of drawers against the door, each clutching a screwdriver in case anyone tried to get in. You get used to so many strange things when you grow up without parents, you soon get so used to having one single person who you love that it's impossible to shake the habit.

Louisa hurt, but Fish hurt more, Louisa hated reality, but Fish really couldn't stand it. Louisa tried drugs a few times, but Fish couldn't stop. Louisa was still seventeen when Fish turned eighteen and wasn't allowed to stay at the foster home any longer. Fish promised Louisa that it would be all right, but Louisa was her only good person, and after enough nights apart, Fish found other types of people. She fled from reality, down into bottles, out into the fog. Adults always think they can protect children by stopping them from going to dangerous places, but every teenager knows that's pointless, because the most dangerous place on earth is inside us. Fragile hearts break in palaces and in dark alleys alike.

Louisa has now been alone on the planet for three weeks, because that was when all the adults lied and said that Fish had committed suicide. It wasn't true. No adult missed Fish when she died, no one does if you're an orphan and grow up in ten different foster homes, it's so easy then to just blame the fact that she took an overdose of pills. But Louisa knows the truth: Fish was murdered by reality. She was suffocated by the claustrophobia of being trapped on this planet, she died of being sad all the time.

You have to know all this about Louisa, otherwise you can't understand what a painting can mean. That there is a speed at which a heart can beat that you can't remember when you've stopped being young. There is art that can be so beautiful that it makes a teenager too big for her body. There is a sort of happiness so overwhelming that it is almost unbearable, your soul seems to kick its way through your bones. You can see a painting, and for a single moment of your life, just for a single breath, you can forget to be afraid. If you've ever experienced that, you know how it feels. If not, there probably isn't any way to explain it.

Because it isn't a painting of the sea. Only a damn adult would think that.

TWO

The old woman hasn't noticed Louisa yet, that's part of the plan. For someone who's surprisingly tall, Louisa is surprisingly good at being invisible. The secret to that is knowing that you don't mean anything to anyone. That you're worthless.

The woman, who feels very important and is therefore very visible, also happens to be fully occupied at the moment, because she's just caught sight of the men and women talking about investments, so she snorts: "Look, Charles! Apparently they let anyone in here these days, even those vulgar new-money social climbers. Look at them! No taste, no style!"

She says "new money" as if it were a terrible virus, because people like her like things to be old, she wants antique furniture and vintage wine and old money. The only things that should be new are sports cars and hip joints. The richer people like her get, the fewer things they like, until eventually they become so rich that they even hate other rich people, and that's actually the only thing Louisa almost likes about them.

The woman looks at her husband in annoyance and asks: "Are you listening, Charles?"

The man replies: "Yes, yes, darling. I'm listening. We'll buy that one of the sea. What's the artist's name? 'C. Jat'? What sort of name is that? Do you think there are any more of those sandwiches anywhere?"

No one notices when Louisa opens the backpack full of cans of spray paint. No one notices when she ducks under the rope and walks closer to the painting. She will never be able to explain what she feels when she sees it. Maybe this is what it feels like to become a parent, she thinks: there are no words. *Miss you, see you soon. —Mom,* it says on the postcard in the backpack. Louisa reaches down to the bottom of the bag.

"You there! What do you think you're doing! You're not allowed to be that close to the painting!" a voice behind her suddenly exclaims.

It's the old woman, she sounds very angry but if one has a face where the skin has been pulled back until the cheeks start just behind the ears, it's hard for anyone else to know what one really feels. The woman pretty much has the emotional range of a lampshade.

That's when Louisa stops following the plan. It isn't the plan's fault, it's just that her brain sometimes gets a bit crowded with both the genius and the non-genius having to live there together. So Louisa turns around with tears in her eyes and snaps at the woman: "It isn't a painting of the sea!"

The woman quickly takes two steps back and stares at Louisa as if she has just been attacked by a piece of furniture. Did it just *speak* to her?

"Are you . . . are you completely out of your . . . Step away from that painting at once!" she commands, well on her way to fainting from the effrontery of it all.

But Louisa remains standing calmly on the other side of the rope, blinking away her tears. She whispers:

"It isn't a painting of the sea. You vulgar new-money social climber."

The woman gets so angry that she almost suffocates, so she grabs her husband so hard that he chokes on a tiny sandwich and almost suffocates as well.

"Chaaarles!" the woman howls, and the old man splutters and spits bread all over her diamonds before pointing furiously at Louisa's white shirt as if he imagines his index finger can shoot fire and thereby instantly instill fear in the world around him.

"You there! Stand still! I want to talk to your supervisor!" he commands.

It turns out, to his horror, that Louisa isn't at all afraid of index fingers, because she isn't an elevator button, so she merely replies quietly: "I don't work here."

Then she searches her backpack some more until she finally finds what she's looking for. A thin, red-colored pen.

"In that case, I want to talk to your PARENTS!" the old man demands, slightly disgusted, looking around for what he seems to be imagining are two chimpanzees holding an informational leaflet about contraception upside down.

Only then does the woman notice Louisa's backpack, and then she understands everything, because she knows all too well what young people and backpacks mean.

"Charles! She has spray paint in that bag! She's one of those *activists*! Get the guard, Charles, she's going to ruin the art!"

"Says the woman who wants to hang it in her ugly summer house . . . ," Louisa mutters.

Then she turns around, and with her thin pen she draws a tiny fish in red ink on the wall right next to the painting.

That wasn't the plan. She was really only supposed to look at the painting, she thought that would be enough. It isn't her brain's fault that now something in her heart suddenly somehow wants the painting to know that she was here. Her and Fish. Stupid, stupid heart.

The woman screams in panic and the old man hurries to fetch the guard. But it was still nice of him, that thing he said, Louisa decides. That he thought that she had parents.

See you soon. —Mom, the postcard in her backpack says. On the front is a picture of the world-famous painting by C. Jat. For as long as Louisa can remember she's wanted to see it in real life, she used to talk about it to Fish all the time, that one day they would be here together. But now? Now she can't even explain the feeling. Sometimes when she and Fish snuck into theaters they would watch movies where women tried to explain what it was like to become a mother, and they always looked just as overwhelmed and lost for words. Becoming a parent? Someone said it's an invisible tidal wave that hits you with such force that you lose your breath and never quite get it back. You spend your whole life gasping, someone else said, because it's a love so immense that it squeezes the air out of your lungs. Everyone else thinks you look like the same person afterward, a third said, but you don't understand any of it, because there's such a clear before and after. A completely new you.

That's how the painting feels, Louisa thinks. But it was still nice of that old woman, she decides, to think that Louisa was planning to ruin the artwork. As if anything could have stopped her then.

Lady, Louisa thinks, if I'd wanted to destroy the painting, this entire building would be ashes by now. I'm insanely good at destroying things, lady. Everyone I love dies.

The guard comes rushing over now, or at least lumbering, a three-hundred-pound body with a tiny, furious head perched on top. Louisa clutches the red pen tightly in her hand.

She hates it when adults touch her, that's what happens if you've never met an adult you can trust. Her dad was gone before she was born, he didn't want to be a dad, but Louisa wonders if perhaps her mom had wanted to be a mom, at least for a little while. If she had felt the tidal wave when Louisa was born. *Miss you*, the postcard says, in terrible handwriting. The only thing Louisa remembers about her mom is her voice singing a lullaby. They came from another country, Louisa remembered nothing about it. She never found out what they left behind, but it can't have been good if this place was better. When Louisa was five years old, she was left with neighbors. Her mom walked out the door and never returned. The police looked for her for a few months but she was too good at being invisible, and that was probably the only thing her daughter inherited from her. Time is a strange concept once you've been abandoned. If you're five years old when your parent leaves you, the leaving didn't happen on one particular day, it happens every day. It never stops. Louisa grew up in foster homes. She only spoke her mother's language, and when she tried to imitate the other children's languages in the foster homes, they laughed at her, or worse. For a long time after that she didn't really speak at all. She remembers that it was hard to sleep in those homes, because things kept hitting the walls, sometimes it was plates and sometimes it was glasses and sometimes it was people. Sometimes it was other people, and sometimes it was her. Nowhere lasted very long, she had to move several times, some of the foster homes were creepy, some were scary, and some were dangerous. Only one was beautiful.

She was six or seven years old then, and of course that particular home was just as full of screaming people and silent fears as all the others, but there was a fridge in one corner of the kitchen covered with postcards of famous works of art. It was her heaven. She never found out who had bought the postcards and left them there, but it was probably someone like her, someone who had passed through the home and wanted to tell the children who came after that there was a different world out there. Art is empathy.

One of the postcards was of the painting of the sea which isn't a painting of the sea. It was the first thing Louisa ever stole, the first really beautiful thing she ever touched. One day a few years later she arrived at a foster home where someone laughed, and it was Fish. They belonged to each other instantly. They slept so close at night, with screwdrivers in their hands, that if Louisa woke up and felt a heart beating in her chest, she couldn't tell if it was her own or Fish's. Fish taught her to understand all the different languages the other kids at the group home spoke, mostly all curse words of course, because when it came to cursing, Fish was truly a citizen of the world. But it was when Fish snuck them into the movies that Louisa learned to speak English like the American film stars. At night she would lie beside Fish and whisper out entire scenes from the great love stories. Still, there were a lot of words in any language she couldn't understand. One day not long after, the police rang at the door to say they had found Louisa's mom.

A child's brain is peculiar, it interprets everything in its own way. Louisa had always dreamed of this, but what the police officer said was incomprehensible. Fish had to explain: "Inform the relatives" meant that you told the people who cared. So Louisa was the relative. "Deceased" meant dead. "Substance abuse" meant her mother had drunk herself to death. Drowned from the inside. A child's brain is so imaginative, Louisa heard this but didn't grow up afraid of alcohol, just horribly afraid of swimming.

The next time they were at the movies they saw a really old film, because Fish knew that Louisa loved those best of all, and a famous singer was playing the main role. In one scene she sang a lullaby to a child and Louisa suddenly recognized it: it had never been her mother's voice she remembered, it was this. Her mother had left the five-year-old alone with the television for so many hours that in the end Louisa didn't know which voice was which, her mom's or the ones in the old films. She cried when she realized that she was a person without memories, but Fish sat beside her and said: "To Hell with that, why should your stupid brain get to decide what happened and what didn't? You can still keep that memory, it's yours!"

So Louisa kept it. Imagination is a child's only weapon. And on the back of the postcard of the painting, Louisa wrote a message, the one she would have wanted, as if she had been longed for and loved: *See you soon. —Mom.*

She put it in her backpack and thought that one day she and Fish would see that painting in real life, and maybe then it would be like when superheroes discover their powers. If she ever got to the sea, maybe she wouldn't be scared of swimming. She imagined it would be like in fairy tales, and that in some magical way everything would have a happy ending.

It won't.

But this is how her adventure begins.

THREE

So Louisa gets thrown out. That doesn't happen very often, actually, because most people who get "thrown out" are in fact led out, or perhaps dragged out. But Louisa isn't like everyone else, so she leaves the church in the air.

Right before the out-throwing in question, she paints a guard, which doesn't mean that she paints a guard on a wall, but actually paints the guard himself. Unfortunately, of course, the guard does not give the impression that he is the sort of person who appreciates symbolism of that sort, he just rushes over, as angry as a wild boar that's been given a habanero suppository, and grabs her so hard that she screams. Shortly after that he screams too.

Because Louisa really, really doesn't like it when adults touch her, so she panics, and that's when she paints the guard. In her defense, it's self-defense, because the only thing she has in her hands is the pen she used to write on the wall, so she stabs the guard's lower arm with it. He has an impressive scream, somewhere between a five-year-old who's fallen off a swing and an opera singer who's found a snake in her car. He doesn't at all appear to appreciate the irony of the fact that the pen is red and that arm is covered in the sort of cool tattooed words that guards love, so that now it looks like an angry teacher has discovered that one of those words is spelled wrong. The guard, three hundred pounds without an ounce of fun, tries instead to grab hold of Louisa again, so she jumps out of the way and snatches up the first thing she finds in her backpack: a can of spray paint. It happens to be white, and the guard happens to be dressed in black, so once she's painted him from top to bottom, he looks like a really angry highway.

When his fists finally close around her arms and lift both her and the backpack up into the air, the brutality is so abrupt that it feels like her collarbones snap like matchsticks, but that isn't what frightens her. It's the fact that he yells, "CALL THE POLICE!" to another guard that leaves her terrified. The police scare Louisa far more than violence, so when the guard carries her toward the exit, she does what every rational person would do in that situation: she bites him on the ear.

They are right by the door at the time and the guard lets out a howl, the three-hundred-pound crybaby, and throws Louisa and her backpack away from himself with such force that she actually flies out across the sidewalk, like the building is spitting out a watermelon seed.

The last thing Louisa hears is the old woman inside crying: "Did you see? She was trying to vandalize the painting! I said so the moment I saw the backpack: she's one of those activists! They only want to spoil things! Like nasty little cockroaches!"

The last thing Louisa yells back is: "It isn't a painting of the SEA, you stupid . . ."

She has a whole series of really solid insults ready for the end of that sentence, but unfortunately she lands on the pavement and has the air knocked out of her. It hurts badly, but she doesn't have time to feel how much, because the guard is already on his way after her, three hundred pounds minus half an ear.

"Call the police!" he yells to the other guard again, so Louisa snatches her backpack from the ground and runs. He runs after her, but of course he doesn't stand a chance, he's a grown man and they don't have a clue about how to run. Grown men don't have enough things they're afraid of on this planet to become good at running.

She races to the end of the block, then turns right, goes around a corner and thinks about the sea. She always does that when she's frightened, so she's thinking about the sea almost all the time. It might seem strange for someone who's seventeen and can't swim, and actually has never even left this city, because it's the sort of city that feels like it's closer to outer space than the sea. She's never even seen it. But she's memorized every inch of blue on that painting. It's her happiest place.

The postcard is in her backpack, but she doesn't need it anymore, because she will never forget what it was like to see the painting in real life. Because what all the stupid adults think is a painting of water is actually a painting of a fishing pier. It reaches out from one corner, like an outstretched tongue of concrete beneath the sky, and at the far end sit three teenage boys. They are so small that adults hardly ever even notice them. The artist called the painting *The One of the Sea*, so that's all anyone looks for. The boys in the middle are hiding in plain sight. Who can paint like that? Who can punch the lungs of someone who merely sees three kids hanging on a wall? Who can make you smell the salt water and weep over someone else's childhood?

Louisa has never met those boys, but they're her people, the only people she has left on the planet. They're maybe fourteen in the picture, possibly almost fifteen, no longer children but not yet grown-up. They're painted as if the artist saw them so intensively and dreamed them so beautifully that he learned how to whisper in color. Painted by someone who must have been completely beaten to pieces inside, because no one could hold a brush so carefully otherwise, no one could paint friendship like this without first having been a completely lonely child. It is a perfect summer day and they're sitting so close to each other, and if you look really closely you can see that they seem to be moving. They're vibrating with laughter, as if one of them has just let loose a really, really good fart.

They don't get any of that, the ignorant, useless rich people back in that old church, because they aren't in enough pain. They walk around in there, happy and content and pleased with the way the world works, so they think it's a painting of the sea. But any idiot can paint the sea, even a *happy* idiot can paint the sea! This is a painting of laughter, and you can only understand that if you're full of holes, because then laughter is a small treasure. Adults will never understand that, because they don't laugh at farts, and how the hell are you supposed to trust the judgment of someone like that with something as important as art?

They've never loved anything so much that it's worth being beaten up by a guard just to get to see it once in your life.

Louisa's face is cold with tears as she runs, but every other part of her is on fire. At the bottom of the painting she saw the artist's signature, and next to it he had drawn tiny, tiny skulls. She would never have known that if she hadn't been able to stand really close to it, just once in her life. No guard would be able to beat that out of her memory even if they tried, because now she has skulls in her whole heart.

She turns right at the next corner too, so that she ends up at the back of the old church she was just thrown out of, because the guard chasing her is just stupid enough not to think of looking there. That too is actually a completely perfect plan. She really is a genius. Except perhaps for the small detail that there's a homeless man standing by a trash can whom she doesn't see, so she collides with him at top speed and falls headfirst to the ground and knocks herself unconscious.

So okay. Maybe not a *completely* perfect plan.

FOUR

Twenty-five years ago, in an entirely different childhood, there was a big sea. The sun shone, the summer was endless, and out into the never-ending clear blue water stretched a fishing pier, and at the end of it sat the best sort of humans. They were fourteen years old, almost fifteen, and not to brag, but Louisa was right: it really was the most excellent fart. One of them let it loose and the friends almost fell into the sea with laughter. That was the moment that became the painting.

If you've had people who can make you laugh like that, you never forget it. If not, words are pointless. Either you have smelled a remarkable fart, or you become one of those adults who stands at an auction a quarter of a century later thinking it's a painting of the sea simply because the painting is called *The One of the Sea*. Adults really are out of their minds.

Those teenagers? Before they were in the painting they only existed for each other. They had one summer on that pier twenty-five years ago which felt like it was going to last forever, because that's how all summers must feel when you're about to turn fifteen, that's the age when friendship is like joining the mafia: you can't leave it, you know too much. When you're fourteen you know every corner of each other, all the weakest and most fragile places, and of course you can't be allowed to become an adult with all that knowledge, because an adult would never be able to keep secrets like that.

One of the teenagers farted and everyone laughed like crazy. If you only get a few summer days like that you're truly lucky, if you only find one friend like that you're insanely fortunate. The pier was so hot that the fourteen-year-olds had to sit on their backpacks to stop their buttocks from getting scorched, and if there were any gusts of wind, they were less cooling than a hair dryer in a crematorium. They were sweating so much that if they went for a swim, the sea ended up saltier, they were so hot that if they burned themselves on a cigarette, the cigarette would scream. And they laughed, dear God, how they laughed, because it was that sort of summer. Their last one together.

Of course it was never supposed to be a painting. The plan was never that anyone would see that signature at the bottom, "C. Jat," with the skulls next to it. There really wasn't anyone who thought that fart would become a world-famous fart, and that many, many years later it would be sold at an auction for so much money that even rich old ladies would have raised their eyebrows if they had enough movement left in their faces. The kids on the pier weren't supposed to be anything at all, they were supposed to be born poor and die poor, because that's how the world is constructed. They got into fights at school and got beaten at home, they knew exactly how a key sounds in a lock when a father comes home dangerously drunk, they knew perfectly well that they were stupid and worthless because they had been told that the whole way through their childhoods.

And that summer twenty-five years ago? They saw death in those weeks, they were chased and assaulted, they experienced more violence than the people at that art auction twenty-five years later would experience in their whole lives. You aren't supposed to have any sort of future at all if you grow up that way, you certainly aren't supposed to end up a world-famous artist, but one day that's exactly what will happen to one of those teenagers. Because in an ugly place, he was born with so much beauty inside him that it was like an act of rebellion. In a world full of sledgehammers, his art was a declaration of war.

One day one of the other teenagers, a boy named Joar, leaned over the artist's sketch pad and whispered, as if the whole thing were magic: "Who the hell can draw so you can see what it's supposed to be? You fucking alien!"

That was the closest Joar got to saying what he really wanted to say: *I love you. I hope you know that.* So the artist replied:

"Thanks."

That was the closest the artist got to saying what he really wanted to say to Joar: *I love you too. I can't live without you.*

It was Joar who found the competition that started it all. His mom used to take home the newspapers she found in the staff room of the nursing home where she worked, because at the end of the month it sometimes happened that Joar's old man had to choose between buying alcohol and buying toilet paper, so it was good to have the newspapers. The first day of summer vacation, Joar happened to read an ad in the newspaper before he wiped himself with it, and that changed everything. The following morning he stood on the pier and explained the rules of the competition, which unfortunately wasn't easy, seeing as he was surrounded by idiots.

"It's a fucking competition for young artists, and anyone can send in a fucking painting, and they hang the best fucking painting up in a fucking museum!" he explained for perhaps the seventh time, possibly the eighth. "*Now* do you get it?"

Naturally his friends understood perfectly well, sometimes they just enjoyed pretending to be idiots because it was so funny when Joar got angry.

"But . . . what do you have to paint, then?" one of them asked for that very reason.

"You can paint whatever the hell you want! You can paint a goddamn boat!" Joar groaned impatiently.

"But . . . we don't have a boat?" was the response.

"Not paint ON a boat, you moron! Paint a picture OF a boat on a . . . painting canvas! Or whatever the hell it's called!" Joar snapped.

Then the friend pretended to understand, only to exclaim:

"But I'm not much good at painting boats, Joar."

"YOU won't be doing the painting . . . ," Joar sighed, and then he finally realized that his friends were grinning, so he muttered: "Idiots, you're all idiots."

The first person to stop laughing was obviously the artist, his joy never lasted very long, his skin was too thin to keep reality out. He scratched himself all over, he always did that when he was nervous, and then he whispered:

"Can't we just forget about it, Joar? I can't paint the way you're supposed to for competitions like that, they're for fancy people with money, I can't—"

Joar interrupted impatiently:

"What do you mean, you can't? Stop that! You're a million times better than all those fucking rich kids, you just need to show them! Paint anything, paint the goddamn sea!"

Joar said it with the best intentions, it was just that no one had taught him how to make his words sound like that. He didn't want to prove to the world how good the artist was, he wanted to prove it to the artist himself. Joar was good at mending engines, because in them he could always see what was broken, but humans are full of crap you can't see. We break in the invisible parts. So Joar didn't know how to say that he loved the artist, and instead he roared:

"Just paint! Just win that fucking competition!"

"It doesn't work like that," the artist whispered, because he couldn't explain why he couldn't breathe, he didn't have words for why he was so sad that summer.

He scratched himself all over and his eyes darted about, the third boy saw it and did his best to distract the others.

"Paint the sea? Difficult," the boy said, and this time it was hard to tell if he was playing dumb or if he really was.

"How is it DIFFICULT? It's just ONE color!" Joar pointed out.

"But it's so . . . big. How would we get enough paper?" came the response.

There was a long silence before one of them started to giggle, then all of them broke down laughing. Even the artist, eventually, and when he did, not even Joar could be angry. That was how all the best things started.

They spent the rest of the day throwing stones at each other, telling stupid jokes, and swimming. Out of all the things the artist would paint for the rest of his life, Joar was the hardest, because it was never possible to paint him the way he felt about his friend. When the sun started to go down that summer day, Joar said irritably:

"You need to get away from this fucking town."

"Don't say that," the artist pleaded, but then Joar got angry:

"But you do! The rest of us are screwed, we're going to have shit lives, but not you, do you hear what I'm saying? Because you're a goddamn world-famous artist, the world just doesn't know it yet! Don't forget that when all the other bastards out there know who you are—we knew you were world-famous first!"

Not to brag, but he was right.

Then they lay on the pier and drank cheap sodas and watched the sunset for free. The summer was still endless and the world-famous artist who wasn't world-famous yet slowly moved his finger across the sky in the last of the daylight, drawing skulls in the air.

Then he asked one of the other fourteen-year-olds: "Do you think we'll all still be best friends when we're grown-up?"

Joar replied calmly: "When we're grown-up, I don't think we'll all be alive."

Not to brag, but he was right about that too.

FIVE

Louisa's head hits the ground so hard that her vision goes dark. For a moment she thinks she's dying, she's unconscious for a few seconds, for just one of those seconds she actually thinks she can hear Fish's voice from beyond the grave. Perhaps that ought to make her happy, but it just makes her angry. Because it was Fish who promised that if they could just survive their damn childhoods, everything would be okay after that. "But *you* were the one who was supposed to survive, not me, because you were the one who was good at being alone!" Louisa yells in her head, and then opens her eyes in fear and realizes that she might have shouted it out loud.

Someone hushes her, unless she imagines that? She presses her tongue against her teeth, and if she didn't know better, she'd say she had cat hair in her mouth. Then she hears the hushing again, and when she blinks up at the sky she sees the homeless man on the other side of the trash can with a finger pressed to his lips. Louisa isn't exactly great at being hushed, she really isn't, but she keeps quiet and holds her breath when she hears the security guard yell a short distance away: "You speak English? Have you seen a girl?"

Louisa sees the homeless man nod quickly and point in the other direction. The guard sighs breathlessly and turns around and runs. Or maybe "runs" is overstating it, but whatever it is, it's slightly quicker than his walking. The homeless man stands there until the three hundred pounds of muscle and zero ounces of detective skills finally disappear out of view, then the man leans over Louisa behind the trash can and smiles tentatively. He has a big red Louisa-shaped mark on his face. Their heads must have collided. Louisa remembers running hunched over, so the man must be really short. Beside him sits a ginger cat, she sees now, the homeless man's clothes are dirty, but the cat looks surprisingly clean and well-kept for a homeless cat. The man looks frightened, but the cat just looks very annoyed, as if Louisa has spilled milk over its stamp collection.

"Sorry," Louisa whispers in the English she learned from the movie stars, and tries to get to her feet, but she lurches and stumbles right into the homeless man.

When they touch, they both jerk as if from an electric shock, the man falls against the trash can, and Louisa trips over the cat. The cat really, really doesn't look happy.

"Sorry, sorry, sorry," Louisa repeats as her backside lands on the ground again.

The man gets laboriously to his feet, his hands are shaking badly and he seems to be in pain, but he smiles as if to say it's all right. The cat really doesn't look like it agrees with him. Louisa blushes with embarrassment when she sees that there's a broken box and dirty blanket behind the trash can, and realizes that she's blundered straight into the man's and the cat's bedroom.

The man looks like he'd like to help her up, but really doesn't want to reach his hand out to her, she recognizes the body language.

"You don't like it when people touch you?" she whispers.

The man shakes his head apologetically.

"Me neither," she says.

He smiles tentatively, as does she. A short silence follows, and unfortunately Louisa is very bad at silences, so she starts babbling. That's because her brain is a bit of a bully and always tells her that if everyone else is quiet, it's probably because Louisa seems so weird, so she should definitely start babbling at once! So Louisa turns to the cat and says:

"I like cats! I actually like cats more than dogs, because cats are much harder to shoot!"

Then Louisa's brain asks her why on earth she said that, and Louisa thinks it was because her brain told her to! Then her brain answers that it's precisely this kind of stuff that makes people think you're weird,

Louisa! And then Louisa feels so embarrassed that her cheeks can't hide it. It really is a bully, that brain of hers.

"I mean . . . ," she mutters apologetically to the man and the cat, "that in films, gangsters always say they're going to shoot their enemies 'like dogs.' They never say they're going to shoot them 'like cats.' Because cats would never sit still long enough . . ."

The homeless man smiles, the cat very much doesn't, but it does look like it might dislike Louisa a tiny bit less now. Louisa's brain immediately tells her to talk more, so she says:

"Plus that people who have dogs often have to stick their hands right down their throats, because dogs are always eating things that can kill them. I mean, should an animal like that really survive? You never see anyone with their hand shoved inside a cat's mouth . . ."

Louisa finally falls silent and her brain sighs in despair. The cat tilts its head and appears to be thinking of furballs. The man doesn't seem to know what to do with his hands, he looks like he's ashamed of how much they're shaking, so he puts them in his pockets. Unfortunately then his pockets start shaking, and he looks even more ashamed of that.

To his relief, Louisa doesn't appear to notice, because she's just caught sight of her backpack, the zipper must have broken when she fell and now her whole life is lying on the pavement: The passport, the cans of spray paint, pens, sketch pads, and a pack of cigarettes. Two screwdrivers. And all the clothes she could carry. It hits her so suddenly and so mercilessly that this is all she owns now, seventeen years on the planet and it fits inside one bag, that her skeleton just folds. As she slumps down in despair and starts to gather her things together, she has tears in her eyes, and when the man starts to help her, he does too. It takes a special sort of heart to feel like that about someone else's belongings.

"Thanks," Louisa whispers, embarrassment all over her cheeks as she returns the cans of spray paint to the backpack, then she adds shyly: "I didn't . . . steal anything in there, just so you know. That isn't why the guard was chasing me. I'm not a thief."

The man looks like he believes her, but the cat appears to harbor certain doubts, so Louisa goes on: "And I didn't vandalize any paintings either! That may have been what that stupid old woman was shouting, but it isn't true! I would never . . . never do that. I was only there because I love that painting. I just wanted to see it in real life, just once. I was supposed to see it with my best friend, but she died, and I . . ."

She bites her lip and her brain starts bullying her again. So she stares down at the ground and mutters some of the worst swearing the homeless man has ever heard. And that's saying something, because he's met drunken sailors and been on boats with drunks and once he heard a pregnant woman yelling at a traffic warden, a man has heard quite a few swear words then. He is therefore able to conclude that this young woman is unusually gifted. Louisa curses and curses and curses, then suddenly she starts crying so violently that her whole body shakes, because she had a completely *perfect* plan this morning, and it definitely *didn't* include her standing in an alley behind a church, crying so hard that a homeless cat gets snot on its fur.

"Sorry, sorry," she sniffs.

The cat looks a little disgusted at the thought of having to wash its fur with its tongue now. The man awkwardly gets to his feet, the knees of his pants even dirtier than before, and holds out her passport. It's open to the page with her photograph, so he can see her name and date of birth. He opens his mouth, but the sound that comes out is so quiet that it hardly sounds like words, more like the rustling of wind through leaves:

"Louisa. Nice name. Happy birthday."

Louisa takes her passport, carefully, as if it has a heartbeat. It was Fish's idea that she get a passport, even though they both knew they would never travel anywhere, because Fish said that a passport is proof that you exist. Now that Fish is gone, it feels like the only proof Louisa has left.

"My . . . birthday isn't until tomorrow," she says.

"I might not see you tomorrow," the man whispers, with kind eyes and a tender smile. She realizes that his voice doesn't sound quiet like that because he's shy, but because he's ill, it hurts him to talk. She doesn't know what to say then, and that's obviously never a good start for her brain, but in Louisa's defense, no one has ever wished her a happy birthday except for Fish. It isn't so easy to sort out all your emotions when a stranger suddenly does it. Say something smart! her brain is yelling, but instead Louisa manages to say:

"The guard said he was going to call the police! *That's* why I ran, not because I've done anything wrong!"

Her brain points out that the homeless man probably doesn't care, but suddenly Louisa cares very much what he thinks, as if it would be a comfort if at least one single person and one single cat in the whole world didn't have only negative thoughts about her. So everything just tumbles out of her:

"It's just that I . . . I've run away. I mean: I'm homeless, but not homeless the way you are, not homeless in a way that you should feel sorry for me . . . I'm homeless on purpose. I mean, I ran away from the place where I was living, so I've probably been reported missing. But I had to, because . . . it isn't a good place to sleep alone. You know? And I . . . I heard the adults talking about my best friend Fish dying, and they said it was just as well. They said she was crazy and dangerous, and that the best thing she could do for the world was to not be in it. So I had to run away, because otherwise I would have killed the idiots who said that, because Fish wasn't crazy! She was the best at nearly everything, and she was my human. She was MY human, she was my HUMAN. And now she's dead and no one even cares, no one even remembers her! So I ran, because if the police catch me, they'll send me back to the foster home because I'm a minor, reported missing. But tomorrow's my eighteenth birthday and then I won't be missing anymore, I'll just be . . . gone."

Her brain tells her over and over again that she's babbling too much, but Louisa's heart is too exhausted to listen to anything higher up now. It's one of the last days before Easter, the weather is like winter and spring are fighting over the temperature like two annoying siblings, one minute the sun is shining, the next an icy wind is finding its way through the alley and under her shirt. So she says, nodding toward the blanket and box:

"I sleep in cars, it's a bit warmer. Plus that I like the sound when you lock the doors from inside."

She feels ashamed at once, because she realizes that the homeless man can't break into cars when his hands are shaking, and besides, he might not have had a friend like Fish who taught him how to do it. Louisa feels sorry for him, she feels sorry for anyone who didn't have Fish.

The homeless man stands silently in front of her for a long time, before that rustling sound comes from his throat again, the softest voice she's ever heard: "I'm sorry."

So she whispers back sadly: "I'm sorry too. For . . . whatever has happened to you."

His eyes look moist and he sniffs, and the cat moves cautiously to the side so it doesn't get more snot on its fur. Neither Louisa nor her brain know what to do with the silence that follows, so she takes a deep breath and holds something out to him. The man takes it, surprised: a postcard.

"The painting in the picture there, that's what I broke into the church to see."

Tears are running down her cheeks, but she looks almost peaceful, or at least as peaceful as anyone can look if they've just been crying on a cat.

"I sometimes think," she whispers to the postcard, "that the artist who painted all that must have been in so much pain, but he must also have been the world's happiest person. It's like he must have felt every single feeling inside himself all at the same time, and it must have been almost unbearable, because otherwise no one would be able to paint like that. You know?"

Her brain is screaming at her that she actually seems super weird now, but it's a bit late for that, so she goes on: "Do you see the kids out on the pier? People think it's a painting of the sea, but it's actually a painting of them. And those kids . . . they're in all the artist's paintings. He never painted them again, but if you *know* they're there . . . you can sort of feel them everywhere anyway. My friend Fish and I always used to talk about going there one day. Jumping from that pier. I was going to learn to swim there!"

Those last words are barely audible over her sobbing. The homeless man looks as if he'd like to hug the postcard as compensation for the difficulty he feels hugging people. He hands it back carefully, but Louisa shakes her head.

"You can keep it," she says.

Because she's seen the real thing now. It's in her brain and her heart forever, no one can take it from her.

"I always think that those kids were poor, like me. But now the artist's paintings get sold for millions, so now he's world-famous and really rich and doesn't have to be afraid of anything anymore," Louisa mumbles, as if trying to hide her envy.

The man looks very envious too, holding on to the postcard. Louisa gets the pack of cigarettes out, Fish was really the one who smoked, but she puts one in her mouth anyway. She offers the pack to the man, and he takes one, very hesitantly. Louisa can't help thinking that's a kind thing to do, taking the risk of getting lung cancer out of sheer politeness.

"Do you smoke?" she asks.

He shakes his head amiably.

"Good," Louisa says, "because I don't have a lighter."

Since Fish died, she just likes holding cigarettes, feeling them between her lips sometimes. Just as she's about to explain that to the man, she sees that his hands are shaking so badly that he can barely hold his. So she asks, in a voice as full of sympathy as it is of curiosity:

"Are you an alcoholic? Is that why you're shaking?"

The man says nothing for so long that she's about to apologize, but then his head moves slowly from side to side and he replies:

"No, no, I don't drink. I . . . spill nearly all of it."

It takes so long for Louisa to realize that this is a joke that her laughter comes out twice as hard. She hasn't laughed like that since Fish was still here. The man looks so happy at having been the cause of that wonderful sound that the next joke comes almost without effort:

"It's . . . it's no laughing matter, I lost my job because . . . because of this."

"What job did you do?" Louisa asks, surprised.

"Tambourine thief," he smiles.

Oh, how she giggles. Oh, oh, oh. The best sound in the world. She waves her hand in the air and exclaims:

"Is that why you don't smoke? Because you always stub your cigarette out by mistake? Are you really homeless, or do you just keep losing your keys?"

Oh, oh, oh, how he chuckles at that. Louisa wishes she could say something else just as funny, but her brain is useless, so instead she says:

"Are you ill?"

He nods, but without sadness.

"Yes."

"Are you . . . dying?" she asks, because he actually looks like he is, as if he might get blown apart if the wind changes direction.

He nods again, but he only looks sad because she looks sad. With a voice full of solace, the man says, out of nowhere:

"Life is long, Louisa. Everyone will tell you that it's short, but they're lying. It's a long, long life."

She can barely keep her balance, hearing that. It's honestly quite a lot to take in from a stranger all in one go, isn't it? Particularly when you haven't spoken to a single human being at all for a very long time. She puts on her backpack just so she can hold on to the straps, so she knows what to do with her hands, and then she looks down at the ground and mumbles:

"My friend Fish couldn't handle being alive. She was hurting too much. But I think I'd like to try, to be alive."

The homeless man nods proudly, and Louisa might be imagining it, this surely wouldn't be the first time, but she can't help thinking that the cat looks a little proud as well.

She doesn't say good-bye, she isn't good at that, so she just raises her hand, and the one-armed man in the tree on her lower arm looks like he's waving. But just as she's turning away, the homeless man suggests:

"Would you . . . would you like to paint something?"

She looks back over her shoulder in surprise, and the man makes a gentle but grandiose gesture toward the back wall of the church, as if it were his living room. Louisa doesn't know what to do, no one apart from Fish has ever asked her paint anything. How can you say no to that?

So Louisa stops and paints. She shrugs off her backpack and uses up almost every single can of spray paint. She paints small hearts and fish that feel no pain. She paints cockroaches, like that stupid old woman in the church called her, but she paints the cockroaches so they are beautiful. So beautiful that their beauty is an act of vengeance. Then she paints jellyfish in guards' uniforms, and the homeless man smiles so widely at that that he almost falls over.

He tentatively reaches for the can of spray paint she's holding, and Louisa looks so surprised when he gently takes it from her hand, without touching her skin. Then he paints, with trembling fingers, and the fact that Louisa is still standing when he's finished is actually quite remarkable. Because her heart has left her body by then.

He paints skulls.

SIX

Twenty-five years ago, the summer he would turn fifteen, the artist painted skulls everywhere. First with his fingertips in the air, then with a pencil in his sketch pad, and finally next to his name when he signed the painting which would become world-famous. Only his friends would ever understand what a miracle it was, not that the painting became famous but that it was ever finished at all. That something so great came out of a boy who thought so little of himself.

Because obviously the whole idea was no good, the boy thought. He couldn't paint, he knew that. The only thing he was good at was running. He had grown up in a neighborhood where children's heads spin like owls' to avoid threats, he went to a school where fights broke out in the blink of an eye, where every recess was about hiding and where everything that could be used as a weapon was bolted to the floor of the hallways and classrooms. Stress was the normal state of his body, and that makes you good at running, because you practice every day.

But art? What the hell did he know about art?

When he ran, his friend Joar was always beside him, but always looking over one shoulder, because Joar wanted to make sure he was the one who got hit if anyone caught them. Unlike the artist, Joar was good at fighting, that happens if you get beaten a lot, and Joar was beaten so much at home by his old man that it was a miracle he still had a skeleton. Whenever Joar got teased at school for being short, the artist always thought that if only they all knew just how put down he had been by that evil man, they would have thought it was a miracle that Joar had grown at all.

The artist? He was good at seeing the beauty in everything, that happens if you're no good at seeing it in yourself. He didn't belong in school, he didn't belong in this town, he didn't belong in his own body. He had cried so much that spring when he was fourteen that he felt hollow. Everyone thought he was insecure simply because he was so quiet, but that was never the problem. It was the things he was absolutely certain of that were the problem: Certain that he was worthless. Certain that his friends were wrong about him. Certain that he was going to disappoint everyone.

But his friends? All they wanted was to make him laugh. Sometimes they succeeded with silly jokes, sometimes with almost-smart jokes, but most often just by running next to him across the whole town, all the way down to the pier, until they were so out of breath that they couldn't think straight. Then they competed to see who could jump into the sea first, and the artist tore his clothes off as he ran and was just about to leap off the edge when a voice behind him yelled: "WATCH OUT!"

He stopped midstride and turned around.

"Watch out when you jump so you don't miss the sea, losers!" Joar yelled as he rushed past his friends and jumped in first.

In his defense, he needed the head start to win: not to be mean, but Joar was the shortest in the group, and he definitely wasn't the fastest. Someone once said he was "two apples tall," but they sure as hell weren't big apples. Even so, he was the bravest and strongest of them all, he may have had the smallest hands but he always had the biggest fists. Whenever Joar left a room, it felt as if twenty people had walked out. If you took your eyes off him for a moment he would already have rushed off, throwing himself into a fight with someone twice his size, or jumping off a cliff that no one else dared jump from with a triumphant cry.

The artist didn't know it then, but that was how he would eventually paint Joar in the picture: his outline blurred, as if you were always on the point of losing him. In the fullness of time the artist would find a way to paint laughter, make everything beautiful, because that was how he wanted to remember those days when they were fourteen. Because there was beauty too.

As an adult, the artist would recognize that the whole of that summer had been full of violence. Full of funerals. When August came, the friends would be different people. By then, Joar would have seen his mother get beaten up for the last time and decided to kill his old man. The summer started and ended with death.

But in between?

In between, the summer managed to be plenty of other things too. It managed to be love and friendship, miraculously loud laughter and magnificently stupid decisions. They put fireworks in mailboxes, rode shopping carts down the steepest hill in town and tried to dry wet socks in a toaster, because what else are you supposed to do when you're fourteen? Die of boredom?

More than anything else, that summer managed to become that painting, and that was how the adventure began for the boy who went on to become the artist "C. Jat." He would often try to think that perhaps that has to be the case: that our teenage years have to simultaneously be the brightest light and the darkest depths, because that's how we learn to figure out our horizons.

The artist would remember being fourteen as feeling like he was always homesick, because he realized as an adult that that was what the emptiness in his chest was: some of us are born in the wrong place, the whole of our childhood is like being shipwrecked on a desert island, we ache with homesickness without knowing what home is yet. That's all childhood friends are, people stuck on the same island. If you find a single one of them, you can cope with almost anything.

So one day in June, the artist whispered: "I can try to paint . . . the sea."

"Good!" Joar replied happily, because he didn't know how to say the truth, that he had seen the pills in the artist's backpack and the cuts on his wrists.

Joar didn't know how to whisper, *You can paint whatever the hell you like, as long as you paint, I'm just scared I'll lose you if you don't.* The artist had no words either, because he didn't know how to explain to Joar that his anxiety made him feel like he was drowning. That he was so scared that if he held on to his friends' hands, he would drag them down into the darkness with him.

They knew each other without words, and sometimes that was unbearable. One day the teenagers would sit in a painting, but that day they were sitting on the edge of a pier, in the longest silence any of them could ever remember existing between them. That was why it was so liberating when one of them suddenly farted.

That laughter? It was a miracle that they didn't break their ribs, all of them. They all yelled, "IT WASN'T ME!" at the same time, and then they all pointed accusing fingers at each other, and then they jumped, one by one, into the water. How could the sea be big enough to have room for their hearts? Incomprehensible.

When, eventually, they were floating on their backs next to each other, the artist turned to Joar and asked:

"Did you mean what you said? That you don't think we'll all be alive when we're grown-up?"

It was a cloudless, wind-free day, the sea hugged them, and Joar smiled back sadly:

"*You'll* be alive. Not all the rest of us, but you'll be alive, because you're going to live forever."

Not to be mean, but he was wrong.

SEVEN

Twenty-five years later, the world-famous artist C. Jat is standing in an alleyway behind a church with his shaking fingers clenched around a can of spray paint, dying. It would take a huge amount of imagination to think anything else. Everyone dies, of course, every single person, but very few get to understand that they're dying. That's why the artist doesn't want people to know that he is, that's why he's hiding from the world, because when it comes to death, the living are pretty crazy. They don't want to see anyone who's ill, they don't even want to think about illness, and if they absolutely have to, they sigh and say things like: "Oh, it reminds you not to take life for granted!"

Not to be mean, but healthy people aren't quite right in the head, the artist thinks. Surely taking life for granted is the whole point of being here, because what else are we doing? We're a bunch of lonely apes on a rock in the universe, our breath consists of eighty percent nitrogen, twenty percent oxygen, and one hundred percent anxiety. The *only* thing we can take for granted is that everyone we have ever met and everyone we have ever known and everyone we have ever loved will die. So how great must our imaginations be for us to even summon up the enthusiasm to get out of bed each morning? Endless! Imagination is the only thing that stops us from thinking about death every second. And when we *aren't* thinking? Oh, those are all our very best moments, when we're wasting our lives. It's an act of magnificent rebellion to do meaningless things, to waste time, to swim and drink soda and sleep late. To be silly and frivolous, to laugh at stupid little jokes and tell stupid little stories. Or to paint big paintings, the biggest you can manage, and to try to learn to whisper in color. To look for a way to show other people: this was me, these were my humans, these were our farts. These were our bodies, and they were small, far too small, because they couldn't contain all our love.

That's all of life. All we can hope for. You mustn't think about the fact that it might end, because then you live like a coward, you never love too much or sing too loudly. You have to take it for granted, the artist thinks, the whole thing: sunrises and slow Sunday mornings and water balloons and another person's breath against your neck. That's the only courageous thing a person can do.

"I . . . I . . . I," says the seventeen-year-old girl in front of him in the alleyway behind the church.

The artist regrets admitting to her that he is ill. He feels sorry for her when he sees that she feels sorry for him, because there's no cause for that at all. He's almost forty years old and he's lived a long life, remarkably long, and anyone who says otherwise is a liar. He has seen the world, fallen in love on white beaches, danced to loud music on warm nights, and wasted slow mornings under soft sheets. He has painted and giggled and sung. All the things he never dared dream about when he was fourteen and had cuts on his wrists and pills in his backpack. He has lived, dear Lord, how he has lived.

"I love the way you paint, especially the cockroaches," he therefore says to the girl in front of him, blinking happily at the wall like he's just woken up.

Louisa, who has just realized who he is, sniffs back:

"I . . . I love the way you paint too! You . . . you're the whole reason I paint at all!"

This is honestly a few too many feelings for her to feel all at the same time. She's already had quite a complicated day as it is, you aren't really in a fit state to meet your idol under circumstances like that. The cat suddenly rubs against her leg, which would probably have been a very tender sign of affection if she didn't suspect that it was trying to use her pants to rub the snot off its fur.

"I'm not your reason, no one is your reason, your art is your own," the artist protests gently.

Louisa gasps for air. She has a million questions which she will never have time to ask. Perhaps that doesn't matter, the artist probably wouldn't have had any good answers anyway, adults are always a lot more useless than teenagers hope. But unfortunately the artist never gets the chance to disappoint Louisa, because at that moment they hear the sirens. They hear the security guard yell, "She's down there in the alley!" and the clatter of ugly shoes with uncomfortable soles echoes so loudly in the alley that they can hardly hear their own thudding hearts. They hear other shouts too, from police officers, and then the artist suddenly starts laughing. Because, of course, what's the alternative? Not taking it all for granted?

"Run," he tells her, perfectly calmly.

"What?" Louisa gasps, panic-stricken.

The artist flashes her a happy, grateful grin.

"Run, Louisa! I hope you learn to swim. I hope you paint every single wall from here to the sea. Now, run!"

He hands her the can of spray paint he had borrowed, shaking all the way from his fingertips to the end of his nose.

"But . . . what about you?" she manages to say, but his grin is so wide that his ears ought to watch out.

"I'm afraid I can't run fast anymore," he whispers, before adding: "But don't worry. What are the police going to do with me? I'm world-famous, didn't you know?"

She's breathing fast, the way you do when the biggest moment of your life is also one of the most embarrassing.

"Sorry . . . sorry I didn't recognize you," she says, looking at the can in his hand, then pleads with a sob: "Can you keep that? So you can give it back to me the next time we meet? I'll come back here to look for you!"

The world-famous artist nods.

"Don't hurt yourself!" he makes her promise, and that's the most loving thing any adult has ever said to her.

The police come around the corner and she hesitates for just a moment, tears dripping down the collar of her shirt, but then she turns and runs. The artist will never give the can of spray paint back, she will never get the chance to tell him what he really meant to her. It doesn't matter, he's with her everywhere now, on every wall.

Life? It's long.

When Louisa's backpack disappears from view around the corner, the artist stands and thinks about a pier under a cloudless sky. About being fourteen and floating on your back in the sea and starting to laugh so hard that you roll over and almost drown. Louisa said she thought the artist was world-famous and really rich and never had to be scared now. She got two out of three right, which isn't bad. But he's always been scared, scared of everything.

He often thinks about the critics who, when he was young, said his art had no value and that he would never amount to anything. When he became famous, he often wished that they had been right. He thinks about how success accelerates everything in your world, and how his heart could never keep up. He thinks about the incredible fame and the unbelievable amounts of money and the constant panic attacks. He thinks about being best in the world at disappointing everyone, because it so quickly becomes impossible to say no to people who are always reminding you of how grateful you should be. He thinks about paintings he left all his breath in, which were then sold for so much money that old men and women no longer even hang them on their walls, they keep them in bank vaults. He thinks about gallery exhibitions where everyone loved him, because that's how they make you feel, that's the trap. He thinks about the men who looked at his pictures with dollar signs in their eyes and asked: "How many of those do you think you can squeeze out in a year?" He thinks about the women who said, "Your pictures really *speak* to me!" and then talked about the furnishings in their summer houses. He thinks about the unavoidable question from all these people: "Where do you get your *inspiration*?"

The artist never dares to look anyone in the eye when he gets asked that. He's never been able to explain that all his paintings are an attempt to show how beautiful he wishes he actually was. He's dreamed of being able to say: "Being human is to grieve, constantly." Because what he really wants to know is: "How the hell do all the rest of you cope?"

Sometimes he wants to yell that everything he paints is about one of his humans dying, can't everyone see that? His best human died, and he can't stop feeling sad, he's sad all the time, sad everywhere. He feels like telling the old men and women who spend fortunes on his paintings that he saw so much violence when he was young that he still feels it on his skin, as if he might get bruised just from existing. Sometimes his nails and eyelashes and hair hurt so much that he scratches himself all over until he bleeds. He hates loud noises. He doesn't like anyone to touch him. He takes pills to sleep, other pills to stay awake, he drinks too much alcohol. Sometimes he cries so much he throws up. There's something very wrong with him, he wants to say, and the only time he doesn't hate himself is when he's painting. That's the only time he ever feels like himself. That's what he wants to explain when they ask about his inspiration, but obviously he can't, because not even women who like pictures that speak to them want to hear that sort of thing in their summer houses. It would be extremely impolite when one has been so very expensive. So instead the artist always just whispers: "I don't know."

Year after year after year. "I don't know." He got more and more expensive, and more and more sensitive, until his heart was made of paper, and tore a little more at the edges when he opened his eyes each morning. Everyone he met said he ought to be so grateful, because his life was every artist's dream, and he felt ashamed, as if he had grabbed the wrong coat from a cloakroom and was wearing someone else's dream. Because all he dreamed about was not being recognized in the street, and not being adult, and about lying on a pier with his best friends and drinking sun-warmed sodas and reading superhero comics. About being no one at all alongside his very best no ones.

You need to know all that about him, because otherwise you can never understand what's happening to him now. What paintings on a church wall can do. That there is a speed at which a heart can beat that you can't remember when you've stopped being young, art that is a joy so overwhelming that you almost can't bear it. How sad it must be, the artist thinks, what an immense loss for anyone who never gets to experience this.

It's one of the last days before Easter, winter and spring are fighting for everything that's alive, the artist is thirty-nine years old and dying. The only people who know that are Louisa and one other person. Well, Louisa and one other person and one cat. The artist hears the police officers behind him, but he doesn't feel scared, he just looks at the paintings on the wall and thinks:

What a lovely day.

The first police officer grabs him by the shoulder, and he really doesn't mean to paint the police officer, but the artist's body is so weak that he loses his balance and accidentally points the can of spray paint upward. The paint happens to be pink, and police uniforms happen to be blue, so when the can finally falls from the artist's hand, the police officer looks like confetti on a giraffe's tongue. The artist hardly feels himself being wrestled to the ground, he hits his head, scraping his forehead so badly that it starts to bleed. The police officers don't see a world-famous artist, they just see a homeless man who has defaced a church. That was half true, of course, because he didn't have a home. He had a huge apartment full of beautiful things until very recently, but he sold everything to buy something else. That was what the box was for, the one Louisa saw behind the trash can. But the artist wasn't dirty because he was sleeping outside, as Louisa thought, he was only dirty because a fairly crazy girl had collided with him and he had landed on the ground, and the ground happened to be made of dirt. It wasn't his blanket lying beside the trash can, and it wasn't his cat either.

It isn't even a homeless cat, in fact, it has a perfectly excellent home in an affluent part of town where it is very spoiled, it is very much a middle-class cat. It just happens to enjoy sneaking out and living a different life as well, drifting around town all night in the company of artists, looking for adventure and getting its fur dirty. Some cats are just like that.

When the police officers pick the man up from the ground, he's like a rag in their arms, he seems to be hanging lifeless, the police officers shout something but are suddenly drowned out by a panic-stricken cry from another man. He's slim and well-dressed, with glasses and thinning, neatly combed hair, and he's just come rushing out from the art auction in the church. He comes round the corner just in time to see the girl disappear at the other end of the alley. When the artist's body slides out of the police officers' grasp, the well-dressed man rushes forward and catches him.

"What are you *doing*? Don't you know who this *is*?" the man snaps, angry and distraught in equal measure.

They aren't the most art-interested police officers in the world, they really aren't, so they shrug their shoulders in a mildly affronted way. To be fair, there are an awful lot of famous people on the planet nowadays, so many that there hardly seems to be anyone who isn't famous anymore.

"He was painting graffiti," one of the officers mutters.

"Are you mad? He's sick! He *definitely* hasn't been painting . . . ," the well-dressed man bellows confidently, but then he sees the skulls on the wall and stops himself, lets out a deep sigh, and mumbles uncertainly: "Okay, hold on, those are definitely . . . his."

Then he looks down at the body in his arms, the artist has lost so much weight to illness that the man could easily have lifted him up. The man whispers sadly: "What happened? I leave you alone for an hour and you get yourself beaten up by the police?"

The artist's eyes are closed but when he recognizes the man's voice, he leans his head close to his chest and gasps: "Don't let them catch her, Ted! She's one of us!"

EIGHT

The cat? Obviously it runs off when the police arrive. Cats may not know much about prison, but this one knows enough, it's an outdoor cat and has no intention of becoming a locked-up cat. Besides, it knows that people will like the man more when they find out he's a world-famous artist, but they'll like the cat less when they find out it isn't homeless. We want to look up to men, but we'd prefer to feel sorry for cats, that's how the world works. So the cat decides it's probably just as well to go home and have dinner now, and wanders off to the other end of the alley, and that's the last time it sees the artist. Animals don't have telephones that ring at dawn, they're very lucky, they never find out that they've lost someone. But at the end of the alleyway the cat stops very briefly, looks around, and runs its tail through the paint on the wall, which hasn't quite dried, and if you didn't know better you'd swear that it had tears in its eyes.

Louisa? She runs until her throat feels like it's about to burst from lack of oxygen and happiness. Just once, she got to paint a wall with her idol, paint with her whole being, and it was incredible that the building was still standing afterward, that her hammering chest hadn't smashed every brick. She runs so far that evening that when she finally breaks into a parked car to sleep, she passes out on the back seat as soon as she's locked the doors. She hasn't slept so deeply since Fish was sleeping next to her.

The artist? He sleeps too, dreaming about a summer and a boy. When he wakes up in the hospital later that night he blinks against the bright light, and can only make out the outline of the well-dressed man in the chair next to him. The artist whispers hopefully:

"You're . . . here?"

The well-dressed man, whose name is Ted, takes his hand tenderly and leans closer, waits patiently until the artist recognizes him. Then the artist whispers:

"Sorry . . . I thought you were Joar, just for a moment . . ."

"I know," the man named Ted says sadly, because the artist says Joar's name in his sleep every night.

The two men have known each other forever, almost their whole lives. If you have loved anyone as much as Ted loves the artist, so much that you're prepared to be mistaken for someone else just to see your friend's face light up for a couple of seconds, then you know what he feels. Otherwise there's probably no way to explain.

"Are we in a hospital?" the artist wonders, looking around the room in confusion.

"Yes," Ted nods.

"Not the police station?"

At this Ted tries to conceal his irritation, not entirely successfully.

"The police thought you were homeless! They thought you were a vandal! What were you even thinking? If I hadn't heard the shouts from the alley—"

The artist interrupts him with a weak voice that's barely more than a gasp: "Did she get away?"

Ted throws his arms up in despair.

"The girl in the alley? Yes, I saw her run off, the police were all busy with you."

"Good, good," the artist smiles, blinking slowly, like an exhausted child declaring that they absolutely, most definitely, aren't remotely tired at all.

"This was on the ground. Is it hers?" Ted wonders, pulling the postcard out of his pocket.

"Yes, yes," the artist whispers unhappily, running his fingers over it.

Ted can hardly bear how slight his friend has become, with his sunken face and almost transparent skin, like thin ice over death. The eyes are all that's left of the person he used to be, the illness has aged his body to that of an old man, but the eyes are still those of a mischievous little kid: playful and loving and dazzling and entirely impossible not to fall in love with.

"What happened? What were you doing in that alley?" Ted asks tenderly as he tucks the artist in.

The artist's fingers trace the bump on his forehead and he thinks for a few moments, then whispers: "I just wanted to see if I could still jump in the sea and miss the water."

He laughs so hard he starts to cough, Ted doesn't look remotely amused, perhaps because he knows how much Joar would have laughed.

"We agreed that you were going to wait in the café at the train station! I leave you for an hour, and you manage to get yourself beaten by the police?" Ted grunts.

The artist brightens up and exclaims:

"Yes! Isn't that great? Like being young again!"

He starts coughing again.

"It isn't funny," Ted says seriously.

"It's a bit funny," the coughing man insists.

"This was all *your* idea! I was going to go to the auction and you had one job: to stay at the station and not draw attention to yourself. How do you think that went?"

The artist breathes deeply through his nose and for the first time looks a little ashamed.

"I know, I know, I just got it into my head that I wanted to see the painting against a big, white wall one last time. I was just going to sneak into the auction for a little while, but the guard wouldn't let me in. He had no idea who I was!"

He says this last sentence with a happy grin. Ted sighs so hard that his spine creaks. The artist's illness means he no longer looks like himself, which is at least a small consolation for a dying man who has always hated being famous.

"So what were you doing in the alley, then?" Ted asks again.

"I went round the back of the church to see if there was a window I could crawl in through, like we did when we were fourteen."

"You're not fourteen anymore."

"What do you mean? Of course I am! So are you!" the artist laughs, then asks: "By the way, what happened to the cat?"

"What damn *cat*?" Ted exclaims wearily, because how much can one person manage to get up to when he's left alone for an *hour*?

"I made friends with a cat," the artist whispers proudly.

"You drive me crazy," Ted groans.

"It isn't very nice to be angry with someone who's dying," the artist teases, and is immediately punished with another fit of coughing.

"I'm angry because you're not taking this seriously," Ted snaps, far more angrily than he intends.

"Oh, I'm taking it seriously, Ted. I'm just not afraid. It's been a long life," he replies, like he has so many times before.

"No," Ted whispers, moist-eyed.

Because it's been a painfully short life, the blink of an eye, a single summer's day. Ted's chest hurts, like crying without oxygen, because grief does so many strange things to people, and one of those things is that we forget how to breathe. As if the body's first instinct is to grieve itself to death. Soon Ted will stand up and discover that he's forgotten how to walk too, that happens to us all when the love of our life falls asleep for the last time, because when the soul leaves the body, evidently the last thing it does is tie our shoelaces together. In the weeks following the death we trip over thin air. It's the soul's fault.

"It's been a long life," the artist insists. "It's been . . ."

He tries to say something else but is cut off by such a violent fit of coughing that his thin frame shakes. Ted is struck by the panic of love and just wants to help.

"Drink some water! Look, the nurses left some food! Eat your vegetables!"

The artist laughs through the coughing and wheezes:

"Vegetables? Do you really think that will make any difference now?"

It's a joke, but that doesn't help, because now Ted's whole chest is shaking. The artist hasn't seen him this desperate in twenty-five years. The artist wants to comfort him, but there's no point, ever since they lay on that pier the year they turned fifteen, Ted has been terrified that everyone he loves will die. Sooner or later he'll be proven right.

"Don't be sad," the artist smiles.

He considers saying that it's actually Ted's fault, because if you live as healthily as Ted does, you only have yourself to blame if you're the last one left. But this doesn't feel like the right moment.

"Don't concern yourself with what I might be feeling!" Ted snaps.

This isn't the first time he's been sitting beside a hospital bed, the artist has been dying for a long time, just very slowly. Now it's happening mercilessly quickly. He's stopped taking his medication, it doesn't help anymore, he's decided that he's had enough. He isn't remotely scared, and it's hard for Ted not to be angry about that. "A long life," the artist keeps saying, but obviously that isn't true. Because Ted could end up living until he's eighty, a whole extra life, without him! It's so hard not to be angry with yourself then, impossible, when all you want to do is cry out: "You have to live, for me."

"On my gravestone I want you to put: 'Enter from other side,'" the artist whispers, because he knows jokes like that drive Ted mad.

"Be quiet," Ted mumbles.

"Or 'Here lies a man who ate his vegetables but died anyway,'" the artist suggests.

He starts coughing so badly that the nurses come rushing in, thinking that he's dying. Ted grunts wearily:

"Don't worry, he's just laughing at his own jokes. There's nothing wrong with his lungs, it's his brain . . ."

Then one of the nurses laughs too. She tucks the artist in, pats him on the cheek, and walks toward the door but seems to change her mind, then changes it once more. She turns around carefully and says softly:

"My husband loved your work. We saw some of your paintings in a gallery once. I loved the way he looked when he was looking at them."

"Thank you," the artist whispers.

"We should be thanking you," she replies.

She could have asked him for an autograph, it would have been the artist's last, she could have sold it for a lot of money. But that would never have occurred to her.

When she has closed the door softly behind her, the artist whispers to Ted:

"I'm sorry my death is so unexciting. If I could have made it a bit more spectacular, the price of my paintings would have gone up. Was a heroin overdose really too much to ask? Or getting murdered?"

When Ted doesn't reply, because he's so angry, the artist tries to give him a pillow and suggest that it isn't too late for that last idea. Ted rolls his eyes. Then he nods toward the box in the corner of the room and says, as if it ought to make the artist feel a bit embarrassed:

"You haven't even asked if I did what you asked me to do. But the answer is yes. I bought it, and it was ridiculously expensive. It cost all you had."

The artist nods gratefully, without a trace of regret.

"Good. Artists are supposed to die poor."

Ted looks at him sternly for a long time before he mutters:

"Easy for you to say, I'm the one who's going to have to pay for the cremation."

Ted makes jokes so rarely that the artist isn't at all prepared for his own laughter this time. When the nurse comes running back in, Ted has to confess that this time he was actually the one being funny. The nurse looks suspicious, like she doesn't believe him. She leaves the door slightly ajar.

"Can I see it?" the artist whispers when they're alone again.

Ted nods resignedly and gets up, then carefully lifts the world-famous painting out of the box. There's a small framed map of emergency exits and escape routes on the hospital wall, so Ted takes that down and hangs up the painting instead, seeing as escape routes are now surplus to requirements. When he turns around, the artist is lying in the bed looking at his own artwork, and crying, crying, crying.

Ted takes his hand gently and promises: "On your gravestone I'm going to write: 'I love you and I believe in you.'"

"I love you and I believe in you too," the artist smiles, resting his head heavily on Ted's arm.

Ted looks at the painting, at himself on the pier, side by side with his best friends that last summer they were children. Then he looks at the signature in the bottom corner, the skulls the artist always drew next to his name, and says:

"I saw the skulls on the wall today. That's the first time you've painted them in . . . I don't know . . . years?"

"I didn't know I'd missed them so much," the artist replies, wearily but happily, like a five-year-old after a long day with a new playmate.

"Who was that girl in the alley?" Ted wonders.

The artist smiles excitedly.

"Her name is Louisa! Her best friend was called Fish! Louisa has run away, she's gone missing, but she turns eighteen tomorrow, so then she'll just be gone instead. She sleeps in cars. And she paints so that . . . so that . . . did you see the wall, Ted? She painted so that . . . so that the roofs blew off the buildings."

The corners of Ted's mouth tremble when he admits: "I've been longing to see you paint skulls again."

The artist blinks calmly: "It's Easter, and a girl who was being chased appeared, and she was nice to a homeless man in an alleyway . . . and she painted a church. It would take less to make you start to believe in God, Ted."

"Yes," his friend agrees reluctantly.

"Don't cry for me, Ted. I got to experience everything. It's been a long, long life, and at the end of it I got to see something unbelievably beautiful."

Ted nods disconsolately. "That girl's paintings?"

"No. You. I got to see you."

Ted's ears are ringing as he lays his forehead against the edge of the artist's bed. Afterward it will feel as if this went on for several days, because that's how death sounds. Once upon a time, church bells used to ring for the dead, now it's telephones, and the more they ring, the more important the person was. When a world-famous artist dies, phones ring on every continent, people talk about him on the news, people who have never met him cry. Art is so big, so unfathomable, that it teaches us to mourn for strangers.

Early tomorrow morning even the most serious critics, even those who have never written a kind word about the artist's paintings, will whisper "Oh no" into their phones when they hear what has happened. And Ted has to forgive them, because in grief we are reminded that we're human beings. In life we might be enemies, but when faced with death, we see the truth: we are one species, all we have is each other, and where you go, I shall follow.

Strangers' phones will ring all around the world, but perhaps most of all the artist's own phone will ring, endlessly, in the darkness, because Ted will call his number again and again. That's the very hardest thing to understand about death: nothing. That the world shrinks without him, because instead of him there is just emptiness. The vibration of his laughter, the smell of his skin, his phone number. How can someone who meant everything to Ted become . . . nothing at all? It's the incomprehensibility of death that drives people mad, so that we forget how to breathe and how to walk, until we spend whole nights stumbling about in dark rooms, calling and calling, trying to understand how there can be a phone number that no longer belongs to anyone.

The artist in the bed closes his eyes and has so little strength left in his voice that Ted has to read his lips: "Write on the gravestone: 'Does this coffin make me look fat?'"

It's been a long, long life, and at the end of it the artist manages to make someone he loves laugh out loud, so that every single wall sings. It would take less to make you believe in God.

If any of the nurses hurrying past in the corridor see what Ted does next, they're merciful enough to pretend they haven't noticed. The almost-forty-year-old man gets up carefully onto the bed. Four hands lace their fingers together, their bodies so close that when one man falls asleep, he does so with the other's tears on his lips. There Ted lies beside the love of his life, and the love of his life isn't afraid, or angry, or even lying in a hospital bed anymore. He is lying on a pier in the sun, with salt water on his skin and Ted's kisses on his eyelashes.

So a world-famous artist falls asleep, and soon telephones are ringing everywhere, soon they are talking about him on the news, at daybreak his death will belong to everyone and everything. But for a very short while that night in that hospital room, it only belongs to Ted. A soft little exhalation through the stubble of his beard, one final little beat of his heart, and then the world is smaller.

The very, very last thing the artist whispers is: "Find Louisa. Give it to her."

NINE

Louisa wakes up on her birthday in one of the strangest ways you can wake up: by noticing that her bed is moving. She blinks up at the ceiling and walls in confusion, and soon realizes that there is a fairly logical explanation for this: the bed isn't a bed, it's the back seat of a car. For a few moments she feels complete panic, because she finds herself thinking that the only reason for this is that she has been kidnapped. But then she sits up, and then the kidnapper, a woman of uncertain age who is happily singing along to the music on the radio, catches sight of her in the rearview mirror and lets out a shriek of terror. Only then does Louisa remember that she actually went to sleep in the car the previous evening, and that the kidnapper is perhaps not so much a kidnapper as a car owner, and that it is now probably more likely that the woman will think she is about to be kidnapped than the other way around.

The woman stomps her foot on the brake and the car stops so abruptly that Louisa hits her nose on the seat in front of her and exclaims irritably: "HELLO? Can you at least try to be CAREFUL?!"

Unfortunately, the woman isn't listening, she's just shrieking. Should she really be this angry, Louisa thinks, seeing as she isn't the one who's been woken up at half past six in the morning? What sort of lunatic drives to work this early, anyway?

"ARRWAUUARWAAAR," the woman cries, or something like that, but to be honest it's hard to know exactly, because suddenly Louisa isn't listening to her at all. She's listening to the radio, so intently that at first her heart can't accept the words she hears.

"Wait . . . hush!" she tells the woman, still not entirely awake, and puts her ear closer to the speaker.

But the woman definitely doesn't wait, and certainly isn't delighted to be hushed by Louisa in her own car either, so in the end Louisa simply leans forward and puts her hand over the woman's mouth. Not unlike what you would do if you were, for instance, thinking of kidnapping someone.

" . . . *as you've just heard, news has reached us that the world-famous artist C. Jat* . . . ," the voice on the radio says.

Then the voice suddenly breaks, as if even the newsreader has lost their professional monotone today and is struggling to hold back tears. A short, trembling breath is heard, followed by: ". . . *died last night. Thirty-nine years old.*"

Perhaps the newsreader has seen the artist's painting in galleries. Perhaps in beautiful books in big houses or in cheap magazines in small waiting rooms. Perhaps on a postcard, on a fridge, in a children's home. They have never met, but it doesn't matter. Art teaches us to mourn for strangers.

If you thought that the woman in the car was having a complicated enough morning already, it really doesn't get any better when the young kidnapper suddenly starts crying all over the back seat. That isn't entirely normal behavior for a kidnapper, it really isn't, so it ends with the woman offering the girl her handkerchief. When Louisa whispers: "Sorry I slept in your car," the woman replies vaguely: "Sorry I . . . woke you?"

When Louisa gets out of the car, the woman asks if the girl would like her to "call someone?" That is kind of her, to assume Louisa has a someone.

On the car radio, and on all other news broadcasts everywhere, serious journalists talk about the death of a famous man. His death belongs to the whole world now. Louisa will never quite be able to forgive the world for that.

What happens next is both stupid and logical, much like most of life, really. Louisa spends the whole of that first day, her birthday, drifting around town, without knowing where to go with all of her grief, and she doesn't even remember the next day, but on the next it's as if her feet take control and start walking without her brain giving them permission. She doesn't know where the artist's funeral is taking place, or how she could say good-bye, so her shoes carry her back to the only place where she can still feel his presence. Soon rich people around the neighborhood will complain to some anxious politician until they send a team of very serious professionals who paint the church wall in the alley white again, but tonight everything is still there: the cockroaches, fish, hearts, and skulls. So Louisa takes out her paints and carries on where she and the artist left off, painting all night through her tears in the light of the streetlamps, getting lost in time. Early the next morning the sun rises without her noticing. She doesn't hear the footsteps, the black-clad stranger approaches so quickly from behind that she doesn't see him until it's too late. So when she hears the deep voice, she turns around instantly and does the only reasonable thing: throws the can of spray paint at his face as hard as she can.

That's how she meets Ted.

TEN

It isn't the best first impression you can make, it really isn't. The can of spray paint sails through the air until it meets resistance, and when it does there's a loud noise, because that resistance happens to be Ted's glasses, and then his eye. The sound that follows contains a fair number of complicated words of the sort used by people who are too posh for ordinary swear words.

Louisa, who heard footsteps behind her and just assumed someone had come to murder her, the only reasonable assumption, isn't really sure if she should apologize or throw something else. The man in front of her is short and thin, the same way the artist was, but he's smartly dressed in a blazer and pants that don't look like he slept in them, his face is clean-shaven where the artist's was bearded, and his eyes are grown-up and serious where the artist's were full to bursting with childish curiosity. The man picks his glasses up from the ground with one hand, holds the other over his eye, and sighs:

"Are you . . . Louisa?"

Her eyes dart from one end of the alley to the other, as if she wants to make sure she can run away from him if she has to.

"Are you from the police?" she says suspiciously.

"If I was from the police, I'd already have thrown you in jail for assault," he replies tersely, his English is perfect but the accent is funny.

Louisa mutters back:

"Assault? You were the one who crept up on me! I thought you were a murderer, and I didn't even throw anything *at* you, I just threw it in your . . . like . . . general direction!"

Ted takes an extremely deep breath.

"Well, I'm sorry if my face happened to get in the way of one of your projectiles," he says tartly, putting his now rather crooked glasses back on.

"Apology accepted!" Louisa grunts, perfectly seriously.

"God, I can see why he liked you . . . ," Ted groans, in a way that really doesn't sound like a compliment.

"Who?" Louisa exclaims.

"Him," Ted says, with the sort of seriousness that adults adopt when they've spent a whole day trying not to cry, and points at the skulls on the wall.

Louisa blinks in confusion and tries desperately to remember how to breathe.

"You . . . you knew him? C. Jat? I . . . ," she begins, but doesn't get any further, it's hard to talk when your lungs and heart are in a little heap on the floor inside you, because now Ted is holding out the postcard she had given to the artist.

"He wanted me to give this back. And the can of spray paint he borrowed. But you can only have that if you promise not to throw it!" Ted says sullenly.

Louisa takes the postcard with trembling fingertips, her vocal cords still frozen with shock so all she manages by way of a response is a nod. Ted's expression becomes slightly more sympathetic then, at least in the eye that wasn't hit by a can of spray paint, so he says rather more amiably:

"He wanted you to know that he really, really enjoyed painting with you. You evidently told him that you'd see him again here, so he wanted to apologize for not being able to come, but I'm afraid he . . ."

Ted's voice isn't strong enough to carry the word "died," so Louisa helps him by whispering:

"I know. I . . . I heard on the news."

They look at each other for just a moment, but neither of them can bear to maintain eye contact.

"He left something for you," Ted says through his teeth, looking down at the ground.

Behind him are a suitcase and two boxes, one large and one small, and when Louisa sees the small one she can't stop herself asking:

"Are those his ashes?"

Ted blinks heavily behind his crooked glasses.

"How did you know that?"

"My best friend Fish died. They didn't let me keep her ashes, but they were in a box like that, and there was a guy at the church who let me hold them for a little while. I was her only human. The minister was nice, he made sure she was buried under a tree, she liked trees. One day I'm going to be seriously damn rich and buy a really nice gravestone for her. Or rather . . . about her. Well, I mean . . ."

Then Louisa's brain points out that perhaps this is enough words out of your mouth now, Louisa? As if it wasn't her brain who came up with all the damn words in the first place! Louisa knocks her head with her fist a little bit in frustration. Ted, on the other hand, doesn't seem to know what to say, so he doesn't say anything, which makes Louisa very jealous. His brain seems a lot more disciplined than the anarchic mush she's got inside her own skull.

Ted takes a deep breath and picks up the large box, it takes an embarrassingly long time for Louisa to realize that means he wants her to take it. He holds it out gently, as if the contents were very fragile, so naturally Louisa takes it so clumsily that she ends up sitting on her backside with the whole thing in her arms. Ted leaps forward and stops the box from falling with a look of such panic in his eyes that it's obvious he doesn't really want to part with it. When he eventually lets go of it, his whole chest seems to be fighting against his whisper:

"He . . . he sold everything he owned so he could buy this back. Everything he earned in his entire career, but even so, I only *just* managed to buy it back at the auction. I told him it was stupid, but he said artists were supposed to die poor. All he wanted when he died was to be able to give it away to whoever he wanted. And he wanted that person to be . . . you."

Louisa stares uncomprehendingly, first at the box, then at the man in front of her.

"What are you, his lawyer or something?"

Ted evades her gaze like a silverfish beneath a bathroom lamp that's just been switched on.

"No, no, I was just his friend."

"I'm sorry," she says at once.

"You don't have to be," he says dismissively.

"I do," she insists. "If you were his friend, I'm sorry. Because the whole world lost an artist, but you lost your human. And I'm sorry you had to share that with the rest of us. You should be allowed to have your grief in peace."

Ted is almost forty years old, but those words hit him as if he were just fourteen. That makes him angry, because he can't cope with being fourteen today, he can't cope with feeling everything in the whole world one more time. So all he manages to pull himself together to say is a curt:

"Thank you."

Then he turns away. He picks up the small box that holds the ashes of his huge, incomparable friend, takes his suitcase, and starts to walk out of the alley toward the train station on the other side of the street. He has completed his mission. But of course Louisa's brain suggests that she ought to shout something else, so she does:

"I've never met a grown-up like him!"

Without looking back over his shoulder, Ted admits weakly:

"Neither have I."

He almost gets to the end of the alley before he hears Louisa's cry echo off the church and around the world, so he realizes she's opened the box and found the painting.

ELEVEN

In Louisa's defense, this really is an extremely odd situation to find yourself in, and there probably isn't any right or wrong way to react, so she reacts in what might be the only reasonable one: noisily.

"NO!!!" she yells at first.

A couple of seconds of silence follow.

"What the hell? NO! NO, NO, NO!" she exclaims after that.

More silence. Her brain is evidently searching for the appropriate words to describe how she truly feels, until eventually it decides upon:

"NOOOOOO!"

Then she lets go of the world-famous painting as if it has burned her, only to immediately pick it up again, terrified that it might get dirty on the ground. Unfortunately, her brain doesn't offer any useful ideas for what to do next, so she quickly puts the painting back in the box and rushes after Ted, clutching the whole thing in her arms and yelling: "ARE YOU TOTALLY STUPID? WHY ARE YOU GIVING THIS TO ME? TAKE IT BACK!"

Ted turns around, with a look on his face like a person would have at the end of a long battle against an insect over a glass of juice.

"I'm not giving it to you. He gave it to you."

"DO YOU KNOW WHAT THIS IS WORTH?"

If Ted weren't such an extremely grown-up and serious person, he might have rolled his eyes, but instead he just mutters:

"I know exactly what it's worth, seeing as I was the person who bought it on his behalf at the auction."

"SO WHY ARE YOU GIVING IT TO ME, THEN?"

Ted looks at her with pity, but unfortunately, this gets drowned out by self-pity. Life is long, his friend had said in the hospital, but he didn't mention the fact that almost every moment hurts when you have to live it alone.

"He wanted you to have it because he . . . because he spent his whole life waiting to meet someone who saw a wall the same way he did."

Louisa is trying desperately to find a way to balance the box in her arms.

"But how can I, what am I supposed to . . . What the hell? No! NO!"

She tries to locate her brain, but it has evidently left her head and slammed the door behind it.

"Sell it," Ted suggests, as kindly as he can.

"SELL IT?"

"Or keep it. Hang it on your wall at home. Do what you like," he sighs.

"I don't have a home!" she replies.

Ted swallows and tries to balance between empathy and irritation.

"Okay. So sell the painting and buy a house. Buy ten houses. You're rich now, I promise."

Louisa's eyes grow wild with terror.

"No . . . no, this isn't . . . Why? You were his friend! YOU have to take it!"

"I can't."

"Why not?"

"Because he gave it to you."

Louisa thinks for a long time, so long that Ted briefly imagines he could just take his suitcase and leave and never see her again, but obviously he can forget about that. Suddenly she yells triumphantly, as if she were a genius:

"I know! You can BUY it from me!"

Ted can't help smiling at this.

"I can't afford it, my dear."

"Aren't you rich?" she exclaims, glancing at his clothes, as if everyone with clean pants must be financially independent.

"I'm a high school teacher," Ted informs her.

This means very little to Louisa, since she's not exactly sure what a high school teacher makes, so she mumbles:

"I can't . . . don't give it to me . . . it's too much, I'm just a damn kid, I don't even have a damn place to live, I've run away from my foster home, I sleep in cars, I can't . . ."

It looks like it weighs a thousand tons in her arms now, even though Ted knows that it hardly weighs anything at all, so he probably has a good idea of the feelings that are making her knees buckle. Nothing weighs more than someone else's belief in you. He could have said that, to console her, but unfortunately his own brain is too crowded with regret and loss. So instead, his jealousy shines through when he snaps:

"I appreciate that it feels like a great responsibility. But he chose you. He chose . . . you. Sell the painting so you don't have to sleep in cars anymore."

"Sell it to who? Everyone will think I stole it!" she exclaims in despair, and only then does Ted realize that she actually has a point.

He swallows hesitantly and adjusts his crooked glasses.

"Okay. So . . . sell it in there, to the same people I bought it from," he says, gesturing toward the church with an expression of certainty on his face that he suddenly doesn't feel at all.

He feels a degree of irritation now, because the artist didn't think this through at all, because the artist always relied on Ted to think about things.

"It's closed! It's Easter! Everything's closed!" Louisa retorts, in a tone that suggests that maybe she thinks Ted is something of an idiot.

"So you'll be rich after Easter, then!" Ted replies, in a tone that suggests that maybe he is starting to feel like one.

"And until then?"

"What do you mean?"

Louisa's whole body is shaking with sobs now.

"I'm homeless and you've just given me a damn painting worth a damn FORTUNE! In this town? I won't survive until after Easter with this!"

Ted hesitates for a moment.

"What makes you say that?"

"Experience!"

He has to admit that he really doesn't have a good answer to that.

"Maybe you could call someone who can help you? Your mom?"

"She's dead," Louisa says matter-of-factly, rather than with any sadness.

Ted absentmindedly scratches his hair, which no longer looks quite so neat.

"I'm sorry, I read the postcard and thought . . . ," he says quietly.

"You read my postcard? You're not allowed to read other people's MAIL!" Louisa snaps back at once.

Ted stares at her in astonishment.

"That wasn't . . . mail. It was a postcard. It's like . . . accidentally reading the slogan on someone's T-shirt."

She rolls her eyes, which Ted finds highly immature.

"Why can't YOU call someone, then? Someone who can take the painting!" she suggests.

"I don't know anyone here. I'm not from around here," Ted admits.

He thinks about the artist, and the medication he had decided to stop taking at the end, and about the journey here which Ted had tried so hard to persuade him not to make because he was so ill. Then he whispers:

"He didn't live here either, we just came here because it was where the painting was being sold. He wanted to buy it without anyone knowing. He was worried someone would find out he really was dying, because then the price of the painting would go up and he wouldn't have been able to afford it. So he sent me into the auction and we didn't tell anyone. I realize now that it was stupid. I have nothing on paper to prove that he wanted to give it to you. I'm sorry . . . I really am. But I have to . . . go."

He turns away again, so weighed down by the demons of adult life that his feet scrape the ground. Grief is a selfish bacteria, it demands all our attention. Ted doesn't want to be rude to the girl, he just wants to be alone, he just needs silence so he can hear the artist's voice in his head again. Feel his breath against his skin. You don't wish for happiness when you have lost the love of your life, because you can't even imagine ever feeling happy again. All you wish for is peace, calm, a long night's sleep. You dream of nothing but being able to forgive time for making us old. For not letting us stay on a pier with our best friends. For letting summers end.

"Where are you going?" Louisa calls after him.

"Home."

"Home? The place he painted? Is that where you came from?" she asks, picking up the painting again, making the frame scrape against the box.

"Yes," he replies, without even turning around, because he knows every inch of that pier anyway.

"You're going to bury his ashes there?"

"Yes."

"Is it far?"

Ted stops and breathes through his nose, so hard and so irritably that Louisa is really impressed that no snot comes out, he must have incredible sinuses for such an old man.

Ted, almost forty years old, sighs:

"Yes. It'll take several days by train."

"Why don't you fly?"

"I like trains," he says in a tone that really doesn't sound like it belongs to a train lover.

"So you're afraid of flying?" she guesses.

Ted exhales so hard that his pants flap.

"*Everyone* should be afraid of flying! Have you *been* on an airplane?"

"No. I haven't even been on a train," she replies calmly.

She feels a little ashamed when she sees how ashamed he is at hearing this, that really wasn't her intention. But train journeys suggest that you have somewhere to go, or someone to travel to, and she hasn't had that sort of life.

Ted turns toward her, but without meeting her eyes, and just mumbles down at the ground:

"I'm sorry, I really am. I hope everything . . . turns out okay for you."

"Can I come with you, then? Where you're going?" Louisa asks, so suddenly that in all honesty, it probably surprises her as much as it does him.

It is obviously an unbelievably stupid idea, but what is she supposed to do? Her brain certainly doesn't help her at the moment, not one tiny bit.

"Definitely, definitely not!" Ted exclaims, horrified.

Then he turns around abruptly and starts to walk off with his suitcase and his friend's ashes, moving so quickly that he stumbles, which embarrasses him, so he stumbles even more angrily out of the alley and into traffic, where he almost gets run over. A car blows its horn and Ted is a man who hates attention, so his face turns so red that it's a miracle his skin doesn't fall off. He stumbles on, the train station is on the other side of the street, and he almost makes it to the entrance before Louisa's brain persuades her to rush after him and yell so loudly that the whole block can hear her:

"WAS IT YOU THAT FARTED?"

Passing strangers look at Ted with disgust, and his face is deep purple now, Louisa isn't really the ideal company for someone who hates attention. Ted smiles nervously and apologetically at the strangers, then he turns to Louisa and hisses:

"What's *wrong* with you?"

Louisa has gathered all her things and pulled on her backpack and she lumbers toward him, sweaty and out of breath, with the box containing the painting in her arms.

"Are you one of them? One of the boys?" she yells, pointing at it urgently.

For the first time since the hospital, Ted looks right at the painting, so it's honestly something of a miracle that he keeps his balance, his shoes really are far too big for a fourteen-year-old. It's cold in the street but he suddenly feels hot, and for a few moments his feet are dangling off the end of a pier, it's summer and nothing terrible has happened yet. He blinks his way back to reality, glances at Louisa, and thinks about what the artist had called her: *one of us*. So he sighs and points reluctantly at himself on the pier.

"That's me."

Louisa's voice is suddenly full of gratitude when she whispers:

"My whole life, every time I looked at the postcard of this painting, I always thought it looked like you were all laughing. How crazy is that? Being able to paint LAUGHTER? And I've always thought it looked like one of you had just . . . farted. It's . . . stupid. Sorry . . . I . . . Sorry! There's something wrong with my brain! I always babble when I get nervous, I . . ."

Ted is breathing faster now, his chest is rising and falling, his cheeks twitching, Louisa thinks it looks like he doesn't know how to cry, like he has only read about tears in a manual and misunderstood the point. Then Ted points at one of the boys in the painting and says slowly:

"That's Joar. He was the one who farted. He had . . . incredible farts. It was like he was completely made out of eggs."

Then Louisa laughs so loudly that it echoes across the whole train station, and then Ted almost laughs too. It's certainly the closest he's gotten since the artist fell asleep beside him for the last time.

"I'm sorry the police came and got your friend, I'm sorry that was one of the last things that happened to him," Louisa manages to say, and clumsily starts to shove the painting back in the box.

Ted smiles sadly:

"Don't be. I haven't seen him so excited in years, he felt young and dangerous again. He was . . . he was such an idiot, you need to know that."

"How long did you know him?" she asks.

Ted blinks slowly and adjusts his glasses.

"I knew him since we were little, I've . . . always known him," he replies, because with the sort of friendship they had, there was never a "before."

Louisa leans over the painting and says, into the box:

"When I was little, I used to think about all of you when I was trying to sleep. I thought I would fall asleep, and when I woke up I would be there by the sea with you. And you'd teach me to swim."

At this point a door slams inside Louisa's head, because now her brain is back, and it wants to tell her she sounds like a damn stalker when she talks like that!

Sure enough, Ted hits a new personal best at looking uncomfortable. He glances at his watch.

"I should probably go now," he mumbles anxiously, then takes out his ticket and goes through the turnstile.

"So can I come with you?" Louisa repeats, simultaneously awkward and shameless, which is quite an achievement, and quickly slips through the turnstile after him.

It is, of course, not the greatest idea she's ever had. Because the combination of Ted and Ted's suitcase and Louisa and her backpack and the box isn't exactly what the engineer who designed the turnstile had in mind. They get stuck like two tennis balls in the mouth of an overambitious golden retriever. Ted has to clamber over his suitcase to get free, and then Louisa climbs out, trying very hard not to touch him, and it really doesn't go very well.

"Leave me alone!" Ted snaps, falling forward as she crashes into him, hitting him on the back of the head with the box containing the painting.

His glasses end up even more crooked. He gets to his feet and grabs his suitcase and the box of ashes and starts to run. As if that were going to help, seeing as Louisa has much longer legs. He stumbles all the way to the end of the platform before giving up.

"WHY?" Louisa yells behind him.

It's a little unclear whether the question is why he's running, or more generally why he's such an irritating person. Ted doesn't answer, he just slumps over his suitcase like a middle-aged man who has seriously overestimated his fitness.

"Why . . . ," Louisa repeats behind him once more, "why did you even give me the painting? You could have just kept it! Or sold it yourself! Why . . ."

Ted stands there, furious and exhausted, his hands on his knees, and pants his reply:

"Because he loved me and he believed in me! And this was his final wish!"

He falls silent because he has to bite his bottom lip to stop it trembling. Louisa sees the train approaching the platform. Say something smart, her brain is yelling at her.

"Is there anyone where you come from who can help me sell the painting?" she shouts, still barely audible above the squeal of the train's brakes.

That was actually pretty smart, even her brain has to admit that, because then Ted does something that he will soon regret immensely. He replies with a groan:

"Yes. Maybe. But she . . ."

"Well, then! I'll come with you and meet her and then we'll sell the painting and share the money!" Louisa nods quickly, as if the matter is thereby settled.

"NO!"

"WHY NOT?"

Ted throws his arms up in frustration.

"Dear God, you can't just ask a strange man if you can go with him to—"

"Why not? Are you planning to kidnap me?" Louisa interrupts.

"What? Of course I'm not going to kidn—"

"Look, I don't want to be mean, but you're pretty small," she points out. "I reckon I could take you."

"What on earth . . . what are you talking about?" Ted wonders, recognizing that the conversation has gone off in a radically unpleasant direction.

"Kidnapping!" she explains instructively, then stands up straight as if to demonstrate her size and how difficult it would be to put her in a box or lock her up in a cellar, for instance.

"I'm not planning to kidnap you . . . but I suppose that's exactly what I'd say if I *was* thinking of kidnapping you?" Ted protests.

Louisa looks at him thoughtfully for a long time. Then she says:

"You seem to know an awful lot about kidnapping."

"What?"

"I'm just saying that for someone who isn't a kidnapper, you know an awful lot about—"

"Okay, I'm going now!" he declares, and walks quickly toward the train that has just pulled up to the platform.

"You're right, we can talk more on the train," Louisa nods enthusiastically.

"No!"

"Why not?"

"Because you're a child! I can't just take a child to . . ."

"Do you have something against kidnapping children? Is that where you draw the line?"

"No! I mean, yes!"

"I've just turned eighteen. I'm an adult. I can go wherever I like."

"Congratulations."

"Thanks. So that means I can come with you?"

"That really, really isn't what it means!"

"But WHY?" she yells, which makes Ted lose control and yell back:

"BECAUSE I CAN'T TAKE RESPONSIBILITY FOR YOU AS WELL!"

And that's the first time she sees him cry.

TWELVE

Twenty-five years ago Ted and his friends lived outside every day, all through summer vacation, inseparable until the sun went down. There is a particular way of missing someone, the way you can only miss your best humans when you're fourteen years old, when you go your separate ways outside your houses and your skin feels cold when they turn away.

"Tomorrow!" one of them always called out.

"Tomorrow!" the others always promised back, before they disappeared into the darkness.

At night the teenagers lived in different realities, but at daybreak they belonged to each other again, at the crossroads between the houses. Every morning Joar was there early, waiting at the junction, and every morning Ted was already sitting on the grass waiting for Joar.

Joar never knew why Ted did that, the two of them were never best friends, the only thing they had in common was the artist. Ted hardly ever spoke, Joar talked almost all the time, Ted was never angry and Joar was never anything else. Joar left home early every morning, at the same time his mother snuck out to go to work, before his old man woke up, hungover and dangerous. Ted? He could have slept all day if he wanted, no one would have noticed.

"Why are you always so damn early?" Joar asked one morning in June.

Ted just shrugged his shoulders timidly, staring down at the grass. It was still only the start of summer vacation, Joar had just found that competition for the artist to enter, the picture wasn't painted yet. All the best still lay ahead of them, all the worst too.

"If I lived in your house I'd sleep until lunchtime," Joar mumbled, and lay back on the grass.

You could tell from his breathing that he regretted saying it at once. Ted's house was quiet for a reason, and Joar knew that. The world is extremely inventive, it has plenty of ways of breaking children.

"Did you bring anything to eat?" Joar therefore asked in a gentler tone of voice.

Ted nodded and pulled cookies out of his backpack. Joar took them, but didn't eat any.

"Good, he likes these," he said quietly, before awkwardly coughing away the weakness in his voice and quickly changing the subject: "What do you think is the best invention in the world?"

Ted shrugged his shoulders again.

"Do you know what my mom said when I asked her?" Joar suddenly grinned, because no one could make him laugh like his mom. "Pockets, she said. POCKETS! What an idiot, right?"

Then Ted smiled, because no one could say "iiidiiiot" with such boundless love in each "i" as Joar, because no teenage boy protected his mother the way he did. His mom was kind, but she wasn't always smart, and Joar was smart, but not always kind, but in this particular instance Ted actually agreed with Joar's mom. Silently, of course, but still. Pockets were actually an awesome invention.

"Pockets!?" Joar repeated accusingly, as if he were a mind reader. "Not planes or medicine or fire or anything? Do you agree with that? In that case, you're both totally stupid! Do you know what my mom said about fire? That it wasn't an invention, just something cavemen discovered. I mean . . . what? You know what I said? I said that if fire was a discovery, then pockets were also a discovery, because pockets are like the ass cracks of pants, some caveman put his hand between his buttocks and decided, 'Hey! I can keep my keys here! We should have these in our clothes!'"

Ted laughed at that, because Joar was good at that, he could fight and play soccer, but most of all he was funny. All his best ideas came from his sense of humor. The only thing he wasn't much good at was being alone, because he hated silence, that was when he got all his worst ideas. That was why Ted always made sure he got to the crossroads before him every morning.

When the artist finally walked over from his house, Joar called out, "Good afternoon!" even though it was still so early that no other kids in the entire town were awake yet. At least not the happy, safe kids, the ones who didn't hate every minute they had to be at school. They didn't long for summer vacation the way Joar did, they were in no rush to get out into the world to do absolutely nothing all day.

"Have you had breakfast? Have a cookie! They're the ones you like!" he commanded the artist, then, without even taking a breath: "Have you started painting the picture of the sea yet? Damn it, you've got to start painting if you're going to win that fucking competition!"

The artist looked like he hadn't slept all night, and ate the cookies in such small pieces that they hardly even counted as crumbs. He didn't answer, because he didn't know how to explain that he already regretted promising he'd paint the sea. Obviously he couldn't do it. He wasn't that good. Joar just wanted him to finish it, and the problem was that Joar thought you needed to start if you were ever going to finish, but that wasn't how it worked. Art isn't chronological. Everything the artist drew came from a place in his head that he could only get to if he wasn't looking for it. If he was told to draw, it was like waking from a dream and trying to dream it again. A lack of self-confidence is a devastating virus. There's no cure.

Ted sat alongside them in silence and wished he were funny, because laughter heals all wounds, but he just sat there, jokeless. Joar looked down at the ground and really did try not to say anything else, but the ultimate expression of love is nagging, we don't nag anyone the way we nag the people we love. All parents know that, and so do all best friends.

"How fucking hard can it be to just start painting?" he therefore repeated at least five times on the way to the sea, but was met with nothing but silence.

Once they reached the pier he kept nagging the artist to eat all the cookies before they went swimming, and the artist didn't protest, because he was used to it. But when Joar took his clothes off and all the bruises became visible, Ted could see the artist's heart break in his eyes, because he never got used to seeing those.

Joar was great at soccer, everyone wanted him on their team at school, because he always threw himself headfirst into every tackle. He had learned that this stopped people from asking where all the bruises came from. Sometimes, many years later, Ted wondered if perhaps that was why it took the artist such a long time to paint the picture of them by the sea: he didn't have all the colors he needed to paint Joar's body.

A lot of children run to the door when they hear their old man come home, but none as quickly as Joar. He would lie in bed at night and count the number of times the metal of the key scraped against the metal of the lock before his old man managed to get it in. The more scrapes, the more his old man had drunk, the most dangerous nights were when he just gave up and rang the doorbell instead. Then Joar would rush to the door so his mother wouldn't have to take the first blow. His old man hit them as if they weren't people.

Sometimes his old man regretted it the next day, promised not to do it again, the way men like him always do. But sometimes he didn't even remember what had happened, he would wake up with blood on his knuckles and go sit in the kitchen without even knowing who he had beaten to pieces the night before.

The fact that Joar was capable of loving anyone at all after that was incredible. That he could love anyone the way he loved the artist? A miracle.

They would be turning fifteen that summer, and everyone who met Ted probably thought he had had his humans all his life, they were such an obvious extension of each other, like the tail on a dog. We never get that age back again, when every friend is a childhood friend, we measure all infatuations throughout our lives against that. But in fact Ted had only had the artist and Joar for a few years, whereas those two had always had each other. Ted felt deeply ashamed that he was jealous of that. Twenty-five years later, he will still feel ashamed.

When they emerged from the water that day in June, Ted carefully took one of the artist's sketch pads out of his backpack and wrote something in it. A short while later, when Joar was lying on his back on the pier and his thin body was drying in the sun, he asked, predictably enough: "What do you think the best invention in the world is?" The artist glanced at his pad and read out loud: "Pockets!"

Joar's eyes widened, and at first he shouted: "How the hell did you . . . ?" before glaring at Ted and the sketch pad, then at the artist again, and muttering: "Idiots! You're all fucking idiots!"

Joar might have been furious with Ted if he hadn't loved the artist's laughter so much, but oh, how the artist laughed, and that was the only thing Ted and Joar needed to have in common. When they all laughed, they belonged together.

Ted had never felt funnier in his entire life.

The artist needed their laughter too, perhaps more than anyone understood, he had laughed less and less that spring, and hardly drawn anything at all. But he tried to draw that day, he really, really tried, because he hated disappointing Joar. Sometimes when the artist got nervous his skin itched, and sometimes one of his shoulders started to twitch, sort of bouncing up and down beneath his T-shirt, and often he felt so ashamed of it that he cried. There was something wrong with him, he knew that, his brain absorbed information in the wrong order. He had never wanted to play with other children when he was little, he had just wanted to sit alone in a corner drawing, his parents were often told their child wasn't normal. They believed that, sadly, which is why they missed out on the incredible joy of having a child who was special.

Adults often think that self-confidence is something a child learns, but little kids are by their nature always invincible, it's self-doubt that needs to be taught. And oh, how the artist was taught, because the world has spent thousands of years practicing how to puncture the lungs of children who are different. In preschool it had taken a long time for adults to realize that the artist didn't like it when anyone touched him, but of course the other children had realized this at once, so they would creep up on him and prod him until he screamed. Sometimes he would flail about himself in panic and couldn't be calmed down, and then his parents would be summoned to talk to the teachers that afternoon. Even as a five-year-old, he had learned to recognize the shame in their eyes.

Soon the other children discovered that he was afraid of confined spaces, so one day they forced him into a storage trunk in the schoolyard and sat on the lid. He lay curled up in there, crying, for so long he thought he was dying. In the end the other children weren't even holding down the lid anymore, but he still didn't dare try to open it.

Then there was a single long howl, followed by another one, and then the sun was suddenly blinding the artist. It was Joar, also five years old, who had thrown open the lid of the trunk while the other kids ran to the teachers crying because their noses and lips were bleeding. That was Joar's first day at preschool, and the last day of loneliness for the boy in the trunk. You do whatever you can to not disappoint a friend after that.

They were twelve years old when they met Ted, when Joar rode his bicycle into him, because Joar was good at a lot of things, but bad at braking. "Meet" is probably the wrong word, no one met Joar, because you don't "meet" a natural disaster, you get hit by it. Joar and the artist had been bored, and Joar had come up with the idea of riding their bikes down the steepest hill in town, through a gap in the fence surrounding the abandoned old harbor, then out onto a pier at full speed and on into the water. The pier was their secret place, forgotten by the world, no one else knew it existed. But on that particular day, there was a strange little boy standing at the end of it. "WATCH OUT!"

Joar had yelled, but it was too late. The bicycle hit Ted and he and Joar both ended up in the water, Joar surfaced at once but the other boy was gone, and the artist had stood on the pier and for almost a minute thought they had just murdered someone. Then suddenly Joar yelled, "THERE!" and the artist dived into the water without hesitation. They pulled Ted up onto the pier and he coughed up enough water to drown a small horse. He blinked at the artist in terror and the artist smiled back and said his first words to him: "Nicely watched out!"

Then Ted smiled. That's how long it takes to become best friends. A whole lifetime, a single second. But then he suddenly looked aghast.

"Your bike!" he whimpered to Joar, and looked out at the water where it had sunk, as if it were Ted's fault it was gone now.

"No worries, it was a disposable bike," Joar said, shrugging his shoulders.

It took several minutes for Ted to realize that meant Joar had stolen it. Joar explained very slowly and patiently that you should never ride your own bike out in this fucking town, surely he understood that? Someone might steal it!

A few days later Joar and the artist went home with Ted after school, it was the first time they had ever known anyone who lived in a detached house. Admittedly, it was probably the cheapest and most ramshackle house in town, but that didn't matter, because Ted had a room of his own in the basement.

"Who the hell is this kid?" Joar muttered. "Some sort of prince?"

The room was cold and smelled of damp, but for twelve-year-olds, having a space of their own is the height of luxury, a staircase dividing them from the adult world is like a moat around a castle. Joar walked around the room, bowing to all the furniture and saying solemnly: "Your Royal Highness the Wardrobe, pleased to meet you! Your Majesty the Wallpaper, delighted!" He thought it was typical of the upper class to have wallpaper, and as he walked through the room he pretended to get lost because it was so big. "Hello?" he called from the bookcase, because that was also typical of the upper class, to have books instead of bottles on their shelves. "Hello? Can you hear me? I'm in the library!" he cried, and the artist laughed out loud. The infatuation was instant, Ted's heart reached out to the pair of them like a plant reaching for the sun.

That evening they went home for dinner, because the artist didn't dare have dinner with someone else's family, and Joar didn't want to leave his mother alone with his old man. On the evenings when his old man was out, Joar still stayed at home, because then he and his mom would watch television shows with celebrities in them, his mom loved those because the celebrities always looked so happy. But the artist went back to Ted's after dinner that first evening, and soon he was doing that almost every evening, always knocking carefully on the basement window, making a sound like lizard's feet on the glass. He never rang the doorbell upstairs and he avoided Ted's parents the way he avoided all adults, because he knew he made them uncomfortable. The artist had been told all his life what he was and what he wasn't: he was a strange boy, not like other boys, not enough of a boy at all. But in Ted's basement, he sat on the floor drawing all the things he didn't dare draw anywhere else, first superheroes and terrible monsters, because Ted liked those. Then, as the night got later, he drew bodies. First with clothes on, then without. Sometimes, when he was really sad, he gave the naked men angels' wings.

Ted got used to falling asleep to the scratching sound of a pencil and his friend's breathing, he always woke to an empty room with a gentle breeze blowing through the open basement window. Then Ted would often sneak upstairs to his parents' bathroom and count the pills in the cabinet. Ted's dad had cancer, that was why the house was so quiet and why Ted was allowed to live in the basement, so his dad wouldn't be disturbed. The bathroom cabinet was full of painkillers, the artist only stole a few pills at a time, it was pure chance that Ted had noticed. The artist kept them in a box in his backpack, as if he were building a bomb. Ted never said that he knew, but a few weeks before that summer vacation when they were about to turn fifteen, the artist stopped drawing, then he stopped eating, and then Ted told Joar. That was why Joar had decided to enter him into that competition, and also why he always wanted Ted to bring cookies each morning.

It's hard to say "I love you" when you're fourteen years old. And completely impossible to dare to whisper: "Don't hurt yourself, because you'd be hurting me too."

The artist's parents were divorced. His father was a bitter man, never violent, just incapable of warmth. His expressions of paternal tenderness extended, at most, to telling his son in a low voice: "Try to behave . . . you know . . . normally." The artist never knew what that meant, just that he always did it wrong. His dad worked at the harbor, sometimes the men he worked with came to the house and sat in the kitchen. They were often drunk and always angry—at their bosses and the politicians and the economy. But late one evening when his lips were lubricated with beer, his dad had slurred: "You know, sometimes I wonder what I did wrong. If it's my fault that the boy is like he is." The other men all told him it wasn't his fault. They all agreed that there was something wrong with the boy, of course, they just objected to the part about who was to blame.

It was a small apartment with thin walls, the artist had been sitting on the other side, knowing that it would have been better if he didn't exist at all.

Ted hated loud noises, he always had, he used to panic at the sound of metal cutlery on plates, or of Styrofoam or cardboard bending. But he would never find a noise he hated more than the sound of paper being balled up.

That day on the pier twenty-five years ago, when Joar had gone off for a pee, the artist had turned to Ted and whispered with moist eyes:

"I can't do it, Ted. I can't draw the way Joar thinks I can draw! And they don't even want a drawing for that competition, they want a *painting*. I don't have any paint, I don't even have any brushes . . . I don't know how to do it. I can't, I just can't . . ."

His shoulder twitched, he scratched himself all over, then he balled up the sheet of paper and Ted would never forget how it sounded. The artist threw it in the water, the sea swallowed the drawing, and Ted would spend the next twenty-five years wishing he hadn't just sat there silently.

When Joar came back, the artist stood up and left, muttering that he was going to pee but mostly he probably didn't want them to see how hard he was crying.

Joar sank down next to Ted and sat for a long time in silence before he said, seriously, with his eyes fixed on the horizon: "We have to get him to paint that picture, Ted, you understand that, right? He's going to die if he stays in this fucking town. But if he wins that competition, he'll be famous and rich and . . . happy. Like the celebrities on TV. Okay? We just have to . . ."

Joar's fingers toyed with a cigarette lighter he'd found on the ground, his arms were covered in bruises and scars. Ted didn't say anything, he just nodded, and Joar nodded back. That was their oath.

On the way home that evening, the teenagers who were going to become a painting walked close to each other, but the artist walked closest to Joar. Ted did his very best not to be jealous, but failed miserably. When you're fourteen years old, friendship and infatuation are the same feeling, light from the same star, so perhaps there ought to be a better word for it. But how do I explain that I'm freezing to death if I'm not seen by you?

When the teenagers went their separate ways at the crossroads between the houses, they called out "Tomorrow!" to each other, and each promised back into the darkness: "Tomorrow!"

Ted looked over his shoulder, his skin feeling cold. None of the teenagers could explain what was going on, they just carried each other in silence. Joar had made it his responsibility to make the artist world-famous, the artist had made it his responsibility not to disappoint Joar. Ted? He had made it his responsibility that none of the people he loved would die. That's a terrible burden for a person. Your shoulders creak, your skeleton shrinks, in the end you can hardly walk.

THIRTEEN

"I can't take responsibility . . . ," Ted whispers at the train station twenty-five years later.

He's holding his suitcase in one trembling hand, the ashes of his best friend in the other. When he backs away from her, Louisa notices for the first time that he's limping.

"Okay," she says quietly.

"Okay?" Ted repeats in surprise, wiping his eyes behind his crooked glasses, deeply ashamed of his tears.

"Yes. Okay. I won't bother you anymore," she says, and turns around.

"Okay . . . ," he nods in confusion, because the strangest thing that can happen to a middle-aged man in the middle of an argument is for him to suddenly win.

She casts a final glance at him and says: "Don't hurt yourself."

Ted really does try not to show that he can hear the artist in her then, dear God, how he tries. He collects himself, like a serious adult would, and mutters curtly:

"Sorry . . . sorry I raised my voice."

He stretches his neck, tries to make himself as tall as her, as if that would make him seem more adult. It reminds Louisa of a small giraffe, which puts her in mind of angels. That might not appear to be the most natural connection in the world, sure, but she doesn't believe in angels, and Fish was *obsessed* with angels. When they first met, Louisa would never draw people, just animals, and most often giraffes, because their bodies looked the way Louisa felt: really tall and really wide, but in all the wrong places. Fish always said that if she died, she would come back to Louisa as an angel, only in the form of a giraffe, so that Louisa would recognize her, and obviously that made Louisa laugh hysterically. A giraffe in the middle of town—even as an angel, Fish couldn't be discreet. She'd be an idiot, forever.

Louisa smiles sadly to herself as she picks up the box containing the painting. She turns toward the other side of the platform where a group of young men dressed in black are smoking uneven hand-rolled cigarettes and drinking from bottles wrapped in paper bags. Then she says:

"Don't worry. You go. I'm just going to go and ask those nice guys over there if they can help me sell the painting instead. They look pretty trustworthy . . ."

Ted sighs so deeply that you really wouldn't want him in the vicinity if you were building a house of cards.

"But . . . no! What are you doing? Don't go and . . ."

He takes two steps after her, and Louisa turns around dramatically.

"Excuse me? Aren't you in a rush to catch your TRAIN?"

Ted hyperventilates, trying to hold back his frustration.

"Are you insane? You can't just walk up to a group of strange men with a painting worth this much!" he hisses.

"Why not? Because they might kidnap me?" she snorts.

Ted can't quite figure out a smart way to reply to that, so on pure instinct he says the only thing that every middle-aged man on the entire planet can think of to say to an annoying teenager:

"Aren't you . . . supposed to be in school? Or something?"

She screws her nose up.

"It's Easter."

"Okay, okay, but you're just a child, someone must be missing you, surely?"

"I'm eighteen. No one's missing me."

"I'm just trying to help you!" Ted persists, and puts down his suitcase and the box of ashes so he can massage his temples.

She nods quickly:

"Okay? So help me, then! You said you were going home, and that there's someone there who can help me sell the painting! Take me with you, we can sell the painting, and then I'll come back here after Easter! No one will even notice I've been gone!"

Ted throws his arms up in a gesture of such resignation that he accidentally hits himself on the back of the head, which is quite a talent, being so clumsy that you're your own most likely cause of death.

"What about the foster home, then? You mentioned that, didn't you? You can go there, can't you?" he tries.

Louisa's eyes darken: "Just help me sell the painting and I'll be gone from your life, I promise! I'll do whatever you want! But I'm never going back to that fucking place!"

Ted is rubbing his eyelids now, he really doesn't even mean to say the thought out loud:

"Once you've sold the painting you can buy that whole place."

She replies so quickly that her words are like a slap:

"I'd only buy it so I could burn it down."

It's hard for Ted not to think of Joar then, sitting on the pier with a lighter in his hands.

"But you must have some sort of caseworker at Social Services that you could call? Or however these things work?" he tries, but Louisa shrugs.

"I don't think they're at work right now."

"Why not?"

"Because it's Easter!"

"It's *Easter*," Ted echoes, frustrated, rubbing his whole face now.

"Are you a bit slow or something? Not that there's anything wrong with that, I'm just wondering," Louisa says, very considerately.

Ted sadly doesn't have time to think of a smart insult to say in reply, because a voice behind them suddenly demands:

"You two! Do you have tickets?"

Ted turns around to find an angry man wearing a thin tie, he has a name tag on his chest that he adjusts as if it were a sheriff's star in an old Western movie.

"Tickets?" Ted says in confusion.

"I saw that girl there push through the ticket barrier with you! Does she have a ticket?" the sheriff grunts, and puts his thumbs in his belt as if he were about to draw an imaginary revolver.

"You can take this as payment! It's worth—" Louisa immediately says, holding the box containing the painting out toward the sheriff.

"NO!" Ted protests.

Louisa turns toward him with a look of perfectly feigned surprise.

"Are you still here? I thought you had a train to catch?"

Ted clenches his fists so tightly in his pockets and screams so loudly inside his head that all his internal organs probably age at least ten years. The sheriff doesn't quite seem to know how to interpret this, so he decides to take charge of the situation by grabbing Louisa's wrist.

"Listen! Do you have a ticket or not?"

Louisa shrieks so loudly that half the people on the platform turn around, she pulls free as if he were burning her. Her sleeve slides up and Ted sees her arm, it's so covered with bruises and scars that even the air must hurt her skin.

"Don't touch me!" she snaps, and backs away, feeling for the screwdriver in her bag.

Ted recognizes the look in her eyes, sees the artist in her, and it weighs so heavily on him it's a wonder he doesn't leave footprints in the concrete platform. All Ted wants in the world right now is to be left alone, but the problem with never wanting to disappoint your friends is that when your friends are in Heaven, they can see everything you do, the bastards. So when the sheriff takes a step closer to Louisa, Ted steps in between them, extremely reluctantly, with his hands raised and his eyes screwed shut.

"Okay. Okay, okay. I'll pay for her ticket!"

The sheriff stares at him in surprise, Ted hunches up as if he's expecting to be hit, the sheriff doesn't seem to know how to react to that.

"Oh? Well, okay then . . . ," the sheriff mutters, slightly disappointed, as if he had been quite looking forward to the chance to give a public demonstration of his authority.

"Okay?" Louisa asks brightly.

"Okay!" Ted repeats, not at all brightly, and searches for his wallet.

The ticket is paid for, the sheriff lumbers away, and Ted could topple houses of cards a mile away with his sighs. He picks up his suitcase and the box of ashes and limps onto the train, but Louisa doesn't follow him. Ted turns in the doorway and grunts:

"Are you coming, then?"

Louisa looks skeptical.

"So I can come with you? Just like that?" she wonders.

"It's exactly what you wanted!" Ted snaps.

Louisa rolls her eyes.

"Oh? So now I'm supposed to just TRUST you all of a sudden? What if you murder me?"

"I'm not going to murder you," Ted groans.

"That's exactly what a murderer would say! I don't even know your name!" she points out.

"Ted."

"I'm Louisa."

"I know."

"Okay."

"Okay?"

"Okay! Now we know each other! Stop being so weird!" she shakes her head irritably.

"Because *I'm* really the one being weird . . . ," he mutters.

Louisa lifts the box onto the train, then climbs into the carriage, looks around, and immediately blurts out: "Wow! These seats are really soft! Fish should have taught me how to break into trains instead of cars!"

Ted blushes and avoids the gazes of the other passengers. Louisa seems to think deeply before she adds: "Do you know that women are most likely to be murdered by someone they know, Ted? So if anyone's going to murder me now, it's most likely that it's going to be you!"

Ted closes his eyes and counts to ten at least ten times, then he finds two empty seats, and Louisa follows him, to a chorus of "ows" from strangers hit in the head by her backpack. Ted tries to put his suitcase in the overhead luggage rack, but can't quite reach, so Louisa asks if he needs help and of course he absolutely, definitely doesn't, because he's a grown man. His suitcase hits him in the head three times before he gives up and squeezes himself, the suitcase, and the box of ashes into the seat closest to the window.

"Are you sure you don't want to put your bag up there?" Louisa wonders helpfully, able to reach the rack without even stretching.

"This is fine!" Ted snaps, with his suitcase on his lap.

"It certainly looks super comfortable," Louisa notes.

She only gets an affronted grunt in reply, so she lifts her own backpack up into the rack and puts the box containing the painting on the floor by her feet. Then they sit there side by side, and in her defense, at least twenty seconds pass before Louisa gets bored and asks:

"Do you like riddles, Ted? Do you know how you get a one-armed man out of a tree?"

Ted closes his eyes and looks like he really wouldn't have anything against falling out of a tree himself, right now. This is going to be a long, long journey, he thinks.

And Heaven laughs. Oh, how it laughs.

Ted takes a small roll of tape out of his suitcase and mends his crooked glasses. Louisa tells riddles and jokes the whole time until the train starts to move, but then she suddenly does something very unexpected: she falls silent. She sits there and stares in wonder at her hometown through the window, this is the first time in her life that she's left it. She blinks hard and takes deep breaths, and just as they reach the end of the platform, she catches sight of it. It happens so fast that at first she's sure she must be imagining it, but there it is, sitting calmly on a bench and looking at her condescendingly. It must have had a bath since she saw it in the alley, because its fur is shiny, but you can't wash away arrogance. Their eyes meet for a moment, and no one will ever believe Louisa if she tells them, but she could swear that it raises its right paw and waves.

Typical Fish humor, to come back as a cat.

FOURTEEN

Art is context.

Because honestly? It isn't a great painting.

It would have been strange if it was, of course, because the artist who would become known as C. Jat was only fourteen years old when he painted it. It's the job of fourteen-year-olds not to be great at things, the only expectation they have to live up to is to be morons, they're put on this earth so their moms and dads will support the headache-pill industry. It really, really isn't the job of fourteen-year-olds to be geniuses.

So the painting was nothing special, not at all. It was the artist who was. An impoverished little nothing from a run-down harbor town with divorced parents and a gang of friends that a teacher once described as "a pack of wild animals." All his childhood the artist had seen adults destroy their surroundings, some with violence and others with silence, sometimes with clenched fists and always with empty bottles. Children have two worlds, the one they have been given and the one they can dream about, but not even the artist had enough imagination to believe it was possible to paint his way out of there. It would take a really, really big idiot to dream anything as grand as that. Thank goodness he had one of those.

Joar was often told he was stupid, he didn't care, but the artist got really angry. Joar wasn't stupid, he just happened to be the sort of person who only thought about one thing at a time, which was why he was so good at fixing engines. The artist, on the other hand, thought about everything all at once, which was why he could draw, but he always did it in the wrong order. From the edges of the paper toward the middle instead of the other way round, sky first, people last. So the world-famous painting wasn't even a painting when he started, it was a drawing, because he couldn't afford paint. And it wasn't even a drawing of the sea to start with, it was a drawing of clouds, because clouds are nothing and that was how he saw himself. Everything else? That was what Joar saw in him. As an adult, the artist would be told that great artistry is something that has to find its way out of a person, but for him it was something that needed to find its way in. Because for him, art was love. Grief. A story.

A context.

If a homeless man in the street had tried to sell the painting of the children on the pier, it would have been worthless, but once it was hanging on a white wall in a beautiful gallery, it cost a fortune. When sufficiently wealthy people want something bad enough, it becomes invaluable, because then art isn't experienced through the eyes, but by the ears, they're not paying for a picture but for its name and history. In their world it isn't the artist who should be admired, it's the owner, because only something which has a price can have any value. That's why the children on the painting are so important that they're protected by guards, but the children on the pier in real life could die without anyone even caring.

The painting that was called *The One of the Sea* didn't become world-famous because it was fantastic, it wasn't coveted because it was a work of genius, but because of everything the artist did after it. The art he one day created, when he called himself "C. Jat" and painted pictures that knocked the breath out of everyone who saw them, but also the man he became known as: he was shy and broken, and the buyers loved that, the more broken the better. *Break some more*, they wished, *go to pieces in front of us!*

When C. Jat stopped going out, he became mysterious, when he stopped giving interviews, he was stalked. The less he had to give, the more everyone wanted. One day he would be called one of the great artists of his generation, and everyone always wants to know what great artists are going to do next, but for some artists it's the other way round: they become so loved that eventually everyone wants to know what they created back at the start. That was how *The One of the Sea* became world-famous, because that was where it all began. That was why it was bought and sold so many times, and that was why one day it was so expensive that it cost the artist all the money he had to buy it back.

For what? Nothing special. The brushstrokes were a teenager's, the narrative a child's. Even so, plenty of people who had seen it once could never quite stop talking about it afterward. Because everyone only saw the sea at first, all that blue, you had to stand there looking for a really long time before you caught sight of the three kids at the end of the pier. A lot of people actually saw nothing at all unless the figures were pointed out to them, and the people who pointed them out always did so triumphantly, as if they were showing the way to a hidden treasure. That was why the newspapers started calling him a genius, because it was as if that fourteen-year-old had planned the mystery precisely so: as if only someone who loved the sea enough, and understood art deeply enough, would look long enough to see the children.

But the truth? It wasn't intentional. Joar found that competition but the artist couldn't even afford paint. He couldn't even explain that to Joar because Joar got very angry at words he didn't understand, and "watercolors" is a difficult concept to grasp. Painting in oils was obviously even harder, because when Joar heard that, he exclaimed: "What do you mean, oil? Everything would fucking end up black, wouldn't it?"

So it was never intentional, any of this, the artist just promised to try in order to make his best friend happy. It wasn't his intention to paint the sea, and it wasn't his intention that anyone would see three children sitting at the end of the pier. If anyone had asked him what art was, he would have whispered that it was probably something for other kids, for the rich, the smart ones, the ones with talent. He didn't know a damn thing about art, his hands just drew for the same reason that some feet dance: they don't know how to stop.

That was why there very nearly wasn't a painting at all. Because right after the first funeral that year, just before the second one, his fingers stopped drawing altogether. If Joar hadn't kept nagging and nagging, they would probably never have started again.

Honestly? It *is* a great painting. Just not at all in the way that the people who called the artist a genius thought.

That June evening twenty-five years ago, when the teenagers were on their way home from the pier, the artist walked closer to Joar than he ever did with anyone else. Joar said quietly:

"I'm sorry I can't tell you it doesn't matter."

"What?" the artist wondered disconsolately, always heartbroken at not being able to be all the things everyone wanted.

Joar took a deep breath and his old man's fingerprints shone blue and purple all over his body in the light of the streetlamps. Then he said tersely:

"I know you want me to say that the competition doesn't matter. That you don't have to win. But I can't say that. You have to win. You have to get away from this fucking town!"

The artist walked on with his eyes fixed to the ground and replied unhappily: "You always talk about me as if I was worth a better life than the rest of you . . ."

"You're not!" Joar replied immediately.

The artist was so surprised that he almost laughed, but Joar just shook his head slowly and went on with devastating seriousness: "You're not worth a better life than us. It's just that you'll never be able to cope with living like us. A normal life? You're too soft for that.

Staying here and working in the fucking harbor like our dads? Getting up every morning and feeling like shit? Being angry all the fucking time? Day after day for fifty years? That's hard. You have to be a hard man. You aren't. You need a different life."

The artist walked in silence for a long time before he dared to ask: "What about you, then?"

Joar smiled dreamily and said: "I'm going to have a normal life. I'll work in the harbor. Get up every morning and feel like shit, be angry all the fucking time. But every so often, on a fucking Sunday, I'll go to some museum somewhere. And deep inside, there'll be a painting by a world-famous artist, and it'll be so beautiful that I can cope with being alive for one more week."

The artist was so happy at that, for a dizzyingly brief moment, because Joar hardly ever spoke about his own future. Joar was always in a hurry for the present. He was in a hurry to love the start and middle of summer vacation, June and July, because that was the best time of the whole year. Because August meant his old man was on vacation from work, and that was the worst. The most dangerous thing you can give evil is free time, because that meant darker jealousy and deeper paranoia and more empty bottles. His mother wouldn't survive another August, Joar was certain of that, and he knew that his own body wasn't yet strong enough to protect her. He was always the shortest of them, but his friends would always remember him as the biggest and bravest. His old man was the opposite, he weighed two hundred pounds but was a tiny, tiny man.

One time a teacher at school said that Joar was "irresponsible," which was the craziest thing the artist had ever heard. Sure, Joar couldn't sit still and couldn't be quiet in class, but only because he was in a hurry. Most children don't know that they're in a hurry, they're lucky. The teachers said that Joar didn't listen, but what they really meant was that he didn't obey. They said he was violent, but he was just better than everyone else at fighting. He was never the one who started fights, but it always looked that way after he had won. They said he was dangerous to have in the classroom, but it was actually the artist who was the dangerous one, because it was always him that Joar was protecting.

The problem was that once Joar's brain got stuck on a thought, all his brain cells flocked around it like ants around a sugar sandwich, but unfortunately it wasn't always the smartest brain cells that got there first. So he got terribly angry at strange things. If his best friend got caught in a door, the door would get a beating, because in Joar's world, there were no inanimate objects, everything was conscious and anything they did was on purpose. He refused to eat cilantro because some people love cilantro and some think it tastes of soap. It didn't taste like soap to Joar, he just refused to eat something that was so damn unfair. Once he heard someone on television talking about "organic meat" and asked the artist what it meant, and the artist suggested that maybe it meant the pigs got better food and were allowed to live outdoors, and maybe be happier? "So they only murder the happy pigs? Isn't that fucking worse?" Joar wondered angrily. The artist had no reply to that. It was hard to argue with Joar's logic, however flawed.

Once when they were in the fourth grade the teacher asked Joar to stay behind, so the artist had to go out into the hallway on his own, and some sixth graders rushed over and snatched his sketch pad from him. At first they just laughed, but when they caught sight of the naked bodies he'd drawn, they yelled that he was fucking disgusting. That didn't hurt him as much as they wanted it to, so they hit him and shoved him headfirst into a locker, but that didn't seem to hurt him enough either. Not until they tore up his sketch pad, the artist had never experienced pain like that, so he screamed. Joar came flying out of the classroom, there were five of the older boys but Joar was a whole gang on his own. They were bigger and stronger, which was fortunate, because otherwise he would probably have killed them. It took a janitor and three teachers to drag Joar away. He was made to sit in the principal's office while they called his parents, and unfortunately it was one of those days when his old man had been too drunk to go to work, so he was the one who answered.

On the way home after being told off by the principal, Joar stopped in the hallway where the fight had taken place. He bent down to pick up all the garbage that had fallen out of the trash can when he had stuffed one of the sixth graders into it. The adults at school thought he was cold and hard, that he didn't have feelings. It was the opposite that was the problem, for God's sake. This was a boy who cared about animals and cilantro and hated fighting. He only fought for those he loved. So the artist lived in constant fear that one day Joar would love someone so much that he would end up in prison.

When Joar got home that evening, his old man almost beat him to death, and if it hadn't been so unbearably cruel, it would have been almost ironic, beating a child because he had been fighting at school. His old man came down on him like an avalanche, and it wasn't even to teach him a lesson. He just did it because when the principal called him, he had had to sit there and pretend to be a proper parent, a real dad. It had reminded that bastard of what he really was: nothing. That was why he beat the boy extra hard.

When Joar came back to school, he played soccer at every single recess, throwing himself headfirst into every tackle, to create excuses for a body absolutely covered in black and blue. After that day the artist always hid his sketch pad extra carefully from the sixth graders. Not to protect himself, and certainly not to protect them, but to protect Joar. Because Joar was dangerous, but the world was always more dangerous. The world is undefeated.

Responsibility? No one ever felt more of it.

So as they walked home from the pier that June day twenty-five years ago, the artist whispered the only thing he dared hope:

"Maybe you could come with me? Away from here?"

"I can come and visit!" Joar lied, because of course he knew that would never happen. He knew that his future was nothing, as empty as the clouds. That was why he let himself promise: "Don't worry about me! You're going to be world-famous and happy, like the celebrities on TV. You're going to paint things people love. And you know what I'll get? I'll get the best thing of all: knowing that I was part of the reason."

When they saw the outlines of their homes on the horizon, Joar kept his eyes fixed on his until he could see the flowers growing in the small tin box hanging outside his bedroom window. His mom grew plants that were a small revolution every day, an armed resistance of tenderness in an apartment besieged by hatred and violence. Joar walked slower, and quieter, until he felt something touch his fingertips. It took several seconds for him to realize that the artist was holding his hand.

The artist was fourteen years old and knew nothing about art, but one day he would be grown-up and celebrated around the world, and would realize that he still only knew the same simple things: Art is a moment. Art is being a reason. Art is coping with being alive for one more week.

It was Ted who called out "Tomorrow" at the crossroads that evening, and when the others replied, "Tomorrow!" one of them added a fart as well. Dear God, how they all laughed, until their spines popped like Bubble Wrap, a fart really is the best chiropractor if you know how to appreciate it.

That evening Joar opened all the windows in his childhood home and watered all his mom's plants, lavender and geraniums, in the tin flower boxes. She kissed him on his hair and said: "That isn't your responsibility." He did the vacuuming and hung the laundry on the radiators and she whispered: "Darling Joar, that isn't your responsibility." Then they talked about what was the best invention in the world, and she said, "Bottle caps," and he got annoyed, so she suggested,

"Bottle openers, then?" and it took him several minutes to realize that she was teasing him. "I'm stupid, but I'm not *that* stupid," she giggled. He wanted to say that she wasn't stupid at all, but instead he said: "Your fly is open." When she looked down and realized he was joking, she exclaimed: "These pants don't even have a zipper!" The way he laughed at that made her think that no mother in the whole world was as lucky as her.

She had bought pizza, she really only did that when they had something to celebrate, but sometimes when she needed to help Joar forget. She was so good at that. She told jokes, he laughed, not at her jokes but at how much she laughed at them herself. He had to help her slice the pizza because one of her arms hurt so badly she couldn't lift it. She had told her colleagues at work that she had slipped on some wet grass and they had laughed, because she was so clumsy. Joar tried to laugh too, but when he couldn't manage it anymore and the look in his eyes grew darker, his mom simply breathed the words: "Darling, darling, it isn't your responsibility."

As if there was anything that wasn't, as if that was the sort of son she had. Joar was the one who dreamed of being a superhero, but she was the one who had superpowers. Her arm was broken, the radiator that Joar's old man had thrown her against was buckled, he had thrown her so hard that there were dents in the metal.

"It's okay, Mom. Now let's eat this pizza before it gets cold," Joar nodded, hanging laundry over the dents. She hugged him with one arm. Then they watched TV, and the happy celebrities, and Joar did his job: he made her think he had forgotten, he was so good at that. When his mom fell asleep, Joar lay awake in his bed with dirt from the flower boxes on his fingers. He listened for the key in the lock, waiting for his old man to come home drunk. Outside the window the lavender and geraniums were growing, it was beneath them Joar had hidden his knife.

Art? It's context.

Soon Joar's old man would be standing at the door. A few days from now his best friend would start a world-famous painting. In twenty-five years perhaps someone would look at it really, really closely and see that the artist had painted something on the pier next to the teenagers.

Flowers.

FIFTEEN

There's a poem by Mary Oliver, "The Summer Day," which ends with the lines:

Tell me, what is it you plan to do
with your one wild and precious life?

Ted heard the artist whisper it to himself at the funeral that summer, over and over again. They were fourteen years old then. It was the first time Ted had lost someone he loved, when you grow up you realize that fourteen is actually quite late, that not losing anyone in all the years before then was really just luck. Ted remembers how he cried sitting in the pew afterward, inconsolably and violently, until his throat stung and his chest ached. Until then he hadn't known that grief is physical, an abuse of the living.

Twenty-five years later he's sitting on a train with a box containing the artist's ashes, in a larger box on the floor is an absurdly valuable painting, and beside him sits a completely strange and wildly annoying teenager. Bad ideas? Ted grew up with Joar, a boy who had once tried to dry his wet socks in a toaster, and on another occasion, when a carton of ice cream was too frozen to scoop, had thought: "I'll just warm the spoon in the microwave!" So Ted has seen some really bad ideas, but none worse than this.

He feels like yelling at the box of ashes that he isn't ready for this sort of responsibility. He wants to remind the artist of the time Ted didn't buy a pair of suede boots because they would require too much maintenance. I can't even look after *shoes*, and you've left me with a *person*, he thinks angrily. Angry at himself, angry at the artist, and most of all angry at death for having such good taste. Always taking the best first.

Just a few weeks ago, Ted had been sitting in the artist's big, beautiful apartment. They had eaten breakfast on the balcony, watching the seasons change, spring was slow but relentless, winter dying an inch at a time. On the other side of the artist's stupid little jokes and sparkling laughter, the illness was gaining ground in much the same way. His hands shook, making him spill his tea, but he didn't care. Ted was so envious, he wished he were able to confront death so nonchalantly.

"How much do you think it costs?" the artist had asked, as if they were talking about something no more important than a bag of potatoes.

They had seen the article in the paper, saying that the artist's first painting was going to be sold at auction. At first Ted had thought he was joking, then he had sputtered:

"You're *serious*? It would cost everything you own!"

"Good. Artists are supposed to die poor," the artist had grinned.

"Stop saying that."

"That I'm going to be poor?"

"You know perfectly well what I mean."

The artist's shoulders had bounced merrily.

"I tried to give you the money. You didn't want it."

"I can't take responsibility for that much money," Ted had whispered.

"Well, then. In that case, I'm going to buy the only thing I want," the artist had laughed.

Then he had started to cough so badly that Ted leapt up to help.

"Are you okay? Should I call the doctor?"

"No, no, stop worrying that I'm going to die every time I cough."

Ted had replied, hurt:

"I'm not worried you're going to die. I'm worried about you being dead. I'm worried about being alive without you."

The artist's smile had been like sunlight between heavy curtains.

"Tell me, Ted, what is it that you plan to do with your one wild and precious life?"

"Stop it," Ted had muttered.

"Stooop it," the artist had teased affectionately.

"Can you try to behave like an adult, just for once?"

"Definitely not! Under no circumstances are we allowed to be adults, Ted, that's fatal! All adults die, sooner or later, haven't you noticed?"

"Sit still and I'll mop up your tea . . ."

The artist's voice was hoarse from coughing as he asked again:

"Please, Ted, tell me. What is it that you plan to do? You've been hiding away in my apartment for two years now. You've been playing hooky from life."

"I've been taking care of you!"

"I know. And for that, I love you. But when I'm gone, you need to live."

Ted had no answer to that. After breakfast the artist felt sick, and when he threw up Ted sat beside him, holding his frail body and stroking what little hair he had left.

"Don't try to talk . . . ," Ted pleaded in vain when his stubborn friend tried to say something anyway.

"Don't tell me what to do, I'm actually dying here!" the artist smiled tiredly with his cheek against the cold porcelain.

Ted sighed:

"You know what? It's actually going to be nice to have some peace and quiet!"

The artist's roar of laughter echoed around the whole apartment. Not many people are blessed like that, with as many giggles and chuckles as he was in his final weeks, with the chance to feel that he stole more moments from death than death had from him. Breakfast on the balcony every morning, popcorn and old films every evening, his best person to hold his hand. Who gets all that? Hardly anyone. That was why he decided to buy back his first painting, no matter what it cost. People always said he was extraordinary, but he was just like everyone else, at the end of his life he only wished for what almost all of us wish for: to have our childhood summers back.

"I want you to be happy when I'm gone," he had whispered to Ted one evening, just before he fell asleep.

It was a lot to ask, of course. Having a heart is heavy, far too heavy for some of us. But Ted had promised to try.

"Joar? Joar . . . is that you?" the artist had mumbled hopefully when he woke up.

"No. It's Ted. Joar isn't here," Ted had whispered back from his chair, trying to accept the disappointment in his friend's eyes.

It's all too heavy, far too heavy for some of us, but we carry on anyway. The days had passed between the two men in that big apartment, breakfasts and old films, fingertips held in palms. And laughter, laughter, laughter. Stupid little jokes, silliness between soulmates, everything else is just meaningless gaps in a life. Sometimes the artist managed to persuade Ted not to be adult, once he threw water balloons indoors and Ted got so angry that he actually caught one and threw it back. Unfortunately the artist ducked and the water balloon flew through the open balcony door and down into the street, they heard a splash and someone shouting angrily in a foreign language. After that they ate breakfast indoors for three days. At least once every morning the artist giggled so hard at the memory that egg flew out of his mouth and spattered the wallpaper, and when the men's eyes met then, it felt like summer to Ted.

Very few people knew the artist was ill, and only Ted and the doctors knew how bad it really was. "Death is public but dying is private, the very last private thing we have," the artist had said, and there had been no fear in his voice, no bitterness. It had been a long life. Wild and precious.

He had painted that picture of his friends on the pier the summer they turned fifteen, when he and Ted had known each other for two years. That autumn, after the funerals, they went their separate ways but without ever losing each other. Everything Joar had dreamed of for the artist really did happen: he was discovered by influential people, got into a prestigious art school, and moved to a big city far away. There he would lie on the floor of a small room, terrified, crying with Ted on the phone all night. No one else understood their grief. The world was so overwhelming, harsh and violent, the boys were too sensitive to have hearts. Sometimes the artist would sit curled up in his window looking at life going on in the street below, and whisper into the phone: "How does everyone else cope, Ted?"

"Maybe we'll learn?" Ted said, trying to sound hopeful.

Perhaps they did, for a while, unless they just got better at pretending. When the artist turned eighteen he was described as a "prodigy" by his teachers, when he turned twenty they said he would be world-famous, by the time he was twenty-eight he wished they had been wrong.

But in the years in between? That was when something altogether remarkable happened to him: he found his voice. It was Ted who suggested that he ought to go traveling and see the world when he finished art school. The artist's parents died, the artist came home to bury them, and Ted was terrified that if his friend didn't leave again at once, he might get stuck there forever.

"You need to see bigger things," Ted told him.

"Come with me," the artist asked, knowing of course that Ted would say no.

Ted wanted an ordinary life, to wake up in his ordinary bed, he definitely didn't want to experience the world. He just wanted to see the look in his friend's eyes when he came home from seeing it. So the artist set out on his own. When he was twenty-two, he went from country to country, chasing paintings, devouring galleries and museums. He hitchhiked, took slow trains, crossed a mountain range on a ramshackle old motorbike. When he was twenty-four, he worked as a dishwasher and cleaner, falling in love with strangers on pulsating dance floors, dancing in the moonlight on endless beaches. Then he met old women who taught him to paint portraits and get paid for it, then he met young men with cans of spray paint who taught him to paint the walls of buildings and run from the police. When he was twenty-six, he had done this on every continent, so he called Ted and told him he was on his way home. The phone echoed as they drowned in each other's laughter, but it didn't turn out the way the artist expected. He sent his new paintings ahead, to his old teachers at art school, and his astonished teachers in turn sent them to important men and women. And everything changed. The artist had seen all the world's art, now he was creating art the world had never seen, that was how he became famous. He never came home again after that. He never again sat on the pier drawing.

Fame was instantaneous and merciless, certainly not something for sensitive boys, the artist had taken the world, but now it took him. When he was twenty-eight, he went traveling again, but differently this time, he was driven in big black cars to crowded airports. Everyone he met told him they loved him, hardly anyone survives that. He was photographed for magazine covers, and lay on the floors of expensive hotel suites all night, breathing through his panic on the phone with Ted. The artist was an observer, he couldn't bear to be observed, the world always gets those mixed up.

When he was thirty, he was taking pills every day, because no one who loved him was around to look in his backpack anymore. For a while he was deliriously happy and unhappy at the same time, always one or the other, until in the end he couldn't tell the difference. So many people appeared in his life, telling him what he ought to paint, how he ought to sell his art. At first those people worked for the artist, but soon he was working for them. Soon everyone was disappointed because he painted too slowly, too strangely, too little. When he was thirty-two, he was having panic attacks so often that he forgot how his body had felt before them. He bought an enormous apartment and filled it with beautiful things, but slept on a mattress in the hall, curled up like a cat. He was tricked out of half a fortune, gave the other half away voluntarily, he looked for love in all the wrong places and got his heart crushed in every possible way. He stopped going out, his skin was too thin for fame, his lungs too small for the top of the world. When strangers recognized him in the street, he would run like a terrified animal. When he turned thirty-five, a rich man came to his studio and bought a painting that wasn't even finished, one week later there was a line of other rich men outside, all hoping to do the same thing. He had become so famous that his unfinished paintings were the most valuable now. He never went to his studio again after that, he lived in his apartment like someone shipwrecked, whispering on the phone to Ted: "Everyone wants me to paint more pictures, but only until they buy one, because then they hope that I never paint again. My art is only an investment now, everyone who owns a piece of me hopes I'll die, because nothing is more valuable at auction than an unfulfilled life."

He hit rock bottom when he was thirty-seven. One night he was so drunk that he almost drowned in his own bathtub, alone in his apartment, surrounded by beautiful, silent things. That was when Ted came to live with him, even though Ted hated traveling and was terrified of big cities. He took the train, saying it was too expensive to fly, but the first thing the artist whispered in his ear when Ted stepped into the apartment was: "Coward!"

Ted snapped back: "You know what they say about bumblebees? That they shouldn't be able to fly? Well, neither should people!"

The artist laughed. So did Ted. Neither of them had done that for a long time. Ted was only planning to stay for a short while, but that turned into the rest of the artist's life. At first they both pretended that it was for Ted's sake, that he had needed a vacation. But really it was the artist who needed a home, and home was Ted's snoring in the darkness, like when they were kids, back in the basement.

From that day until his last, the artist was neither unhappy nor too happy, just everything in between, calm and safe and contented. Everything a person can wish for. They giggled, danced, made food, and read poetry out loud to each other. That lasted several months, a handful of moments, an eternity. Then the artist got sick and Ted stayed. In twenty-five years of friendship, they only lived with each other for four: two years as teenagers, two years at the end. But if you don't believe that boys' souls can be connected across a great distance, you know nothing about them.

Toward the end of his illness, the artist slept a lot, and Ted would sit beside his bed and read. The artist's bookcases were full of poets, like the bookcases of anyone trying to find out how everyone else copes.

Ted read Bodil Malmsten: "There is no death, only a lot of dead." Then he read Joan Didion, about her first memory of coming home from the hospital after her husband died: "I remember putting his cell phone in the charger on his desk." Then he read Bodil Malmsten again: "That is what death is, that you are never answering again."

Then he read Maya Angelou, "When Great Trees Fall":

Our memory, suddenly sharpened,
examines,
gnaws on kind words
unsaid,
promised walks
never taken.

Then he read Bodil Malmsten, over and over again: "The heart is always unguarded." He fell asleep in the chair and when he woke up, the artist was gently holding his fingers.

Just before Easter that last spring, the artist's doctor said that he definitely must not travel anywhere. The following day, Ted helped him sell all his belongings, then they traveled all the way to the auction and Ted bought the painting, and behind the church the artist met Louisa.

Now Ted is sitting on a train, with a box of ashes and a famous painting and a teenager clearly out of her mind. It really is a remarkably bad idea, all this. Worse than socks in the toaster.

SIXTEEN

Ted manages to accidentally doze off, in that way that means he wakes up surprised, not knowing how long he's been asleep. Just a few seconds, maybe? Minutes? What time is it? That's when he realizes how exhausted he is, as he blinks groggily up at the lights in the ceiling of the train. He was woken by a drumming sound. He looks around for a while before he figures out what it is: Louisa is tapping her fingers on the armrest, restless as a wasp in a jar.

"When's the train going to stop again? I need to pee!" she hisses.

He stares at her as if she's joking, but she most certainly isn't.

"There . . . there are toilets on the train," he says, as gently as he can, because he doesn't want her to feel stupid.

"Are you kidding? I thought they only had those on trains in movies!" she says loudly, apparently not feeling stupid at all, and then he can't help thinking that it might be appropriate to feel a *little* bit stupid after all. But he points toward a door with the word "Toilet" on it, and she bounces away as if someone had yelled, "Free marshmallows!"

Once she's gone, Ted sits alone and marvels at how silently an eighteen-year-old can get to her feet, without so much as a single groan or creak of the spine. When you grow up and see how naturally a teenager moves, you realize the logic of Stone Age people dying when they were twenty-seven, because from then on, the body does everything it can do to die. You think you're going to be young forever, but suddenly you reach an age where getting up from a chair can't be taken for granted, it requires planning, and Ted has now reached that age. Not so long ago he had gotten a stiff neck when he sneezed. "You're starting to get old," the artist had grinned, and Ted had felt so insulted that he blurted out: "Says someone who's actually dying!"

He had instantly felt so ashamed that he covered his mouth with both hands, and oh, how the artist coughed then, because he was laughing so much.

Ted nudges the box of ashes and his voice breaks as he says:

"I can understand what you saw in her. I know who she reminded you of."

The train gains speed, the world flickers past outside, first houses and roads, then farms and fields. Soon trees and darkness. It's a long way from here to the sea, unbelievably long.

The toilet door flies open and Louisa comes back. Ted wipes his cheeks and tries to hide by looking out the window. She lands on the seat beside him as if it were the long-jump pit at the Olympics.

"Why do you look so sad? Have you been crying?" she asks.

He wipes his eyes hard with his wrist and mutters irritably: "No."

"Is it because of your hair?" Louisa asks with deep sympathy.

At first he doesn't understand at all, but then she looks just a few seconds too long at the top of his forehead, so he mumbles: "No. No! No? Why . . . why do you say that?"

She shrugs her shoulders nonchalantly.

"I just guessed. You were sitting there looking at your reflection in the window, so I thought it was because of your hair."

"I wasn't looking at my *reflection*!" Ted declares.

Then he does his very best not to look as if he's looking at the reflection of his forehead while looking at the reflection of his forehead to check how far back his hairline has actually crept now. He thinks of what Joar used to say: *You know you're old when you have to use soap on your head and shampoo on your ass.*

Louisa interrupts him amiably enough with a far more important question:

"Where does the poop go?"

"Excuse me?"

"The poop people poop on the train, where does it go?"

Ted clears his throat the way the most uncomfortable man in the world would clear his throat.

"I . . . I assume there's some sort of container beneath the train."

"What happens if that gets full, then? Do they just empty the poop onto the tracks, or what?"

He looks almost shocked by the idea.

"I don't know. Maybe."

She thinks for a long time before asking, very seriously:

"What if it's really windy outside? So if you were walking next to the rails, you'd get a poop tornado right in your face?"

"I've never thought about it," he confesses.

"How can you *not* have thought about it? It's *all* I can think of now!"

He sighs so deeply that it's a miracle the fields of wheat outside the train window don't get flattened.

"Maybe . . . maybe we could have a little silence break for a while?"

She shrugs her shoulders and mutters:

"Okay. Sure."

She takes a sketch pad out of her backpack, makes herself comfortable in her seat, and puts her feet up on the backrest of the seat in front of her. Ted really, really tries not to point out that that isn't allowed, but soon every field all the way to the horizon gets flattened when he sighs:

"Can you please take your feet down from the seat?"

"Why?" Louisa asks, uncomprehendingly.

"You'll make it dirty," he says.

She looks at him, then at the back of the seat, then at him again.

"What if I take my shoes off, then?"

"That isn't what it's about."

"So what is it about, then?"

"It's about not sitting with your feet on the back of the seat in front!"

"Why not?"

"Because only badly behaved kids do that!"

She looks at the back of the seat, then at him.

"Okay. Backrest police."

The train brakes, creaks, and rocks as it pulls into a station. Louisa notes that Ted keeps looking at the time.

"Why do you keep looking at your watch?" she asks.

"To check if the train is on time," he replies, more irritably than she thinks is strictly reasonable.

"Are you in a hurry?"

"No."

"So why do you care if it's on time, then?"

"I always care about things being on time."

She looks at him as if he were crazy, which he really doesn't appreciate. He contemplates going to the bathroom, then realizes what a nuisance it would be to stand up, and decides that it isn't worth it. Louisa takes a cigarette out of her backpack and balances it between her lips as she draws.

"Are you out of your mind? You can't smoke in here!" Ted says instantly.

"Look, for someone who wanted to sit in silence, you're making an awful lot of noise," Louisa points out.

"Surely you understand that you can't smoke in here," Ted hisses, so she hisses back:

"I haven't even lit it! I don't even have a lighter! I don't even smoke!"

"Why do you have cigarettes, then?"

"They're not mine! They belong to my friend Fish!"

They stare at each other, the thirty-nine-year-old and the eighteen-year-old, with funerals in their eyes. It's hard to cope with seeing yourself in someone else.

"Okay," he mumbles.

"Okay!" she mumbles.

"You shouldn't smoke, you're too young," he persists sullenly as he looks out the window.

"Why?" she says, looking down at her drawing.

"Because it will kill you."

"If you wait until you're old enough to smoke, you die even if you don't smoke," she replies, which is irritatingly hard to argue with.

But she does at least take her feet down from the seat, and removes the cigarette from her mouth.

"Thank you," Ted says quietly.

"Are you married?" she asks, without raising her eyes from her drawing.

"No."

"Do you have kids?"

"No."

"What a waste."

"Sorry?"

"I said it's a waste, being as annoying as you are, you might as well be someone's annoying dad."

Ted sighs and closes his eyes, in the futile hope that she will too.

Louisa stays quiet for as long as she can possibly manage—so something like a minute and a half—before she asks, "What sort of flowers are they?"

Ted opens his eyes and wrinkles his nose with such surprise that his glasses slip off.

"Flowers?"

Louisa carries on drawing, lets her hair fall down and hide her face, as if the question embarrasses her.

"On . . . on the painting. The ones lying next to you on the pier. What sort of flowers are they?"

It's the first time he's heard her sound uncertain, as if she's worried she's wrong and might appear stupid. Ted's shoulders slump, it's a burden to hear yourself in others.

"Hardly anyone ever sees those flowers," he admits gently.

"I didn't see them until I saw the painting in real life, you can't see them on the postcard, you have to stand really close," she says quietly.

Ted nods thoughtfully, then leans forward, lifts the painting carefully out of its box, and looks at the tiny pink and purple marks next to the teenagers on the pier. Then he whispers:

"Geraniums and lavender. It was Joar's mom who—"

Louisa suddenly forgets to feel embarrassed and changes back into an overexcited child again, and exclaims:

"Joar? The one who farted?"

Ted's brain strongly disapproves, the way an adult brain is supposed to, but the corners of his mouth can't help twitching.

"Yes . . . yes, Joar used to do incredible farts. He could blow holes in his jeans. Maybe that was why his mom grew so many flowers, now I come to think about it, it was probably the only way to survive when you have a son who's like a chemical weapon."

He laughs, so does Louisa.

"She sounds like a good mom," she says.

Ted nods, but sadly now, his muscles unable to maintain the laughter. His face isn't used to it. When you get old, gravity pulls the corners of your mouth down, the road to a smile grows longer.

"Yes, she really was remarkable at growing things, everything smelled so good around her. She managed to help everything . . . survive."

His mouth drowns in wrinkles at the end of the sentence.

"You must all have liked her very much if her flowers were included in the painting," Louisa declares.

Ted cleans his crooked glasses to give himself a chance to blink more slowly.

"Yes. Everyone loved her. We couldn't understand how her and Joar's home could smell so good, that something so lovely could exist in a place where someone so evil lived. Because Joar's old man was . . . he was big and strong, but he was a tiny man. He used to beat Joar and his mother like they weren't even human beings, he . . ."

Ted falls silent again, firstly because he doesn't know how to describe men like that, but then because he realizes that Louisa probably already knows all about them.

"I understand," she whispers.

"I'm sorry that you do," he whispers back.

She smiles at that, strangely enough. She's young, it's still so easy for her, it doesn't cost her body anything.

"Geraniums and lavender," she repeats dreamily from behind her hair, the words falling down onto her sketch pad, and then she says something quite remarkable:

"Thank you."

"What for?" Ted wonders.

She shrugs her shoulders.

"For telling me things. And for letting me come with you."

Ted says nothing for so long that she almost taps him on the nose to see if he's still breathing. In the end he blinks and mumbles:

"Joar was actually the shortest of us, but he looks tallest in the painting."

Louisa looks up and tucks her hair away from her eyes.

"Even shorter than you? Seriously? What are you, hobbits?"

"I . . . ," Ted begins, feeling a little insulted, but she quickly explains:

"I mean, hobbits are people in *The Lord of the Rings*, they're really short!"

"Thanks, I know what hobbits are," Ted sighs.

Louisa rolls her eyes.

"Well, sorry I tried to explain, then! You're really old, so how am I supposed to know what films you've seen?"

Then she disappears behind her hair again, adding quickly:

"Maybe Joar was bigger in the painting because that's how you saw him. Fish felt big to me, even though I was much taller. People think it's bad if someone makes you feel small, but it really isn't."

Ted doesn't respond. He just looks down at the box of ashes and concludes, however much it annoys him, that the artist was right. She's one of us.

SEVENTEEN

It's strange, the things you remember from your childhood, but perhaps what you forget is even stranger. When you think about summers growing up, it feels like the sun was always shining, there's never any wind or rain in nostalgia.

At the end of the artist's life, when he was thirty-nine years old and knew he wasn't going to reach forty, he often whispered Joar's name when he woke up. He talked in his sleep about birds and chili sauce, about stolen bicycles and shopping carts going full speed down steep hills, because those were the things his brain clung to. But sometimes Ted saw his friend swimming in bed, as if he were looking for something out at sea, and from time to time the artist would yell out into the darkness: "Where's Ali? Where's Ali?"

It's funny, the way our memory tricks us. Ted was twelve when he met Joar and the artist, almost a teenager, but he could hardly recall life before them. For more than a year they had no one but each other, but despite that, that isn't how Ted remembers that time. In his mind, there were always four of them.

Twenty-five years ago the friends always cried "HERE!" to each other when they emerged from the water. They would run along the pier together and jump right into the sea in different directions, down into the darkness. Down there they were alone, flailing wildly against the deep as their thin bodies grew heavy, as if invisible claws were pulling at them from the depths. Then, just as inexplicably every time, the claws would suddenly let go and they would fly up toward the surface. "HERE!" the first friend would cry out as soon as they opened their eyes toward the sky and the air reached their lungs. "HERE!" the next would cry. "HERE! HERE! HERE! HERE!" they would all cry. In winter, when the sun hadn't risen by the time they set off for school, they did the same thing at the crossroads: "HERE!" they would call between the buildings before they caught sight of each other in the darkness. "HERE! HERE! HERE! HERE!"

Four cries. Joar's, then the artist's, then Ted's. But first of all: hers.

The summer they turned fifteen, the morning after Joar had lain awake with a knife hidden in the dirt beneath the flowers, listening for the sound of his old man's key in the lock on the front door, his friends waited for him at the crossroads until the sun was high in the sky. But he didn't appear. His old man had been out all night, even more drunk than usual, he had been defenseless. The bastard couldn't have opened the front door to the apartment even if it had been unlocked. Joar had lain in bed, feeling the weight of the knife in his hand and the hatred in his heart, hour after hour.

The next morning, his friends sat on the grass by the crossroads, waited as long as they possibly could, then they began to walk toward his home. They saw the tin flower box outside his room from a distance, the window was open, the wind playing through the geraniums and lavender. The friends stopped in the street, stood and looked up at his window, unable to summon the courage to call his name. Friendship is special when you're a teenager, you can feel in your skin when there's something wrong.

"Here," the voice suddenly whispered from the doorway.

The friends' eyes jumped in surprise from the window to the door. There stood Joar, with dirt on his fingers, wearing a crumpled shirt. His old man really had been more drunk than usual last night, so drunk that he hadn't even come home, a workmate from the harbor had let him sleep on his sofa. That morning, Joar's mom had looked in Joar's room and seen that her son was lying awake. When she told him that his old man hadn't come home the night before, she didn't see relief in Joar's eyes, but something far more terrifying: disappointment. She saw the darkness in Joar's eyes and his clenched fists, and noted that the window was ajar. She never saw the knife, she didn't need to, because being a mother is special too: you can feel in your skin when there's something wrong.

"Mom got it in her head that we needed to repot all the plants in the apartment this morning, I had to help her," Joar said to his friends by way of explanation.

His friends could obviously see that he was hiding something, but it's hard to find the right words when you're fourteen years old, so they said the only one they had:

"Here."

"Here," Joar smiled.

As they set off toward the pier that day, he was clutching the straps of his backpack so tightly that his knuckles turned white, because that was where he had hidden the knife now. He had realized that he couldn't kill his old man if his mom was home, she was too suspicious, he needed a new plan. Ted was walking unhappily by his side, feeling his friend's pain but unable to do anything about it, so instead Ted did something thoroughly unexpected: he was funny. A squirrel ran past them and scampered up a tree, and Ted shouted:

"Artichoke!"

If you had heard his friends laugh then, you would never have guessed at what, but a more liberating roar had never tumbled over those streets. Because when Ted had first gotten to know Joar and the artist when they were twelve years old, he had hardly dared speak at all, always so frightened of pronouncing words wrong. He was an immigrant kid who could barely remember the country he was from, just young enough when he left to not speak his old language fluently, but just old enough for his accent to always be noticeable in his new one. He had gotten used to the fact that whenever he heard the mocking laughter of other children, it was usually directed at him. But Joar and the artist had laughed in a different way, without any of the malice, so with them was the first time Ted ever dared to babble. There was no greater security for a child.

One day he told them he had found his new language so difficult that he didn't learn to read until he was ten, before then everything had just been a chaos of consonants in his brain, and his big brother had tricked him into believing that the word for "squirrel" was "artichoke." So for several years, whenever Ted saw a furry little animal running through the park, he would think, There's an artichoke. The first time he was in a supermarket with his mom after he learned to read, he read the words "artichoke hearts" on a tin and didn't dare open his mouth. He just went home thinking that the people in this country were the cruelest in the world.

His friends had laughed so hard that they fell over when he told them about this when they were twelve, and now they laughed even harder when they were fourteen.

"When I was little, I tricked my mom into thinking that people who were allergic to fur can't eat kiwis," Joar giggled, and when the others were having trouble breathing, he added: "She still believes that!"

His laughter carried all the way to his home, to the open window and into the apartment. His mother stood there with dirt on her hands, smiling from ear to ear. Being a parent is so strange, all our children's pain belongs to us, but so does their joy.

As the friends walked on toward the sea and the pier that day, it turned out to be one of the best afternoons of the whole summer. Perhaps they would even remember it as one of the best of their lives. There would be other days, much darker, but this one was something else. The artist was clutching his backpack, because it contained all the pills he had stolen from Ted's father's bathroom cabinet. Joar was holding his backpack even tighter, because it contained the knife. But Ted emptied his backpack of cookies, and the artist forced Joar to eat one too, and they were the driest cookies they had ever tasted.

"These cookies are so dry, it feels like they're eating me," Joar said through clumsy lips, as if he had run out of saliva.

They giggled, spraying crumbs like snowflakes, and at that moment it probably felt as if everything could turn out all right. They walked through the streets, away from their homes, crossing the big parking lot where Joar's old man's car was parked. Before that summer was over, they would come running from the other direction and see a police car parked there instead. One day the men who worked at the harbor with Joar's old man would stand beneath the window of Joar's room with empty eyes and hearts full of shame. The apartment would smell of geraniums and lavender and there would be a body lying on the floor.

But not yet, not today, because it's only June. The sun is still shining over the sea, the pier still smells of farts, and the artichokes are still chasing each other through the trees.

Joar looked around, then turned to the artist and Ted and asked:

"Where's Ali?"

It's strange, the things we remember from our childhoods, funny how obvious some things feel in hindsight. As if there had always been four friends, not three. Or as if the world-famous painting was called *The One of the Sea* from the beginning. Because of course that wasn't the case, not at first. The painting should really have been called *The Boys and Her.*

"HERE!" a voice roared somewhere behind the boys that summer's day.

Then Ali came flying around a corner.

EIGHTEEN

Everyone should be allowed to be fourteen for far longer than a year. There are so many other ages we could skip instead: thirty-nine, for instance, is an age that Ted would happily have done without. He feels a sudden urge to pee far more often now than he was prepared for, his body has started to wake him at night, he presumes it's getting its revenge because it's annoyed he's keeping it alive. One time the artist read an article suggesting that people will soon be able to live until they're one hundred and fifty, which Ted thought sounded unbearable, because at this rate he wouldn't be doing anything by then except peeing.

The train shakes and rocks and groans, as if it really hates being a train. Its movements aren't helpful to someone who needs to pee, so in the end Ted gives up and decides to go to the bathroom after all. It isn't a decision he takes lightly, the various parts of his skeleton sound like sugar cubes being trodden on as he unfolds his body and squeezes past Louisa. The bathroom is cramped and the seat is too narrow in a way that you really don't think about when you're young. He wipes every surface before he sits down, hitting his head on various parts of the furnishings four times, and when he is finished he closes the lid carefully before flushing. Then he hears the artist's laughter inside his head, because he was always amused by Ted's fear of germs. The artist refused to believe that if you flushed with the lid open, all the germs got sprayed about, which drove Ted mad. Something else that drove him mad was when, after he had been living with the artist for two weeks, he was going to wash the bedspread and the artist had exclaimed: "You're supposed to WASH it?" He'd been using the same one for years. When he noticed that Ted looked ready to throw up at the very thought, he promised: "I'll wash it tomorrow!" but Ted dismissed the idea gently, saying: "No need. I'm going to burn it tonight."

The brain is so peculiar, the things that get stuck in it.

He leaves the bathroom and weaves back to his seat. Louisa stands up so he can squeeze past, back to his seat by the window. He hopes naively that he might pretend to fall asleep, but there's no chance of that, he doesn't even have time to close his eyes before she asks:

"Do you normally celebrate Easter?"

"No," he sighs.

She nods understandingly.

"Don't you like Jesus? Some people who don't like Jesus don't like Easter. But you know who else probably didn't like Easter? Jesus."

"I have nothing against Easter. Or Jesus," Ted says.

She considers this for a moment, then asks:

"Don't you like eggs? Some people don't like eggs. I mean, I don't LOVE eggs, but we painted some at school when I was little and I liked that. One time I asked the teacher if I could paint my eggs like ninjas, and when she said yes, I just painted all the eggs white. She didn't get the joke."

Ted doesn't respond, and she takes that as a sign that he's definitely interested in hearing more.

"Fish didn't like eating eggs, because she thought it was disgusting to eat an unborn chicken. But you know what she did eat? Chicken! And then she said *I* was the weird one, because when I was little I thought that Santa and Jesus were the same person. I got reeeally confused the first time I heard someone talk about the Crucifixion."

"Okay," Ted nods tersely, in the hope that that might suffice to end the conversation, which of course it absolutely doesn't.

"Why do you have a limp?" she asks.

"I don't have a limp," he says, as a subtle signal that he doesn't want to talk about it.

"Yes, you do! I noticed it earlier, when you ran along the platform!"

she replies, as if she wouldn't recognize a subtle signal if it hit her in the face.

"I was in an incident a few years ago," he sighs.

"What does that mean?"

"An accident."

"Hello, Mister Complicated, have you ever thought about just saying the words you actually mean? What happened?"

He massages his eyelids.

"I fell."

She waits for him to go on, but nothing happens, so she mutters:

"Great story! Really engaging!"

He bites his lips, first the top one, then the bottom one.

"It's a long . . . ," he begins.

"Oh no, not a *long* story! Not when I have so much to *do* right now!" she retorts with a dramatic gesture around the train carriage.

He glares accusingly at the box of ashes, as if this is the ashes' fault. He feels exhausted. His heart has broken. He doesn't know what gets into him, but before he knows it he finds himself telling the truth:

"I got stabbed."

Louisa's eyes grow as large as rich men's wristwatches.

"Are you kidding?"

Then Ted looks up and does something very, very strange. He makes a joke.

"If I was kidding, I would have asked you how to get a one-armed man out of a tree."

Louisa is so surprised by this that at first she sits there in silence, then when she does start laughing, she sprays saliva on Ted's jacket. He panics and tries to wipe it off with his sleeve, and then she laughs even louder:

"Stop it! You're just rubbing it in! You're making it worse!"

He certainly isn't laughing when he asks:

"Can't you even laugh like a normal person?"

Louisa rolls her eyes.

"Do you always moan this much? Is that why someone stabbed you?"

"No!" he snaps.

She shrugs her shoulders apologetically.

"Okay. Why, then?"

He carries on rubbing his jacket, and regrets every single word the moment he opens his mouth:

"It was . . . it was a student at the school where I worked. He tried to stab another student. I intervened."

"Not so smart," she says, trying to sound funny even though she's actually a bit impressed.

"No, not so smart," he agrees, and closes his eyes.

It's somewhat ironic, perhaps, that more than twenty years after Joar hid his knife in the flower box, another teenager had stabbed Ted. He was already fragile before that, but afterward he thought that even the wind had sharp edges. He still has nightmares about both knives.

"Did you come close to dying?" Louisa asks.

"No," he lies.

Louisa peers at him skeptically.

"You got *stabbed* but didn't come close to dying?"

"It was . . . it's a long story . . . I lost a lot of blood," he grunts.

"But you didn't die," she concludes.

"You should be a detective, nothing gets past you," he concludes in response.

She doesn't seem offended by his sarcasm. He can't help thinking that she ought to be a little offended. Typical teenagers—for a generation that seems to take offense at everything, they really are pretty hard to insult.

"So you saved that student's life?" she asks.

"It's hard to answer that," he sighs.

"Why?"

"Because it's a hypothetical question."

She doesn't seem particularly concerned about what a hypothetical question is.

"Were you scared?" she asks.

"I can't answer that either," he says.

"Because it's another one of those hypnotic questions?"

Ted finally stops rubbing his jacket, his chest rises and falls with a resignation that you probably need to have begun losing your hair to understand.

"No. Because the question presupposes that I stopped being scared."

Louisa says nothing for all of three minutes after that. Possibly a personal record, actually.

"When did it happen?"

"Just over two years ago."

She looks at the box of ashes.

"Was that when you went and lived with him?"

Ted polishes his glasses to give himself an excuse to blink a thousand times. Then far more words pour out of him than he is expecting:

"Yes. He . . . he'd been asking me to come and live with him for several years, but I always said that I actually had a proper job, I didn't live in a little Peter Pan world like him. But when I got out of the hospital, I didn't know what to do, I was too frightened to go back to school. I . . . I really needed a Peter Pan world just then. So I went. And when I got there, it was the first time in forever that I slept through a whole night."

His fingers are shaking as he puts his glasses back on, the tape has started to come loose and they're crooked again. When he woke up after the operation, the artist was the first person he called, and it wasn't until long afterward that the artist confessed that he had been so drunk that he had almost drowned in his bathtub the night before.

"Then what happened?" Louisa wonders, after waiting patiently for all of like twelve seconds.

"I stayed with him for a few weeks, then they turned into months, and then he got sick, so . . ."

He bites his top lip, then his bottom lip, then his tongue.

"So you never went back home?" Louisa says.

"He was my home," Ted whispers.

Louisa is quiet for an eternity, maybe almost a whole minute, before asking:

"Were you the only person looking after him?"

"No, no, he had his doctors at the hospital, nurses, loads of . . ."

She shakes her head.

"No, I mean the only one of his friends. I just . . . assumed that if someone is as famous as he was, then they must have loads of people taking care of them."

Ted glances out the window. He thinks about the beautiful apartment, furnished by a famous interior designer at incredible cost. He remembers the vast dining table with sixteen chairs around it, only one of them slightly worn.

"People worshipped his art. He was loved by millions of people. But there's a difference between being loved and receiving love," Ted says, but quickly checks himself, as if this time it's his brain that is starting to slam doors shut and pointing out that surely this is enough personal information now?

Louisa recognizes that look.

"Can you sleep through the night now?" she asks curiously.

"No," he admits.

"Me neither. Not the way I could sleep when Fish was in the same room, I got used to hearing her breathing."

Ted looks down at the box of ashes. Then he glances at Louisa, smiles weakly, and says:

"He used to snore."

"Fish too! Like, really badly! It sounded like someone strangling a dinosaur!"

Ted laughs loudly. It makes his throat hurt, as if his body has forgotten how to do it properly.

"Why aren't you still living in his apartment?" she asks.

"We sold it. We sold everything he owned to have enough to buy back that painting. That's his entire inheritance," Ted says softly.

Her voice sounds heavier when she replies:

"He should have given it to someone else. I don't know anything about art."

Ted glances at her sketch pad. She's been drawing cockroaches.

"How long have you had that postcard of the painting?"

"All my life, pretty much."

"How many different foster homes have you lived in?"

Her face disappears behind her hair again.

"Don't know. Loads. It doesn't matter."

"And you never lost the postcard?"

"Never!" she exclaims in horror, as if it were insane to even think such a thing.

Ted nods slowly.

"Then you know all about art. More than anyone I've ever met."

It's a good thing she's sitting down then, otherwise she would have fallen over.

"He should have given the picture to someone else, someone who's been to one of those fancy art schools, someone who's *good* at painting . . . ," she whispers.

"He didn't want to give it to someone who was good, he wanted to give it to you," Ted replies.

It takes a few seconds for Louisa to realize that's a joke. Then she bursts out laughing, spraying more saliva on his jacket, and Ted regrets being funny.

"Sorry," she giggles.

He takes a breath so deep that he almost ends up in the seat behind his before he replies:

"He often used to say that the only time he felt like himself was when he was painting. Everything else, life, reality, that was just an act. Only art was real for him. And when he met you . . . well, he saw himself. I hadn't seen him draw skulls for several years until I saw that wall in the alley. He told me at the hospital that he loved your cockroaches. He said he'd never seen anyone paint insects so beautifully."

The thirty-nine-year-old and the eighteen-year-old avoid each other's eyes for a long time after that. Her fingertips stroke the sketch pad on her lap.

"There was an old woman, one of those rich assholes at the auction, who shouted that I was a cockroach when I got thrown out. But cockroaches are survivors. That woman is going to die in her ugly summer house, but the cockroaches will live on."

Ted smiles.

"You're one of them now, you know?"

Louisa frowns.

"One of what?"

"You're a rich asshole," Ted smiles, nodding at the painting.

Louisa screws her whole face up. Then she nods, suddenly much more cheerful.

"In that case, I'm no longer homeless! Because when rich people sleep outdoors, it isn't homelessness, it's camping!"

She feels like telling him that she really likes his laugh, but she doesn't quite know how to say that.

"Camping," Ted repeats with a chuckle.

He feels like telling her that the artist didn't give her the painting because it was his inheritance, he gave it to her because he realized that she was the inheritance. Art is what we leave of ourselves in other people. But he doesn't quite know how to say that.

The train rattles on. Louisa says nothing for maybe four and a half minutes. Okay, probably closer to four, to be honest.

"Do you want to ask me anything?" she asks.

"Maybe not right now," Ted sighs toward the window.

"Bit rude. I've asked you loads of things," she points out.

Of course, it is practically impossible to argue with that, so Ted looks at the time, takes a deep breath, and asks:

"Okay. Why was your friend called Fish?"

Louisa brightens up, as if she has just found out there are toilets on trains.

"Because her eyes were, like, really far apart, so some idiots at our foster home called her 'the Hammerhead Shark,' and she hated it, because sharks are predators and she didn't want to be one of them. So she and I decided she should be a fish instead!"

Ted tries really, really hard, but unfortunately he can't stop himself from saying:

"Sharks are fish."

"No. They're mammals," Louisa corrects amiably.

"No. Dolphins and whales are mammals. Sharks are fish," Ted corrects, rather less amiably.

"You're kind of spoiling the story," she points out.

"Okay," he sighs.

"Okay!" she goes on cheerily. "So: she wanted to be a fish because fish are like birds, only underwater. They're free. If you get what I mean?"

He nods, a little less unfriendly now, but doesn't ask anything more, so she replies to the question she thinks he should have asked instead:

"Do you know what Fish called me? The Giant! Because everyone else called me 'Monster' because I was the biggest girl in the house, and I hated it, but when she said 'Giant,' it sounded . . . kind of powerful."

The train lurches and the box of ashes on the floor rocks. Ted bends over and catches it, then can't quite bring himself to let go of it. His brain certainly thinks there have been more than enough questions for one day, but despite that, his lips move tentatively, and out comes:

"What happened to your parents?"

Louisa looks up as if she'd like him to ask again, just because it felt so nice that he cares.

"My dad took off before I was born. He's dead now. He got killed in a fight in a bar or something. He wasn't a good person, so I'm probably lucky he didn't want to be my dad."

"And your mom?" Ted asks.

Louisa draws harder and harder on her sketch pad.

"Well, I don't think she was a bad person. I remember she used to sing, or at least I think I remember that she sang. And we had a TV! So she can't have been a completely bad mom, because then she would have sold the TV."

"What happened to her?" Ted hears himself ask, because now his brain has evidently given up all hope of stopping this conversation from continuing.

Louisa spins her pencil between her fingers, faster and faster.

"When I was five she left me with some neighbors and disappeared. She wasn't a bad person, I think, she was just . . . broken. Like some bits of her were missing, if you get what I mean? The neighbors were nice, but they didn't want a child. And then there was a problem, because when they called the police, the police thought they'd kidnapped me. And then they ended up in prison. Not because of me, though! They ended up in prison because they stole stuff. But they weren't bad people either, I don't think. I think we only had a TV because they'd stolen it for us."

Ted's voice is gentle, like he's trying not to scare a bird, when he asks:

"How do you know all this?"

"A woman from Social Services told me. She said everyone deserves to know their background."

"How old were you then?"

"Seven, maybe."

She's still sitting in a train seat, but for just the blink of an eye, Ted can see her sitting on a pier.

"That's very young to find out all about yourself," he says.

She shrugs her shoulders.

"I think the woman from Social Services drank quite a lot. Like my mom."

"I'm sorry," Ted says, honestly.

The pencil spins and spins in Louisa's hand.

"Don't be. My mom drank herself to death without me. If I had been with her when she drank herself to death, maybe no one would have found me."

"So you ended up in foster care?"

"Yes."

"What was that like?"

"It was okay," Louisa says, in the way you do if you have so many bruises and scars all over your body that eventually you can't be bothered to think it might not be normal.

"I'm . . . sorry," Ted repeats.

If he had been more comfortable touching people, perhaps he would have given her a hug. If she had been more comfortable having people touch her, maybe she would have liked it. But as it is, they remain seated where they are, with ten inches of air between them.

As many as seven minutes may pass this time, Louisa deserves credit for that. But then the conductor goes past, a man roughly the same age as Ted, but with more gray in his beard. Ted watches him, and Louisa watches Ted watching and grins. When Ted notices, he blushes.

"What sort of men do you fall in love with?" she asks.

"That really is none of your business!" he exclaims so abruptly that the other passengers in the carriage turn around, and the conductor glances over his shoulder, and Ted blushes so hard that you could have cooked waffles in his wrinkles.

"Okay, okay, oh my God, sorry for asking," Louisa grins, then she looks at the conductor and declares confidently: "No, I get it, you could probably never fall in love with someone like him. He's not your type."

Affronted, Ted glares at her and mutters back:

"He might be! I mean, you don't know anything about that!"

Louisa shakes her head thoughtfully.

"No, because there are loads of men like him, if you could fall in love with one of those you'd have found one already. Then you wouldn't be alone."

The way Ted looks at her isn't entirely dissimilar to the way you would look at a spider on a sandwich. Then he looks at the box of ashes, as if the person inside has just said something about unwashed bedspreads. Then he takes such a deep breath that the paint almost peels from the walls of the carriage, before quickly wiping his eyes and admitting quietly:

"The geniuses. I only fall in love with the geniuses."

Louisa's face lights up.

"Fish was like that too!"

Ted nods slowly and says:

"That was why she loved you."

The words come so quickly that at first Louisa doesn't understand what he means.

"No, I mean, Fish fell for BOYS who were . . . ," she protests.

"I know what you meant. I'm just saying you're wrong," he says.

That sets a new record for the kindest thing an adult has said to her.

The conductor leaves the carriage and Ted does his best not to look at him as he goes, which doesn't go very well. Louisa does her best not to ask any more questions, and that doesn't go well either.

"What are you going to write on his gravestone?" she asks, nodding toward the box of ashes.

"I don't know," Ted lies.

She wrinkles her nose.

"He was super famous, it has to say something! Like, something poetic!"

"He was also an idiot, so he suggested it should say: 'Here lies a man who ate his vegetables but died anyway,'" Ted sighs.

Louisa laughs, then says slightly disappointedly:

"You'll never put that. It's a shame that the boring one out of the pair of you survived."

Ted does his best not to smile.

"I love you and I believe in you."

"What?" Louisa wonders, rather shocked.

"That's what I'm going to put on the gravestone. 'I love you and I believe in you.' It's something we always used to say to each other."

Louisa is so taken aback that all she can manage to say is:

"Nice."

"Thanks."

"What subject did you used to teach?" she asks.

"History."

"Seriously?"

"It would be a pretty strange thing to lie about," he points out.

"Tell me one, then!"

"What?"

"A history."

"About . . . what?"

Louisa leans forward and carefully lifts the painting out of the box again.

"Tell me about him! Tell me about the painting! Tell me about how he became world-famous, tell me about . . . I don't know! I've thought about all of you so much that Fish said I was a bit of a psychopath. She said it wasn't normal to fantasize about three strange boys on a pier this much, because you could be murderers or anything!"

"Or kidnappers," Ted points out.

He presses desperately against the window to save his jacket when she starts laughing. Then she points toward the pier in the picture.

"So that's you? And that's Joar? And that's . . . him."

Ted sadly shakes his head.

"No. That's Ali," he corrects.

"What?"

Ted sighs so deeply that the sigh has another sigh in the middle of it.

"If you want to hear the story of that painting, really hear it, then

I'll have to start by telling you that you're wrong. Everyone who looks at it is wrong. Those aren't three boys sitting on the pier."

Louisa stares at the painting, stares at Ted, stares at the painting. And then Ted does something he never thought he would do again. He tells the whole story, right from the beginning.

NINETEEN

"We'd never met anyone like her."

That's how Ted starts, with his eyes fixed on the glass of the window. It's so strange, he thinks, how we choose to tell a story. We hardly ever start at the beginning. Because there were four best friends on the pier that summer when the artist painted the picture, Ali joined the gang last, but if you think that makes her least important, you don't understand a damn thing. Then you've never been addicted to another human. Ted got to know Joar and the artist when he was twelve, Joar and the artist had known each other almost all their lives, but none of them could remember a childhood without Ali. They had just turned fourteen the autumn she crashed into their lives, but the idea that there could even have been a time before her stupid, stupid giggling? Impossible.

"Her laugh sounded like a swarm of insects," he tells Louisa, because it did: a wild buzzing from her stomach to her lips, that girl was chaos, from her uncombed hair to her unbridled heart. She was their second life.

"When she was in a good mood, she used to sing in French, which was both wonderful and unbearable, because she was great at French but terrible at singing. Joar used to say that she sounded like her fan belt needed replacing. Which may have been true, because Joar didn't know anything about singing but an awful lot about fan belts . . . ," Ted reminisces, and then a swarm of insects emerges from Louisa too.

"Obviously it didn't matter how she sang," Ted goes on, "because when Ali was happy, she would dance so hard that she left marks on the pier, and you can forgive someone almost anything then."

He goes on to explain that that was fortunate, because she often needed forgiveness, because she was a wholly unreliable little lunatic. When Ali got an idea, her eyes would look like someone had set fire to a honey badger and let it loose in her brain. Joar had a lot of bad ideas, it has to be said, but only at an amateur level. After a couple of months with Ali, he was a professional idiot. Or "iiidiiiot," as Joar pronounced it, and then he and Ali laughed so much that Ted can still hear the echo inside him on the train twenty-five years later.

"Those birds there," Ted says to Louisa, pointing at the picture. "He painted them for Ali, because she loved birds. And that red haze there on the sky, do you see it?"

"Hmm," Louisa says, wide-eyed, her nose so close to the picture that she's almost pushing through it.

"I remember reading a load of stuffy art critics in serious newspapers who said that was genius, the way he caught the light with that red. But it wasn't light, or genius, it was just Ali."

"What? He caught her light?"

"No, I mean it *was* Ali. She loved coming up with stupid games, and that summer when we were fourteen she came up with one where we had to put chili sauce in our mouths and lean our heads back, and then we would try to make each other laugh. Joar won. And Ali sprayed chili sauce all over the picture."

Louisa stares at the painting for a long time, and looks like she's trying really hard not to reach out one finger and taste the sky.

"So he just painted the three of you, not himself?" she asks, looking at the box of ashes.

"Yes," Ted says, almost caressing the air above the picture. "He said he was all the rest of it, everything around us, the water and the air."

"He was the light," Louisa whispers.

Ted thinks once more that the artist was right. *One of us*. So he tells her:

"All of the best and worst ideas we ever had came from Ali. She got Joar to do so many stupid things. One time they stole a car together.

And another time she got Joar to try drying wet socks in a toaster, and he almost burned down my mom's house! But it was also her idea that the painting should be of . . . us. That was her very best one."

He breaks off. It's so strange, he thinks, the way we remember things. What we try to remember and what we fight to forget. As the train rolls on toward the town by the sea where he grew up, he tells Louisa the story of his friends, but not all of it. He tells her what he can bear to, but not everything that actually happened. He tells her all his best memories of Ali, that she was the one who gave the artist the idea for the painting. But he doesn't mention that she was also the one who gave Joar the knife.

"We had just turned fourteen," he says instead.

It was September, he tells her, the school year had just started when she came around a corner. It was the end of the lunch break, Ted and Joar and the artist had been hiding at the far end of one of the hallways, because they went to a school full of predators where everything was always just a countdown to being chased. You become good at hiding then. But they had heard a furious scream and a loud bang, and then Ali came running, like a blinding light, like a heart attack. They had never met anyone like her, because hardly anyone has that much luck. She had one black eye and blood on her knuckles, and the door she had slammed behind her belonged to the principal's office. Ted happened to catch her eye and the first thing she yelled at him was: "WHAT ARE YOU STARING AT?"

Was there ever a time before her? Impossible. Ted and the artist stood there like their mouths were full of glue, so obviously it was Joar who plucked up the courage to open his:

"Hey, Ali. Who won?" he asked cheerfully, nodding toward the girl's bloody knuckles.

Her eyes filled with hatred so fast that Joar backed away, which was an almost exotic occurrence, not even the artist had ever seen him take a single step back in his whole life. The girl was only half a head taller than Joar, but she seemed ten feet tall as she leaned forward and growled: "What did you call me?"

Joar threw his arms out, shocked and affronted and terrified, all at the same time.

"Ali! Like Muhammad Ali! The boxer! I just wondered who the hell you'd been fighting, what the hell's wrong with you?" he gasped.

The girl stopped midstride. She tilted her head to one side, like a surprised pit bull. Then her face cracked and out came a huge laugh.

"Ali. I like it," she smiled. "Ali . . . Ali . . . Aliii."

She was trying out the name as she looked at the boys one by one, letting them bounce around in her pupils. The boys had no way of knowing that she was fourteen years old and alone on the planet, it was always incomprehensible that someone like her could be. They didn't know she had stood on a rooftop and almost jumped a few months before. They knew nothing about her darkness, how much pain she was in, that her thin body was a raging fire inside. They didn't know that she had just moved to their town and that she had decided that very morning to either die or find a new life. New friends, new jokes, new . . . everything. Maybe even a new name, if anyone was offering one.

Ali? That would do. The boys? They had no idea of all this, they just happened to be the luckiest boys in the world.

Ali ran her fingers over her black eye and muttered: "I got into a fight with a boy in gym class because he said I threw the ball like a little girl."

Joar glanced at her knuckles and noted: "You don't fight like a little girl. Did he notice that, or what?"

"He noticed it quicker than diarrhea," Ali grinned.

Joar's laughter thundered through the hallway at that, and from then on, they belonged to each other.

Twenty-five years later, Ted falls silent for a moment on the train. That was in the autumn when they had just turned fourteen, after that came a winter and a spring, and then that summer when they turned fifteen. Their last summer as children. Ali really was Joar's second life. They only had each other for a little more than a year. Who has time to get to know someone, really know them, in that time? If you so much as ask the question, you weren't there, you've never fallen that madly in love, never been addicted to another person's breath. It wouldn't have made any difference if Joar and Ali's love had lasted eighty years, it was already everything right from the start, bright light and loud bangs and heart attacks.

Ted glances at Louisa, smiles weakly and says:

"You said it looked like we were laughing in the painting, like someone had farted. You said you couldn't understand how anyone could paint . . . laughter. That's because it was Ali's laugh he painted."

"And the chili sauce?" Louisa grins.

"And the chili sauce," Ted laughs.

They were in parallel classes at school, Joar and the artist in one, Ted in another, and Ali in a third. They didn't look for each other after school, they just floated together in the crowd anyway, as if they were inevitable to each other. They never talked about Ali going with them to the pier, she just did. They lay there on their backs with their heads on their backpacks, with the sea on three sides, on the last hot day of the year. The following day, autumn would tear September out of the exhausted hands of summer. Ali smoked their cigarettes and asked, impressed:

"Where did you steal these?"

Joar, who in all honesty had stolen pretty much everything in his life except cigarettes, blew smoke rings the size of doughnuts and replied happily:

"We bought them."

"Are you rich, then, or what?" she wondered, because she had met rich kids before, and if these three were rich, she was thinking of throwing them in the sea.

"No. We got the deposit back on Ted's dad's beer cans," Joar informed her.

Then Ali turned to Ted and looked him in the eye so directly that he blushed. They were lying with their cheeks on their backpacks, with the world at a ninety-degree angle and their faces so close that he could feel her breath on his eyelashes.

"My dad drinks a lot of beer too," she said.

Ted replied the way he always did, so shyly that the first words disappeared down into the water:

"My dad can't drink it anymore. He's going to die. But our pantry is still full of beer, so my big brother drinks it."

That was the first time Ted said it out loud to anyone. Both the bit about the beer, and the bit about dying.

"That's sad, but also nice," Ali said.

And Ted had thought then that perhaps it was nice, somehow, that his big brother drank their dad's beer alone in the kitchen at night, and that Ted secretly got the deposit back on the cans. Slowly, slowly, they emptied the pantry, a silent but shared act of grief between two brothers.

"Thanks," Ted had whispered, and then she had put her fingers as close to his arm as you can get without actually touching someone.

He can still feel her on his skin, twenty-five years later. He sits on the train and suddenly laughs, happy mist forming on the train window.

"I remember thinking that she was a perfect person. For a while. But then I saw her swim, and it passed. She used to swim like an octopus with a cramp . . ."

He laughs as he talks about the first time they watched her jump into the sea from the pier in her underwear, and Joar jumped in after her because he thought she was drowning. She got furious, and it was the first time she and Joar had a fight, but definitely not the last.

Ali had moved around her whole childhood, because every time her dad ended up unemployed, they moved to a new town, and her dad could hold on to a hot waffle pan for longer than he could hold on to a job. So no adult had ever really had time to check what Ali could do at a certain age, and what she couldn't. Now she was full of ridiculous knowledge and incomprehensible gaps. She could make a sound just like a dolphin, but she didn't know her multiplication tables. She had learned fluent French by watching foreign children's television programs, but she couldn't tie her shoes properly. Instead she would make up her own knots, and had invented her own way of swimming, and somehow it worked, because she was a genius idiot. That was why she got on so well with Joar, because he was an idiotic genius. On one of their first days together, she appeared with some fireworks she had stolen from her dad, then she taught Joar the joys of blowing up mailboxes. It was lucky he had taught her to tie her shoelaces properly by then, because they had had to run away from a lot of angry mailbox owners.

Joar's eyes sparkled as he watched her light the fuses. Her eyes sparkled back when she realized that Joar, no matter how tough he pretended to be, was ridiculously scared of explosions. It turned out that one of Ali's many unexpected talents, apart from sounding like a dolphin, was being able to shape her lips and make a sound like a burning firework. When they got to the pier, she had fun pretending to put something in Joar's backpack, and when he heard the noise, he leapt into the sea in a panic. When he climbed out, he chased her like a mongoose after a snake, then they had another fight, and then they were best friends again. They were like two little machines with engines that were far too big. Uncontrollable. One time they ran away from a mailbox so fast that Joar forgot to drop the firework in, he ran off with it in his hand and only realized what was happening at the last moment.

"Iiidiiiot!" Ali yelled as they both threw themselves out of the way of the bang.

"I thought YOU were holding it!" Joar yelled.

"So what did you think YOU were holding, then?" Ali snapped back.

"I . . . I don't know!" Joar admitted.

"It's unbelievable that evolution even gave boys penises, because you can't be trusted with anything," Ali muttered.

When they got to the pier, they had a contest to see who could do the ugliest run, and Ali staggered as if she had been shot in the ass with a tranquilizer dart. Joar's jaw ached from laughing so hard in a way he hadn't even known he could laugh before her, an all-encompassing laugh that his body seemed to have been keeping in reserve, just in case he met a completely perfect idiot. Every time Ali heard it, she looked like her body had been saving an extra pair of eyes just for him, unused until that day.

That's how suddenly it happened, falling in love. They stumbled halfway into autumn without realizing, because the only thing the three boys really knew about Ali in those first few months was that she didn't want to go home.

"Was her home like Joar's?" Louisa asks on the train when Ted falls silent.

"No, no, hers was . . . different," Ted says sadly, then adds, as if the memory has just popped into his mind: "She hated dresses."

"What?" Louisa says.

"She hated dresses, but she loved the choir," Ted mumbles.

"The choir?" Louisa repeats.

A small laugh slips out of Ted.

"God, she really couldn't sing . . ."

"Can you tell a story like a normal person?" Louisa asks.

Ted blinks at her in surprise. Then he blushes.

"Sorry, I . . . I was just thinking out loud."

So he tells her that when the four friends went their separate ways at the crossroads each evening, they would always call "Tomorrow!" to each other. When the weather was too bad to go to the pier they would sit in Ted's basement, Ted reading comics, the artist drawing, and Joar and Ali watching superhero movies. Joar always kept an eye on the time, because he had to get home in time to eat dinner with his mom, it took several months before the boys realized that Ali was the same, only the other way around. Sometimes weeks would pass without her coming to Ted's, sometimes she would be there five nights in a row, but the times she stayed really late were because she was counting the hours between the time the people in her home were getting drunk and the time they'd have fallen asleep. The children of addicts always know what the time is.

On those evenings, the artist would often sit on the floor drawing birds for her. She was envious of them, not because they flew south for the winter but because they flew back home again in spring, that they were so confident they knew where their home was. Sometimes when she looked at the time, it was as if she were counting the days until her dad told her they were moving again, she had never lived anywhere on the planet for longer than a year.

Ted often fell asleep to the sound of their breathing in his room, and he had never slept so soundly. One night when the artist was climbing out the window, Ted mumbled in his sleep: "I love you." It wasn't intentional, it just slipped out. But the artist replied as if it were the most natural thing in the world: "I love you too." When Ali crept past, Ted mumbled to her as well: "I love you." Ali stopped abruptly, shocked, and hesitated for an eternity, because no one had said that to her before. So she leaned forward and whispered: "I . . . believe in you."

Autumn turned to winter, and school was approaching the Christmas break. The four friends found a place in the schoolyard, behind an old shed, where they could smoke between classes. Ali and Joar would tease each other, getting into fights almost every day, scrapping wildly and then making up in a moment. When Joar wanted to provoke Ali, he called her "girl," which she hated, because the only thing she hated more than girls were boys. When she wanted to provoke Joar, on the other hand, she told him he smelled. One morning, when he had stolen some new aftershave that he was very proud of, the first thing Ali asked was: "Is it supposed to smell like that? Sweat?" Joar snapped: "It doesn't smell like sweat!" Ali sniffed the air: "Well, something smells like sweat." Joar roared: "In that case, it's my sweat that smells like sweat! Not the aftershave!" Ali pretended to be surprised, she was good at that: "So what is it that smells like shit, then? Is it the aftershave? Have you gotten ahold of shit aftershave?" Then they fought, but never hard enough for either of them to get hurt.

Ali was usually better at making Joar angry, he had more weak points, but one winter's day Ali said that she'd applied to join the school choir, which was due to perform at the end-of-term assembly. So Joar replied that her singing voice would be "like a chain saw in a symphony orchestra." Ali snapped, "Shut up," as usual, but Joar wasn't observant enough. He didn't hear that her voice had become more fragile. So when Ali announced miserably that the choir leader had decided that all the boys should wear white shirts and all the girls dresses, Joar burst out laughing. He didn't have time to see the tears before she clenched her fists, and when they fought this time, it was different, because she was trying to hurt Joar. She elbowed him across the nose, he staggered back, blood gushing, and she stood there, her whole body shaking, yelling: "You're GARBAGE, Joar! Did you know that? You're just mean fucking GARBAGE!" The collar of her shirt was dark with tears. She ran off and didn't appear at the pier or at Ted's house for several days.

The morning of the last day of term, the boys saw her standing alone at the other end of the schoolyard. She was shivering in the winter cold, wearing just a thin dress. The boys had never seen anyone hate an item of clothing so much, as if the fabric had nails sewn into it that were scratching her skin. She tugged and pulled at it in embarrassment and tried to cover her knees, and every other second she glanced at the school gate as if she planned to run away, but when an adult voice called out, she followed the rest of the choir inside the school anyway. Only then did the boys realize that someone who hated a dress as much as that must really, really love singing.

"Come on," Joar grunted.

The boys slipped out of the gate like eels in dark water and ran home. It was the start of Christmas vacation, they were free, no one saw them disappear. Unlike Ali, the boys did everything they could to escape being noticed at that damn school. Attention was lethal, that was how you ended up being bullied and beaten. They would never have dreamed of getting up onstage like her.

Ali spent the whole morning practicing with the choir, the loneliest person on earth. When it was time for the performance, the choir was standing behind a curtain listening to the audience file into their seats, and Ali threw up in a corner. Just as she was thinking about running away, the curtain went up, and it was too late. There she was, standing in the glare of a spotlight in her thin dress, with white knuckles and red cheeks. Terrified and defenseless. She heard the audience start to giggle. Only a faint noise at first, when everyone was trying not to laugh and it was coming out through their noses, but soon it was a roar. Ali tugged and tugged at her dress to cover her knees, panicking that they were laughing at her. But then she heard something else: the rest of the choir. They were also laughing hysterically now. Only then did Ali look out at the first row of the audience. There sat her friends. Joar, Ted, and the artist. Wearing dresses.

They had run home and borrowed them from Joar's mom's wardrobe. Obviously all the dresses were too big, because all the boys were too small, and they would be teased about it every day for the rest of their time at school. Joar would get into so many dress-related fights when spring came that the principal might as well have moved Joar's desk into his office. Joar didn't care. It was worth every blow if Ali realized she wasn't so damn alone, at least not all the damn time. Who gets a friend like that? Hardly anyone.

On the way home that day, Ali for the first time told the boys how her mother had died. How she used to sing and laugh and call Ali "my heart." She had strong opinions about television programs and she loved cheese. She was a whole person, and then suddenly she wasn't anymore. She had been riding her bike and gotten hit by a car, she had left home one day and never come back, she was alive and the next second she was dead.

"My mom loved the fact that I was in a choir when I was little," Ali told the boys. "She loved singing, so when I sing it's like she's . . . with me. I know it's stupid. Typical of a little girl, thinking—"

Behind her, Joar interrupted irritably:

"Do you have to walk so fucking FAST?"

Because it really isn't easy to walk fast in a dress if you're not used to it. Especially not if it's a bit too big, Joar kept tripping over his, and Ted kept having to pull the fabric out of his behind, and the artist's shoulder strap had come loose. Ali turned and looked at her boys for a long time, then muttered: "You're all garbage, all three of you. You know that, right?"

They nodded. She wiped her eyes with the back of her hand. Then the artist mumbled to Ted: "You look good in that color."

"Thanks," Ted smiled.

"You look nice in that color too!" Ali grinned to Joar.

"Do you want a fucking fight or something?" Joar snapped.

She laughed so hard that she tripped and fell into a bush.

They walked to the pier, it was covered with snow and the sun was already going down, but Joar made a small fire and they sat there until dusk. They pulled their jackets as tightly as they could around the dresses, and huddled so close to each other that they had the same skin. Then Ted suddenly plucked up the courage and whispered into the darkness: "I love you."

The fire crackled, the waves lapped, the wind crept under their dresses. Then Ali whispered: "I believe in you."

"I love you *and* I believe in you!" the artist smiled.

"Garbage," Joar muttered.

They went home happy. The next day, down at the harbor, Joar's old man was told that Joar had worn a dress to the end-of-term assembly. The other men laughed at his old man, teasing him, so when he got home that evening, he beat Joar harder than ever. Beat him as if he was dirt, as if he had no pulse. The first days of that Christmas vacation, Joar just lay on the bed in Ted's basement the whole time. He hurt so badly that he couldn't even go down to the pier. That was when Ali gave him the knife.

TWENTY

Ted doesn't mention that last bit to Louisa. Nothing about the knife.

Joar hid it at the bottom of his wardrobe that winter, and when spring came he hid it in the dirt under the flowers in the flower box outside his bedroom window, and then in his backpack. He didn't touch it until the summer, when August was approaching and his old man would soon be on vacation from his job in the harbor. Joar kept hoping that he would think of something else, that someone would come and save him and his mom, like in Ted's superhero comics. But no one came, and there was no way they would survive another summer.

The train stops for a short while at a gray station. A plastic bag dances in the wind on the platform. In the painting on the floor, the birds fly in the sky, chili sauce glints in the light, the three friends on the pier laugh at a fart, and the artist is all around them. In every brushstroke. Ted watches the plastic bag's erratic flight on the other side of the window and bites his lip, he has never told anyone the story of his childhood, there's a kind of boundary for the sort of emotions you're prepared to share with others when you're hardly comfortable sharing them with yourself. After all, Ted is the kind of man who can hardly bear waiters asking him how the food is, because he thinks it's slightly too intimate a question.

"I like Ali!" Louisa declares beside him.

"What a surprise," Ted replies.

"Why is it a surprise?" Louisa asks seriously.

Ted lets out a middle-aged sigh, which is a quite particular type of sigh, it takes far more effort than a teenage sigh.

"Doesn't your generation understand irony?" he says.

"Does YOUR generation understand irony?" she asks back at once, and he can't work out if she's being ironic or not.

So he presumes she wins.

"You have a lot in common. You and Joar too. They would have liked you," he admits.

"Thanks!" Louisa exclaims.

"That isn't altogether a compliment, they didn't have five functional brain cells between them, those two," Ted replies sullenly, but the corners of his mouth are bad at lying, so she has time to notice the smile.

"Still, thanks," Louisa grins.

Then she goes on drawing behind her hanging hair, and Ted looks at his watch, a little frustrated. The train has been standing at this station for so long, they're behind schedule now. The plastic bag dances along the platform, as if mocking his anxiety, as if trying to say: *Look here! See how easy it is for me to make myself happy!*

The artist and Joar and Ali would no doubt all have laughed at that, if they were here—the fact that Ted is so neurotic that he can feel envious of a plastic bag.

He goes to the bathroom again. He seems to have reached the age where he needs to go even though he hasn't drunk anything since the last time, as if his body is inventing its own liquid, when you're approaching forty perhaps you start to melt internally. Louisa sees him come back out, but to her surprise he turns the other way and disappears into the next carriage. For a moment she starts to panic because she thinks he's going to get off the train, because where else would he be going? When he comes back after a while with a newspaper and a Coca-Cola, she stares at him as if he's just pulled a rabbit out of a hat.

"Where did you get THAT from?" she exclaims, because she can't see a damn hat anywhere.

"The restaurant car," he replies, as if it were the most natural thing in the world.

"I thought those only existed in films," Louisa mumbles in astonishment.

"No, they exist in . . . trains," he says.

"I really, really ought to have learned to break into trains instead of cars," she declares.

"I don't know if you like Coca-Cola?" he says, as if he's never met a teenager in his entire life.

"Are you kidding?" she says, snatching it out of his hand like a happy raccoon.

She and Fish used to steal Coca-Cola from the shop occasionally, but only when they had something to celebrate, for instance, if a really idiotic guy had just moved out of the foster home. Or, come to that, any guy at all. The soda is ice-cold on her teeth and she laughs when she gets brain freeze. Ted laughs too, without any sound, she just sees his chest rocking in the seat beside her.

"Have you heard of the internet?" she asks, staring at the newspaper in his hand.

"I like newspapers," he mutters.

"Do you think that might be because you're so damn young? Do you find traveling by train difficult too? Do you miss a horse and buggy?" she asks.

"Funny," he says.

"It's called sarcasm, didn't your generation have that?" she grins.

He is about to say something smart in reply, like that newspapers are better than the internet because you can't roll up the internet and hit someone in the face with it, but he doesn't have time. Because they're interrupted by the conductor entering the carriage to check the tickets of new passengers. Louisa looks up and hisses, a little too loudly:

"You should talk to him!"

"Sorry?" Ted says, insulted.

"The conductor! You should give him your phone number!" Louisa suggests.

"I most certainly should not," Ted informs her.

Louisa nods eagerly.

"Yes, because you should meet a man who isn't a genius! Do you want me to talk to him?"

"No! Absolutely not! And what do you mean by that? You don't know anything about him! Maybe he *is* a genius!" Ted whispers, his voice nervous now, like when you see a monkey carrying a bomb. Louisa snorts.

"He's got tattoos on his hands, I don't think he's a genius . . ."

"There's nothing wrong with his tattoos," Ted grunts, but regrets it at once.

"So you've checked out his tattoos?"

"No! And I'm not giving him my phone number!" Ted hisses.

"Why not? What if he's the love of your life?"

"Stop it!"

"Isn't he your type? Are you worried you aren't his type? That he doesn't like geeks?"

"I didn't say . . . What do you mean by that . . . Stop it! Just stop it!"

Louisa peers thoughtfully first at the conductor, then at Ted.

"I think you're worried he's the sort of person who only likes slightly dangerous men, and you're worried you aren't dangerous enough."

"Don't do anything stupid, plea—" Ted manages to say, but by then it's of course already too late, because as the conductor walks past, Louisa raises the can of soda and says:

"Hello! Cheers!"

The conductor smiles in surprise.

"Hi, cheers to you too."

"We're celebrating!" Louisa nods triumphantly.

"Oh?" the conductor smiles.

"We're celebrating the fact that Ted here just got out of prison!" Louisa says.

The conductor's eyebrows bounce so high, they could reasonably be described as bangs. He clears his throat for so long that he has a whole new voice at the end of it.

"O . . . kay. Well, congratulations, then!"

Louisa nods cheerfully. Ted does nothing, because of course he's already sunk into the ground and burned up in a river of lava. The conductor looks around nervously and mutters beseechingly: "New passengers?" toward the other passengers, and hurries on. Ted's face couldn't be any redder if he had been missing his skin.

"Why did you do *that*?" he hisses furiously.

"Now you seem dangerous!" Louisa informs him helpfully.

"Thanks, thanks a lot," Ted says ironically.

"You're welcome," Louisa replies, without a trace of irony.

Ted tries to think that he should at least be grateful that she didn't say he'd kidnapped her.

"Ali and Joar really would have loved you," Ted grunts toward the picture.

"Thanks," Louisa smiles.

"That still isn't a compliment."

"But it's still a thank-you. Can I ask something?" Louisa says quickly, without waiting for a reply, because every word that comes out of her mouth is already rushing downhill. "Was Ali raped?"

Ted turns and stares at her, so shocked that even Louisa is a little taken aback.

"Why . . . why do you ask that?" he manages to say.

Louisa disappears behind her hair and shrugs her shoulders.

"I just wondered. There was something about the way you told the story. That she said 'I believe in you' when you said 'I love you.' When you've been raped, that's pretty much the biggest thing you can do, I think. Believing in someone, like really . . . believe in them. Trust them. Especially a boy."

The train is standing still, so it takes a long time for Ted to realize that he's the one rocking.

"Were you . . . ?" he whispers, but Louisa quickly shakes her head.

"No. But Fish was, in the foster home where she lived before we met. That's why we always slept with screwdrivers in our hands."

Ted's voice isn't entirely steady when he goes on:

"Ali was . . . She . . . she loved my mom's lasagna. My mom worked nights, so she used to make meals and leave them in the freezer before she left home. Ali liked coming up to the kitchen with me to watch while I heated them up in the microwave. She would open the cabinets and look at all the canned foods and packs of spaghetti as if they were magic, because in her home, all the cabinets were empty except for the ones full of bottles. When you clicked the switch on the wall in my house, a light came on in the ceiling, because everything in our house worked. My mom was just as poor as everyone else on our street, but she . . . held everything together, you know? Everything worked. Ali had never experienced that. That was the first time I realized something was wrong. And then my big brother came home one time, he opened the front door when we were in the kitchen, and Ali reached instinctively for the cutlery drawer. That was the first time I had seen anyone apart from Joar do that, look for . . . weapons. Eventually she explained. It took a long time, everything she said came out a little at a time, one story could take several weeks. Her dad didn't get violent when he was drunk, not like Joar's. Ali's dad just loved having fun. He was good at dancing and drinking wine, but even better at not opening bills. He didn't want Ali to call him 'Dad,' he wanted to be called 'Buddy,' because he didn't want to be an adult. Because adults like him don't understand that adults have to be adults so that children can be children. So their house was always a lot of fun, always full of strangers, at the end of one party or the start of another. Groups of women smoking in the kitchen, and men singing as they stumbled from room to room. It was an insecure environment for Ali when she was seven, threatening when she was ten . . . dangerous when she hit puberty. She . . . she told me late one evening when we were on our own. About . . . about one of her dad's friends, and the soda that tasted funny, and how she woke up naked with the man on top of her. She said she didn't even remember what happened, she just saw the bleeding scratch marks on the man's cheeks and couldn't understand at first that she was the one who had made them. Then . . . then she just exploded. Like a monster waking up in self-defense. The man was drunk and slow, and Ali said she must have struggled so hard she got sweaty, and suddenly she slipped out of his grasp. She fought and kicked as hard as she possibly could, until he screamed and fell over. Then she grabbed a blanket and jumped through a window, from the first floor, she sprained her ankle as she landed but still ran off into the forest to hide. She was gone for almost twenty-four hours, her dad didn't even notice. When she went home, he had just woken up, hungover, and thought she had been at school. She never told him. One night she stood on the roof of their apartment building and almost jumped. The next night she stood there again, a bit nearer to the edge. Night after night, nearer and nearer, until one day she got back to the apartment and found moving boxes everywhere. Her dad had gotten tired of the town where they were living all of a sudden, he said it wasn't fun anymore, far too full of people who wanted him to repay the money he had borrowed from them. So the next day, there were only bills left in the apartment, Ali and her dad were long gone. That was how they ended up in our town. That was how she found us."

Ted falls silent. He remembers the look on Ali's face so clearly, the way she sat on his bed in the basement and told him all that. The big tears on the small, angular cheekbones, the way she threw out her hands like a sad magician and whispered: "And hey presto: now I'm here."

He remembers her telling him she always slept with a knife under her pillow. Ted was so naive that he asked if that wasn't dangerous, didn't she cut herself on it while she was asleep? Ali just smiled and said that was the cutest thing she'd ever heard.

"You're probably right," Ted whispers to Louisa on the train. "She said she believed in us, never that she loved us, because that meant more to her than love."

He still doesn't mention the knife.

"She and Fish would have liked each other," Louisa says behind her hair, drawing the most beautiful cockroaches in the world on her sketch pad.

"Yes, they probably would have," Ted agrees.

"Can I ask one more thing?"

"Yes," Ted says, as if you ever have a choice with someone like Louisa.

She nods toward the box with the painting.

"Why did he always draw skulls next to his signature?"

"He stole them."

"The skulls? Who from?"

"From a janitor."

"What?"

Ted adjusts his glasses.

"He used to say that art is coincidence. A beautiful painting is the sum total of a person, what has happened to them, blessings and curses alike. Coincidences."

"So he stole the skulls from a janitor? When?" Louisa asks, a little frustrated, because she's starting to think that the old man tells stories as if he were reading fortune cookies.

"In the spring, back when we were fourteen. Just before the summer when Joar found that competition in the newspaper," he remembers.

"What *competition*? Can you just begin at the *start*?" she says in frustration.

Ted smiles weakly.

"There was a competition for young artists. That was how Joar got him to paint that picture to begin with. But that's an entirely different story, Joar had . . ."

"Wait! Just wait! I don't know if I want you to tell me!" Louisa suddenly exclaims.

"Why not?" Ted wonders in surprise.

Louisa's gaze slips away from him like butter in a frying pan, she strokes the cockroaches on her sketch pad as if they were asleep.

"Fish used to love fairy tales, I've heard tons of them, so I'm not really sure I want to hear how this one . . . ends. Because this one really happened. And I know what happened to you, I know you survived! So now . . . now I know the other bit too."

"What other bit?" Ted asks.

Like someone who has never had the chance to get used to happy endings, Louisa whispers sadly:

"Now I know that everyone else you're talking about might have died."

Ted hadn't thought of that. Because for him, everything in the story has already happened, but for her, it is all happening now.

"Do you want me to . . . ?" he begins, but she takes a deep breath, closes her eyes tightly, and replies seriously:

"No, no. Tell me! It's too late to turn back now!"

TWENTY-ONE

So Ted tells her.

"Joar was always told that he was the sort of boy who went looking for trouble, but that was hardly ever true. He often got into fights, but not because he went looking for them, but because if you started a fight with Joar, you were the one who was in trouble . . . ," he begins.

Then he tells her how all the school bullies had a go at Joar, and how badly they regretted it. He says that when Joar's eyes darkened, it made Ted think of one of his comics, where a man ended up in prison and was threatened by the other inmates. That was a bad move on their part, because they didn't know how dangerous the man was until he fixed his eyes on them and said: "None of you understand. I'm not locked up in here with YOU. You're locked up in here with ME."

The only thing that saved the bullies' lives that year was probably the fact that Joar's old man beat him senseless every time the principal called home after a fight, and the fact that Joar's friends couldn't bear that. Every time Joar defended the people he loved, he got hurt worse and worse, love would be the death of him one day. So his friends begged him to stop. Which forced Joar to be creative.

"If that hadn't happened, the painting would never have been what it was. Art is coincidence," Ted says.

Louisa strokes her cockroaches, repeating the words quietly to herself:

"Art is coincidence. Fish would have liked that."

Then she nods at Ted to go on. So he explains that in the spring, just before the summer when the picture was painted, Joar found out that a gang of older girls were bullying Ali. They wrote on her locker that she was ugly and disgusting, as if that was why they hated her, but the truth was the complete opposite: they hated the way their boyfriends looked at her. The older girls did all they could to get the boys' attention, but Ali, who did all she could to escape it, got it for free. They could never forgive her for that. So one day, the meanest and most popular girl in the gang had a simple idea: she pretended to be nice, and made everyone in the line for lunch step aside for Ali, just so they could call after her, "Let the little poor girl through, she doesn't get any food at home! Look at her clothes, her family treats the dump like a mall!" The whole cafeteria laughed. As Ali ran out, they threw coins at her.

Naturally Joar's initial suggestion was that maybe he should make a nice new jacket out of that girl's face, but Ali wouldn't let him. So Joar did something better. The next time he saw the girl in the hallway, he called out cheerily: "Hi, Red!" She didn't understand a thing, but the next day he did the same thing: "Hi, Red!" After a week, her friends angrily caught up with Joar, yelling: "Why do you call her Red?" Joar stared at them in surprise: "Don't you know? Because she blushes so easily. Haven't you seen how red her face goes at the slightest little thing?"

Joar wasn't big on difficult words, so he had probably never heard of a self-fulfilling prophecy, but no one understood the meaning better. That girl had never blushed before then, but if all your friends tell you why you're called "Red," it happens. Soon the girl would blush if she so much as saw Joar, then she started blushing just because she was arriving at school, and soon even her friends were calling her "Red" behind her back. She never called Ali a little poor girl again.

One evening not long after that, Joar, Ali, and the artist were sitting in Ted's basement, eating heated-up lasagna and reading comics. They were discussing which superpower they'd like to have, and the responses were predictable. Joar wanted to have super strength so he could protect his mom; Ali wanted to be able to talk to the dead so she could communicate with her mom; the artist wanted to be a shape-shifter who could change his appearance so then perhaps he could be what his mom wanted him to be: *like all the other children.*

Ted sat in silence, hoping he wouldn't have to say what he wanted his power to be, and he was lucky, because Joar asked him to say "something smart" instead. That meant that Joar wanted to hear quotes from superheroes. So while his friends lay on the floor, so close together that only dreams could fit between their bodies, Ted read out some of his favorites: Spider-Man's "With great power comes great responsibility." The Flash's "Life doesn't give us purpose. We give life purpose." Wonder Woman's "Which will hold greater rule over you? Your fear or your curiosity?" Then he thought for a little while, searching his memory for the words, before he came out with Iron Man's "Heroes are made by the paths they choose."

The fourteen-year-olds lay in silence on the floor, resting in each other's breath for a long time, before Joar said tentatively: "Can you do that one . . . the one I like?"

He didn't often sound as vulnerable as that. So Ted replied gently, because he knew exactly which quote Joar meant, it was from Beta Ray Bill: "If there is nothing but what we make in this world, brothers, let us make good."

Joar closed his eyes as if he was really trying to memorize it. He wasn't scared of death, because he had never expected to live a long life. He knew that happiness existed, but not for him. He believed in Heaven, that good people lived forever, just not that he was one of them. All he wanted was for his mom to be safe and for the artist to have a big life.

Later that evening Ted tried to explain what an "antihero" was, and Joar suddenly got very angry, because "anti" meant "opposite," for God's sake. So "antihero" must mean "villain." Ted said that an antihero was a good person who sometimes did bad things, but Joar thought it was the other way around, and a villain who does good things is still a villain.

"My old man taught me how to fish. He taught me to repair car engines. And once upon a time he made my mom fall in love with him, he didn't beat her at the start! But evil is evil, you can't fucking balance it out with a few good deeds, it isn't a fucking soccer match!" he roared.

Then Ted said the kindest thing anyone had ever said to Joar:

"You're nothing like your old man."

Joar shook his head and whispered:

"You don't know what it's like. When I hit people, I don't feel anything. I don't even regret it."

"You never start fights, you never hit anyone who's weaker than you . . . ," Ted tried, but of course he knew that was a lie, because almost everyone was weaker than Joar.

"I have to get home," Joar muttered quickly, looking at the time.

"Tomorrow!" Ted called after him in the darkness, but Joar didn't answer.

Twenty-five years later Ted falls silent on the train. He realizes he may have said too much, more than he was prepared for. He nods toward the box of ashes and says to Louisa:

"Joar tried to save everyone he loved. It was like he knew he had a clock inside him, counting down to destruction, so he was in a hurry to fix everything for . . . all of us."

"Because of his dad?" Louisa nods gloomily, more a statement than a question.

Ted nods too. Takes a deep breath.

"Yes. But he never called him his dad. Just his 'old man.' He needed a way to describe him that was different from what the rest of us called ours."

Then he goes on to say that people who had never seen violence close-up, never lived under tyranny, might have asked Joar why he didn't call the police about his old man. As if the police hadn't already been to the apartment a dozen times because the neighbors had complained about the noise. But no one dared testify against that man, Joar's mother didn't dare leave him, and Joar didn't dare leave his mother. What could the police do? Lock the old man up forever? Because if not, the world wasn't big enough for Joar and his mother to run away when he got out again. Tyrants can't be beaten, only destroyed, and no help was on its way.

"Real life isn't like comic books," Ted says there on the train, almost as if he feels ashamed.

"No," Louisa says, looking down at her sketch pad, because of course she knows all about that.

Then Ted glances at her, unable to bring himself to tell her the other thing Joar had decided, apart from making the artist famous: in August, Joar's old man would be on vacation, and before then Joar was going to kill him, or die trying, and then he would either be in prison or in his grave. That was why he was in such a hurry that summer, obsessed with the artist becoming famous. Because he knew he was running out of time to protect him.

But Ted doesn't have the heart to tell all that to Louisa, not yet, possibly more for the sake of his own heart than Louisa's. So instead he says:

"The next day, when we went to school, Ali realized that I had never said what superpower I wanted. So she asked, and I lied and said I wanted super speed."

"Why did you lie?" Louisa wonders.

"Because I was afraid I'd cry if I told the truth."

"What would you have wanted to say?"

"I wanted to be able to stop time. So my mom would never lose my dad, so Joar wouldn't get beaten by his old man, so . . . so I would never run out of people."

Twenty-five years later he still wishes the same thing, that he was fourteen years old and that the world was full of broken clocks. He blinks hard, takes off his glasses, they're wet. He feels shame creeping up his spine as his vision blurs. He should never have said that last bit.

"Are you okay?" Louisa asks cautiously.

"Yes," Ted manages to say, but his chin is trembling.

No one tells you when you're young that when you're middle-aged, you can't cry attractively anymore, the slightest little emotion can make you look like you've fallen through ice.

"You're not having a stroke, are you? Your face looks pretty chaotic," the teenager tells him.

Ted runs his hands over his cheeks and wants to say: *Love is chaos.* But instead he mumbles:

"Sorry, I haven't thought about those days for a long time, I got . . . nostalgic."

She looks concerned, the way you do about very, very, very old people, but then she smiles:

"I liked the superhero quotes."

Ted tries to regain control by breathing through his nose, then he nods toward the box of ashes and smiles back weakly:

"He liked Batman best: 'I wear a mask. And that mask, it's not to hide who I am, but to create who I am.'"

Louisa covers her face with her hair again at that.

"Fish and I liked Batman. He was an orphan as well."

Ted glances down at her sketch pad, then points and asks without thinking first:

"Are those butterflies, there above the cockroaches?"

Louisa suddenly snatches the pad away, as if Ted's hand were an unsteady glass of milk. He looks away, shamefaced.

"Sorry. I didn't mean to . . . "

"They're not finished yet!" she snaps, angling the sketch pad so he can't see.

Ted sits in silence, marinating in his own clumsiness for a long while. Then he says quietly, down toward the box of ashes:

"Sorry. They just reminded me of his. Before he painted the skulls, he often used to draw butterflies. He liked anything with wings. Birds, dragons, angels . . . "

She hides her pad and mumbles:

"Tell me more. Just . . . don't look while I'm drawing."

So he looks out the window and talks about spring.

They were still fourteen. Joar hadn't found the competition yet, and the artist hadn't started painting the picture, but in many ways the work of art had already been started. One day when the snow had just started to melt, Ted got into trouble. There was a boy in his class who, for all the obvious reasons, was called "Bulldog." One afternoon he forced Ted inside a locker and left him there for a whole class period. When Ted was eventually released, half the school was standing there laughing because they could see he'd been crying.

When Joar found out what had happened, his eyes turned so black that they looked hollow, but Ted whispered desperately: "If you kill him, that doesn't make you a hero, it makes you a weapon."

"Who said that?" Joar asked, furious.

"Superman," Ted said, wiping his cheeks.

Joar didn't respect many authority figures in his life, but not even he could argue with Superman. So instead of fighting, he calmly sought out Bulldog in the schoolyard and said: "I heard you're going round bragging about stuffing a guy into a locker? I think you're lying!" Bulldog tilted his head to one side, as if the thought were too heavy for his brain, then he snapped: "What the hell do you mean, lying? Want me to show you?" So he led Joar to a locker, but Joar just grinned: "You're going to put *me* in there? I'm the shortest person in the whole eighth grade! You'd never get someone as tall as you in there! So are you lying or what?" So Bulldog lost his patience and put his head and one leg inside the locker to prove how spacious it was. Two seconds later it was clear that he might not have been a liar, but he was definitely an idiot. He banged on the inside of the door as Joar put a padlock on the locker, and it took more than half an hour before the janitor managed to cut it off. When Bulldog emerged into the hallway, someone at the back of the giggling crowd of teenagers called out: "Look! He's peed his pants! Bulldog isn't housebroken!"

On the train Ted cleans his glasses again, on both sides of the lenses, even though only one side is wet.

"Fish was the same as Joar," Louisa suddenly says beside him.

"In what way?"

Louisa's pencil scrapes sadly against the paper, like the sharpened blades of a pair of skates on fresh ice. Not drawing, but dancing.

"Fish didn't think she was a hero either. She always said that I was the main character in our story."

"Perhaps she was right?" Ted says encouragingly.

Louisa's jaw moves sadly from side to side.

"No, she wasn't . . . ," she mumbles, but someone opens the door to the carriage at that moment and her words get lost in the noise.

"Sorry?" Ted says.

"Nothing, forget it," Louisa quickly whispers and stares down at her sketch pad, then swiftly changes the subject: "What happened to Bulldog? Did he get his revenge?"

"What makes you think that?" Ted wonders.

"Bullies always have small hearts but good memories," she replies.

The train still isn't moving. Ted looks at his watch, for the first time in his life he wants time to go faster, only someone who still has all their people left wants to stop time. He replies slowly, because the memories are coming in fits and starts, like water from a frozen pipe:

"I asked Joar not to protect me anymore. I really did. Obviously I knew that Bulldog would try to get back at him for that business with the locker. If Joar was going to get beaten by his dad for protecting someone, I told him it shouldn't be me. Do you know what he said?"

They had walked home from school slowly that spring day, Ted and Joar side by side, which hardly ever happened. Joar had nodded to the artist who was walking ahead next to Ali, although they weren't really walking, they were trying to see who could run the ugliest. The artist won, declaring that he was imitating an artichoke on ice.

"Look at that happy idiot!" Joar grinned. "When he's happy, the whole world is . . . good. When he draws, everything is . . . damn, then everything's good! That's why I have to protect you, Ted. Because the only thing I can do is fight, and when he's grown-up he won't need me anymore. But he'll need you."

Ted had never heard anything more ridiculous in his whole life.

"Why would he need me?"

Joar turned and said:

"Because loyalty is a superpower."

On a train that isn't moving Ted's glasses are still rocking.

"Is that another superhero quote?" Louisa asks.

"In a way," Ted nods.

Louisa says nothing for a long time before asking:

"Joar came up with it himself, didn't he?"

Ted nods again.

"You're right, then. It counts as a superhero quote," she says, then asks: "What happened to Bulldog?"

"He and Bulldog fought in the schoolyard the next day until they were both bleeding," Ted says.

Bulldog started the fight, Joar finished it. Bulldog fought like a madman, but Joar fought like a whole gang. When Joar got home his old man broke the radiator with him. Joar couldn't even play soccer the following week, he was limping so badly, but he still didn't regret a moment.

Because that day when Bulldog was shut in the locker and the janitor had to cut the lock off, the janitor's sleeves slid up, revealing his tattoos: skulls. That was the first time Joar saw them, and he would never forget it. Because without the janitor, nothing would have turned out the way it did. When you're fourteen years old, a single person can be like wind beneath a butterfly's wings.

"Art is coincidence, love is chaos," Ted says.

Louisa thinks that Fish would have liked that too.

TWENTY-TWO

Ted's story is interrupted by a sneeze. From him. Obviously he starts to panic at the first tickle in his nose, the way almost-forty-year-old men do when that happens in public, because men of that age can no longer sneeze just once.

"What's *happening* to you?" Louisa says in horror when he's sneezed six times in a row.

"I don't know," Ted sniffs, after which he sneezes once more.

"I've never heard anyone sneeze more than three times in a row," Louisa says, impressed.

"When I was young I never used to sneeze more than twice," Ted declares, red in the face.

"Maybe it started when you got stabbed? Perhaps you're allergic to nickel or something?" Louisa suggests.

It's impossible to tell if she's being sarcastic or not, young people really are the worst. Ted sneezes again.

"Bless you!" says the conductor with the tattoos, because of course he is going past just then, seeing as the universe really is the worst too.

Louisa turns around seriously and explains:

"Ted caught a cold one night when he was in prison, you know! There was a terrible wind blowing through the bars!"

The conductor smiles with the uncertainty you feel when there's a fifty percent chance the person you're talking to is joking, and a fifty percent chance that she's a psychopath. When he's disappeared into the next carriage Ted sniffs:

"Stop saying I was in prison!"

"I'm telling you, it makes you seem dangerous and attractive," Louisa explains amiably.

"If you want him to think I'm dangerous, maybe you should tell him I got *stabbed* instead?" Ted hisses.

Louisa shakes her head very patiently, as if she's talking to someone who wears their bicycle helmet into the grocery store.

"The fact that you got stabbed doesn't make you seem dangerous, it just makes it seem like you're a dangerous person to have as a friend."

Ted sneezes again, but misses the crook of his arm, spraying the whole of the back of the seat in front of him.

"Don't say it," he begs, mortified.

But it's too late, Louisa is already pretending her hand is a phone that she's talking into dramatically:

"Yes, hello? Is that the backrest police? I want to report an incident! Yes, that's right, the man who said I mustn't put my FEET on the back of a seat—"

"Move, I need to go and blow my nose," Ted grunts with a degree of desperation, holding his newspaper in front of his face.

He struggles out of his seat, while Louisa comments:

"You know this is why male serial killers always get caught, right? DNA everywhere! Have you ever thought about that? That female serial killers never get caught? And now you're thinking: 'But hold on, there aren't that many female serial killers?' That you *know* about, maybe! Because they never get . . ."

Her voice is drowned out by another sneeze from Ted before he reaches the bathroom, louder than all the previous ones, and the other passengers all turn around. When Ted closes the bathroom door behind him he feels so ashamed that he's actually short of breath, and he blows his nose so hard that it feels like his brain is trying to smuggle itself out of him. He accidentally looks in the mirror, which is never a good idea, the jacket of the man looking back at him is all wrinkled, and his face is as red as a priest in a brothel. He feels embarrassed, not only because of the sneezing, but also because he's been talking too much. He shouldn't have told Louisa that story. He can hear his mom's voice from his childhood: "Don't babble like an old woman, you're making a fool of yourself."

It was always important to Ted's mom that he and his brother not act like old women. They had to be men. They weren't allowed to cry, or get hysterical, or ever come across as weak. Their mom had such clear definitions of her sons' masculinity that Ted can only assume it was because she knew what this world does to girls. When her husband got cancer, she had to be both mother and father to the boys, and no doubt she did her best, and that's the worst thing about being a parent: that almost everyone does their best, but almost all fail regardless. Ted's mom saw it as her job to make him tough, she saw softness as a luxury, something only princes and princesses could afford.

He's still holding the newspaper, he hasn't even opened it yet, because he knows they will have written about the artist. He bought it out of habit, the way he always bought all the newspapers when they wrote about his friend, even though the artist hated it. Ted was too proud, he cut out all the reviews and articles in secret. But today he can't read a single word, because in the face of death grown men are like children, we think that if we close our eyes, we become invisible. We imagine that if we don't open the newspaper, nothing terrible can have happened yet.

He tosses it in the trash can, glances at the mirror, an anxious and overwhelmed man with skin as soft as room-temperature cheese glances back. He's never liked himself much, but even less today. He regrets babbling to Louisa, the way you regret things you said when you were drinking, but in his case it was grief that dulled his judgment. He should never have brought the girl with him at all. He's terrified of responsibility, because he knows he's a failure of a man. Everyone he loves keeps dying. The thought occurs to him to abandon Louisa here, it'd be so easy now, just sneak out of the bathroom and run off down the platform. She'd be okay on her own, wouldn't she? Surely better than with him. He's bad luck, he's sure of it.

Unfortunately, he doesn't even get a chance to try, because when he opens the bathroom door, he hits Louisa in the head with it, because she's standing right outside.

"Ow!" she exclaims, the way you do when you lack a basic understanding of how doors work.

"Why are you standing there?" Ted asks, which is a reasonable question.

"I'm waiting for you!" she replies, entirely unreasonably.

Ted looks into the bathroom, then at her, and frowns.

"Where did you think I was going to go? That I was going to flush myself away?"

"What are you talking about?" she says, and only then does he realize that it hadn't even occurred to her that he might leave her.

Ted can't help feeling slightly insulted that she hadn't even considered it.

"Why isn't the train moving?" he therefore asks, the way you do when you want to regain your authority.

"Technical problems," Louisa replies, as confidently as if she'd had time to take an engineering exam while he was blowing his nose.

"What does that mean?" he wonders.

"Do I look like a train driver?" she asks.

Ted frowns unhappily, but she thinks it's another sneeze and leaps out of the way. He groans:

"Who said it was technical problems?"

"The conductor. He said we can go out and stretch our legs if we want. I said you have such short legs that you can pretty much have them outstretched when you're sitting down. But maybe you'd like some air anyway? Old people usually love getting some air."

Ted looks out the window. A man with a black dog is walking on the platform.

"I'll wait a bit. But you go," he says firmly.

Louisa looks at the dog, then at Ted, and tilts her head to one side.

"Are you scared of dogs?"

"No. I just prefer being where dogs aren't."

"How many phobias do you actually have, Ted?"

"I have just enough!" he snaps.

Louisa grins, but doesn't judge, because she understands him, her own phobia concerns people. Ted is scared of touching them, but she's scared of being touched. So they wait until dogs and people alike have gone past.

"Fish and I always wanted pets, but you're not allowed to have them in foster homes. But one time we did have a fish! It lived in a really big bowl under our bed," Louisa explains brightly.

Ted tries to stop himself from sounding interested, but fails:

"So . . . Fish had a fish?"

"Yes."

"What was the fish called?"

"Buster."

"Good name for a fish," Ted admits reluctantly.

"It is, isn't it? I was the one who came up with it!" she smiles triumphantly.

The dog disappears. Louisa peers out from the train rather more dramatically than Ted thinks necessary, then waves to him as if they were secret agents, and creeps out onto the platform as if she is trying to avoid laser beams.

"Little brat," Ted grunts.

"Miserable old man," she grins.

The platform is full of other passengers wandering about aimlessly to stretch their legs. Ted looks around as if he is still working out an escape plan, just in case he decides to leave the little brat behind after all. There's a road on the other side of the track, and a bus stop, but it has no roof and it's starting to get dark and cold. Who knows how long a miserable old man would have to wait there for a bus? He imagines how much the artist would have laughed at the fact that one of the last things Ted said to him was that it would be nice to get some peace and quiet.

"Are you going to sneeze again?" Louisa asks.

"No!" Ted promises.

"Your face looks really weird," she informs him.

Ted doesn't reply. He walks along the side of the train with his hands behind his back, like a ski jumper, and Louisa bounces along beside him like someone who has never had a sore neck in her whole life.

"Does it hurt? Where you got stabbed?" she wonders, looking at the leg he's got the limp in.

"No."

"I broke my arm once, that hurt really badly. But you could draw on the cast! Did you get a cast when you got stabbed?"

"No."

"Poor you."

They walk on in silence. Eventually Ted's curiosity wins out over his grouchiness.

"How did you break your arm?" he asks.

"A guy in the foster home threw me through a window."

She says it like she is telling him that someone once threw a pencil at her.

"What?! What happened?" Ted exclaims, shocked.

"I had to move. They said I should have paid for the window."

"The one you got thrown out of? That's the most ridiculous thing I've ever . . . ," Ted protests, but she smiles weakly.

"No. The other window. The one I threw the guy through afterwards."

Her sleeve has ridden up and he can see the network of scars.

"I'm sorry," he says.

"No need, I wasn't badly hurt."

"No, I mean I'm sorry that you talk about that like it was normal. I'm sorry you didn't have a better childhood. It isn't your fault."

She bites her cheeks and concentrates on kicking a small stone in front of her.

"Are you going to be a teacher again when you get home?"

The question hits Ted as if she has fired it from a catapult.

"I don't think so," he says, his voice suddenly more brittle.

"Shame," she says.

"Why?"

"You were probably good at it."

"What do you base that on?" he snorts, more unpleasantly than he actually means to.

"You weren't the one that student was trying to stab. You got hurt trying to protect someone else. All the teachers I've ever met would have run away."

Ted clasps his hands tightly behind his back so she won't see that they're shaking.

"It isn't a teacher's job to protect their students," he mumbles, not that he believes that, but because he heard a colleague say it once.

"Yes it is," she replies calmly.

There are people sitting on all the benches they pass, so when they finally reach one that's empty Ted sits down out of instinct. After taking a handkerchief out of his pocket and carefully wiping it first, of course. Louisa sits down next to him, without a handkerchief, and blurts out:

"So, instead of sitting on the train, you'd rather come out here and . . . sit?"

"You were the one who wanted to go outside!" he points out.

"Well pardon me for thinking you might need a bit of air! Here, have a free paper!" she groans.

Ted takes the newspaper in astonishment.

"Where did you get that?"

"It was lying on the bench."

Ted lets go of it as if it has teeth.

"You picked up a newspaper that was lying on the *bench*?"

"You're the one who likes newspapers."

"Not from *benches*! Anyone could have touched it!"

"Says the old man who sneezes on people!"

Ted blushes.

"I sneezed on the seat. Not on anyone. I—"

"People have to sit on that seat!" Louisa points out.

Ted breathes through his nose and tries to think of something smart to say, but stops himself when he notices the sketch pad in her lap. She takes it with her everywhere. The artist was the same. So instead of something smart, Ted says something honest instead:

"I . . . I'm sorry I looked at your sketch pad while you were drawing earlier, that was wrong of me."

"Don't worry about it," she mutters quickly, but her voice is weaker and her grip on the sketch pad tighter.

"Yes, it does. I should have known better," Ted says, because he really should have.

When they were teenagers, the artist never wanted to show anyone anything that wasn't finished. Art is a nakedness, you have to be free to decide when you're comfortable with it, and with whom. Louisa weighs her words with her tongue for much longer than usual before she replies:

"It's just that until I show a drawing to someone, it's only mine. You know? It isn't too late to fix it. I'm not good at drawing, I'm slow, people who are *good* at drawing are just good . . . all the time. Their worst drawings are still great. If you saw my worst drawings you'd realize that I'm actually just a fraud. But . . . before the drawing is finished it isn't too late. That's the only time I . . . like myself."

Ted looks up at the sky, the corners of his lips trembling slightly, and the dimples in his cheeks grow deeper and fill again, grow deeper and fill again.

"I don't know anything about art," he confesses.

"Me neither," she whispers.

"But I don't think the most important thing for an artist is being able to draw, but having something to say," he says, more to the sky than to her.

"You just said you don't know anything about art!" she points out sullenly.

Then Ted sets a new record for the kindest thing he's said to her:

"I think you're like the drawing, you're not ready yet. But one day I think you're going to do something important. One day you'll paint someone else's postcard."

Louisa quickly wipes her face with the back of her hand. Then, to Ted's horror, she reaches down and picks up the newspaper from the ground. She leafs through it, although the wind on the platform does its best to stop her. She's just about to tell Ted that if old people love newspapers, they must really hate reading, but then she turns a page and sees the artist, and all the air goes out of her. "Dead," the headline reads. "No known family," it says lower down. Beside the picture of the artist is a photograph taken outside his home, on a beautiful tree-lined street in the most expensive part of a big city. There are little candles and hundreds of roses on the sidewalk, left by admirers of his work. Louisa can feel Ted looking over her shoulder, but they ignore each other, just resting there in shared grief.

"PLEASE GET BACK ON THE TRAIN! DEPARTURE IN THREE MINUTES! ALL ABOARD!" a voice suddenly cries.

It's the conductor. So the moment is ruined. You can always trust reality to do that.

"Come on," Ted says softly, and gets to his feet with effort.

Louisa looks at the picture of the roses outside the artist's home before carefully folding the newspaper around her sketch pad.

"Was that where you lived with him at the end?" she asks.

"Yes."

"It looks nice."

"It was."

"Do you wish you could have stayed there?"

"No."

"Why not?"

They're walking slowly alongside the train, Ted with his hands behind his back and Louisa with her arms wrapped around herself. Then Ted explains just how bereavement feels:

"I could never have lived there without him. I would just have lain awake all night waiting for him to come home. I would have had to throw away all the eggs, because he was the only one who ate them, but I would have forgotten not to buy them. I would have forgotten that he didn't exist, all the time. I would have gotten angry because the light in the bathroom was turned off, because I used to get so annoyed with him for always leaving it on. I would have saved all his shoes, all his shirts, and I would have been angry with the spring and hated flowers when they appeared because they drowned out the last smells of him. I would have always laid the table for two on the balcony. I would have had to eat all the popcorn myself. I would never have been able to pick a film."

The entrance to the train fills with a slow line of frustrated passengers, the man and the teenager stand on the platform and wait till last, anxious that they might touch or be touched by some stranger in the throng.

"Can I ask something?" Louisa wonders, clutching the newspaper photograph of the artist in her arms.

"Has anyone ever been able to stop you?" Ted says, with half a sigh, half a smile.

Louisa thinks that she was right, he would have been a good parent.

"Were you a . . . couple?" she asks tentatively.

"No."

"Because he was in love with someone else?"

Ted nods softly, his chin heavy with loss, but not bitterness.

"We were as close to a couple as you can get, maybe. It's probably hard to understand."

Louisa shakes her head slowly.

"No. It isn't hard at all. You loved each other so much that you were scared of accidentally breaking each other."

She rubs her lower arm, where the man in the tree is waving. She has known love like that too. Once all the other passengers have gotten on board, Louisa and Ted follow the conductor into the carriage and squeeze into their seats. When the train slowly starts to move along the rails Ted leans his forehead closer to the window, and his face cracks into wrinkles when he says:

"I could never have lived there on my own. I would have frozen to death in that apartment without his eyes on me."

Louisa pulls her jacket around herself more tightly and whispers:

"That's exactly how it feels."

Then he's glad he didn't leave her.

TWENTY-THREE

Now that the train is moving again, Ted feels envious of all the people living in the houses it passes, because they're already home. He gets slightly annoyed at people saying that the world rushes past outside the train windows, because it's the train that's doing the rushing, the world is standing still. Ted gets annoyed at quite a lot of things, which always amused the artist. He used to tease Ted by saying that he "hated adventures," but of course that isn't true. Ted loves adventures, he just absolutely doesn't want to participate in them. He wants to be one of the people in the houses, reading about adventures in a book, like a normal person. He wants to hear the artist's sleeping breath at the other end of the room. He wants to be home.

He falls asleep, just for a couple of minutes.

"Do you want one?" Louisa says when he wakes up, unless perhaps it's her voice that wakes him? He opens his eyes and reluctantly drags his brain back to reality. It's dark out now, he can't see any houses anymore, just trees. Louisa lands on the seat next to him as if the law of gravity has just discovered her, she's holding two cans of Coca-Cola. It suddenly occurs to Ted that she must have been quiet for a long time for him to fall asleep, which is a pretty big compliment to him, because she babbles when she's nervous. He no longer makes her nervous.

"How . . . how did you pay for those?" Ted wonders, glancing at the cans. It's the most diplomatic way he can think of to ask the question.

"You're wondering if I stole them?" Louisa says, affronted.

"No," he lies.

"I'm not a thief!" she hisses.

"Okay," Ted says, slightly sheepish.

"I got the money from your bag when you were in the bathroom earlier," Louisa goes on, as if she's now expecting an apology.

"So . . . you stole my money?" Ted asks.

"It isn't theft when you're friends!" Louisa exclaims, as if the very idea is shocking.

Ted isn't sure how to respond to that, seeing that this too is a compliment. Louisa offers him one of the cans of Coca-Cola, because real friends offer you half of what they've bought with your money, but Ted declines. It isn't as if he doesn't have to pee enough as it is.

"Are we nearly there yet?" Louisa asks.

"No. There's a long way to go," Ted replies.

"So tell me more, then," she asks.

"About what?"

"About the janitor and the skulls. About the painting. About . . . everything."

Ted closes his eyes lightly, opens them heavily. He thinks about his friend and sighs:

"He was like you, he didn't think he could paint either."

Then he tells the whole story about the janitor and the skulls, the way the artist once told everything to him. It isn't entirely straightforward, because the story starts with a lie: that people can't fly. Most of the rest of us get fooled, but the artist was lucky, because that spring when he was fourteen he met the janitor. And the janitor had had the truth revealed to him by his mom when he was little: "All children are born with wings," she had whispered. "It's just that the world is full of people who try to tear them off. Unfortunately they succeed with almost everyone, sooner or later. Only a few children escape. But those children? They rise up to the skies!"

The janitor had grown up feeling lost and different, rejected at school, never normal like other children. But his mom always reminded him: "You feel strange because you still have your wings, rubbing beneath your skin. You think you're alone, but there are others like you, people who stand in front of white walls and blank paper and only see magical things. One day one of them will recognize you and call out: 'You're one of us!' And then you won't feel lost anymore. You'll realize that you've always been able to speak a secret language, one that has no boundaries, because you have no nationality. Art is your homeland."

His mom always thought her son would end up an artist, but she was wrong, he changed the world instead. Because one day he became a janitor and repeated his mom's words to a fourteen-year-old who would come to be known as "C. Jat," and nothing inside the fourteen-year-old was ever the same again.

"But that isn't where it all started, not really," Ted says suddenly, correcting himself. "It actually started with a dog! Well, no, it really started with a broken foot. No, hang on, that isn't true either. The foot wasn't actually broken. I mean . . ."

He takes a deep breath and pulls himself together. Sorting the memories as if they had been lying on a windowsill in a cross-draft.

"It started one day in the spring of the year when we were fourteen," he eventually recalls.

Ali had found a bottle of dish soap in her dad's hall closet, because a dad who liked having fun also liked having parties, and if you had parties a little too often, you also had to mop the floor after someone had a bit too much fun. So Ali had taken the soap to school in her backpack, Joar had cut a hole in a fence and used the wire to make a ring, then he and Ali and the others spent the afternoon blowing bubbles in an empty part of the school stairwell. They had slipped about, laughing and chasing each other down a hallway, until Ali slid into a gang of older boys and girls who snapped irritably: "What are you doing? You fucking idiot!"

The older boys and girls shoved Ali aside like she was a pile of leaves. When they walked past Joar, Ted, and the artist, one of the girls cast a disgusted glance at their stained clothes.

"They stink like they're homeless," she hissed to her friends as they went around the corner.

Joar took this very badly, because he was covered in soap, for God's sake, his clothes had never been cleaner! Ali snorted:

"Did you see that girl's hair, it was perfect! How does she get it to look like that? Does she sleep standing up or what? Do elves fly in through her window every morning and sew her clothes onto her body?"

"Elves can't fly, you idiot," Joar replied confidently.

So an argument broke out between him and Ali about whether or not elves had wings. Ali was convinced that they did. Joar was sure they lived in the forest and had bows and arrows. Ali muttered something to him, possibly involving the words "stupid donkey," so they had a fight. As usual. They were interrupted by a shriek, but it wasn't from Ali or Joar, it came from the stairwell. It turned out that the girl with the perfect hair had slipped and fallen, because some idiot had left soap all over the steps.

And that was how it all started. Coincidence.

The following day the girl with the perfect hair came to school with a pair of crutches. "My foot's broken!" she told the teachers very seriously, because she had quickly realized that was a way of getting out of gym class. Because the girl with the perfect hair hated gym class because you had to share a changing room with girls who weren't perfect, and that could be contagious. So her foot was broken for two whole days, until she sadly suffered sudden memory loss because a cute dog walked past the window of the cafeteria. The girl with the perfect hair ran out to pet it, but forgot to take her crutches with her.

It was, in her defense, an insanely cute dog. Even Ted, who felt much the same about dogs as the girl did about gym class, had to admit that. It looked like a teddy bear made of flesh, which might not sound very cute, but it really was. Either way: this was a school, and if there's one thing everyone knows about schools, it's that a pair of crutches left unattended in a room will, sooner or later, end up on a roof. Which some of the classmates of the girl with the perfect hair and the not-so-broken foot quickly accomplished.

That's why a very old man who worked as a janitor at the school had to climb up and get the crutches. This was in the spring, but no one had told winter, so the temperature was still below freezing at night, and there was still ice on the roof. So the elderly janitor ended up in the hospital after falling and breaking his foot for real.

And *that* was how a young man who would change the world got a job as a temporary janitor.

TWENTY-FOUR

His name was Christian. He was twenty years old, he had a tender heart and a broad smile. He had only gotten the job because his mother knew the principal, and the principal had only agreed on the condition that Christian promised to wear long-sleeved shirts that hid all his tattoos. On his first day at work, Christian was told to paint a wall behind the gymnasium white, but unfortunately that was impossible, because Christian hated white walls. So he came around the corner with his arms full of colored paints, and at that moment a crazy fourteen-year-old came rushing straight into his chest from the other direction. They collided like they were in a cartoon, with the cans of paint hanging in the air for half an eternity before the fourteen-year-old got up from the ground with so much paint on his face that it covered the tears on his cheeks. When the janitor got to his feet his sleeves had slid up, revealing his tattoos: skulls.

The boy had never seen anything so beautiful in his whole life. They both laughed, and it was like standing on the prow of a ship and seeing the outline of your homeland on the horizon.

"Sorry, you're covered in paint!" the janitor said when he saw the stains on the boy's shirt.

"Don't worry, it was already dirty," the boy said shyly, picking up his backpack from the ground and accidentally dropping his sketch pad.

The janitor smiled, like someone waving through fog.

"Oh! You draw?"

The boy nodded in horror.

"Come with me!" the janitor said.

The boy followed him around the corner behind the gymnasium, squeezing between the wall and a fence, to a space so hidden away that not even the school's smokers had found it. The janitor was talking so fast that his eyes were darting about and his jaw carried on moving after he spoke, as if his voice were dubbed.

"My mom got this job for me. I promised to behave. But the principal told me to paint this wall white! What sort of monster does that? Is there anything worse than white walls?"

"No!" the boy replied at once.

Then he smiled shyly, overwhelmed by the smell of paint and a stranger's breath, and leaned against the wall as if he might be able to fall right through it. White? It was anything but white. The janitor had painted angels and birds and butterflies and dragons. Then he told the boy who would one day become a world-famous artist what his mother had said about wings, and about all children being born with them.

"If you feel strange, like you don't belong anywhere, that's because you still have your wings. They're rubbing beneath your skin," the janitor smiled. He patted one of the dragons on the wall and added: "I'm going to paint over them, the principal will go crazy if I don't . . ."

"NO!" the boy shouted, then added, "Don't do it. I've never seen anyone paint like this."

"Pah," the janitor grinned. "I bet you can paint better!"

"I'm really bad," the boy mumbled, and looked like he was about to run off.

So the janitor put a brush in his hand, without touching his skin, and said:

"You know what Mom always says? You can be whatever you want to in life, as long as you don't become a critic! Not of other people, and not of yourself. It's so easy to be a critic, any coward can do that. But art doesn't need critics, art has enough enemies already. Art needs friends."

The boy didn't reply, but he painted a dragon.

"I've never . . . seen anything like that," the janitor gasped when he saw it.

The boy misunderstood, of course.

"Sorry, it's childish," he whispered, and tried to paint over it.

"No, no, don't you dare! You're amazing!" the janitor said.

"You don't have to lie," the boy said, so upset that the janitor laughed.

"Picasso said it took him four years to learn to paint like Raphael, but a whole lifetime to learn to paint like a child."

"I don't know who those people are," the boy admitted.

The janitor smiled and said it didn't matter. Then he pulled out some cans of spray paint and pointed to an empty white area. The boy filled it tenderly with naked men with wings. The janitor looked at them and thought of his mother, because when she saw a beautiful painting she used to say that her heart leapt in her chest so that she could see her blouse move. Great art is a small break from human despair, she explained to her son. It took him twenty years to understand what she meant.

"One of my mom's favorite painters was a man called Ragnar Sandberg," he told the boy gently without taking his eyes off the wall. "Sandberg once said that art should be without purpose, and irresistible. You have to paint like the birds sing."

That was how the wall felt, he tried to explain. Then the boy asked him to paint skulls again, and the janitor did, and as he was doing so he quoted Georgia O'Keeffe: "It never occurs to me that skulls have anything to do with death."

Then he laughed and explained how his mom had been so angry when he got his first tattoos. He had suggested that perhaps she should get some herself, to which his mom had retorted angrily, quoting Marina Abramović: "I don't have tattoos, I have scars."

The janitor scratched his arms.

"She's tough, my mom, but damn, she really knows how to love things. She loves them with her whole body. She used to drag me to art galleries when I was little. I hated it, I hated having to stand in line, I hated not being allowed to run and play. But now all my best memories are from those places."

"Was it your mom who taught you to paint like this?" the boy asked with an envy that you have to have grown up in a home full of blank walls to understand.

"No. No one teaches anyone to paint, all we learn are rules and limitations, what we *aren't* supposed to do. I went to art school, but I was lucky, I got thrown out before they had time to teach me anything."

"Why did you get thrown out?" the boy asked.

"They didn't like what I was painting on."

"What were you painting on?"

"Drugs."

Their smiles were rather brittle then, both of them, the janitor instantly regretting being so honest and the boy not knowing how to respond. He was still wearing his backpack, every time he moved, the pills he had stolen from Ted's dad's bathroom cabinet rattled, a sound like stones rolling down a cliff. Perhaps the janitor heard them, perhaps he just saw something in the boy's eyes, or the red marks on his lower arms, because he suddenly whispered:

"Don't hurt yourself."

It was such a nice thing to say that there was hardly any space for all the words inside the boy who would become world-famous, so he was forced to grow several inches instead. They carried on painting in silence, falling for each other's talent the way you fall through a hole in reality. They were both in pain, but just then they were no longer held captive on Earth. For the janitor it was a blessing, for the boy who would become an artist it was a miracle. Because all that spring the boy had wanted to die.

TWENTY-FIVE

No one can explain why some fourteen-year-olds want to die. Nature gains nothing from unhappy children, yet they are still walking around everywhere, without the words to describe their anxiety. Because how could you even begin to explain such a feeling to someone who has been happy and secure all their life? Should you say it's like a monster sleeping heavily on your lungs, so that every breath feels like you're drowning? That it's a voice in your head screaming that everything about you is a mistake?

Forget it! No one will understand! the voice in our heads hisses to us. Then it repeats the same lies that all broken children have to listen to: *There's something wrong with you! No one else feels the way you do! People can't fly!*

Ali and Joar and Ted were fragile too, but the artist was like a paper boat heading for a waterfall. Sometimes Joar would tease him that his only facial expression was looking like he'd just found a strand of hair in a cream cake. It was a desperate joke on Joar's part, because really he was trying to say: *You're not giving us enough oxygen, we're suffocating without your laughter.*

The artist tried to be happy, he really did, but he had been scared all his childhood.

"He gets it from his mom," his dad sometimes said when he was drunk, in the kitchen with his workmates from the harbor when he thought his son was asleep. They got divorced when the artist was little, he never got to know if his mom's depression started before or after that, if it was the cause or the effect. Sometimes she was almost like all the other moms, but sometimes she would spend all night cleaning manically, whispering to things that didn't exist. The son loved his mom, but he only knew her as a shadow of a person, the world is full of them, their hearts beat and their eyes are open, but they live like they're enclosed in glass bubbles. The son never saw his mother as emotionally cold, just shut off, unreachable. There was food on the table and a roof over his head in his childhood home, but no eye contact and very few words. No "Good night, little man" or "Good morning, darling," no "Aren't you clever?" or "You're so good at drawing!" The only thing she snapped at him desperately when he got beaten or bullied at school was: "Try to be like all the other children! Try to do what all the other children do!" That was probably how she had survived, by never standing out from the crowd, going to work and coming home, watching TV and going to bed. Sometimes she forgot things, sometimes she got lost on the way home from the shops, sometimes she talked to people no one else could see. She had demons in her head, children learn to recognize that at an early age. One doctor prescribed strong medication, she washed the pills down with alcohol, she spent almost all her time sleeping. But if she woke up when the artist crept home from Ted's in the evenings, she sometimes called out: "Did you have fun?" Because she had heard other moms ask that. Then the artist always said yes, he had. And then she would mumble: "Just be like all the other children. Just try to be normal."

Then she would fall asleep again, and her son would tuck her in. Sometimes they would eat breakfast together, often just water and dry toast, because his mom was almost always nauseous. She would respond when spoken to, as would her son, but because neither of them initiated conversations, they hardly ever had one. So his childhood passed. When the artist went to his dad's, not much was said there either, except when his dad was drinking with his workmates, because then the artist could sit on the other side of the kitchen wall and hear the truth. "He isn't normal, the boy," his dad said when the alcohol turned his eyes into marbles. "He was an accident," he went on. "She never wanted to be a mother." That was the kindest thing the artist could remember his dad saying about him, because at least he never said that he didn't want to be a dad.

The following morning the artist would clear away all the bottles in the kitchen, first at his dad's, then at his mom's. He would never have let anyone say they were bad parents, he understood that it was practically impossible to be a good one, children are so fragile that if you're the least bit fragile yourself, it's hopeless right from the start. At least one of you will fall apart.

The artist got beaten up at school when the other children saw he was drawing naked men with wings. He got called terrible things, because children's brutality knows no limits in its inventiveness. He often wished he had been what his parents wanted, a normal child like all the others, but how was that supposed to happen? No one was like him. His mom and dad never saw him hunched over his sketch pad with his pen darting across the paper. What a treasure to miss out on. They never understood how special it is to be abnormal.

The older he got, the worse school became. His shoulder had started twitching when he was nervous, so the artist started wearing the biggest hoodies he could find, and always pulled the hood over his head. He stopped eating, as if he could make himself invisible if he just got thin enough.

He never knew just how obvious it was to his friends that he was falling apart, and how not being able to stop it tormented them. Alone in their rooms at night, Ali was desperate, Joar furious, while Ted knelt at the side of his bed and prayed. Other children prayed to God, but Ted prayed to the demons, because maybe God decided which people would die, but the demons in children's heads decided which ones had the strength to live. So Ted prayed loudly into the darkness, for mercy, for the demons to let go of his friend.

The demons didn't listen. They laughed.

The artist was scared in all his classes at school, because at any moment a teacher could force him to speak, but he was most scared during art lessons. Adults never understand that for a child who uses drawing to escape from reality, being made to do it on command is unbearable. In the eighth grade they got a new art teacher, a hateful little man who hissed that "art isn't about drawing!" Now theory was going to be as important as practice, and everyone was expected to "give a written account" after every exercise. At the end of the first lesson the teacher glared at the artist's work and snarled that the boy "didn't listen to the instructions." The boy didn't dare reply or look the teacher in the eye, and some men take that as a declaration of war.

They had been told to draw a flower, but the artist couldn't explain that he couldn't draw a flower without first drawing everything around it, he just hadn't had time to draw the flower yet. The teacher took his silence as a provocation. Joar was sitting next to him, so he tried to protect his friend the only way he knew: by drawing attention to himself.

"Can YOU draw a damn flower, you damn owl?" he yelled at the teacher.

It happened so fast that it must have been an act of genius, the way Joar took no more than a second to identify what a person was most ashamed of about their appearance and then stab it with a finely honed comment. Perhaps it was the teacher's big eyes, or the shape of his head, or his thin lips or small nose, no one had thought of it before, but just hearing the word "owl" once was enough for everyone to see it.

The teacher hesitated for just a moment, that was all Joar needed, like blood in the water. He yelled: "Come on, Owl! Draw a flower so we can see who's best!"

Ten seconds later the whole class was shouting: "DRAW! DRAW! DRAW!" and the Owl's face changed color, first from humiliation, then from rage.

Joar grinned: "No, no, now you've painted your face as red as a tulip, little Owl, but you're supposed to paint on the PAPER!"

The whole class roared with laughter and the Owl never stood a chance of regaining control. Obviously Joar already knew that the man at the front of the class would get his revenge, teachers always do, the problem was just that Joar didn't know who it would be aimed at.

Bullying happens so horribly fast. Soon the whole school was calling the teacher "the Owl," and it became so common to hear "hoo-hoo, hoo-hoo!" followed by roars of laughter in the hallways every time he walked past that no one even remembered it was Joar who first came up with it. But the teacher never forgot. It became a game among some of the older students to leave dead mice on the Owl's desk, which might sound harmless, but if it carries on for long enough it does something to a man. Joar might have been hard to hurt, but the artist was easy, so he was the target of the Owl's revenge.

Drawing meant freedom for the artist, so the Owl turned it into a prison cell. He came up with a thousand rules, and ten thousand ways to fail. That's how quickly the man regained his authority. The artist wasn't supposed to be creative, he was supposed to obey, to carry out precise tasks and demonstrate exact results. Obviously he couldn't do that. If you told him to draw a house, he would draw how the house felt. The Owl was intelligent, you don't have to be in order to be cruel, but it helps. So one lesson, when the artist had really failed with a task, the teacher made him stand in front of the whole class. The Owl disguised it well, he leaned over the boy's drawing and pretended to be impressed, which made the other students curious. They called for him to show what the artist had done, chanting his name, and the Owl snatched the drawing with a malicious grin and held it up in mock admiration. The room fell completely silent. Then someone giggled: "Looks like something a three-year-old could have drawn . . ."

They all laughed except for Joar, who started fighting with the two boys who were laughing loudest. The artist's face was so red that someone yelled: "Get the fire extinguisher!" and everyone laughed again. That was how easily the teacher proved that Joar was wrong: this boy was mediocre.

It's so easy to crush a heart, soon the artist was only a shadow of a person. The Owl could have stopped there, backing off when he had already won, but the feeling of power probably felt too good. So the lessons only got worse. The Owl's criticism became a torment, the artist was banned from having his hood pulled up, he wasn't allowed to use his own pencils. The Owl defended himself by saying the rules were the same for everyone, the boy really shouldn't think he was anything special. As if the boy had ever done that.

One day the Owl told the class to draw a box. It wasn't a difficult task, they were even given rulers, but when the lesson was over, the artist's paper was still blank, he felt so dizzy he was almost sick. The teacher should have realized then, should have known better, because once in his life even that bastard must have loved something. He should have seen in the boy's eyes that he couldn't draw a box without first feeling like he was inside it. The teacher should have asked him to draw the world outside the box instead, all the things he had felt that time when he was released from the storage trunk in preschool: sunshine and oxygen. He should have asked him to draw Joar's laughter and the feeling of having a best friend for the first time.

But instead the Owl chose cruelty. He mocked him. It doesn't take any strength at all to crush someone's self-confidence if you know where to stomp. The artist did what he always did, he pulled his hood up, stood up, and fled for the door. But the Owl stood in the way, grabbed the boy by the arm, and roared: "YOU'RE NOT GOING ANYWHERE!"

The artist tore free with such surprising force that the teacher lost his balance and stumbled into a desk, hitting his head. It was easy to interpret it as aggression, because no one saw that the boy was crying. It was so easy for the teacher to tell the principal afterward that he had been "attacked," to claim that the artist was one of "a group of hooligans who are like a pack of wild animals," especially as Joar had picked up a chair and smashed up half the classroom on his way out after his friend. But the teacher never told the principal that Joar also had tears in his eyes then, or what he had said:

"Do you think he needs your fucking help? Do you think he needs help to hate himself? You're no owl. You're just a swine."

Two other teachers came running in, Joar had to fight and claw his way out, but by the time he had reached the schoolyard the artist was already gone, like water through cracks in the floor. He was lost, Joar knew that. A backpack full of pills and a head full of demons, hardly any child would survive that. The most dangerous place on earth is inside us.

But the artist? All he would remember is that he ran. He didn't even notice where until he collided with something and tumbled to the ground. Ted had prayed to the demons for mercy, the demons had laughed, but maybe Heaven had listened. Because that day the wings grew out.

Joar, Ali, and Ted spent all afternoon looking for their friend. It was pure coincidence that they caught sight of him when he and the janitor were going to the storeroom to get more paint. The friends hardly recognized the artist's face then, his smile was in the way. When he led them shyly around the corner of the gymnasium to show them what he had painted on the wall, all three of them were so overwhelmed, they had to sit down on the grass.

"Now you know," Joar said happily.

"Know what?" the artist wondered.

Joar leaned so close to the wall that he got paint on his eyelashes.

"Now you know that you don't want to die."

TWENTY-SIX

Ted is interrupted by a sneeze. Not his own this time, but from a baby. The train has stopped at a small station and a young mom has carried the little snot machine on board.

"Bless you!" Louisa calls.

"Thanks," the mother smiles with the exhaustion that only a new parent or someone who's survived in the jungle for three months after a horrible plane crash can exhibit.

"What a cute baby!" Louisa says when they sit down on the other side of the aisle, then she turns to Ted: "Isn't it, Ted?"

"Really cute," Ted says, more or less the way you might say about a shark.

Louisa stares at him.

"Don't you like babies? Come on! Everyone likes babies, Ted!"

Ted feels like replying that that's the silliest thing he's heard since one of his colleagues at the school where he used to work once said she loved going to the gym. But instead he says: "I don't have anything against babies."

Dear Lord, he hardly likes people, and of course babies are the very worst-functioning versions of people. What exactly does she want from him?

"Everyone likes babies, Ted!" Louisa repeats, as if that would make it any more true.

Ted folds his arms, worried that if he doesn't, she might make him touch it. Louisa, on the other hand, leans across the aisle and makes faces at it, causing it to laugh.

Obviously the artist would have done the same thing if he'd been here, because he liked children too, the lunatic. One time he told

Ted that even wild animals were careful with newborns, that it's a biological instinct, because babies are what remind us that life goes on. "Babies teach us not to be scared of death. That's how we realize we can't wish for eternal life. Because if no one died, we would have to ban new people from being born. And when the playgrounds are empty, when the last pair of rain boots has been grown out of, when the last puddle has been jumped in . . . What would we want eternity for then, Ted?"

He had drunk a fair amount of wine the evening he said that, Ted recalls, but he has to admit that the artist probably had a point nevertheless.

"Don't you think?" the mother suddenly says in Ted's direction, as if he's part of the conversation.

He looks up and realizes to his horror that everyone is looking at him: the mother, the baby, Louisa, and the conductor, who has appeared to check tickets and is evidently extremely fond of human beings of all sizes.

"Sorry?" Ted mumbles.

The mother's eyes sparkle so that the dark circles beneath them are hardly visible. She nods first at the conductor, then at Ted, and repeats:

"He was asking if traveling with a baby was difficult, and I said that my mom told me that all parents feel the same: the days pass slowly but the years fly by. Don't you think?"

Ted gawps as if he doesn't understand what she's insinuating.

"You're asking me?"

The mother looks at him in surprise, then at Louisa.

"Oh, sorry, I thought that . . . that you were . . . Aren't you father and daughter?"

If anyone was asleep on the train at that moment, even if they were seven carriages away, they were woken by Louisa's shrieks of laughter. It comes so abruptly that the baby starts laughing too when it hears it.

"No, no, we're just friends!" Louisa says.

"Oh," the woman says, more uncomfortably now, looking a lot like someone who's trying to figure out the age difference.

"I mean, not *friends*-friends," Louisa declares immediately. "We're just ordinary friends! Ted doesn't even like girls, he likes conductors!"

"Louisa," Ted hisses to shut her up, but obviously there's no hope of that, her mouth has a longer braking distance than the train.

"And even if it looks suspicious, you should know that he hasn't kidnapped me! Or *has* he?" Louisa goes on, winking merrily at the conductor and the young mother.

"LOUISA!" Ted snaps, and quickly adds in despair: "She's joking! She's joking! Tell them you're joking, Louisa!"

Louisa turns to him in a sudden attack of teasing that he certainly doesn't appreciate.

"Oh, am I? Are you an expert at humor now, all of a sudden? Tell us a joke, then!" she demands.

"I . . . Oh, stop it . . . ," Ted mutters.

Somewhat unexpectedly, the conductor steps in to rescue him.

"I know a joke! My nephew told it to me yesterday! Do you want to hear it? Okay: you shouldn't get angry with lazy people. They haven't done anything!"

Louisa laughs, the mother laughs, the baby laughs. Ted smiles.

"I mean . . . lazy people, not doing . . . ," Louisa immediately explains considerately.

"I get it," Ted says.

"It doesn't look like it," she points out.

"I get it!" Ted insists.

"So tell us a joke, then," Louisa suggests.

Then Ted feels so crowded by everyone's stares, perhaps by the baby's most of all, that he actually does as he is told. He clears his throat, collects his thoughts, then says:

"Okay. Okay. The police stop a car for a routine check. Inside the car are one man and four penguins. The policeman asks the man: 'Why on earth have you got penguins in your car?' The man replies: 'They don't like being home alone.' The policeman says: 'But you can't do this to penguins, surely you understand that? You really should take them to a zoo!' The man looks surprised, but promises to do as the policeman says. The next day the policeman is standing in the same place when the man drives past again. The policeman stops him and sees that the penguins are still in the car with him, only this time they're all wearing sunglasses. The irritated policeman says: 'Didn't I tell you to take these penguins to a zoo?' The man nods happily and replies: 'I did! And today I'm taking them to the beach!'"

Ted falls silent. He clears his throat again. Louisa and the mother and the baby definitely aren't laughing. But the conductor? Oh, he's laughing, so hard that he drops the little machine that he uses to check people's tickets.

"Seriously?" Louisa says, looking at him accusingly.

"That's really funny!" the conductor exclaims.

Then Louisa turns to Ted and sees that he's giggling too, at his own joke.

"God, you two really would be a good match," Louisa says, but it definitely isn't a compliment.

Ted blushes and the conductor lowers his gaze.

"New passengers?" he mutters toward the other end of the carriage and walks on.

The mother hesitantly leans across the aisle and asks Louisa:

"Sorry, this is really nervy of me, but could I ask you for a big favor? Would you mind holding her while I go to the bathroom?"

All the color disappears from Louisa's face for a moment.

"Me?"

"Yes?" the mother says, holding out the baby.

"You're going to let me hold her?"

"If it isn't too much trouble?"

"It's no . . . no trouble," Louisa tries to say, but her voice cracks, as thin as a soap bubble.

Then she sits there with the baby in her arms, hardly daring to breathe, the way you do when someone has said the nicest thing one person can say to another: *I trust you. I trust you so much that I trust you with the start of life.* Louisa glances at Ted and looks so proud that even he admits:

"It is cute. For a baby."

"Can you tell me the rest of the story about the janitor now? But hurry up!" Louisa says, with her forehead close to the baby's smile.

"Why should I hurry up?" he asks.

"Because it sounds like a story that isn't going to end happily for everyone. And it's easier to cope with sad endings if you're holding a baby," Louisa replies.

TWENTY-SEVEN

The fourteen-year-old boy and the twenty-year-old janitor spent three days painting the wall behind the gymnasium. They painted butterflies and dragons, angels that reached down to touch Joar and Ted when they came to look late in the afternoon, birds that took flight so that Ali's hair moved in the flow of air. But most of all they painted skulls, skulls everywhere, beautiful and alive.

As an adult, the artist would think that this was the best work of his entire career. He was glad his friends had gotten to see it, because hardly anyone else got the chance.

"It reminds me of Basquiat," the janitor said on the third day, pointing to the wall filled with the boy's imagination.

They were alone then, he and the boy, standing on ladders in a world without clocks. The janitor's gaze flickered occasionally, his hands shook from time to time, and a couple of times his nose started to bleed suddenly. He said it was his allergies.

"I don't know who that is," the boy confessed.

"That doesn't matter," the janitor smiled, squinting in the sun as if the light hurt his eyes. Then he trotted out everything he knew about Basquiat, which was an awful lot.

"Did your mom teach you all that?" the fourteen-year-old wondered.

"Yeah. Mom's a teacher, she isn't even quiet when she's asleep, if you taped up her mouth she'd find a way to talk about art through her ears," the janitor said, rolling his eyes.

"Nice," the fourteen-year-old whispered honestly.

The janitor looked ashamed at that, sometimes you don't appreciate your own blessings until you see the envy in someone else.

"I mean . . . she's great, my mom. I was just a handful as a kid, that's all. I always hated it when she pointed to paintings and asked, 'What does that say to you?' It felt like a test in school. But now I'm starting to realize that it's pretty much the nicest thing you can say to anyone. One time I asked her why she was so obsessed with what I was thinking, and she got angry and yelled: 'Because I want to know what's happening inside you! Because you happened to me! You happen to me every second I'm alive!'"

The fourteen-year-old, who came from a home where no one happened to anyone else at all, was holding a brush over a naked body he had painted in one corner of the wall. As if he regretted it and was about to paint everything white.

"My parents don't like me drawing. They're ashamed. They say I should try to be normal," he said.

"They're wrong," the janitor replied, like it was the most obvious thing on earth. "You're an artist."

Sometimes that's all that's needed.

"I'm not an artist, I'm—"

The janitor interrupted him so sharply that his ladder wobbled:

"You're an artist if you create something! You're an artist if you don't see the world the way it is, if you hate white walls! No one else decides what art is, no one can stop you loving whatever you like, the cynics and critics can have control of all the other crap on the planet . . . but they can't decide how hard your heart beats! Become whatever you want, but don't become one of them. Art is a fragile enough light as it is. It can be blown out by a single sigh. Art needs friends, with our bodies against the wind and our hands cupped around the flame, until it's strong enough to burn brightly with its own power. Until it's an inferno. Unstoppable."

The boy hesitated for a long time before saying:

"I can't paint the way the art teacher wants. I can't paint *things*. There's something wrong with my brain."

"That's because you don't paint things the way they look, you paint them the way they feel," the janitor replied.

Then he quoted Frida Kahlo, who said she painted flowers so they wouldn't die. And Leonardo da Vinci, who said that art was never finished, only abandoned. The sound of the doors being unlocked inside the boy then should have been heard around the world, the ground should have shaken, that's how much everything changed inside him. They went on painting the wall until the sun abandoned them.

One day, many years later, a woman wrote in a newspaper that the most beautiful thing about the artist's pictures was that they felt inevitable. "Once you've seen his art, you can't imagine a world without it," she wrote. But for the artist it would never feel inevitable, merely improbable. His first painting had friends before it even existed. Who has luck like that?

"Can we paint again tomorrow?" he asked as darkness fell.

"We can paint every day!" the janitor promised. Because that's what we do, promises like that aren't lies, they're acts of rebellion against death. Then he quoted his mom's favorite poem, by Mary Oliver: "Tell me, what is it you plan to do with your one wild and precious life?"

The boy didn't answer. But he painted a window on the wall, and inside it he painted a child holding a paintbrush, so it looked like the child was painting from the other side of the wall. As if the janitor and the boy were inside the child's painting, as if they were the art. Then the janitor looked him straight in the eye and the boy would never forget it, that a look could feel like that.

"Here," the janitor said, handing him a piece of paper. It said "Christian," with skulls above both i's, followed by a telephone number.

The janitor peered up at a streetlamp that had just come on. His nose was bleeding again.

"Are you okay?" the boy asked anxiously.

"Yes, yes, it's just a nosebleed. That's my mom's number, I don't have a phone at the moment, but if you ever need help, call her. She's the best. I'm going to tell her about you!"

The boy held the piece of paper to his chest. When they parted he called:

"Tomorrow?"

"Yes! See you tomorrow for more painting!" the janitor grinned, and just before he disappeared into the darkness he turned around and called: "Don't hurt yourself!"

The first time the artist saw the janitor's mom, she was standing outside the church. And then the boy wished her all the art in the world, because he had never seen such a desolate person.

"Make sure you keep that job, please, Christian. The principal only gave it to you because we're old friends," his mother had said to her twenty-year-old son when he got the janitor's job.

Then she had sighed to herself, muttering something about who was she trying to kid? He could never paint a wall white, her boy.

Christian hadn't said thank you, hadn't said he loved her, because of course he was far too smart for that. Instead he had grinned and said: "You happen to me, Mom. You're my art."

How could she be angry with him then? She had been pregnant with Christian when she fled from a war, he was already improbable right from the start. When he was little, the other children used to tease him at school, calling him "refugee," but when he didn't know where he belonged she would tell the truth: art was his homeland. Hers too. That was how they survived reality.

Every time they argued the mother would think of Frances Harper, who said that "every mother should be a true artist." When Christian was standing in front of a painting, she always wanted to know what he was thinking, and when he got annoyed she would quote Marcel Duchamp: "Art is completed by the viewer." When her son thought she was embarrassing because she talked too much and laughed too loudly, she would throw Émile Zola's words at him: "I would rather die of passion than of boredom!"

So perhaps it was her fault, she often thought, that Christian later sought passion everywhere. Art is nothing for people with armor, you need a thin skin, but someone like that isn't only sensitive to beauty, but to everything. Seeking out euphoria is a life out of balance. So her little boy grew up, even though she forbade it, and she lost her grip on him.

When Christian was born, his mother held the newborn little body and only felt a single heart beating, first in him and then in her, one and the same. From then on she became twice as scared of the dark. When he became a teenager and disappeared out into the night, she always slept with the light on and her hand on the phone. When it rang, she always answered on the first ring.

He started taking drugs, she hoped he might stop when he got into art school, but it got worse. And how was she supposed to protect him against the world, she who couldn't even keep hold of her own glasses? When Christian was young, he used to carry around an extra pair for her to use whenever she was looking for the first pair. Once, in a gallery full of sculptures, she left her glasses on a stool. When they got back a group of tourists were taking photographs of them because they thought they were art. Her son's laughter echoed up into the roof, and that would never leave her dreams.

"It's a lie that people can't fly, Christian, don't forget that," she said as they walked home that day, and he answered: "Yeah, yeah, Mom, I know." Then he held her hand, and her skin still tries to remember how it felt, all the time. You can't love someone out of addiction, all the oceans are the tears of those who have tried. We're not allowed to die for our children, the universe won't let us, because then there wouldn't be any mothers left.

She helped him get into a rehabilitation program, he made all sorts of promises and broke every single one. He was drawn to parties like smoke finding its way toward the sky, he loved music, lived for dancing. Sometimes he cycled home, sometimes he traveled in a police car, sometimes in an ambulance. She knew he was living too fast, he was running out of time, but it was like trying to stop sunshine. New treatment centers, new promises, but it never worked.

But then, in the end, she managed to arrange a job for him as a janitor at the school. There he failed to paint a wall white, but succeeded in something much bigger instead. He managed to start a story.

When the phone rang late one night the mother answered on the first ring, always ready for it to be the police and for something terrible to have happened.

"Is it my son?" she yelled into the receiver, still half asleep.

Christian laughed drunkenly on the other end and said: "Yes? Sorry . . . what time is it? Were you asleep?"

Asleep? She hadn't slept since he was born, the little brat, she felt like replying. But instead she whispered: "No, no, has something happened?"

He breathed softly and easily into her ear: "I've found one, Mom."

"One what?" she asked.

"One of us."

Then he told her he had found a boy who saw things on a white wall that Christian could never have imagined. Christian had borrowed a stranger's phone at a party, just so he could call his mom and tell her, and his voice was bubbly. His mother's heart was beating so hard then, it was a wonder the buttons on her pajamas didn't burst off.

Christian shouted happily at the other end of the line: "I've never seen anyone paint like this, Mom. You'll see, you're going to love it!"

Then he quoted Ragnar Sandberg, whose words his mom had quoted to him throughout his childhood: "He paints like the birds sing."

His mom nodded with wet cheeks, of course she could hear that her son was high on something, so she just said: "I love you."

Her son laughed, her only boy, wild and precious. Just before he ended the call, he said: "I love you, Mom. You're the best."

When the phone rang the next night, his mother was sleeping so soundly that she didn't answer until the second ring. That time it was the police.

———

The fourteen-year-old artist sat with his back against the wall behind the gymnasium and waited the whole next day. When it got dark his friends came and got him, then he sat silently on the floor in Ted's basement drawing all night. His friends sat around him as if their bodies were shielding a flame from the wind. The next morning they found out what had happened.

"He had a heart attack," Joar explained, crushed.

They were sitting in a window in the hallway in school, close to the stairs they had covered with soap what felt like a thousand years ago.

"What do you mean?" the artist whispered.

"I heard two teachers talking about it. They said he was a . . . junkie. He was at a party, dancing, and his heart just stopped beating . . . ," Joar tried to say as gently as he could.

"WHAT DO YOU MEAN?" the artist yelled.

He didn't actually want to be given an explanation of how Christian had died. He wanted an explanation of how he could be dead. Because that was impossible. No one can be so alive, and then not.

"Wait . . . ," Ali pleaded, but it was too late.

The artist had already started running, down the stairs, across the schoolyard, and around the corner behind the gymnasium. As if it might all be a lie, as if Christian had to be there? But instead the artist stopped abruptly in shock, because there were two old men in overalls standing there with ladders and cans of paint. They were painting the wall white.

As the artist looked around in desperation, he made eye contact with the Owl. The man was standing in the window of his classroom, the only place in the entire school with a good view of that wall. The Owl had reported it to the police as "graffiti" and "vandalism," he had personally called the two men in overalls, because rules were rules, and they had to apply to everyone. Perhaps he had once been a different sort of man, but now he was nothing but ashes.

All the things that the wall had been filled with over the course of a few wonderful days, angels and dragons and birds and skulls, were disappearing, little by little. Before the day was over it would all be white.

Christian's mother remembered screaming into the phone when the police called, but not how it sounded, her ears seemed deaf afterward. She hardly remembered the funeral, only the coffin, because all she could think was: How can Christian fit in there? He was far too big, her whole world.

She didn't see them when she came out of the church, but four fourteen-year-olds were standing behind some trees.

When the mother got home, her phone rang, just once. She answered immediately, but heard nothing but sobbing on the other end before the other person ended the call. The next morning there was a drawing placed on top of the grave, it showed Christian on a ladder, with a smile so big it was a miracle the paper could contain it. She had never seen anything like it. At the bottom, in pencil so faint it was almost illegible, it said: "Like the birds sing." She slept with that drawing on her bedside table, next to the phone, trying with all her strength to force it to ring once more. But it didn't, not for several months.

Joar and Ali and Ted went to the pier with the artist every day. They tried to get him to draw again, anything at all, but he couldn't do it anymore. At the end of the spring term he got an F in art. No one ever notices it when summer vacation begins, but there are torn-off wings lying all over schoolyards everywhere then. The artist didn't speak, barely ate, and his friends were all thinking the same thing: he's never going to survive this.

But they were lucky, they were wrong. The first day of the vacation Joar found a damn ad in a damn newspaper, about a damn art competition. That was how everything started, again.

TWENTY-EIGHT

The baby is clutching Louisa's finger tightly. It's the first time she's been hugged since Fish was around.

"Do you believe in God?" she asks quietly.

"Sometimes," Ted replies.

"Sometimes I do too," she says, with her nose against the back of the baby's neck.

The mother comes back from the bathroom, as grateful as only a parent who has been able to go to the bathroom undisturbed can be. She gently takes the sleeping child from Louisa's arms. Louisa looks like she's freezing when her body is alone again.

"What was the competition? The one Joar found in the newspaper?" she asks.

"It was for young artists, you were allowed to paint whatever you liked, and the first prize was having your painting hung in a museum," Ted replies.

"That's all?"

Ted smiles down at the box with the ashes.

"That's exactly what Ali said. She kept saying it sucked. She thought you should win money or a car or something, like on game shows on TV. But mostly she just nagged because she thought it was fun to annoy Joar. Deep down she knew that it didn't matter. We weren't trying to get him to win, we were just trying to get him to paint."

Louisa frowns.

"Still a pretty useless prize."

Ted shakes his head slowly.

"No. It was a fantastic prize. Because we thought that if he could just see his painting there, on a big white wall beside other artists' paintings, just once . . . then he'd realize he belonged there."

Louisa says nothing for so long that he almost starts to worry, before she concedes sullenly:

"Okay, then. Not completely useless, maybe."

Ted looks out through the train window and sees a whole life. It's strange what our memories do to us, editing our feelings.

"All summer, I tried to get him to laugh . . . ," Ted remembers.

"Did you tell him the one about the penguins?" Louisa groans.

"No," Ted says, but he can't help smiling.

Because he remembers now that this was how they dragged the artist back to life after Christian's funeral: one giggle at a time. He tells Louisa how one day at the start of summer vacation, the artist whispered that he could try to paint the sea, even if he would only be doing it to make Joar happy. But it wasn't until the end of June that he actually started.

That was after Ali had lain beside him on the pier, saying: "I know what you should paint. You should paint us!" Joar immediately pointed out that Ali was so self-centered that what she actually meant was "paint me," but Ali had just shrugged nonchalantly and said: "You can be in it too, you're so short you won't really be seen anyway!" Joar chased her into the sea then, and she laughed so loudly that you could still hear it when she was underwater. And that was how the artist decided to paint them, not the way they looked, but how they made him feel. He decided to call the picture *The One of the Sea*, just to tease Ali, because she really did think it should be called *The One of Ali*.

On the last day of June, the artist went to Christian's grave, sat there alone for several hours, and drew the first pencil sketch of what would one day become a famous work of art. Then he went to the pier with his friends, took all the pills he had stolen from Ted's dad's bathroom cabinet out of his backpack and threw them one by one into the water. Then all his friends felt, just for a brief moment, that perhaps everything could be all right.

"I believed in God when I saw him paint," Ted says on the train.

He has so many memories of the artist, he realizes, but his brain almost always picks one where he's smiling like a child who's just found a coin. That last period in his big apartment, he would often lie on the sofa next to Ted, showing him photographs of all the places he had been in the years between art school and becoming famous. They showed him standing on boats and beaches and next to walls full of imagination, always with paint on his clothes, cans of spray paint in his hands and eternity in his eyes. He had danced and painted his way right around the world, and when he was lying there on the sofa he would smile at Ted and say that he didn't care what people said about him when he was gone, just as long as no one said he died young. Because he had lived for a thousand years.

"I've never prayed to God," Louisa suddenly says.

"Sorry?" Ted says.

Louisa is drawing in her sketch pad, her eyes hidden behind her hair again.

"I said, I've never prayed to God. But I prayed to the demons, like you did. But they still took Fish."

Her pencil dances between explosions on the paper as two tears land there.

"I'm sorry," Ted says.

"Sometimes I can't bear the fucking thought that she isn't here," she whispers.

Ted nods to the box containing the painting.

"He carried on painting those skulls, because then it felt like Christian was still alive in his fingertips. Perhaps it's like that for you too. Art is what we leave of ourselves in other people."

Louisa draws tiny falling flakes.

"Did it snow much in winter where you grew up?" she asks.

"Yes."

"It hardly ever got cold enough where we were. But one winter, nature seemed to sort of short-circuit, you know? So one night there was an insane amount of snow. Fish and I snuck out that evening and had a snowball fight. I hated having such a big body then, because I was so easy to hit, but of course it didn't matter because Fish was so bad at throwing. Seriously, she couldn't have hit a box from inside it, a snake would be better at throwing snowballs than she was! Then she made a snowman and I mean . . . it was so ugly it gave you a migraine. I had to ask if she'd ever actually seen a snowman before. Had she even seen a *man*? She said it was a modern snowman and that I didn't understand art. I laughed so much my voice went hoarse. Then we made snow angels everywhere, all over town. Every time I think of that night, it feels like it lasted a whole winter. It was like we gathered up a hundred days of memories all at once. If I lay them all out, I think I've got enough to make a happy childhood . . ."

The train disappears into a tunnel and the world stops. Ted cleans his glasses for a long time and puts some new tape on the frame. When the tunnel spits them out on the other side, he says:

"Maybe that's enough? Sometimes I think that my whole childhood lasted two years, between when I was thirteen and fifteen," he says.

"Would you swap those two years for a whole childhood? I mean, like, a *happy* childhood, only with different friends?" Louisa wonders.

"I wouldn't have swapped those idiots for a thousand childhoods."

Louisa nods, and draws a million snowflakes.

"Fish said she'd read in a book that in Heaven you could choose a moment in life when you felt really good, and then you got to feel like that for all eternity. She said it didn't matter if we lived to be eighty years old, because that's only a billion different nows, and one really good now is enough."

"And that night in the snow is your now?"

Louisa nods.

"What's yours?"

"Any day on the pier."

"Have many people you've loved died?" she asks, out of nowhere.

"Yes."

"I've been lucky, really," she says.

"How do you mean?"

"I haven't loved many people."

Ted glances at the mother and baby on the other side of the aisle. He thinks about what she said, about the days passing slowly but the years quickly.

"What I hate most isn't that people die. What I hate most is that they're dead. That I'm alive, without them."

"Maybe you should start smoking after all?" Louisa suggests helpfully.

"They would have liked you," he laughs.

"Who?"

"All my people."

In the seat beside them, a baby is sleeping in her mother's arms, the mother dozing in her baby's breath. Perhaps she was a different sort of person once upon a time, but now she's one of those who will always answer the phone on the first ring.

Louisa glances at them too, then she asks Ted:

"You said the janitor's mom was a teacher, didn't you?"

"Yes. She taught art history at the university. But I think she liked fiction better than history, to be honest. She talked much more about myths than facts."

Louisa raises her eyebrows.

"What do you mean, myths? Like, fairy tales?"

"Yes."

"So why don't you just say fairy tales, then?"

"Because they aren't quite the same thing."

Louisa frowns.

"Tell me a myth, then."

Ted sighs.

"Well . . . okay. Here's one: In ancient Greece there were two artists, Zeuxis and Parrhasius. They challenged each other to a contest to see who was best. Zeuxis painted a picture of some grapes, and it was so true to life that birds flew down from the sky to try to eat them. So he turned to Parrhasius, confident of victory, and said: 'Now do you admit I'm the greatest artist?' But Parrhasius just smiled and said: 'Pull aside this curtain, my painting is behind it!' So Zeuxis went over and took hold of the curtain, but he couldn't, because the curtain was the painting. So Zeuxis had to admit he'd been beaten, because he had only fooled the birds, but Parrhasius had fooled Zeuxis."

Ted falls silent. Louisa looks confused.

"Is that the whole myth?"

"Yes."

"So a myth is just a slightly rubbish story?"

"Well, no . . . ," Ted begins, because he wants to explain the moral of the story, but he doesn't have time to before Louisa says:

"People do that with cakes now. There are TV shows. You think it's a shoe, but it turns out to be a cake. You think it's a car, but it's a cake. You think it's—"

"Okay, okay, I get it," Ted sighs.

"I'm just saying, since you seemed pretty impressed when it was just *grapes*," she snorts.

"It must have been loads of fun having you as a student," he notes.

"Did you tell that myth to your students when you were a teacher? Has it ever occurred to you that that might be why you got stabbed?" she asks, not unkindly.

"When I got stabbed, I'd just been teaching them about how Julius Caesar died," Ted replies instantly.

Louisa grins, and he feels a little proud of her then, because she realized it was a joke. Then she asks:

"Do you really think you'll never go back to being a teacher?"

Then Ted thinks about the ceiling in the school, and how he had lain on the floor of the classroom looking up at it while everyone screamed. The boy who had stabbed him had run off, leaving Ted lying there, he could hear the sirens in the distance but hadn't realized they were for him. When the ambulance arrived, he had tried to stand up, because he didn't want to be any trouble. When he got to the hospital, he was laid on his side so the doctors could feel and squeeze every part of his body, and only then did he realize there was so much blood everywhere that they didn't even know how many times he'd been stabbed. When he woke up after the operation, he cried, first with shock, then with guilt. All the best people on the planet die all the time, die of nothing, but he doesn't even die when someone stabs him with a knife?

"No," he whispers, "I'll never go back to teaching."

"What are you going to do instead? Become a comedian?"

"I'm going to become a politician. And pass a law saying that annoying teenagers shouldn't be allowed on trains," he grunts.

"HELLO?" she exclaims.

"See? I'm funny," he yawns.

She rolls her eyes so hard that she almost falls off her seat. Then she asks:

"How do you know all that about the janitor's mother? That she was a teacher and liked myths and all that?"

Ted yawns again, almost as loudly as he sneezes.

"I met her, we all met her, at the end of that summer. It was actually because of her that I became a teacher. But that's a long story . . ."

"Oh no! And I'm so busy!" Louisa says, gesturing toward the silent train carriage.

Ted looks at the time.

"We should try to get some sleep. We have to change trains later."

He closes his eyes, which Louisa lets him do for about ten seconds.

"Okay. But don't lie," she says.

"About what?" Ted says, half asleep.

"You didn't become a teacher because of the janitor's mom. You became a teacher because of the Owl. Because you're one of those people who want to make the world better," she says, almost annoyed that he hasn't realized that himself.

"Thanks," he says quietly.

"Is that who we're going to see? Christian's mom? You said when we met that there was someone in the town where you grew up who can help us sell the painting? Is it her?"

"Yes. If she's home," Ted admits.

"You haven't called to say we're coming?"

"No."

Because he would never do that to her. Every time her phone rings, she still thinks someone has died.

"So what will you do if she isn't home, then? Or if she can't sell the painting?" Louisa asks.

"I don't know. But I'm sure you'll think of something."

"Me?" Louisa blurts out in horror.

"Yes. I believe in you," he yawns.

A new record for the kindest thing he's said.

The trains rocks on through the darkness, the world lies silent, but just as dreams are taking him, Ted mumbles to himself: "Good night, ghosts." Louisa wants to ask what that means, but he's already asleep, exhausted and huddled up in his seat. So she sits beside him for a long time, just drawing in the silence, waiting until his breathing becomes slow and calm, then she whispers:

"I'm sorry."

Ted sleeps deeply and soundly for the first time since the artist was around. He dreams his best memories, of being fourteen years old and lying in the sun on a pier by the sea, of smiles and fingertips seeking each other. He doesn't even notice when the train stops. When he wakes up, there's a drawing on the seat next to him and Louisa is gone.

TWENTY-NINE

Fish always said that kind people were the worst, because at least with mean people you know what you're dealing with. There's no limit to how dangerous someone who seems kind can be.

Louisa slips off the train and out onto the platform, it's easy to be invisible when you know you don't matter, her outline dissolves in the darkness like sugar in warm water. She turns around and sees Ted's sleeping face on the other side of the train window one last time. She raises her hand and waves, which might seem silly, but she feels she should make the most of the opportunity. She doesn't know when she'll have someone to wave to again.

She's left the painting on the train with him, she was never thinking of keeping it, she just knew he wouldn't accept it voluntarily. Now he has no choice. It isn't a perfect plan, Louisa doesn't have a perfect brain, she had actually been thinking of leaving him a few stations back. To be honest, she only really stayed because she wanted to hear the rest of the story about him and his friends. She would actually have liked to stay a few more stations, but doesn't dare, because right now, Joar is still alive. And she knows how stories about people like him end.

"Don't run. When you want to disappear, you walk, like you're just going to the bathroom!" Fish whispers in her head. Fish was the best at disappearing, she got chased by security guards and the police hundreds of times after various break-ins, but always slipped out of their grasp. "The trick is relaxing and making all your muscles soft, that makes you slippery, pretend you're a bar of soap!" Fish had explained, and when Louisa pointed out that bar soap isn't particularly soft, Fish had snapped: "Liquid soap, then! Stop spoiling my story!"

She liked stories, she would have enjoyed being on the train with them, and that's why Louisa knows she has to run away now. It felt too nice, sitting there next to Ted. Nothing that nice happens to someone like Louisa unless it's a trap.

She hurries away from the tracks without even knowing which station she's at, it doesn't matter, she has nothing to go back to. If she's going to disappear, she may as well disappear here.

Be soap! Fish is giggling in her head, and Louisa wants to yell at her that this isn't the right time to be making jokes. But instead she whispers, "I miss you, you moron," right into the darkness. Then she walks through the deserted ticket barrier and turns a corner very nonchalantly, skipping down some steps without noticing the echo, and doesn't see the two men until it's too late.

THIRTY

"There's nothing more dangerous than being noticed by men," Fish said, even though she herself was really bad at that. Because everyone noticed her, of course. Sometimes, when she was a bit drunk or high, she would lie in bed with the screwdriver in her hand and mumble to Louisa: "You can't trust them, have you ever seen the floor of a men's bathroom? And those creatures are actually allowed to make political decisions? And drive cars? Do we really want to put people who can't even piss straight in charge of all the horsepower in the world? We shouldn't even put them in charge of *one* horse!" But when she was sleepy and sad, she would whisper in the darkness: "You can't trust men, Louisa, they're far too easy to love."

Fish was always in love with someone, her crushes were like the drugs she took, happiness on credit. Her heart paid the debt, with interest. The world was too thorny for her, she kept getting scratched. She tried to seem cynical, always telling Louisa not to trust anyone, but deep down Fish's big problem was that she believed in happy endings. That was why she was so easy to hurt. She fell for men who were geniuses, but quite a few who weren't, and the kind ones were the worst. They picked her up in their cars and sometimes they gave her gifts. Louisa wished it had only been jewelry or watches, but often they gave Fish something far crueler: promises. They said they would leave their wives or girlfriends, that they would have a life with her, but of course that never happened. While Fish lay asleep beside her at night, it was incomprehensible to Louisa that all the wives in the world didn't get left for this person. That no one realized she was the best. Or almost, anyway. Okay, maybe not in the morning,

The only bad thing about Fish was that she was terrible in the morning, because she always woke up happy, and that's a complete misunderstanding of what a morning is. Louisa, who was a normal person, always woke up to find Fish bouncing on the bed as if it was going to be the best day ever. Then she just got sadder and sadder with each hour that passed, until in the evening she was like a wilted flower, you had to make the most of the light if you wanted to see her blossom.

On her eighteenth birthday, early that spring, the sun had shone all day and she had sat on the back of a wobbly old bicycle laughing wildly as Louisa rode her around town, chasing the light as if the shadows had teeth. When the sun was going down and Louisa saw her friend wilt, she did the most magical thing she could think of: she broke into a library. Because that was where all the fairy tales were.

Naturally, Louisa wasn't as good at breaking into places as Fish was, so in purely technical terms it wasn't actually a break-in, it was more like them getting shut in on purpose. Which is possibly, in purely technical terms, still a break-in. But it wasn't the break-in that was the present, it was the plan, when Fish realized how much time Louisa must have spent working out how it was all going to happen. "I didn't know I took up this much space in your brain," Fish had said. "You're everywhere in my brain all the time," Louisa had replied. "Is that where I left my gloves? I've been looking for them everywhere!" Fish had grinned. "Shhh!" Louisa had replied, because they had just heard the security guards.

The plan was as simple as it was stupid: they had hidden in one of the bathrooms when the library closed, in the last stall. But of course the guards had come in and noticed that one stall was locked, and the girls had sat huddled up together on the cramped toilet seat, holding their breath.

First the guard yelled and banged on the door of the locked stall so hard that Louisa wanted to crawl out of her skin. When there was no response, he went and got some tools, then stood outside for several minutes removing the screws, and when the lock clicked Louisa jumped so hard that she almost cried out. The guard threw the door open triumphantly with his fists clenched, and Fish held her hand over

Louisa's mouth, their hearts beating so hard that it was incomprehensible that the guards couldn't hear them.

"I told you! The lock must have clicked shut by itself!" the other guard had grumbled.

The first guard just stared in surprise at the empty stall.

"I could have sworn I heard . . . ," he mumbled.

"Come on, I want to get home, the game starts soon," the second guard said.

So they left. Not to brag, but the plan was so stupid it was genius. Louisa had figured out that if all the doors were unlocked, the guards would check all the stalls, but if just one door was locked, they wouldn't bother opening the others. Because what sort of idiot tries to hide behind an unlocked door?

"You're the best, Giant! Have I ever told you that?" Fish had grinned a couple of minutes later when they emerged from the bathroom and wandered out into the dark, empty library. She had lit a cigarette and Louisa had looked prouder than a cat that has just left a mouse in its owner's cereal bowl.

"I wanted to give you something no man has ever given you," she smiled, and then Fish had held her hand.

They wandered about in the sea of shelves between waves of books, and Louisa had never been in a quieter space. It was crazy, really, that Fish loved quiet places yet was friends with Louisa, who always needed noise. Who always *was* noise, actually. If Louisa wasn't talking she was humming, because she was scared of death and death is silent. But for a few moments even she embraced the silence.

Then they played games. They pretended they were in a zombie film where humanity had been destroyed, and then they switched to hide-and-seek, which was a ridiculously stupid idea because Fish was so good at it that Louisa started to panic. "I give up, just come out!" she hissed desperately into the darkness, only to be met with a "WHAT DID YOU SAY???" when Fish jumped out, frightening the life out of her. Louisa yelped in terror and Fish hissed, "SHHH!" Then they lay on the floor and Fish read out loud, because her favorite thing in the library was the fairy tales, but Louisa's favorite thing was Fish's voice.

"Don't worry, she's the main character, so she isn't going to die! The main character never dies in fairy tales!" Fish explained when she read one that she particularly liked.

She was wrong. Because in their fairy tale it was Fish who died.

When they got hungry during that night in the library, they drank Coca-Cola and ate muffins in the deserted cafeteria. Fish pointed out that, in purely technical terms, it wasn't theft: "We're in a library, aren't we? So it's a loan." They would probably have stayed there all night if Fish hadn't gotten curious and opened a door that said "Emergency Exit." Then the alarm went off. Louisa had been in the bathroom, and came rushing out with her pants around her ankles to point out that that hadn't been the smartest thing to do. Then Fish muttered: "I just wanted to see where it went!" When Louisa demonstratively pointed to the sign that said "Emergency Exit," Fish said: "Okay, but exit to WHAT?"

Considering that they were geniuses, they weren't always geniuses, those two, so it was lucky that they were good at running. At least they were once Louisa had pulled up her pants.

On the way home they held hands tightly, and when the first light of dawn burned in Fish's eyes, she said: "If I live until I'm eighty, it won't matter, because this is my now forever." That's what Louisa misses most, because every day may not have been the best day, but with Fish at least you knew that the day had a chance.

"You mustn't be frightened of death, Giant!" Fish had said when they had almost reached the foster home, and then she had pointed at the sky: "Look at the sun, do you get how crazy it is that it rises every morning? Do you get that, Giant? How crazy it is that we are here?" Then Fish had growled and howled and made faces at Louisa to show how insane it was that a human being could do all that, how impossible a body is. "Isn't it like, totally unbelievable that we even exist? So it won't be a tragedy when we don't exist anymore! It's just cool, really cool, that we happened at all."

Almost every night since she died Louisa has woken up screaming into the darkness: "I give up! Just come out!"

The curse is the same for everyone who has loved someone who died of an overdose: we think that if we could just have been with our human every moment of every day, then it would never have happened. It never stops being our fault.

Louisa and Fish had a life together, but at the end they also had two separate lives. Louisa tried to be like the girls at school, doing her makeup like them and dressing like them, but of course they just laughed. The clothes they wore didn't even come in Louisa's size. She envied their self-confidence most of all. They knew who they were, because they had families, they had inherited a belief that they belonged in every room they walked into. Louisa felt like a rat born in a laboratory. The girls came back from school vacation talking about trips and restaurants and visits to the sea. They could all swim, and they could roller-skate and eat with chopsticks. One of them asked Louisa if she liked "sashimi," and Louisa thought it was a cool new band, so she said: "Yes! I listen to them all the time!" Their laughter was like shotgun pellets.

Once she got invited to a birthday party, by mistake, of course, someone's mom had asked all the girls in the class without checking if they were all the same. But for a few hours it was still great, they drank Coca-Cola and watched films and gossiped about boys, Louisa didn't say a word but still felt almost normal. Then someone's wallet went missing and everyone looked at her. The wallet reappeared, it had fallen behind a bed, but by then Louisa had already seen what she was in their eyes: not one of them, not really. She stopped trying after that, loneliness was better than disappointment.

Fish tried to belong in other places. She stopped going to school, disappeared into dark alleyways and down into black holes instead, finding older friends in a fog of bottles and pills. Sometimes Louisa felt hurt that she wasn't allowed to go with her, but Fish joked: "Who's going to look after me tomorrow if we're both hungover?" When she got back to the foster home at night she would only get undressed if all the lights in the room were switched off. She slept in long-sleeved shirts. One time she said: "I don't want you to see the worst of me, Giant. I just want to be the best version of myself in your brain."

Fish hated reality too much to bear it, trying to save her was like catching smoke with a net. The girls shared a bed but still slipped away from each other. Soon after Fish's eighteenth birthday, the adults at the home found all the gold jewelry and watches in her backpack. Of course Fish refused to say where she'd gotten them, so the adults called the police. One of the necklaces had come from one of the kind men, but it actually belonged to the man's wife, and after he gave it to Fish he had reported it stolen to get the insurance money. The police had started an investigation. Fish wasn't allowed to stay in the foster home, the adults there didn't want to be responsible for her. So she got swallowed up by the town and the night. Louisa wanted to run away with her, but Fish forbade her, because Louisa was still only seventeen and the police would look for them. God, how Louisa hates herself for doing as she was told. The last thing Fish did was kiss her on the cheek and promise: "Don't worry. Everything's going to be fine. Our fairy tale has only just begun."

A few nights later a cleaner arrived at the library, just as the sun was rising. She found Fish curled up on the floor among the fairy tales. The policeman who called the foster home said the doctor had declared it an overdose, but said that Fish had drifted off peacefully in her sleep. Her body full of happiness on credit.

THIRTY-ONE

Louisa stops abruptly on the steps. She sees the two men by the car down in the street, can smell their cigarettes, she can't hear what they're saying but she can tell by the harshness of their laughter that it isn't anything good. A bad foster home teaches a child a lot of things, but most of all to identify danger. She tastes blood in her mouth before she realizes how hard she's biting her lip. She glances back up the steps but realizes there's no point trying to run back up there, any moment now the train will thunder away from the platform, she'd never get back in time. Down here there isn't anyone else in sight, the nearest houses are a long way away, the world shrinks until it consists of just her and the men. There is nothing more dangerous.

"Wait! Wait! Quiet . . . ," one of the men down in the street suddenly exclaims.

"What?" the other one grunts, Louisa can hear that he's drunk.

"I thought I heard something. No. It was probably nothing," the first one says.

The brain does a lot of stupid things when it's stressed. It won't cooperate at all. Suddenly it starts reminding Louisa of her trick in the library bathroom, snaking on the floor, through the gap beneath the side wall, into the next stall, and how disgusted Ted would have been if he'd found out about that. She has to put her hand over her mouth to stop herself from laughing out loud. Stupid, stupid brain. It's sheer luck that the shadows on the steps are kind, wrapping their long arms around her. She pads down the steps, two at a time, to the street, staying close to the wall and hurrying away from the car. She doesn't know if the men have seen her, but as soon as she's beyond the streetlamps, the night is a dark hole.

———

She can't see the train behind her anymore, doesn't hear it leave the platform, but she hopes that Ted won't hate her for leaving him and the painting. The worst thing about Ted isn't that he seems kind but might be mean, it's that he might be kind for real. She wishes he hadn't said what he did about believing in her. That's too much responsibility. All she can give him is disappointment.

Sunrise is still many hours away, beyond the lights of the train station the road is pitch-black and absolutely silent, she clutches the straps of her backpack tightly. She's eighteen years old and alone, not missing, just gone.

Then she hears a man yell. Then another one. And she runs.

THIRTY-TWO

Ted is dreaming a lovely dream, about a day without a name. Because a really good summer vacation should only really have two days: the first, and the last. All the ones in between should be nameless, it shouldn't matter if it's Tuesday or Sunday. In a good summer, everything is all just bicycles and comic books and salt water, time being wasted with the sun on your face. One or two small farts, one or two little giggles.

"Aren't you going to color it in?" Joar wondered early one morning on the pier, when he saw the artist's first sketches of what was going to become the painting.

"I don't have any paints," the artist confessed unhappily.

In the dream all the others are fourteen years old, but Ted is grown-up, perhaps because he already felt like that back then. He's the one who asked:

"What does paint cost?"

"Too much," the artist said.

"How fucking much can some paint cost?" Joar snorted, and started feeling the pockets of his shorts with an optimism that really was admirable, because there were kangaroos that had money in their pouches more often than he did.

So the artist took a deep breath and told them exactly what it cost, because there was a shop that sold art supplies in town and he had memorized every single price tag in the window. Then his three friends looked like they were having at least six heart attacks.

"For PAINT?" Ali shouted.

"Are all damn artists damn millionaires, or what?" Joar marveled.

"Forget it, just forget it," the artist whispered unhappily, and that's how close the painting came to not existing at all.

"And then you need one of those damn cloths too, right? The thing you paint on? How much does that cost?" Joar asked.

"You mean canvas?" Ali mocked.

"'You mean caaanvaaas?'" Joar mimicked sullenly.

"Why are you even asking how much it costs? You can't actually count, anyway," she grinned.

Joar held up his middle finger and told her to count that. Ali replied that she'd seen bigger matches than that cute little finger. Joar didn't actually know why he got so angry about that.

"Just forget it," the artist repeated quietly, but no one heard, because Ali threw a small stone at Joar.

It wasn't really that hard of a throw, but it hit him on the ear, and Joar had sensitive ears. So he chased her into the water. When they were lying beside each other on the pier again ten minutes later, exhausted and soaking wet, Ali suggested:

"Maybe we could try getting a job?"

"What sort of job? Robbing wishing wells?" Joar suggested.

It was, astonishingly enough, Ted who had an idea at that point. And it was, astonishingly enough, not a bad idea at all.

In the dream they are suddenly just there, in the big parking lot outside the supermarket. But in real life they must have walked all the way. Or cycled? In that case, was it Joar who stole the bikes? Ted's memory lets him down, but dreams don't care. In real life they were all full of fears and sorrows, and soon there would be another funeral, but that summer they are still happy.

"There! Ask that old lady!" Joar said, pushing Ali forward.

"Okay, okay!" Ali snapped, then she told Ted and the artist to hide, but instructed Joar: "You just stay exactly where you are!"

Joar did as he was told, which was a minor miracle even in a dream. The supermarket kept all its carts chained together like an iron centipede, and to free a cart you had to insert a coin, which was where Ted had gotten his idea from. Ali walked up to the old woman, smiled her most childish smile, and said:

"Excuse me, I only have bills on me, could you possibly lend me a coin for a cart?"

The woman looked skeptical, so Ali quickly nodded toward Joar and said:

"Our mom sent me and my little brother to do the shopping. But she forgot to give us a coin. She has trouble remembering things since the accident . . ."

Credit where credit's due, Ali was a great actor, both in the dream and in real life, with real tears in her eyes and everything. The woman gave her a coin and when Ali came back Joar just stared at it as if it were unicorn poop

"What the hell is this? Free money? Why didn't you think of this before, Ted?"

He patted Ted gently on the back and Ted swung in confusion between compliment and accusation. Then Ali said eagerly:

"There! Go ask her!"

So Joar went up to the next woman, and it went well. A little too well, actually. The woman thought Joar was so cute that she pinched his cheek and offered to go with him into the store and do his shopping for him, but Joar got the distinct impression that she really wanted to take him home and lock him in her cellar. Then there was an old man, so Ali approached him, and if the man's wife hadn't appeared she would probably have gotten his whole wallet. As it was, the old man got yelled at instead. Ted had roughly the same lack of success with both old men and women. The artist only asked one man, who was on his own in a car, and the man had smiled and started to look in the glove box. He said he had cash at home, and asked if the artist wanted to go with him. He reached out his hand through the car window and stroked the artist's cheek, and the boy froze to ice. Ali was standing sixty feet away but she could recognize that sort of man a mile off, so she yelled: "WATCH OUT!"

It doesn't matter where you are, those are magic words, they stop time for a moment. Every single person in the parking lot stopped and looked around, and the man let go of the artist in horror, and the artist took his chance and ran.

The teenagers took a break after that. A security guard came out into the parking lot looking suspicious, so they decided that the least suspicious thing they could do was to go into the supermarket. It was Ted who pointed out that they ought to take a cart, seeing as all the old ladies they had asked for coins would see them in there.

"Sometimes you're damn smart," Ali smiled.

It was a miracle that Ted didn't hit his head on the top of the door, given how tall he walked after that.

Joar sat in the cart, the artist steered it, Ali pointed at things on the shelves and Ted ran and got them. They spent some of the coins so the guard wouldn't think anything was wrong, put a small packet of cookies and some cans of soda in the cart, but even more in their backpacks. They turned a corner and the artist asked tentatively if they could buy some pastries, and it was the first time in months they had heard him say he was hungry. Ted would love Danish pastries for the rest of his life.

Joar stopped at one shelf to smell all the different deodorants he liked, then they passed an entirely different shelf and he suddenly asked:

"Hey, Ali, how do these work?"

Ali stared at the small packs of tampons he was pointing at.

"Are you kidding? How do they *work*?"

Joar blushed, but his curiosity overcame his embarrassment and he grunted:

"Yes! Is that a really stupid damn question or something? I mean . . . do you just shove them in . . . I mean, all the way up?"

For a moment Ali probably felt something like sympathy for his almost admirable stupidity, so she said, not entirely patronizingly:

"How else do you think they would work? That you would swallow them and wait for them to make their way down?"

Joar muttered:

"But . . . don't they fall out? Like, when you walk? I was thinking maybe they have little hooks or something?"

Ali blinked so slowly that her eyelashes looked like they were about to brush her socks.

"What sort of . . . hooks? Are you completely stupid? What the hell would the hooks even be attached to? Why would the tampon fall OUT?"

By now Ted and the artist had caught up with her, obviously they hadn't heard any of the conversation, but Joar didn't think that a complete lack of context ought to stop anyone from having a firmly held opinion, so he said:

"Ted! How do you think tampons stay in?"

Ted looked so uncomfortable that he almost melted and ran down a drain by sheer effort of will. Then he mumbled:

"They . . . squeeze, maybe?"

Ali looked so disappointed that Ted ducked instinctively.

"You think girls go round squeezing the WHOLE TIME while we're having a period? Is this your first day on Earth or something? Your balls must be bigger than your brains!" she snapped.

All three boys looked very confused by this, the way you do when you're not entirely sure if you've been insulted or not. She muttered that she hoped none of them would ever have children, because they would be the stupidest children in the history of the world. Joar peered at her as if he was trying to work out if she was joking. Then he said, in the tone of a very patient teacher:

"Are you stupid or what? Boys can't have children."

Ted nodded helpfully:

"Only girls can have children. I think that's why you have periods."

Ali sighed so deeply that the shelves swayed.

"I-diii-ots."

Then she threw a pack of tampons fairly hard at Joar's head, and he got angry and threw a deodorant at her. Then they had a fight.

"Typical of a girl to be so sensitive," Joar said when they eventually made their way to the checkout.

Ted looked like he was about to say "Yeah, really," but the artist took hold of his arm warily and shook his head. So Ted didn't say anything and Ali let him live.

When they reached the checkout, the security guard was standing by the door looking suspiciously at their backpacks. The cashier, on the other hand, glanced cheerfully into their cart.

"Oh, I wish I could eat Danish pastries for breakfast! How do you stay so slim?" she chirruped.

In the meantime, the guard was talking to one of the women who had given the teenagers a coin, she was pointing angrily in their direction, and the teenagers didn't even wait for the guard to yell.

"How do we stay so slim? We run a lot!" Joar said simply.

And then they ran, with the cart and everything, out into the parking lot. To confuse the guard, Joar rushed off in one direction and Ali in another. When the guard had almost caught up with her she yelled, "WATCH OUT!" which gained her a second, and she darted sideways, and when the guard tried to grab hold of her he lost his footing and fell. By the time he got back on his feet she had already caught up with the other teenagers on the far side of the parking lot, with the artist pushing the cart and Joar clinging to the front like a pirate captain. He threw a Danish pastry at the guard like a Frisbee and yelled: "You look very pale! You should eat something!"

They ran straight across a busy road, almost getting run over by a truck, and they didn't see the hill until they were already on their way down it. Ali and Ted tried to slow the cart by jumping up onto it, which might not have come very high on the list of the smartest things they could have done, and soon the cart was moving so fast that the only thing the artist could do was either let go or go with them. That was how four idiots ended up riding a shopping cart down the steepest hill in town.

Ted dreams of the blind terror, metal rattling beneath their backsides, cars blowing their horns, the wind roaring in one ear and Ali shrieking with joy in the other. At the bottom of the hill the cart tipped over and the pavement scraped their elbows and cheeks, but it didn't matter, they just lay there in a happy heap, giggling, until Joar swore:

"Goddamn it. Now I've got dirt in my pastry."

When autumn came that year, the supermarket would replace its shopping carts with a type that didn't take coins, just a sort of token you had to get from the checkout. A few years later, adults hardly ever carried cash at all. Yet more evidence that society hates teenagers, if you were to ask the teenagers.

They took the cart with them to the pier, all joining in to push it, then all jumping into it as it flew over the end straight into the sea. Perhaps that is Ted's moment, he dreams, his "now" that Louisa was talking about. When they were in midair. He has probably never felt better than he did then.

The shopping cart hit the water so hard and sank so quickly that everything went black for all four of them. There is a certain point down there in the darkness when panic sets in, the water stops being transparent and suddenly you just feel the whole weight of it. You try to turn upward but are just forced down, your pulse is pounding in your ears, your eyes hurt like they are bursting. When you finally manage to get your bearings and feel that you're floating up, you think you're never going to reach the light. When you break the surface that first breath is nothing but pain. It took several seconds before Ali managed to gasp: "Here!"

"Here!" Ted panted.

"Here!" the artist called.

Then: nothing. Just silence.

"HERE!" Ali yelled again.

"Here! Here!" Ted and the artist replied.

Silence.

"Here!"

"Here!"

"Here!"

"HELP!"

The other three had already started climbing up onto the pier when they saw Joar out in the water.

"HELP!" he screamed once more.

His nose was barely above the surface, he was taking two strokes forward and one back, as if something was pulling him down. The first time he disappeared below the surface, his friends laughed as if he were joking, but the second time they immediately jumped in after him.

Ted will never understand how they managed to get hold of Joar, but it wasn't until they started to pull him through the water that they realized what had happened: his foot was caught in the chain of the cart, where you insert the coin, it was wound around his ankle, and in the water the cart weighed as much as an elephant. The more Joar had panicked and tried to free himself, the more trapped he had become. They only managed to drag him halfway to the steps up to the pier, with the cart lurking beneath the surface like some lethal sea monster.

"GET IT OFF ME!" Joar yelled desperately.

Ali was splashing alongside, and looked thoughtfully first at the chain, then at Joar, before asking: "How did you even get your foot caught in there? Just how small are your feet?"

Ted was sitting on the steps holding on to Joar, and he gasped: "You got your foot in but can't get it out? You're like a tampon!"

Joar just grabbed him by his shirt and tried to strangle him.

"GET IT OFF ME!"

Ali was paddling alongside him with all the sympathy she could muster as she looked at him, then called out very, very seriously: "Sure. Have you got a coin?"

That laugh? A tsunami.

They eventually managed to free their friend. Joar was so relieved that he wasn't even angry. That day? Perfect. No one needs more moments than that. They lay on the pier drying out in the sun, and as they walked home that evening with pastry crumbs around their mouths and laughter in their stomachs, everything was still possible, everyone was still alive.

"Tomorrow!" they called to each other as they went their separate ways at the crossroads.

What Ted remembers most of all is the sound when he got home and opened the front door. A small creak, a withheld sob. At first he didn't understand what it was, then he peered into the gloom of the living room and saw the outline of his big brother, sitting on the stool by the old piano. Ted couldn't remember anyone in the family sitting there in several years. His big brother wasn't playing anything, he was just staring down at the keys, and there were empty beer cans on top of the piano. He didn't say anything, he didn't need to. Ted understood at once that their father was dead.

THIRTY-THREE

"Are you okay?"

Ted wakes up but can't see anything, he blinks against the lights in the ceiling of the train, his cheeks cold. The most frightening thing about his dad dying that summer when he was fourteen wasn't the grief he had felt, but the anger. He's thought so many times as an adult that it's a lie that people are scared of being alone, because what we fear is being abandoned. You can choose to be alone, but no one chooses to be left. Sometimes he imagines that mankind invented God just to have someone to be angry with, because you can't be angry with a dad who's dead, not even a little bit. Ted was most angry with God because he didn't get more memories. All he could remember of his dad's voice was: "Good night, ghosts." A man walking quietly around the house at night, while Ted was still very young, turning out all the lights and sending a whispered smile into each room: "Good night, good night, good night." That stopped when he got ill. Ted doesn't have any images of his dad as a person after that, when the man was alive, all he can remember is someone lying in bed, dying. The cancer went on for Ted's whole childhood. Yet the most remarkable thing about losing a parent is that you don't even need to miss them for their loss to be felt. The basic function of a parent is just to exist. You have to be there, like ballast in a boat, because otherwise your child capsizes.

"Are you okay?" the voice asks again, gently.

It's the conductor, leaning over the seat. Embarrassed, Ted wipes his eyes and face with his palms, hiding behind them for a moment too long, as if he's playing peekaboo.

"Yes . . . yes . . . excuse me, excuse me."

The conductor smiles awkwardly.

"I'm the one who should be apologizing. I promised her I'd let you sleep, but . . . it sounded like you were crying."

"It's my allergies," Ted lies behind his hands.

"Oh," the conductor says. "Would you like me to see if anyone on the train has any medication?"

"No! No! Please, it's fine, really," Ted pleads.

The conductor smiles again, and touches Ted's shoulder fleetingly, and Ted doesn't hate it. That's quite a big thing.

"Let me know if there's anything I can do. The train's having mechanical trouble again so we're going to be here for a while," he says.

Ted nods silently and thinks that the conductor has beautiful hands, beneath the old tattoos and the first wrinkles of middle age, small maps of a life. The baby sneezes on the other side of the aisle, then it laughs, astonished at its own bodily functions. The conductor turns and laughs too. Only then does Ted look around and realize that Louisa is not there. There's a drawing on her seat, it's of the artist, but as a young man, not yet sick. It's astonishing that she has been able to imagine him like that. In the bottom corner she has drawn some skulls and written: *For Ted. I hope the birds sing for you.* The paper rustles as his fingers start to shake, he stands up but finds just an empty luggage rack. The box containing the painting, the box of ashes, and Ted's suitcase are still on the floor, but Louisa's backpack is gone.

"Where . . . where's . . . ?" he begins, still confused and half asleep, before he blurts out to the conductor: "Wait! What did you mean when you said you promised her you'd *let me sleep*?"

The conductor glances over his shoulder brightly.

"Your friend? She was getting off at this station. I asked if she was going to say good-bye to you, but she said it was better if you got some sleep."

"What are you talking about? Getting off? Getting off the train? Why would she get off the *train*?" Ted splutters, with sudden panic in his chest, like beer cans on a piano.

The conductor looks a bit like Ted has asked him how gravity works.

"Well . . . you have to get off the train to . . . get off the train. How do you mean?"

"Why would she get off HERE?"

The conductor really does his best to understand the question.

"I don't know. I did actually ask, because it isn't a very safe area at this time of night, but she said she needed to get going. Sorry, is something wrong?"

Ted glances out the window, but the platform is silent and dark, holding on to all its secrets.

"How long is it since she left?"

"Ten minutes, maybe."

"Ten MINUTES?"

"Yes, we should have moved on, but like I said, we're having mechanical issues again," the conductor says apologetically, as if this was primarily a question about the timetable. Then he calls out: "Wait! Where are you going? We're going to be leaving soon!"

But Ted has already run off the train, out onto the platform, into the darkness. The only thing he's holding is her drawing. He calls out her name: the first time as an order, the second time as a negotiation, the third time as a prayer. The way a parent would scream at the sea.

He gets nothing back, the darkness is a wall. All he can hear deep inside his head is the artist's laughter:

"It's a miracle that you manage to close the bathroom door when you pee, Ted, you're so bad at being alone! It's like you're an introvert, but terrible at it."

During their last year in that big apartment, the artist was often amused that Ted would sit in a corner reading, without saying a word, but if the artist went into another room he would always turn around after a while and find Ted sitting there reading instead. He didn't necessarily want to be with his people, just near them. At exactly the same times every day he would look at his beautiful gold watch, close his book, and say: "Time for your pills!" The artist, always busy with something more interesting, like building houses out of playing cards or eating cheese, used to groan: "I should have given you anything else for you birthday other than that damn watch . . ."

Even so, that watch was the only thing he wouldn't let Ted sell when they were getting the money together for the painting. He had engraved all their initials on the back: Joar's, Ali's, Ted's, and his own. So that they would always be with him.

"LOUISA!" Ted yells as he runs across the deserted platform and through the turnstile. No response. He slips down the steps to the road in the darkness and almost runs into a stranger.

"Okay there, everything all right?" the man says amiably.

He's young, with a lilting dialect, and Ted is reminded how far from home he is.

"Excuse me, I . . . I'm looking for my friend. A young woman, eighteen years old, very tall . . . talks all the time! Have you seen her?" he explains, carefully picking up the drawing which he had dropped on the ground.

The young man shakes his head apologetically.

"Sorry."

"Thanks anyway," Ted nods quickly, looks at his watch, as if he's trying to work out how far she might have gotten. The man calls after him:

"Do you want help looking?"

"Oh . . . that's too much to ask, I . . . ," Ted mumbles, because he suddenly realizes that he doesn't even know where to start.

"It's no trouble! Come with me, my friend's parked over here."

He takes Ted gently by the elbow and leads him toward a car. A man is standing next to it, smoking. Ted will never really be able to explain why, but he instinctively folds Louisa's drawing and puts it in his pocket.

"He's looking for a girl, we can help him, can't we?" the young man calls.

"Sure, sure," the other man by the car nods, and stamps out his cigarette beneath his shoe.

Ted tries to slow down, but the young man has his hand on the small of his back now, guiding him toward the open car door.

"It's okay, really, I don't need any help! I'm sure she's gone back to the train . . . ," Ted attempts.

The other man has already grabbed hold of Ted's arms. When Ted resists, the first blow lands, and he lets out a shriek of anger. The second time as a negotiation. The third time as a prayer.

They don't manage to get him into the car, but they do take his watch. They search his pockets for his wallet, but it's still in his suitcase on the train. Perhaps he screams again, perhaps that's why they get so angry that they kick him in the head, he thinks. Even then, his brain tries to figure out how this might be his fault. Then everything goes black. The last thing he hears is a ringing in his ears, like the sound of telephones, and Ted realizes that tomorrow they will be ringing for him.

THIRTY-FOUR

What was it Louisa said on the train? That sometimes you don't want to hear the end of a story because when you find out who survives, you know that all the other characters in it might die?

Throughout his life, Ted has been frightened of men. When he was young, his big brother, six years older, used to beat him up like it was a game. Even the fact that Ted used to curl up rather than fighting back would provoke him. "Fight back, you coward! FIGHT BACK!" his big brother would roar. When Ted still wouldn't, he would hit him even harder. Once he threw Ted down the basement stairs so that he hit his head and lost consciousness. At the hospital their mother had to lie and say he had slipped, the doctor had looked suspiciously at the bruised younger brother, but Ted had lied so well that even he began to think it was true. From then on he took his socks off every time he went up and down the basement stairs, so he wouldn't slip again.

Some children are born lucky, they're the children who ask things like: "What's the most dangerous animal in the world?" But Ted never did, he was a child who always knew the answer. Once when he was eight or nine, their mom had been at the hospital with their dad, so Ted's brother had stolen their dad's beer and sat in the kitchen drinking with some boys from school. When they got drunk, they shouted for Ted and forced him to come into the kitchen. At first they just pointed to things and asked him to say what they were called, so they could laugh and make fun of his accent. His big brother, who had the same accent, didn't encourage them, but he didn't stop them either. Ted had tried to escape to his room, but the drunkest guy in the kitchen, known as "the Ox" for all the obvious reasons, stopped him from leaving.

"Do you like girls?" the Ox asked with a grin, and Ted was smart enough to nod. "Really? You like pussy? Or are you a little fag?" the Ox snarled, his grin gone now.

"Shut up! My brother isn't a fucking fag!" Ted's big brother slurred from the other side of the table. It sounded nice, as if he were defending Ted, but he was really only defending himself. Being what they were accusing Ted of was such a serious crime where they grew up that it would threaten the honor of the whole family.

"Maybe you're a fag too? The fag brothers?" the Ox grinned, standing up and stretching out his arms so that his body looked like if he got hit by a truck, it would mostly be the truck's problem.

But Ted's big brother replied stubbornly:

"You really do talk a hell of a lot about fags. Do you think about them when you're jerking off too?"

The violence was an explosion. The Ox flew over the table in an instant to grab hold of Ted's brother's face, but didn't have time, because by then something had flared up inside Ted's head. He grabbed a full can of beer from the table and threw it as hard as he could.

"DON'T TOUCH MY BROTHER!"

The can hit the Ox in the eyebrow, and the huge fifteen-year-old yelled so loudly that it must have been heard across the whole block. Ted was shaking with stifled sobs even before the blow was struck. He could have run, but there wouldn't have been any point, the Ox's fist was like a sledgehammer when it hit his little chest. Ted lay on the floor, unable to breathe, the Ox stood over him raining blows on his back, as if Ted were a lump of meat. People who have never been beaten up don't understand the recklessness demanded of the person doing the beating, what must be missing from someone like that, or what happens inside the person getting beaten.

Lucky children often ask what the most dangerous animal in the world is, but all other children already know. It isn't the lion or the hippopotamus or the snake or the spider or the shark. The most dangerous creature on the planet is, and has always been, a young man. And the worst thing about a young man? That until very recently he was just a boy. No one gets any warning when he stops being one.

Ted doesn't even remember how he got away from the Ox, or how he crawled to his room. He just lay there shaking beneath his bruises, as if he had a fever. Late that night, before their parents got home, his door opened and his big brother came in with grilled cheese sandwiches. Ted had eaten in silence and his big brother had asked anxiously: "You're not going to tell, are you? That I took the beer?" He wasn't at all worried that Ted would tell about the rest of it.

One day not long after that, Ted heard his mother talking to a friend. She had walked into his big brother's room without knocking and caught him looking at porn. She sighed into the phone to her friend and said: "Well, I suppose it's just natural? That's what boys his age are SUPPOSED to do, isn't it? Get into fights and look at porn, that's what men do. Otherwise I suppose I'd worry that he was . . . you know . . ."

Ted has been frightened all his life.

He hears the kicks to his body now, on the pavement beside the car below the train station, but he no longer feels them. Perhaps his brain is protecting him by blocking the pain signals, like when the Ox beat him up in the kitchen, and when he got stabbed in the classroom many years later. Enough adrenaline becomes insulation, the world stops, like when you stop fighting against water and just let yourself drown.

But then he hears a cry, far beyond the ringing in his ears, at first he thinks it's his own, but it sounds different. His body slumps when the kicking stops, he falls onto his back, blinking at the only streetlamp, a short distance away. Then he hears the cry again, it's one of the men, like an animal caught in a trap. No, Ted suddenly realizes, it isn't even a cry of pain. It's a cry of shock, like an animal encountering a more dangerous animal.

Louisa may be alone when she comes rushing out of the darkness, but she's like Joar, she fights like an entire gang. She's holding a metal pipe in her hand, later she won't even remember where she found it, only that she snatched it up out of pure instinct.

In the fullness of time she will hate herself for this, and how natural this violence is to her. What must be missing inside her. Most people never find out what they're truly capable of, but she will never forget. She swings the metal pipe and hears it break the first man's arm, then hits the second man as hard as she can across his calves, knocking him screaming to the ground. All Ted hears after that is the clatter of the metal pipe hitting the ground, and Louisa shouting:

"RUN!"

So they run. Ted staggers and she drags him. Up the steps, through the turnstile, out onto the platform. They get there just in time to see the lights at the back of the train as it thunders away along the tracks and disappears into the night.

THIRTY-FIVE

You don't realize how loud a heart is until you've run the whole length of a train platform and you're left standing in the cloud of silence that the train spews out as it abandons you.

"WAIT!" Ted bellows desperately at the lights, but that's about as effective as throwing marshmallows at a whale and thinking it will change direction.

No one on board hears him, the train doesn't care, that's how everything goes to Hell. There goes a world-famous painting along with the ashes of the man who painted it.

Ted does a pirouette of anger.

"Why did you get off the train?" he snaps, with his lip split and blood dripping from his nose.

"Why did YOU get off the train?" Louisa retorts instantly, and when she clutches the straps of her backpack he sees how bruised her knuckles are.

"I was worried about you," he confesses.

"Yeah, wow, I'M really the one you should have been worried about," she snorts with a wild gesture toward his face.

Ted's chest is thudding with exhaustion, it takes an awful lot of energy to shout at someone else when it's yourself you're angry with.

"Why . . . why did you get off the train?" he repeats.

She jumps up and down with anger at that.

"Because I . . . I can't take responsibility for such a valuable painting! Why can't you understand that? Why couldn't YOU just keep it?"

Ted sighs, spraying more blood from his nose. His entire body hurts when he talks:

"Because he gave it to you!"

"Why the hell are you so STUBBORN?" she demands to know.

"I'M stubborn? You were the one who . . . ," Ted yells, but falls silent when he sees her whole face crumple.

"Things like this . . . they just don't happen to people like me, don't you get that?" she sobs angrily. "This is too good to be true, and that's always dangerous. I'm just . . . I'm just trying to survive in this goddamn world . . ."

Then Ted jumps up and down with anger as well, which hurts tremendously, even though he doesn't jump very high at all.

"I'm just trying to survive too!" he shouts, before quietly adding: "Ow . . ."

Her cheeks are wet.

"You don't get it."

His are too.

"What is it I don't get?"

"THAT YOU CAN'T TRUST MEN!" she yells.

"DO YOU THINK I DON'T KNOW THAT?" he yells back.

They stare at each other with furious desperation. Then Louisa looks down the tracks and blinks, full of regret.

"I didn't mean for you to lose the painting," she whispers.

"I know," he whispers back.

So the pair of them, two broken dolls, stand on the platform, faces streaked with tears. And sure, it might not have been a totally genius idea, Louisa can admit that. But everything had actually been going very well until she *didn't* hear the train leave the station. She had gotten off the train, run out through the turnstile and down the steps, snuck past the men by the car and off along the road into the darkness. But there she had stopped, just for a few minutes, to listen for the train to disappear. It was stupid, but being stupid is human, and today she was extra human. So she stopped to listen, because she needed to lose hope. She needed to hear the train leave the station so she knew it was too late to change her mind and run back. Because she has never abandoned anyone, so she doesn't know if she can. But being abandoned? She's world-class at that.

But she didn't hear the sound of the train. Instead she heard Ted yelling her name, then she heard him call for help, and now they're standing at the end of the platform and the distance between them and the painting is growing at over one hundred miles an hour. So no, it wasn't a perfect damn plan, it really wasn't.

"If I'd known that you can't be left alone for five minutes without getting beaten to death, I'd have locked you in the bathroom before I left," Louisa mutters.

"Ten," Ted replies sullenly.

"What?"

"You were gone ten minutes," he insists.

She lets out a laugh at that, reluctantly, as quietly as a creaking door. Then she holds something out to him.

"Here."

It's Ted's glasses. In the middle of the insanity and violent tumult down on the road she had seen something glinting on the ground, dropped the iron pipe, and picked them up.

"Thanks," Ted manages to say.

"Oh, don't mention it, they're probably scratched and broken now, I . . . ," she begins, but he's shaking his head.

"No, I mean . . . thanks for coming back. I . . . I thought I was going to die."

She looks down at the platform and hides her feeling behind an insult, as usual.

"Oh. Well. Those glasses suit you. You see less of your face when you're wearing them."

He starts to adjust the tape holding them together and replies:

"It suits you, that laugh. I'm glad they didn't manage to take it from you."

"Who?"

"All the people who have tried."

She looks him in the eye, only very briefly, perhaps she's thinking of saying something smart, or perhaps something honest. But instead they hear voices from the other end of the platform, and suddenly the faces of the two young men appear over by the steps. One man's arm is dangling uselessly by his side, broken, but in the other he is clutching the iron pipe. His eyes hardly belong to a human being anymore, he and his friend are no longer muggers, they're hunters.

"Run!" Louisa snaps.

"Where?" Ted gasps.

"THERE!" she calls, and jumps down onto the tracks.

Before Ted even has time to think about it, he's limping down after her.

THIRTY-SIX

Ted has read so many books with explanations of what fear does to the human body, but always gets annoyed by the most basic supposition: that fear is described as something abnormal. As if we shouldn't be afraid all the time.

When you get chased, your brain immediately channels power to what matters most, like a backup generator in a power outage, so the parts that govern logical thought and strategic planning shut down. A million thoughts get filtered down into a single one: survival. When Ted gets nervous, he loses all sensation in his nose, that's why he puts his glasses on and takes them off so often, why he pretends to polish them, because fear changes our blood flow and the heart supplies the biggest muscles first. When someone is being chased, their hands go cold and their digestive system shuts down to save energy. It might sound remarkable, that the body is biologically prepared for something as unlikely as being chased, but of course the opposite is true. This is exactly what we're built for. Throughout our entire existence we have been on the run, first from wild animals, then from each other.

"RUN!" Louisa yells as Ted limps across the train tracks.

She jumps over a small fence on the other side as if it were nothing. Ted, on the other hand, struggles to get over it and tears a hole in his pants on the barbed wire, lands with a *thud* on the ground next to her just as another train appears. For a few blessed moments it forms a wall between them and the men on the platform, but as it roars past just a few yards from them and the ground shakes, Ted curls up as if he's about to get kicked again. Eventually a body can't handle any more fear, any more flight, and he closes his eyes and just wants to sleep now. Louisa doesn't let him.

"COME ON!" she demands, tugging at his dirty suit jacket. "They're going to get their car and drive round the station and chase us on the other side, we need to hide!"

They slide down a grass bank toward a small square and a deserted parking lot. Louisa looks desperately for somewhere to hide, heads over to a thick clump of bushes, and shoves Ted straight into it. Soon they see the headlights of a car slowly coming closer. Somewhere in the distance a dog barks.

Ted can't remember a time in his life when he wasn't thinking about death. The brain is so strange. As he huddles in the bushes, with the smell of the earth in his nostrils and the sound of barking dogs in his ears, he remembers his dad's funeral twenty-five years ago. The minister in the church had kept it brief, some might even have called it "unsentimental," but it was probably actually the opposite. It would only have taken the slightest note on the organ, one sob, the smallest change in the air, for every person in the pews to have broken into a billion pieces that day. The fact that the minister said so little was an act of mercy, his audience couldn't bear to feel any more than they already did. Grief is a luxury for those living an easier life.

It had been early July, during the night a storm had passed over the town and the rain remained as a cold curtain, after the funeral the adults hurried to their cars, hunched up. The only person who remained in the church was Ted, no one noticed he was missing because no one noticed he was around. He was like a piece of lint on clothing, Joar used to joke, you could go a whole day and suddenly you would catch sight of him and think: Oh! How long has *that* been there?

Ted's mom hadn't said a word after she got home from the hospital the night his dad died. Ted's big brother had sat in front of the empty beer cans on the piano every morning, but never played anything. The only thing he had said to Ted before the funeral was: "We mustn't cry. We have to be strong, for Mom's sake." Ted had promised. He and his brother had sat there in the front pew and been what they thought men should be, strong and silent.

Afterward, when Ted was sitting there on his own and the tall roof of the church left him in an echo with no content, he could only hear silence upon silence. He remembers thinking that if he stayed in there, his dad wasn't dead, not really, as long as he didn't go out into the rain and reality. He tried to remember his dad's voice, or his laugh, but there was nothing but emptiness inside him where those sounds should have been. He had realized then why his big brother and his mom were so angry all the time, why they hated Ted so intensely, because Ted was only fourteen years old. He could only remember the dad who had been sick. He hadn't lost the happy dad, the one who existed before, the dad who had played the piano. That must have been much worse, Ted thought.

"Good night, ghosts," he had whispered into the emptiness.

Only then did he cry.

He didn't hear the church door open. Exactly when they came in or how long they had been there before he noticed them, he had no idea, but suddenly they were all around him: Joar, Ali, and the artist. Like lint on clothing. They had no words, so they let him cry, only not alone.

"Shhh!" Louisa whispers in the bushes.

Ted realizes, to his shame, that he has been sobbing out loud. His brain is so stupid, it can no longer tell the difference between threat and reality, he's just frightened of everything all the time. The young men's car comes slowly along the road, they're staring at the fence by the train tracks where Ted tore his pants when he climbed over. One of the men leans out the window and peers toward the bushes where they're hiding, but he's unlucky, because at that moment a taxi comes along from the other direction. It stops right in front of Ted and Louisa. The men in the car are blinded by the taxi's headlights and swear loudly.

The taxi driver, an old man with the body of an oversize duvet squeezed into a too-small bag, gets out like an elk getting out of a ditch. Then he stands next to the bushes, legs apart, right in front of Louisa and Ted, and starts to undo his belt.

Louisa whispers:

"No . . . no, no, no, tell me he isn't going to pee . . ."

He most definitely is. Louisa shuffles backward, deeper into the bushes, dragging Ted with her. But just as the taxi driver has undone his pants, one of the young men in the car calls out:

"Hey, you, old man! Have you seen an old guy and a girl?"

The taxi driver turns around in surprise.

"Here? Not a person here, no! Why else I'm having a piss here, you think?"

The men appear to consider this for a few moments. They certainly don't give the impression of being particularly quick-witted, but eventually one of them can be heard swearing again. Then the engine revs and the car skids away and disappears.

The taxi driver fiddles with his belt for a good while before he finally looks over his shoulder and mumbles:

"Safe now. Safe for you two to come out now, I think."

When Ted and Louisa don't emerge at once, the taxi driver leans closer to the bushes and says:

"My friends, I have many, many children. I am very, very good at hide-and-seek."

So Louisa gives up and cautiously sticks her head out, but she's clutching a stick in her hand.

"Back off!" she demands.

The taxi driver obeys with his hands raised.

"Backing off, backing off. But if hiding, I'm just saying, maybe hide with a more agile friend than your friend in there, yes? Saw him limping from the tracks from a mile away, I did. As agile as a fridge, that one."

Louisa holds the stick in her hand as she crawls out of the bushes. Only then does she realize that the taxi driver actually isn't an old man at all, but an old woman.

"So you . . . you weren't going to have a pee? You were just pretending?" Louisa deduces.

"Pee? In bushes? Not an animal, am I?" the taxi driver snorts.

Louisa gets to her feet, looks the taxi driver up and down, and finally drops the stick. Ted comes crawling out on all fours.

"Are you okay?" Louisa asks.

"Great. Tremendous. Never been better," he grunts, getting to his feet with all the grace of a pony in high heels.

The taxi driver grimaces with sympathy when she sees how bruised his face is.

"Ouch! Lucky you were, yes? Isn't safe round here at night, it isn't."

"Thanks, we noticed that," Louisa points out.

"Got off at the wrong station, yes?" the taxi driver wonders, gesturing off toward the train tracks.

"You could say that," Louisa admits, then she nods toward Ted: "He left something on the train. Something . . . important. Could you help us catch up with it?"

The taxi driver smiles a smile where roughly every fourth tooth seems to be in the right place.

"Catch up with *train*?"

Louisa sighs when she realizes how stupid her question was. But it isn't so damn easy to know, she hasn't been in a car that many more times than she's been on a train. Ted takes the roll of tape out of his pocket again and nervously begins to repair his glasses.

"We have to . . . ," he begins, without having the slightest idea how he's going to finish the sentence, but the taxi driver interrupts him:

"Catch up with TRAIN!"

"Excuse me?"

The taxi driver's eyes sparkle as wildly as a badger's after a double espresso.

"Yes! Catch up with train, we will! Come!"

Louisa lights up as if someone has given her ice cream and fireworks.

"Really? Yes! We'll catch up with the train! COME ON, TED!"

Ted puts his glasses on.

"I don't know if this is such a great idea . . . ," he whispers.

Louisa immediately misunderstands and bites her cheeks.

"Sorry. You don't want me to come. I get it. It's . . . "

"No. I mean, yes! Of course I do! What are you talking about?" he groans.

Her hands are shaking. She wishes she were as good at abandoning people as she is at being abandoned, but it feels too late now.

"I understand that you're angry. But I just want to help you find the painting and the ashes, I don't want it to be my fault that—" she begins.

"I know, my God, of course I know, that isn't what I meant . . . ," Ted insists.

"What the hell *did* you mean, then?" Louisa says in response. Her talent for switching from defense lawyer to prosecutor in an instant really is unsurpassed.

"I mean that maybe it isn't such a good idea for us to jump into a *stranger's car*," Ted whispers, so the taxi driver won't hear.

"Do you want the painting back or not? Are you worried we're going to get robbed by an OLD LADY or something?" Louisa whispers back, which she obviously does so well that the taxi driver only manages to hear absolutely everything. The woman laughs at Ted.

"Scared? Scared of me? I'm old, very old. Dangerous as a meatball, I am."

"Ted's scared of everything," Louisa informs her helpfully.

"No I'm not!" Ted protests, affronted, but at that moment, unfortunately, the dog barks in the distance once more and he jumps as if someone has put pins in his underpants.

"Scared of dog?" the taxi driver wonders.

"Reaaally scared of dogs," Louisa nods.

Ted turns toward them with his feet wide apart and puts his hands on his hips like a very angry and very short Superman and snaps:

"I am definitely not scared of dogs!"

THIRTY-SEVEN

He is definitely scared of dogs. Terrified. But he wasn't always, not before his dad's funeral.

Twenty-five years ago he was sitting in the church with his friends. They heard footsteps behind them and Joar turned around like he always did, fists clenched, prepared for war. The minister walking down the aisle jumped in surprise.

"Terribly sorry, you startled me," he smiled.

"Don't creep up on people in churches, you psychopath!" Joar roared back at him.

"I . . . work here," the minister said in his defense.

"Like I care, you psychopath!" Joar pointed out.

The minister looked like he didn't exactly know what to do with that information. So instead he turned sympathetically toward Ted and said:

"I'm very sorry for the loss of your father."

"What for? Was it you who killed him?" Joar snapped, so quickly that even Ali gasped. Joar turned to her, first sullen, then surprised, and added: "Well? *Was* it?"

Then Ted laughed, out loud, and then they all joined in. Dear Lord, how Ted needed that.

The minister had taken all this with admirable calm, the teenagers had to give him that, with just a little twitch of the corner of his mouth and a fleeting glint in the corner of his eye. Then he nodded to Ted and walked on along the aisle without any hurry, gathering up the hymnals and forgotten umbrellas. But Joar, who was strong enough to control anything except his tongue, couldn't help calling out:

"So was it *God* who killed him?"

"Sorry?" the minister said in response.

Joar held up his hands as if he were being mugged:

"Don't get mad, okay? But when someone gets sick and recovers, you always say that it was God who did that, so it's pretty damn cowardly for Him to escape the blame when someone dies!"

It would be wrong to say that the minister looked amused by the question, but he didn't look unamused.

"I think that God's plan sometimes involves a meaning that we can't see," he said tentatively.

"So God murdered him on purpose? As part of His plan?" Joar persisted.

The minister may have then looked a little like he wished he'd gone home for his lunch instead, but he replied with all the patience his training could muster:

"I don't have all the answers, I'm afraid. That's why it's called 'faith.'"

Joar, who hadn't been to a single science lesson all term, snorted with a confidence that was pretty impressive under the circumstances: "Right. If you want answers, we have something called *science*."

If the minister felt insulted, he hid it well.

"Perhaps the one doesn't necessarily rule out the other," he suggested.

"Have you met God?" Joar asked.

"How . . . how do you mean?"

Joar shrugged his scrawny shoulders.

"I mean, God talks to you, right? Is it like watching TV, or is it more like talking on the phone?"

The corners of the minister's mouth danced at that, albeit reluctantly.

"I'm probably the one who does most of the talking, I have to admit."

Joar couldn't have looked more disappointed if Santa Claus had turned out to be a dentist.

"So you're full of shit, then?"

"Sorry?"

Joar's arms flew out from his sides so fast that he almost hit his friends.

"What? This whole thing, with a big fancy church and asking people for loads of money, and you haven't even TALKED with GOD? I thought you could, like, ask for favors and stuff! What sort of shit religion is this?"

The minister took a thoughtful breath, smiled briefly, and replied:

"Perhaps you should ask God yourself?"

Joar stared at him in genuine surprise, as if he were expecting the minister to hold out a tin can on a piece of string, with God sitting at the other end.

"How the hell am I supposed to do that?"

The minister gestured amiably toward the roof.

"God belongs to you as much as to me. You can ask whatever you want."

Joar pursed his lips thoughtfully for a long, long time. Then he looked up at the roof, cleared his throat seriously, and said:

"Okay. Can you stop giving people cancer, you fucking bastard?"

The way Ted laughed at that, on that day of all days, probably saved his life. And the way Joar looked when he heard that, he had probably never felt so proud. If the minister heard it, he pretended not to have, and if Heaven existed, God was probably prepared to overlook it too.

"Come on. Let's go and buy some pastries," Ali whispered to Ted, and they stood up. And only then did it feel like Ted's dad was really dead. That's why he always thinks of himself as an adult when he thinks back to that summer, because he was never a child again after that day.

On the way out of the church, the artist dropped a page from his sketch pad, the sheet of paper drifted down the aisle and landed in front of the minister's feet. The man leaned over and picked it up. He held it tight and was lost for breath.

"Is this . . . ?" he mumbled in astonishment, looking up at the high walls of the church.

"I'm sorry!" the artist said, out of instinct, as if he had committed a crime.

The minister stammered:

"No . . . no, no, don't apologize! I've never . . . never seen anything like this. Did you just draw this, while you were sitting here? Incredible!"

It was a drawing of the church windows, of Jesus on the cross, his naked, bleeding body. The minister looked at it one final time, as if he really wanted to memorize it, before he handed it back gently and said with a smile:

"One day you'll be someone whose work sells for millions."

The boy squirmed uncomfortably and said down toward the floor:

"You can keep it, if you like."

It was the first time someone other than his friends had said his art was worth anything. The first time an adult, apart from a janitor called Christian, had said what he drew was anything other than shameful and embarrassing. The minister held the drawing gratefully as the boy walked out of the church and disappeared into the rain with his friends.

"What did the minister say?" Joar asked outside, and the artist told him the truth.

So a moment later, the church door flew open again and Joar rushed back in and snatched the drawing out of the minister's hands. The boy's eyes looked apologetic, but all that came out of his mouth was:

"Not if it's worth MILLIONS!"

Then he rushed out again, and the minister laughed and laughed and laughed. Perhaps God did too.

The four teenagers crossed the churchyard and jumped over the low wall on the far side, going past the parish hall where a happy family had just had a party. That morning, before Ted's dad's funeral, the minister had conducted a christening. Many years later Louisa will sit on a train and say that the best thing about babies is that they remind us that life goes on, but just then Ted didn't do much thinking at all, he was busy with the noise Joar made. They walked past the kitchen door of the parish hall, where the cleaners had left some black trash bags, and Joar kicked every single one, because he was one of those kids, everyone knows one: a kicker. The first bag sounded like it was full of paper, the second full of plastic, but the third sounded . . . different. Joar and his friends stopped dead and stared at it.

"Was that . . . ?" Ali whispered.

"It sounded like . . . ," Joar agreed.

He cautiously kicked the bag again, the sound was as easy to identify for a kid as the ice cream truck coming around a corner: the bag was full of drink cans and plastic bottles.

"Deposits!" Ali hissed.

The next moment, Joar had slung the bag over his shoulder and the four friends set off, running as fast as they could, their whole bodies laughing. One of the cleaners shouted angrily after them, but didn't bother trying to chase them.

"How many paints and canvases and shit can we buy with this, do you think?" Joar grinned to the artist.

It was a good day, a really good day. Or at least it was until they ran past a house with a large garden and Ted caught sight of another black trash bag which looked exactly like the one Joar was carrying. That could only mean one thing: more deposits.

"Ted! Wait!" Ali cried, but it was already too late.

It wasn't that Ted was particularly desperate for the money, it was more that he wanted to succeed at something. He wanted to do something, just once, that was worth a damn. He wanted to be the big hero, instead of it always being just Joar. So he climbed over the fence and ran toward the house to grab the trash bag. In his defense, it went pretty well, not a single person inside the house saw him. The only problem was that the big black bag wasn't a big black bag at all. It was a big black dog. That was how the four friends found out that Ted really, really needed glasses.

Ted has never run so fast, before or since. He ran like a ferret on fire, with a barking, howling wild animal hot on his heels. It was never dogs he was scared of after that, it was death. From the corner of his eye he could see the tongue lolling between the razor-sharp teeth, and could imagine the sound they would make as they sank through his flesh and crushed his bones. He would dream about that a thousand times. If Joar hadn't run along the fence and distracted the dog for a few moments, Ted never would have gotten away. Unfortunately, the only way Joar could think of doing that was to throw the whole bag of cans and bottles onto the lawn. The noise confused the big black beast, and when Ted jumped over the fence, Ali leapt up and yelled as loudly as she could:

"AAAAARRRRGGGGHHHH!!!"

The dog hesitated, just for a moment, then went on barking like a lunatic, but it still backed away a couple of paces. Ted would always remember that as the moment when Ali scared death itself into retreat. Not even death had the energy to argue with that girl.

While Ted stood there on the right side of the fence, bent double and gasping for breath, and the other three stared longingly at the treasure scattered across the grass around the furious dog, Joar muttered:

"Almost all those damn bottles are from that fizzy water! What sort of morons pay for WATER?"

"It's called mineral water," Ali corrected.

"You're a mineral poo," Joar informed her.

So they had a fight. Then an adult who had heard the dog barking yelled something from inside the house, and they ran off again.

"Sorry, sorry," Ted kept repeating, but his friends just laughed it off.

"We'll find the money for paints some other way," Ali promised.

Joar nodded exultantly:

"It's a good thing it was you the dog was chasing, Ted, because you've got such a tiny ass! If it had been chasing Ali, she'd have been bitten right away!"

Then Ali looked at Joar and did the kindest thing the boys had ever seen her do: she stayed quiet and let him win. Just that once. You couldn't possibly love anyone more when you're fourteen years old.

Twenty-five years later Ted is standing in a parking lot near a train station staring at a taxi. His suit jacket is crumpled, his shoes are full of dirt, his face is bruised, and his wrist is bare when he raises it to see what time it is. Somewhere out in the darkness, a dog is barking, but dogs are not what Ted is scared of. They never were.

THIRTY-EIGHT

Human beings are capable of such unbelievable stupidity. We speak of the birth of a child as a miracle, but really the miracle is everything that comes after. The artist used to sit in a big window in his apartment looking at the people down in the street and muttering: "The dinosaurs died out, but you and I and all these idiots managed to survive? We do nothing but try to find ways to destroy everything that's keeping us alive, but we're still here?"

Then Ted used to go to the stereo in the living room and play some opera, to remind them that humans are also capable of . . . that.

"How can there be enough room inside a person for something this beautiful?" the artist had whispered once when they were listening to Maria Callas.

Then Ted had thought about the myth of Zeuxis and Parrhasius, and the curtain that wasn't a curtain, and he thought that Maria Callas's voice sounded like the artist's paintings felt. As if they were more real than reality.

"But there isn't enough room. Art is what can't fit inside a person. The things that bubble over," Ted had said.

"Sometimes you're really smart," the artist had replied.

Unfortunately, that wasn't true. Everything Ted has done in his life since then suggests the opposite.

"TED?" Louisa repeats, making him jump.

"What are you yelling for?" he snaps, looking around the parking lot in panic.

"You're not listening!"

"I'm listening . . . now."

Louisa gestures toward the taxi.

"I said: if you're worried about being robbed in the taxi, you don't have to worry. You don't have anything left to steal!"

"Really? You think so?" Ted replies, affronted, and holds out his arm where his watch used to be.

Louisa rolls her eyes toward the taxi driver.

"Ted's generation is very ironic, you know."

"Ah," the taxi driver says understandingly.

Ted breathes in through his nose irritably, which is much more difficult now that there's so much blood in his nostrils. Deep down he wants to point out that in this particular case, he was actually being sarcastic, not ironic, but instead he just sighs:

"Okay."

"Okay?" Louisa says suspiciously.

"Okay."

"I mean . . . okay? Or okay-okay? Or okay-okay-okay?"

Ted frowns.

"What are you talking about?"

"What are *you* talking about?"

He groans.

"I said okay! Let's get in the taxi. And try to catch up with the train. We might die, but what does that matter, this day can't really get any worse anyway . . ."

"I'm sitting in the front!" Louisa exclaims quickly, then shrugs off her backpack and rushes around the car.

"Then you'll have to sit with Albert," the taxi driver nods to Ted.

"Excuse me?" Ted says, but it's already too late.

Albert is sitting in the back seat. He's a plant. A very, very, very large plant. The taxi driver explains that her house is very dark at this time of year, and Albert needs a lot of sunlight, so she takes him to work with her. Ted looks out the window: pitch black.

"Good idea," he says, trying to avoid getting one of Albert's leaves in his eye as the car turns around in the parking lot.

"Ironic?" the taxi driver whispers to Louisa, while putting her foot down on the accelerator as if it were trying to steal her breakfast.

"No idea, Ted is very complicated," Louisa replies, and squeals with delight as the taxi flies along parallel to the train tracks.

"We're driving very fast," Ted points out in terror from the back seat.

"THANK YOU!" the taxi driver cries.

"He probably didn't mean it as a compliment," Louisa says.

"You're right, very complicated. Youngsters these days," the taxi driver snorts, like it was a swear word.

"Did you hear? She called you a youngster!" Louisa grins toward the back seat, but Ted is fully occupied regretting every one of his life choices.

Louisa looks around the car curiously, pressing all the buttons. The taxi driver isn't the least bit annoyed, just smiles.

"Like my children. Pressed everything, they did."

Louisa's expression swings between embarrassment and enthusiasm.

"I've never been in a taxi before. I mean, I've been in police cars a few times, and they're a bit like taxis, right? Only there, the doors are locked!"

She carries on pressing buttons, and accidentally turns the stereo on. Terrified, she tries to switch it off, but the taxi driver shakes her head calmly and turns the volume up instead. She hums along to the music.

"What's that?" Louisa wonders.

"Opera! In Italian!" the taxi driver yells.

"What are they singing about?"

"Love!"

"It must be nice to speak Italian," Louisa says dreamily.

"Italian? Can't speak a word of it!"

"How do you know they're singing about love, then?"

The taxi driver chuckles, turns the volume up until the speakers rattle, and promises:

"My friend, all opera, always about love!"

Albert is asleep on Ted's shoulder in the back seat. Ted shuts his eyes tightly and tries to think happy thoughts, he isn't very successful. People say that anxiety is fear for no reason, but Ted's brain is very helpful when it comes to providing suggestions. Once he read a book that said that people with neuropsychiatric disorders need to "make friends with their brain," but Ted and Ted's brain are not friends, they're classmates, forced to do a group assignment called "life" together. And it's not going great.

Ted shouldn't be here, his brain says. He shouldn't be the only one left. What sort of selfish God deprives humanity of a world-famous artist and leaves behind a neurotic high school teacher? Ted can't look after Louisa, he can't even fall asleep without her going missing. He can't take responsibility, not for art and not for people, he can't even walk off a train without getting beaten up. One person can achieve a lot of stupid things, but managing to lose his best friend's watch, his best friend's painting, and his best friend's *ashes* in the same evening surely must count as some sort of record?

Maria Callas is singing on the radio. Albert is good at keeping secrets, no one will know that Ted cries on him then.

"Is that your husband?" Louisa asks in the front seat, pointing to a photograph on the dashboard.

"That's my man, yes, yes," the taxi driver smiles, waving a wrinkled finger and a worn ring.

"How long have you been married?"

"Forty years."

"Wow," Louisa gasps, because that's a length of time that no eighteen-year-old can comprehend, the fact that they've been with each other for more than twice as long as she has been with herself.

"Secret? You know, everyone ask: What's the secret? Do you know? Holding hand!" the taxi driver nods.

"Holding hand?" Louisa repeats.

"Everyone say: Don't go to bed angry! But you know, if you hold hand, very hard to be angry for long, you know? So you hold hand, when you go for walk, when you watch TV. You hold hand, so you know: You and me. Always."

"That sounds simple," Louisa smiles.

"Other thing, important! In restaurant, he orders food I like, always. Halfway through meal, we swap plates. You understand? You must live with each other, not only alongside each other."

Louisa nods. She's never been to a restaurant, but when she and Fish stole ice cream, they used to swap halfway too.

"Is that your children?" she asks, pointing to another photograph taped to the dashboard.

"Yes, yes, seven children!"

"SEVEN? Have you and your husband ever tried just going to the movies one night or something?" Louisa exclaims, and then Ted leans forward between the seats and scolds:

"Louisa! You can't say that!"

"What? I'm just asking. I mean, I like babies and all, but . . . seven?" Louisa points out.

The taxi driver just grins.

"Seven children. All grown-up now. Two dead. But: have grandchildren now! And Albert! A person needs to keep something alive, you understand? Otherwise: we are not people."

Louisa nods seriously and adds:

"Ted hates children. He's scared of babies."

"I'm not scared of babies!" Ted protests, so annoyed that he accidentally hits Albert.

"No, no, you're really brave," Louisa giggles, and the taxi driver chuckles, and then Ted glares at the pair of them.

"Well, the conductor on the train believed I'd been in prison!" he snaps.

You say a lot of stupid things when you're feeling stupid.

"Sure. But for some financial crime or something. Or for riding a bike on the sidewalk, maybe," Louisa informs him.

"I could very well have been in prison, and I'm not scared of babies," Ted says, and it's hard even for him to decide which lie is biggest.

Albert lurches as they go around a bend and ends up lying in Ted's lap.

"Or dog! Also not scared of dog?" the taxi driver nods encouragingly.

"I'm just not hugely fond of them . . . ," Ted grunts, carefully putting Albert back in his seat and fastening his seatbelt.

Then the taxi driver puts her foot down and clutches the steering wheel tight, and every bit of metal in the car shrieks.

"NOW! THERE!"

They can hear the train in the distance. The taxi driver skids to a halt by the steps of the station and Louisa, who has already taken her seatbelt off, jumps out of the car while it's still moving, scraping her shoes so that bits of rubber swirl like snow around her feet.

"This certainly, certainly isn't a good idea!" Ted says to Albert, because Albert is really the only one listening to him nowadays.

Then Ted jumps out of the car too, and runs as hard as he can. Or limps, anyway. He can see Louisa far ahead of him, she flies up a flight of steps and rushes out onto the platform, waving and shouting like someone possessed. The train thunders into the station and thunders straight past her.

"WAIT!" Louisa roars, but the train doesn't care. It's already thrown itself into the darkness and been swallowed up by the night.

That's how quickly it's all over.

Ted stands with his hands on his knees, so out of breath that it hurts to even think. He hears Louisa screaming furiously at God and the universe and everything, but what does that matter now?

When they eventually stagger back down the steps, Albert and the taxi driver are still there waiting. They look apologetic, or at least the taxi driver does. Albert just looks like Albert.

"Come! Next station! We go!" the taxi driver shouts encouragingly.

"We'll never make it in time," Ted sighs.

The taxi driver laughs.

"No, no, of course, never make it. What you think I am? A moon rocket?"

"Then what's the point in even trying?"

The taxi driver shrugs her shoulders.

"Next station: lost and found. Maybe someone leave what you lost there?"

"I doubt it, it's very valuable," Ted says disconsolately.

The taxi driver shrugs again.

"Maybe people surprise you? What to do without hope? Eh? Come on, I drive you!"

So they get in the taxi again, driving at a more civilized speed this time, following the train tracks into a small town where the main street is paved with cobblestones, so Ted and Albert bounce around like pinballs in the back seat. Most of the shops look like they're boarded up, but there's a small hairdresser's and a small café, and at the far end a small sporting goods store with bathing suits in the window. Optimistic at this time of year, Ted thinks.

"Only Easter now! But in summer, all tourists come!" the taxi driver informs them.

Louisa peers out into the darkness in the hope of understanding what would attract tourists, but sees nothing but buildings. They could be anywhere.

"Wow! What happened there?" she asks as they pass a parked car with its windshield covered in white splotches.

"Bird shit. Really big birds here. Worst thing about living close to sea," the taxi driver replies.

Louisa splutters as if she's just choked on air.

"Are we . . . near the sea?" she manages to ask, astonished.

"*Near* the sea? If I turn right here, we *in* the sea!" the taxi driver grins.

But she turns left instead, toward the next train station, and adds:

"The birds are like tourists. They screech and make a mess, but you're not allowed to shoot them . . ."

When the car stops Louisa opens the door and breathes in deep, astonished mouthfuls of the darkness outside. It tastes of salt.

"The sea," she repeats.

Ted doesn't hear her, he's busy checking his pockets with growing panic.

"Oh God, I don't have my wallet! It's in my suitcase on the train!" he wails in despair.

"I've got money," Louisa says calmly and pulls some crumpled bills from her pocket. "I got it out of your suitcase on the train."

The taxi driver takes the money, moves Albert to the front seat, then turns to the pair of them.

"You take care of yourselves now, you hear? Don't forget: hold hand!"

Ted and Louisa really, really don't look like they're planning to do that, but Louisa hugs herself and calls brightly:

"Thank you for rescuing us! And thanks for the lift! And thanks for the love story about you and your husband!"

Ted is a little more restrained.

"Thanks for . . . everything," he says, and really tries to look like someone who isn't scared of dogs.

The taxi driver takes one last look at him, up and down.

"How do you say? The first day of the rest of your lives, this? So live this life!"

Ted feels fully occupied just trying to get through the night, but the taxi driver glares at him until he doesn't dare do anything but nod. Then she and Albert drive off around the corner, on a long road toward sunrise. Ted watches them go and thinks exhaustedly that it doesn't matter if life is long or short, it isn't time that's the problem, it's the speed. Far too much happens when you're alive, everything goes so damn fast, how are you supposed to have time to be a human being?

Louisa clears her throat twice behind him.

"Aren't you going to say thank you to me? For paying for the taxi?" she asks.

Ted's eyebrows bounce.

"With my money?"

"You can still say thank you, right?" Louisa points out, affronted, and starts heading toward the sign on the station that says "Lost and Found."

Ted follows her with a sigh that could have toppled trees. This is the first night of the rest of his life, and it starts with a squelch.

"Watch out for that dog shit!" Louisa calls, precisely one second too late.

THIRTY-NINE

It's funny what the body remembers, long after the brain has forgotten. The smell of the sea, the sound of a squelch.

"WATCH OUT!" Ali called, one second after Joar stepped in the dog shit.

"Aaarrrggghhh," Joar roared.

"There's dog shit there," Ali informed him helpfully.

Joar responded by jumping around on one leg and trying to wipe it off on her, then on Ted and the artist, as they squealed with terror and laughter. They were halfway through July at the time, those hours every year when you suddenly wonder where all the others have gone, like you've been mugged. The middle of summer vacation is a quite specific sort of sadness.

"What's that?" the artist suddenly asked, and they all stopped laughing.

That was the day they found the dead bird. It was the beginning of the end of summer.

It had been raining for several days, but that day had given them a brief window of sunshine. They had run to the pier that morning, competing to see who could strip down to their underwear fastest and throw themselves straight out into the sky. Afterward they had dried off in the sun, eating cookies Ted had brought with him from home and drinking Coca-Cola Joar had stolen.

"It always smells so good after it's rained during the night," Ali had said.

"Petrichor," Ted had replied.

"What?" three gawping mouths had replied at the same time.

He had evaded their gazes, always shy about explaining something, worried about seeming patronizing.

"Petrichor. That's what it's called. The smell of rain. People usually say it's the soil that smells, but it's actually most evident near pavement and rocks."

"And on a pier, maybe?" Ali had said, patting the pier as if it were a big, living friend.

"How the hell do you know stuff like that?" Joar had wondered.

"I read it in a comic. It said that people can smell rain more clearly than a shark can detect the smell of blood," Ted had replied.

"You ought to be a teacher," Ali had suggested.

"Yes, you should," the artist had agreed.

And perhaps that was enough for that to be what happened.

"Why the hell would sharks need to smell rain?" Joar had muttered.

Then they had all laughed, first at him, then with him.

"Did you watch TV last night? The show about that millionaire who lost all her money?" Ali had asked.

"Yes, serves her right," Joar had snorted.

"Don't say that, I felt sorry for her," Ali said.

"Why? Why feel sorry for her for that, almost all people are fucking poor!"

"Yes, but we've been poor all our lives. She's only just started."

They had argued about that for quite some time, as usual. That was how you knew that Joar and Ali had boundless imaginations, because otherwise two people who loved each other so much could never have found so much to fight about.

"So how are we going to get enough money for the paints and brushes and canvas and everything for the painting?" Ted had asked.

"There's no need . . . ," the artist had mumbled quickly. "We can just forget about the competition."

But he could forget that, of course.

"Maybe we could hire Ali out as a singer? People could send her to someone they hate!" Joar had suggested.

"Maybe we could sell one of your two brain cells, Joar?" Ali had shouted back, getting to her feet to fetch some stones to throw in the water, one of her favorite pastimes, apart from throwing them at Joar.

"Maybe we could sell your face to someone who wants to dress up as an ASS!" he had answered.

She had sighed disappointedly.

"What are you even talking about? Is that your best insult?"

Joar had blushed.

"Maybe it isn't so easy for you to understand an insult, because you're an ASS!"

They had carried on like that all day. You can have worse days when you're fourteen, far worse. The artist had lain on his back with the sea in his nostrils and his friends' voices in his ears, and it was that feeling that he would paint the sky with, eventually. Heaven is a summer.

And then, on the way home, they heard a squelch. That was when Joar stepped in the dog shit. When he tried to wipe it off on Ted, Ali teased:

"Ted isn't scared because it's shit, he's scared because it's DOG shit!"

"No I'm not!" Ted protested.

A little more than a week had passed since his dad's funeral, when he discovered he needed glasses after being chased by a trash bag. Every evening he had gone home to a dark house, walking quietly through echoing rooms and collecting empty beer cans. Every morning his friends had teased him relentlessly to stop him drowning in the silence, because they didn't know what else to do.

Ali pretended to be very serious.

"Perhaps it's human shit, Ted? Does that make you feel better?"

"No!"

Joar roared:

"*Urgh*! What if it *is* human shit!"

Then he took his shoe off and scraped it against the edge of the sidewalk. Which only resulted in him getting a tiny bit of shit on his finger, which made him look very much like he wanted to scrape his whole hand off. Ali laughed at that, but unfortunately with her mouth full of cookies, so the crumbs hit Ted's face like a sprinkler. He looked so disgusted that even the artist giggled:

"Oh no, crumbs in the face, Ted would probably rather have gotten dog shit on his pants!"

They laughed so much that Ali accidentally pushed Joar into a large bush. He disappeared, then jumped up again at once like a stripper out of a birthday cake. That was when the artist caught sight of something.

"What's that?" he asked.

Deeper in the bush lay a bird, tangled in a net.

"Is it breathing? Lay it on its side! Should we give it mouth-to-mouth?" Ali said in a confused torrent, because she was good at a lot of things, but not much good at anything when she was stressed.

"You shouldn't give it mouth-to-mouth with that breath, anyway . . . ," Joar grunted, moving his head away from hers.

"It's the cookies . . . ," Ali muttered, putting her hand over her mouth.

Ted reached forward to pick up the bird, but Joar quickly knocked his hand away.

"You mustn't touch birds! Their mothers won't take them back then!"

Ted leaned closer to the bird and said tentatively:

"This bird looks like it's old enough to be retired. It probably doesn't have a mother."

The artist leaned forward too and added quietly:

"Besides, it's dead."

Joar stuck his head into the bush and conceded:

"Okay. Maybe it does look a bit gray around the feathers."

"And dead!" Ali pointed out.

Joar gently freed it from the net. The artist dug a small hole in the ground and they buried it there. Joar thought they ought to say something, and then everyone looked at Ted, because he was the one who was responsible for words. So Ted repeated, as well as he could remember them, the words the minister had said at his dad's funeral:

"There is a time for everything. A time to be born and a time to die, a time to plant and a time to uproot. A time to weep and a time to laugh. A time to mourn. A time to dance."

When he fell silent, Joar wiped his eyes and Ali did a few sad little dance steps. The artist covered the grave with soil. Only then did they hear a peeping sound from the bush, and that was how they found the second bird, the one that was still alive.

It was caught in the net, emaciated and abandoned. The friends hesitated just a moment.

"You do it . . . ," Ali whispered to the artist, seeing as he was the only one who could lift the bird out of the net without it struggling.

Some people have those sorts of hands, as if all living things instinctively know when they are being touched by someone who would never do them harm. He gently held it up toward the sky, but the bird didn't fly off, as if it didn't realize it was free.

"Maybe it's hurt inside?" Ted said sadly.

"It's probably just frightened!" Joar said.

"That's the same thing," Ted pointed out softly.

"Have we got something we can put it in?" Ali asked.

"I have," the artist said, and carefully took the box out of his backpack with his free hand.

The other three glanced at it, a little concerned, even the bird, but Ali was the only one who dared ask: "Is that the one you kept all the pills in?"

"Mmm," the artist admitted.

"What the hell difference does it make? If there are any left, they might be painkillers! We're, like, better than vets!" Joar declared, and helped the artist lay the bird in the box in a way that a vet definitely never would.

Joar carried the bird all the way home, when it started to rain he protected the little box with his body, and when they could almost see their houses he said decisively:

"I'll take it home, my mom will know how to save it."

None of his friends had the heart to disagree. But even Ali, the queen of bad ideas, knew that this was a bad one.

Behind them the rain and wind took their whole childhood and disappeared.

FORTY

Ted is an idiot, the lost-and-found office is closed. Of course it's closed, it's the middle of the night, what was he thinking? The only positive with the darkness is that no one can see him blushing at his own stupidity.

"I can break in," Louisa assures him enthusiastically.

"We definitely aren't going to break in," Ted snaps.

He tries the locked door once more, as if it might suddenly change its mind. Then he screams a very, very bad swear word inside his head. He is so tired of traveling, so tired of himself. He thinks about how strange the artist was: every time he talked about the trips he made in his twenties, his voice always sounded like it was carbonated with joy. Madness, Ted thinks.

"I'll be fast! This isn't even a difficult lock!" Louisa insists.

"We *aren't* going to break in!"

"So what are we going to do, then?"

"I don't know, because you keep talking all the time, so I can't think!"

"Okay. Have you finished thinking?" she says after maybe nine seconds.

"No."

Fifteen seconds pass.

"How about now?"

"No!"

"Well, hello? Can't I just break in while you're thinking?"

She's taken her screwdrivers out of her backpack and is ready.

"Can you just try to . . . not be yourself for two minutes?" he implores.

"Wouldn't it be easier if you just weren't *you*?" she suggests, walking toward the door.

"No! Wait!"

"I'm just going to—"

"Stop it, I said!"

"But it will be quick! I'm just going to—" she insists, and then he loses his temper.

"What's wrong with you? If it's closed, how would anyone have left anything here since we got off the train?" he blurts out, a lot angrier than he means to be.

"Oh," she says, reluctantly putting her screwdrivers down.

"Just . . . stand still! This is all YOUR FAULT from the start!" he snaps, so unexpectedly that she flinches, as if he has thrown something at her.

Ted has never regretted anything so instantly in his whole life. Louisa backs away so quickly that she trips over herself.

"Do you think I don't know that?" she whispers, biting her bottom lip so he won't see it trembling.

"Sorry, I didn't mean . . . ," Ted says, but it's too late.

She throws her arms up and blinks hard.

"No, no, you're right. It's my fault! That's why I didn't want the damn painting from the start. I knew you'd be disappointed in me, sooner or later, so it was better that I just . . ."

She searches for words, trying not to cry, her tongue trying to find somewhere to hide as her teeth chatter. Ted has never carried a heavier guilt, because it's himself he's looking at then, every time his mom raised her voice. It is an act of violence when an adult yells at a child, all adults know that deep down, because all adults were once little. Yet we still do it. Time after time, we fail at being human beings.

So when Louisa can't find the words to explain how she feels, Ted fills them in for her, in a voice so crushed that it vibrates on every consonant:

"Better that you just . . . left me right away? Is that what you were going to say? That it's too scary trying to be liked by anyone? It's easier to just give up?"

"Yes," she whispers.

He breathes so deeply that his rib cage rattles beneath his suit jacket. Then he confesses:

"I thought about leaving you, long before you left me. I was thinking of getting off the train when I went to the bathroom."

That prompts a new record in silence between them.

"We suck at abandoning people," she eventually mutters.

"We should practice," Ted smiles.

She smiles too. They probably have more to say to each other, but they don't have time, because instead they are interrupted by a voice behind them in the darkness:

"There you both are!"

Unfortunately, the voice doesn't know what sort of night they've had, or what effect a voice in the darkness on a deserted train platform will have on them right now. Ted spins around in panic, red in the face like only a middle-aged man who really can't cry attractively can be. Louisa turns around with a screwdriver in each hand and her eyes wide open with wild rage, ready for war. The woman in front of them on the platform almost falls onto the tracks.

"I . . . I . . . ," she stammers.

It's the mother from the train. A little farther away, a man is standing with a stroller, he looks sleepy and terrified, two emotions that really aren't easy to combine. Louisa clears her throat the way you do when you've almost attacked someone's mom with screwdrivers by mistake, and quickly hides them behind her back. Ted wipes his face with the sleeve of his suit jacket.

"Er . . . hello there," Louisa manages to say.

"What . . . what are you doing here? In the middle of the night?" Ted wonders.

"I'm waiting for you!" the mother smiles eagerly when she regains her balance, before she catches sight of Ted's face and exclaims: "Oh my, what happened?"

At first Ted honestly doesn't understand what she means, then he looks at himself as if he's borrowed his body from someone else. His pants are torn from the fence he climbed over, his jacket looks like he found it in the forest, his taped glasses are holding on to his nose for dear life, and his face isn't just streaked with tears, but also full of bumps and bruises.

"It's a very long story . . . ," he begins with resignation.

"Are you okay? Should I call a doctor?" the mother asks, the way mothers do.

"Don't worry," Ted says.

"Are you hungry? I've got some cookies in the stroller! You need to eat!" she says, and without waiting for an answer calls out: "Honey! Can you bring me the cookies?"

The man with the stroller approaches very, very warily, as if he has just read a "Do Not Feed the Animals" sign at a zoo.

"No thanks, I'm not really hungr—" Ted tries to say.

"EAT!" the woman says tenderly, albeit in capital letters.

The man gives Ted a look that indicates clearly and concisely that he really recommends that Ted eat. So Ted eats, as does Louisa.

"You're going to be a good mom . . . ," she says.

"What did you say?" the woman smiles sternly, clearly disapproving of her talking with food in her mouth.

"Nothing . . . ," Louisa mutters, and shoves another cookie in.

The man clears his throat discreetly at his wife.

"Honey. Perhaps you should . . . ?"

At first the woman looks horrified, then she chirrups:

"Oh! Yes! Sorry! The conductor saw you both get off without your things! And my husband was going to pick me up from this station anyway, so I was going to take them with me and leave them in the lost-and-found office. But of course that was closed. I'm so forgetful. I'll just have to blame baby-brain!"

She smiles as if they ought to know exactly what that means, so Louisa and Ted just nod politely and eat more cookies. They're exhausted, their brains aren't exactly working brilliantly either, so it takes a few seconds for them to realize what she's actually saying. Only then do they see what she's got with her: Ted's suitcase and the box containing the painting.

"YES! YES! YES! YES!" Louisa exclaims, showering the stroller with crumbs, her voice echoing around the station.

She's so relieved that she feels sick, then she starts laughing hysterically, and would probably have thrown her arms around the woman's neck if that hadn't required physical contact.

"Excuse me," Ted says, so quietly that no one hears, because the woman exclaims in delight:

"I hope nothing is broken! That box looks like it contains something fragile!"

"It's perfect, everything's perfect!" Louisa assures her, looking down into the box.

"Excuse me . . . ," Ted repeats, to no avail.

"And here's your suitcase, Ted!" Louisa blurts out, looking through the pocket as if she were thinking of pointing out that someone has stolen his money, before she realizes that it was her.

Ted adjusts his glasses, shifting his weight from one foot to the other, and eventually manages to say:

"Excuse me . . . there was a small box too. It was next to my suitcase, about this big . . ."

The woman turns to him, unconcerned.

"Yes, but that was empty, wasn't it?"

Ted rocks as if the world is moving.

"Excuse . . . me?"

The woman tilts her head to one side.

"Oh no, it wasn't empty? It was so light. I thought it was . . . trash."

Ted's mouth opens, but the scream is silent. Louisa looks from Ted to the woman to the painting, then collapses like a punctured bouncy castle.

“What . . . what happened to it?” she asks, without daring to listen to the reply.

The woman scratches her hair nervously.

“I think the conductor threw it away. Was it important? Oh no, now I feel stupid . . . oh, it’s this baby-brain . . .”

Ted composes himself, but his voice is breaking when he whispers:

“No, no, please. Don’t think that. You’ve done more than enough, really. This big box is the most important one. The other one was . . . oh, don’t worry. Thank you, really. I wish I could give you some sort of reward, but . . .”

The woman shakes her head.

“Certainly not! I’m just happy I was able to help. You helped me go to the bathroom in peace on the train, a mother never forgets a thing like that,” she smiles to Louisa.

Louisa takes the box containing the painting in her arms, silently paralyzed by the realization that the artist’s ashes are gone. So Ted repeats in a thick voice:

“Thank you. Thank you very much.”

He puts his hand gently on the box, almost touching Louisa’s hand, trying to comfort her.

The woman smiles happily, then writes her address and phone number on a piece of paper and hands it to him.

“If you’re ever passing through here again, do get in touch. We have a guest bedroom you’d be welcome to stay in.”

Ted doesn’t really know what to say in response, so he writes his own name and phone number on a scrap of paper and hands it to her. What would anyone want that for, he thinks, embarrassed.

Then the woman and man wave, turn away, and steer the stroller off into the night. Ted is left standing there with the piece of paper, and Louisa looks at it as if it is an unbelievable treasure. A *guest bedroom*, did these people live in a palace or something?

“Come on!” she mutters, taking a firmer grip on the box containing the painting and beginning to walk.

"Where are you going?" Ted calls.

"We need to find a taxi and follow that train! We have to get those ashes back!"

But Ted doesn't follow her. He remains standing where he is, he could swear he hears the flutter of wings as a flock of birds takes off toward the sky some distance away.

"No, no, wait . . . ," he says.

Then Louisa turns around and misunderstands again. Not to brag, but she really isn't bad at misunderstandings.

"Don't you want me to go with you? I know everything is my fault! Just let me help to . . ."

Ted slowly moves his hands as if he's trying to wave down an airplane, which is probably roughly the same level of difficulty as getting Louisa to stop talking. He nervously takes off his glasses and puts them on again, several times. He is going to need an awful, awful lot of tape when all this is over.

"No, no, Louisa, it isn't your fault. I should never have said those things before. I'm sorry that none of this turned out the way you imagined. You dreamed about the painting and the children in it all your life, and the only one you got to meet was . . . me. And I've just been . . . myself, the whole time. You should have gotten to meet the others instead. You would have liked them."

"I like you," she whispers, as if she is on the point of being abandoned.

He scratches his receding hairline.

"The last thing my best friend asked me to do before he died was to look after the painting and you. I've failed at both. I'm sorry it didn't all turn out like a fairy tale for you. What was it you said you felt when you saw the postcard of the painting when you were younger? That you dreamed you could fall asleep and wake up on that pier? And that you would . . . learn to swim?"

Louisa wipes her eyes on the box in her arms.

"I'm sorry you had to take responsibility for me, Ted. I'm sorry that

I'm . . . me. Okay? I'm sorry for everything! But just, *let's go*, now! We need to find a taxi and go after that train, and . . ."

But Ted doesn't move from the spot. He just sticks his hands in his pockets and looks up at the night sky, taking deep breaths and noticing the smells of the sea and dog shit. He thinks of everything that has died, but even more about all the things that are still alive.

"Can you really break doors open?" he asks after a while.

"Yes, of course I can," she sniffs, as if all normal people can do that.

"Come on, then. I've got a better idea," he says, and starts to walk off in the other direction.

"No, we need to go after the train! We need to find the box of ashes!" she cries.

Ted replies, and his voice sounds like it's carbonated:

"It's okay. He was always going on about how much he loved traveling."

So they don't chase after the train. They go to the small street of shops instead and look for the sporting goods shop. Louisa breaks in, they leave money on the counter, Ted writes an apologetic note. They take towels and bathing suits out of the window display.

The sun will soon be rising. They walk to the sea. He teaches her to swim.

FORTY-ONE

After they found and buried one bird and saved the life of another, the four friends went their separate ways at the crossroads, calling out: "Tomorrow! Tomorrow! Tomorrow! Tomorrow!" Ted looked over his shoulder and kept Joar's body in his eyes for as long as he could. They didn't know it then, but they would only swim in the sea together one more time.

A little while later, Joar was sitting on the floor of his room with his mom, and asked nervously:

"Should we puke on it?"

Joar had been so convinced that his mom would know exactly what to do with an injured bird, but she was standing next to him now and in every way possible looked like she didn't.

"Puke?" she said.

"Don't mother birds do that to their kids? They eat and then fly to the nest and throw up the food into their kids' mouths?"

"I have no idea," his mom smiled happily, because that was how happy she was every time Joar knew something she had never heard of.

"Ted said this bird probably isn't even a kid, but then how the hell are you supposed to know that?" Joar said, peering suspiciously at the bird, like a bouncer trying to guess if the bird had shown a fake ID.

"Oh, darling, you're asking me, when I'm such an idiot?" his mom laughed.

"You're the one that keeps everything alive," Joar answered very seriously.

Because she did. Plants and him and herself, against all the odds, in a home where everything ought to die.

"How lucky am I?" she whispered then, hugging him tight.

"Mom . . . ," he groaned, and rolled his eyes.

But she was right, of course, because most teenage boys don't hug their mothers back. So how lucky was she to get to be his?

"Do you think it's hungry? We've got cake! Someone at work had a birthday, and there was some left over . . . ," she suggested.

Joar laughed: "Maybe we should start by just giving it water, Mom?"

She sighed at herself and let her hands take turns hitting each other.

"Yes, yes, of course, I'm such an idiot, I just get so *nervous*, darling, and then I say such silly things . . ."

She was always nervous, always felt stupid. She called from the kitchen to ask if Joar wanted cake if the bird wasn't going to have any, and Joar replied: "Do bears shit in the woods?"

Then she laughed loudly and called back: "Is water wet? Do one-legged ducks swim in circles?"

They had been telling the same silly, silly jokes since Joar was little. In a way, it was their equivalent of Joar and his friends calling: "Tomorrow!" A gentle reminder that they still had each other, in spite of everything.

"You're not stupid, Mom, you just have . . . poor judgment," Joar said softly when she came back with cake and water.

"I don't really know what that means," she smiled in embarrassment, but then she added proudly: "But I can't be completely stupid, you know, because then I couldn't have had such a smart son! And I haven't puked on you one single time, unlike some mother birds . . ."

Joar admitted: "I don't really know what the hell it means either, I just heard Ted say it about his big brother one time . . ."

Then they both laughed, such a miraculous sound in that house that the walls must have been shocked every time. When his mom gave the bird water, she did so by putting one finger at the end of a straw, so she could feed it drop by drop, and Joar thought that was so smart he wished everyone who thought she was foolish could have seen it.

Because plenty of things could be said about Joar's mom, and sadly most people said them all the time. Never directly to her, of course, it was actually pretty remarkable that such a small woman could have a back large enough for half the town to talk about her behind it. But Joar, as Ali often said, had "insanely big ears for such a small head." So unfortunately he had already heard everything at a young age. The neighbors in the street and the moms at soccer practice and the teachers at school, they all sniggered the same sort of things his paternal grandmother used to say before she died: Joar's mom wore heels that were too high and blouses that were cut too low, she talked too much and wasn't ashamed enough. She was too old for the way she dressed, too adult for her giggle, wore far too much makeup to be someone's mom. "Poor child," Joar had heard old women whisper in the supermarket, because that was the worst sort of gossip: the sort that is disguised as concern. Joar's grandmother had been better at that than anyone, and it often made Joar sad when he thought of her death, because she had been so very old then, and he was worried his old man would live just as long.

Because they were right, the old women in the supermarket, Joar was a poor child. But not because of his mom. She was all that was good in the world. Definitely not an idiot.

But did she have poor judgment? Do bears shit in the woods?

When Joar was little, his mom didn't have a child seat on her bicycle, so she used to put him in the basket on the front like he was a small dog. She never told him to go to bed, it wasn't unusual for her to suggest ice cream for breakfast, and when Joar occasionally forced her to eat healthy food, she would call him "boring." Sometimes Joar would tease her about the time she accidentally set him on fire when he was seven, which was obviously an exaggeration, she just happened to set a small part of his pants on fire. She had been trying to mend a hole in them, because even if she was not so great at cooking, she was most excellent at sewing, but unfortunately they'd had their electricity shut off that week, so she had done it in the dark and accidentally knocked over a candle. In hindsight, sure, it might have been better if she had asked Joar to take his pants off first, but you can't think of everything.

At an early age she would take the boy to the movies and smuggle him into R-rated films. Well, maybe not "smuggle," the guy at the ticket booth might have had a crush on her and pretended not to notice. All men everywhere fell a bit in love with her, not even Joar could blame them for that. Sometimes they saw several films in a row, sometimes a really bad one ten times, all so they could stay there in the darkness where the world smelled of popcorn and always had happy endings. Of course most children get tired of being best friends with their moms, so she did everything with Joar as if it were the last time. But it never was. How lucky was she?

In the winter, on nights when Joar's old man wasn't home, they would head out and climb over a fence down by the ice rink and go skating in the light of the streetlamps. His mom used to be a figure skater when she was young, every time she swept out across the ice it took Joar's breath away. It was the only place he knew where she wasn't afraid. He got good at skating as well, so good that he had had to pretend to really suck at it when the school organized an ice hockey competition when he was nine. He didn't want anyone to tell his mom that he ought to start playing on a team, because they couldn't afford it, children who played ice hockey in their town didn't get their electricity cut off and didn't use newspapers as toilet paper at the end of the month. It didn't matter, of course, Joar wouldn't have wanted to play on a team anyway. They were run by a bunch of angry dads shouting at their kids, and if Joar needed to be around a raging fucking moron, he had one at home.

Sometimes the boy and his mom would lie on their backs on the ice rink at night and she would point out the constellations to him, she knew every single one, because she wasn't dumb at all. Joar could have ended up with any idiot for a mom, but he got her. How lucky was he?

When he had just turned twelve, she taught him to drive a car. Apart from the fact that he could barely reach the pedals, it had actually gone pretty well, at least to start with, but then Joar asked what one particular traffic sign meant. When she said, "No idea, darling," he asked: "Didn't you have to learn that to get your driver's license?"

"Oh, I don't have a driver's license, darling," she replied, quite unconcerned, then said: "Turn left here."

"You don't have a DRIVER'S LICENSE?" Joar shouted.

"No, no, but how very sweet of you to think that I did," she replied, evidently moved that he thought so highly of her.

"But what . . . what the hell, Mom? How did you learn to drive, then?"

"My mom taught me."

Joar stared at her, and to his own surprise heard himself ask: "What do you do if the police stop you?"

His mom had looked at him so proudly, because that was the most law-abiding thing he had said in his entire life. Then she had admitted:

"Oh, I've only been stopped once. And then I pointed to you in the back seat and said you had an inflamed appendix and that we were on our way to the hospital."

"I REMEMBER that! I thought you were JOKING!" Joar exclaimed.

"You're so sweet, darling," his mom replied. They had driven around town in the darkness all that night, and if she had let him, Joar would have just carried on driving, as far away as possible. But she didn't dare leave her husband, and Joar couldn't leave her. Their prison was invisible.

Now Joar was about to turn fifteen, and they were saving the life of a bird. His mom patiently gave it drop after drop of water, and Joar gathered twigs and leaves from outside the house to make a soft bed for it inside the box. How lucky was that bird?

"Did you know that birds don't have nests? Not for themselves, I mean. They only build them for their kids," Joar said.

"Did Ted tell you that?" his mom smiled.

"His brain is like poop. Everything sticks!"

When his mom laughed really hard, she would fart, no one apart from Joar knew that, because no one apart from Joar made her laugh like that.

"Open the window! Open the window! You're going to murder the bird!" he coughed with tears in his eyes, and she laughed and laughed and laughed.

She stopped when she turned around. They hadn't heard the key in the lock. Joar's old man was standing in the doorway of the room looking at them, at first puzzled, then with hate in his eyes. He was six or seven beers into the day, he was breathing unevenly through his nose, his eyes couldn't quite land on anything. But he saw the bird, he saw how happy Joar's mom was, and the boy knew at once that there wasn't going to be a happy ending to that.

FORTY-TWO

Louisa and Ted are sitting on the rocks wrapped in towels, shivering in the sunrise.

"Is it always that cold in the sea?" she wonders.

"No. Sometimes it's much colder," he smiles.

"I've never felt like this, my skin feels different . . ."

"There's nothing like the sea. Now your skin knows that. Now it's going to miss it, always," he promises.

Louisa sways from side to side, between euphoria and melancholy.

"I would have liked to tell Fish about this. Sometimes I'm so . . . angry. She never got to see the sea."

Ted cleans his glasses for a long time.

"She saw the sea every night with you, on the postcard. And she's seeing the sea now," he says.

"Thanks," Louisa mumbles.

"I should thank you."

"No, I mean, thanks for teaching me to swim . . . ," she says.

"No, really. I haven't been swimming in the sea in twenty-five years. So I'm the one who should be thanking you. Besides, it was much easier to teach you than Ali . . ."

She smiles. He does too.

"I'm sorry we lost the ashes," she says sadly.

"I'm the one who lost them," he corrects her.

"Okay. I'm sorry you lost them, then," she says quietly.

"Well, it was a little your fault too!" he retorts.

She has just enough time to feel very badly insulted before she realizes that he's joking.

"Very funny," she mutters.

"I thought so," he grins.

She looks at the box containing the painting between them on the rocks.

"Do you think he would have been angry? About us losing him?" she asks.

"No. I think he would have laughed. He liked hide-and-seek."

Her eyes light up.

"Maybe it isn't such a bad idea to get your ashes scattered on a train, after all? That way you're always on your way somewhere!"

Ted looks absolutely horrified.

"Ugh, don't say that. Can't we even stop having to travel when we're *dead*?"

Louisa laughs.

"Where do you want your ashes scattered, then?"

Ted thinks for a good while before deciding:

"In a library. You don't have to put up with reality there. It's as if thousands of strangers have given away their imaginary friends, they're sitting on the shelves and calling to you as you walk past. There's an author called Donna Tartt who describes why a person falls in love with art: 'It's a secret whisper from an alleyway. Psst, you. Hey kid. Yes, you.' That's what libraries feel like for me."

Louisa has to pretend to have sea water in her eyes at that.

"How many damn books have you actually read?"

"Not nearly enough."

Louisa disguises a sob with a cough.

"Fish liked libraries too."

Then she takes Fish's cigarettes from her backpack, because Fish always said she had heard that a cigarette after a swim is the best one of all. Louisa doesn't light it, she just smells the tobacco, and to her surprise Ted gently reaches out his fingers and asks:

"Can I borrow one?"

Louisa wrinkles her whole face in surprise.

"Seriously?"

"Not to smoke, just to . . . smell. My mom used to smoke that brand."

She hands him one. So they sit by the sea with the painting, each with a cigarette under their nose, a mild breeze in their hair, and the first light of morning on their cheeks.

"Are you like her? Your mom?" Louisa asks cautiously.

"Yes, I think so."

"Was she very kind?"

Ted's laughter echoes off the rocks. He shakes his head.

"No . . . no . . . I don't think 'kind' is a word anyone would have used about her. She was a hard woman when I was a child, very hard, Joar once said she could headbutt a diamond and break it."

"Hard in what way?"

Ted looks sadly at the cigarette.

"Mom had very definite ideas about . . . everything. She didn't want my brother and I to show our feelings, not whine, never cry. It was important to her that we always behaved like . . . men."

"So she isn't like you at all," Louisa exclaims angrily.

Ted rolls the cigarette back and forth between his fingers, taking deep breaths of the smell of tobacco and salt and a summer that's on its way.

"It's incredibly difficult being a mom, Louisa. It's difficult being a human being. I think my mom was very like me at first, because she was a romantic when she was young. But there's no harder person on the planet than a romantic with a broken heart."

"Did she hit you?"

"No."

"But you got hit?"

"Yes, dear God, yes. My big brother hit me every day when we were little. One time he threw me down some stairs and I got knocked unconscious. It took me a long time to even remember that, I thought I had slipped . . ."

"Were you scared of him?"

"Yes. It's hard to be little."

"It's hard to be everything."

"Yes. That's true. It's hard to be everything."

Shivering, Louisa pulls the towel more tightly around herself and asks:

"What's your best memory of your mom?"

Ted smells the cigarette. The memories are slippery, hard for his brain to get a grip on.

"Of Mom? Us . . . playing cards."

"Cards?"

"Yes. She used to work nights so she could look after Dad during the day. I was bad at school, I had trouble with language, trouble reading and writing. One teacher told Mom that I was being bullied, and I wished he hadn't, because I could see Mom thinking it was her fault. That evening I heard her on the phone to a friend, telling her that she couldn't bear being at home with nothing but death for company. The next day she woke me with her hand on my forehead and whispered: 'You've probably got a fever.' I can't remember her ever actually touching me before then. It was like . . . the sun. As if she had been possessed by an overfriendly demon. And that whole day we played cards at the kitchen table. It sounds stupid, but that's my best memory, because then she just felt like my mom. That first day she pretended I was ill, the next I pretended on my own, and then I went on pretending for several months. We hid away from reality, both of us, it was . . . wonderful. But after a while Dad got worse and had to spend more time in the hospital, and Mom kept going back and forth, and it was too much work for her to have me at home then. In the end the school called and said I'd have to retake the whole year if I didn't go back, so one day when I woke up Mom had already packed my backpack. When I got back to school I was like an animal that had grown up in a zoo, only to suddenly be released out into the wild. I got teased more than ever, I got beaten up a lot and went home battered and bruised . . . and I remember how disappointed Mom looked then. I was ashamed that I kept causing problems, so I said I'd fallen. She knew I was lying, but just asked if I was hungry. That evening I heard her talking on the phone, I could hear the sob in her voice as she told her friend that it was probably her fault that I was so weak. That I wasn't anything like my brother, who could fight and defend himself. Mom said she must have spoiled me, made me soft. She said she was . . . worried. That I would never be a . . . real man."

Ted falls silent. Louisa looks away so he can wipe his eyes in peace.

"When did your mom's heart break? When your dad got sick?" she asks.

He considers his answer for a long time.

"Yes. But perhaps it didn't break. Maybe it got worn out. We didn't have much money when Dad got sick, we only had just enough to keep the house, she probably always felt like she wasn't enough. She worked in a factory, was always tired. The sound I remember most from my childhood is being hushed, because either my mom or my dad was asleep, or both of them. That's why I got the room in the basement, so I wouldn't be in the way."

"Are you sure about that?" Louisa asks.

Ted raises his eyebrows, somewhere in the borderland between surprised and insulted.

"How do you mean?"

Louisa's shoulders bounce.

"I just mean . . . maybe you got the room in the basement so you wouldn't see how sick your dad was the whole time? And how sad your mom was? And maybe your mom was trying to protect you from your big brother?"

Ted stares out across the sea, squinting at the sun with shame washing through him. All these years and he has never even considered that. It's hard to be little, hard to be big, hard to be everything in between. So he turns toward Louisa and says:

"It wasn't only bad. It was a love story at first, my mom and dad's marriage . . ."

Then her eyes grow wide in anticipation, because she loves love stories. So he tells it to her the way it was once told to him.

FORTY-THREE

Ted explains that children know hardly anything about their parents, even if they live with them their whole lives. Because all we know about them is as moms and dads, nothing about who they were before that. We never saw them young, when they still fantasized about all the things that could happen, instead of regretting all the things that never did.

He tells her that at the end of that day when he and his friends had found the birds, Ted got home to a house with all the lights turned off. It had just started to get dark, and in the street stood a rusty car whose headlights blinded him, he couldn't see who was sitting in it. He walked past it on tiptoe, his eyes darting about, his body so tense that when the driver suddenly touched the accelerator and the engine growled, Ted's heart beat so hard that he jumped in the air.

He heard mocking laughter. When he squinted past the headlights he saw a broad-shouldered man in his twenties, with fists the size of shovels, sitting in the driver's seat. The Ox.

"Were you scared, you little fag?" the man yelled through the open window. A cloud of heavy smoke billowed out after him.

The door on the passenger side opened and closed, with the heavy *thud* you get used to if you live on a street where everyone has twenty-year-old cars. Ted's big brother got out and weaved through the beam of the headlights toward the house, too intoxicated to walk straight. Ted hurried after him, hunched over, but jumped in fear again when the car horn sounded. The Ox's mocking laughter disappeared into the darkness with the rumble of the engine.

"Bastard," Ted whispered with his fists clenched, furious with himself for being so easily startled.

His big brother opened the front door with some difficulty, stumbled through the hall into the kitchen, but managed to kick off his shoes out of sheer muscle memory along the way. Wearing shoes in their mom's kitchen was nothing less than a suicide attempt, they had known that since early childhood. He opened the fridge but found no chilled beer, so he fetched two warm cans from the pantry. On his way back to the living room, he bumped into Ted, who flinched automatically as if he were about to be hit. Muscle memory, that too.

His big brother's body was so hard, he strode into every room with such confidence, a honed knife cutting through air. Ted always moved like he was facing a headwind and driving rain.

"The Ox is a fucking idiot sometimes," his big brother slurred, and it came so suddenly that it took a long while for Ted to realize what he had just heard. He would never come closer to hearing his brother say he was sorry.

Ted shocked himself by replying:

"So why are you friends with him, then?"

He was expecting to be hit, but nothing happened, his big brother just looked surprised.

"We've known each other since we were little."

As if that's any kind of answer, Ted thought hopelessly, but of course in that town it kind of was. Friends were something a man like his big brother simply acquired one day in the schoolyard, without quite knowing how it came about, and then he stuck to them, because in this town boys didn't survive long if they were alone. Especially not an immigrant child of the age his big brother was when they arrived. Boys were defined by their surroundings here, the person you were when you started high school was usually the person you remained, either someone who hit, or someone who cowered. Hardly anyone could afford to move away, and no sensible person moved here voluntarily, so around here young men didn't feel that they'd chosen a life, just that they had been allocated one. Life was an allotted period of time, like a prison sentence. After high school the Ox had gotten a job in the harbor, then he had arranged for Ted's big brother to get one too, he had vouched for him and promised that he was "the right sort of guy." That meant he was the sort of man who stood his ground, who didn't back down, and who knew how to keep his mouth shut if the police showed up.

Now Ted stood in the kitchen looking at his big brother's swollen red knuckles and realized that it had been another long evening of being the right sort of guy. Ted usually didn't dare even open his mouth in the vicinity of his brother, but he heard himself say:

"You're not a bad person."

His big brother's eyes narrowed suspiciously.

"What the hell did you say?"

Ted hunched up and looked down at the floor hesitantly:

"I said you're not a bad person. You just pick bad friends. You pick people who are worse than you, because you think that's all you deserve. You ought to pick people who are better than you."

His big brother swayed from side to side, bewildered.

"Not everyone can be as lucky with their friends as you."

Ted was so surprised that he happened to make eye contact, something which all his life had always been rewarded with violence, but this time nothing happened.

"I . . . I didn't even know that you knew I had friends," he said quietly.

His brother grinned.

"Did you think I don't notice that you and those three little hyenas come up and empty the fridge of Mom's food every other evening?"

Ted lowered his gaze again.

"You're right. I'm lucky."

Then his brother shook his head and mumbled:

"No. It's your friends who are lucky."

Then his brother turned and went out into the living room, sat down at the piano, and drank beer. Ted stood there, overwhelmed. He leaned against the fridge and managed to knock off a note that was stuck to it, otherwise he might never have seen it. A short handwritten message from their mom: She'd gone to see a friend. There was food in the freezer. It didn't say when she'd be back, or even if she would.

She hadn't said a word to Ted after the funeral, the whole house had been a coffin.

Ted thought for a while, then he opened the freezer and took out all the ice cubes he could find. He filled two bowls, one for beer and one for his big brother's hand, then went into the living room and put them on the piano. His big brother looked up, as if he didn't recognize Ted at first, as if they were little kids who had been pretending to be grown-up and had suddenly been pretending all too well. Ted turned to go down to the basement as usual, so his brother's soft voice came as a shock:

"You want a beer?"

Ted really didn't, but he nodded anyway. When he took it, his big brother held on to it a second longer than necessary. Holding that beer at the same time was probably the closest they had ever come to a hug.

Ted sat down next to him at the piano. Not too close.

"Do you like your job?" he asked awkwardly because he so desperately wanted to know something about his brother but didn't know where to start.

"At the harbor? No one fucking likes working at the harbor," his brother grinned, but when he saw Ted look sad, he added: "It's a job, Ted. All jobs for people like us are shit. But with my salary and Mom's, we can probably keep hold of the house . . ."

That was how clear it was to him, that it was his duty too, not just hers. Ted sat and looked at the piano for several minutes before he plucked up the courage to ask:

"Can you . . . play something?"

His brother's fingers touched the keys.

"Mom's asleep. We mustn't wake her."

"She isn't home, there was a note on the fridge," Ted said.

His brother tried to hide his surprise, perhaps even his disappointment, not at the fact that she had left him so easily, but that she had left Ted. That's how mercilessly great the responsibility of being a parent is, that you have to be able to take her for granted. Like food in the freezer. Like ballast in a boat.

"What . . . what do you want to hear?" his brother asked quietly.

"Something Dad used to play," Ted asked.

So his big brother played and Ted tried to conceal his envy. He would have liked to be able to play too, but who would have taught him? By the time he was big enough to sit at the piano, their dad was already sick.

"He always used to play this for Mom when she was angry with him," his big brother slurred, his lips slippery with alcohol but his fingers surprisingly assured.

It was a sad song. His brother sang hoarsely: "*Every day, a small eternity. Had I known how much the world had to offer, I would have asked for less.*"

When he was done, he said gently:

"Mom always forgave him when he played that. She used to come and sit on his lap. They never said 'I love you' to each other. They just said 'But, but, but.'"

"What?" Ted smiled, carefully, as if he was afraid of disturbing the incomprehensible magic of his brother actually telling him things.

"I don't know if you've ever noticed, but Mom isn't so good at expressing her feelings," his big brother smiled.

"Nooo," Ted said, sarcastically.

His big brother laughed, and it was wonderful.

"One time they were in the car, and Mom got angry because Dad complained about her driving, so she told him to shut the hell up. Then she lit a cigarette and almost drove off the road, so he had to reach over and grab the wheel, and that made her even angrier. And then Dad got so damn frustrated that he said: 'For God's sake, I LOVE you, but . . .'"

He fell silent. Ted whispered in astonishment:

"How do you know all this?"

"Dad told me. Before he got sick. He used to talk a lot. It's a shame you don't remember that. Actually, maybe that's good. Hell, maybe I'm actually a bit envious of the fact that you . . . don't remember."

Ted sipped his beer and touched a key without daring to press it.

"Was that the first time Dad told Mom that he loved her?"

His brother coughed.

"He told me it was probably the first time anyone ever said that to her. She didn't even say anything back. It was kind of too much for her. But that night, when they'd gone to bed, she whispered: 'But, but, but.' And after that they never said 'I love you.'"

"But, but, but," Ted whispered slowly down into his beer.

"But, but, but," his big brother repeated down into his.

He still had his accent from their home country, it was more noticeable when he was drunk, but Ted's was nearly gone. Slowly, slowly, their inheritance was being polished away.

"Does that hurt?" Ted asked, looking at his brother's battered knuckles, soaking in the bowl of ice.

His brother shook his head.

"It wasn't us who started it. There were some fucking idiots arguing with the Ox. We were just defending ourselves. I . . . don't start fights anymore."

He said it as if it was important to him that his little brother knew that.

"Play that song again," Ted asked.

So his brother played, and when he was finished he asked:

"Have you noticed that one of the basement steps is taller than the others? Dad used to trip over it EVERY time he went up or down. Mom used to go insane because he never looked where he was putting his feet. Sometimes she left things on the floor, boxes or forks or small buckets of water, anything at all, just to see if he would walk straight into them. And he stumbled straight into EVERY single damn one! Mom used to say he could walk through a damn minefield unharmed because he never lifted his feet. She used to call him 'the Worm.' So when he got home from work late, he would step on every creaking floorboard in the hall on purpose, so she would know he was home."

His brother fell silent, perhaps because he remembered that he had once thrown Ted down the basement staircase he was talking about, but his little brother just giggled.

"The Worm!" Ted repeated.

Then his brother smiled gratefully and went on:

"This house was the cheapest in the whole town when they bought it. It was practically falling down, of course, even worse than it is now . . . but one of the neighbors said it was so cheap because it was haunted. Dad thought that was hilarious, so he went around all the rooms calling to the ghosts, and Mom said: 'You know you're so annoying that even GHOSTS can't cope with you?' So then Dad started playing a game. He would wait until she wasn't expecting it, when she was brushing her teeth or cooking, and he would stand next to her and jump like he was terrified of something. And then she would jump too, of course. And then he'd say: 'I thought I saw a ghost.' She never learned. And he never got tired of it."

"I didn't know he was so funny," Ted whispered with embarrassment.

"He was seriously damn funny."

"I've never heard Mom laugh," Ted admitted.

His big brother probably didn't know how to respond to that. So he drank more beer and said:

"She's just tired, Ted. Everyone has had a day when they're so exhausted that they can hardly think, but she's been having that same damn day for the past ten years now. That's hard. She's done her best. She tried to make you and me tough, because soft people don't survive in this town. One time . . . hell . . . one time I got into a fight at school, and she was called in to see the principal, and the principal said I 'maybe needed male role models.' Can you imagine? What a damn psychopath. Dad wasn't even dead then, just sick. Do you know what Mom said?"

"What?"

"She said: 'Male role models? How well do you think that's worked out so far, purely historically, for you men?'"

"What did the principal say?"

"He was so taken aback that the next time I got into a fight, he didn't even call Mom."

Ted laughed, even though he shouldn't have. His brother had never known how to handle grief other than with anger. Who would have taught him?

"So Mom was funny too?" Ted asked.

"Really funny, when she wanted to be! One time she put rotten fish in the mailbox of a neighbor who was always complaining that you and I were too noisy! And she wasn't always this . . . this hard. When I was little I used to have nightmares, I would wake up screaming so hard I lost my voice. And she would come in with a blanket and pillow and lie down on the floor right in front of the door to my room. So the nightmares couldn't come in, she used to say."

Ted sat next to him wiping his eyes on his sleeve, then he asked:

"Tell me something else."

So his brother took a deep swig of beer and said:

"Dad told me that his favorite time of the evening was going round the house turning all the lights off. Because that's the sort of thing dads do, Dad said. Last of all he would go from room to room whispering: 'Good night, ghosts.'"

Ted sipped his beer, then suddenly brightened up.

"I . . . I remember that. I remember I used to lie awake in my bed waiting to hear that before I could get to sleep. It's the only thing I remember of his voice. Or . . . sometimes I think I just dreamed it."

His brother's red, battered fingers moved beneath his gnarled knuckle, and played a few scattered notes on the piano. Ted was so amazed that those hands were capable of both things: brutality and beauty.

"He sang pretty good, Dad."

"Why didn't he become a musician?" Ted asked, but regretted it at once, he could hear for himself how naive it sounded.

"That isn't a job," his brother replied calmly.

He meant "for us," that it wasn't a job for people like us, Ted realized that. Their dad had worked at the factory, just like their mom, to give their kids a better life. Trying to be a musician, following their passion, that sort of thing was for parents who only wanted to give themselves a better life.

Ted's gaze swept across the wall above the piano, he saw photographs of himself when he was little, until his eyes came to rest on another picture: his parents' wedding. No fancy clothes, a simple ceremony in the town hall, his mom was pregnant. But she was smiling in that picture, she was beautiful, she looked as if she was still dreaming about big things.

"Do you think it was romantic? When they fell in love?" he asked shyly.

It was stupid, of course. His brother snorted instinctively.

"What sort of damn question is that?"

"Sorry, sorry, sorry . . . ," Ted whispered at once, hating himself for ruining the magic, he should have known that real men didn't ask questions like that.

He huddled up on the edge of the stool, getting ready to be hit, but something far stranger happened: a little gust of wind. That's what happens when a hard man tries to stifle a sob. His brother didn't cry any tears, just let out a long, ragged exhalation. Then his voice was stern but his words soft:

"It isn't like it is in movies, Ted. It's different in real life. But Dad once told me, when he was really fucking drunk, that he and Mom weren't like two magnets. They were like two colors. Once they were mixed together, there was no way of separating them."

Ted had never, before or since, heard anything more romantic. He peered up at the wedding photograph, trying to focus, it would be a few more months before he admitted to his mother and brother that he really, really needed glasses.

"Tell me something else," he asked apprehensively.

His brother sighed. He tapped the top of the piano with the beer can. Smiled faintly.

"Dad always drank the same beer. He said Mom liked that, because men who never swap beer brands aren't very adventurous, so they don't swap wives either. When he got sick, Mom carried on buying beer every week. As if he might suddenly just get up and go get one."

That's an extra cruelty that cancer brings, Ted thought, when you're waiting for everything to go back to normal again. Until one day you realize that the illness has become the new normal.

"Did Dad like Mom's cooking?" he asked, without really knowing why, maybe just because the frozen meals in the freezer were the closest thing he had come to real tenderness from his mom in recent years.

"Are you kidding? He loved it! I think the whole reason she learned to cook was because she liked to see him eat," his brother grinned, then glanced at his little brother and added: "I think she feels like a good mom when she puts meals in the freezer for us, Ted. When she makes sure that we eat. That's probably the only time she feels like she's . . . enough."

Ted leaned over his beer as if it were a chasm. He asked:

"Do you think Dad was scared when he died?"

Rather than giving him a lie for an answer, he just said nothing for so long that it was an answer in itself. His breath sounded ragged again.

"The night Dad died, one of the nurses phoned home to us here. I suppose she wanted you and me to know right away, and I think she understood that Mom couldn't cope with . . . words."

More ragged breathing.

"What did she say? The nurse?" Ted wondered.

His big brother smiled.

"She said that Mom had very gently curled up on Dad's bed at the end. And that Dad died in her arms."

They said nothing more to each other after that, the brothers. They just sat there at the piano in the empty house, drinking their dad's beer and glancing at each other with their mom's eyes. When the cans were empty, Ted took them into the kitchen and rinsed them. Then he got a meal out of the freezer, ate it even though he wasn't hungry, and left his plate unwashed on the counter.

That evening he lay in his bed in the basement and heard his big brother stumble drunkenly through the rooms upstairs, stopping in every doorway and whispering good night to all the ghosts.

The night was warm, the basement window was open, Ted smelled his mom's cigarettes when she came home. She got out of her friend's car, sat down on the steps and inhaled deep drags, gathering the strength to go back to a life full of responsibility. She probably never knew how to explain that she loved her boys, and they had no words either, because who would have taught them? But when their mom walked into the house, she intentionally stepped on all the floorboards that she knew creaked, so they would know she was there. And when she went into the kitchen she saw the unwashed plate that Ted had left on the counter so that she would know he was full and that she was a good mother. So she washed it and felt like one, just for a moment.

When she lay in bed that night she heard a shuffling sound outside her bedroom door, then a small *thud*, it was the big brother, who had gone to sleep on the floor in front of the door to her room. So her nightmares couldn't come in.

Ted lay in his own bed in the basement and had almost fallen asleep when he heard a different noise at the window. It was barely a knock, just a scrape, and when he looked up he saw small red marks on the glass. Joar was sitting outside. His hands were covered in blood.

FORTY-FOUR

It's hard to tell a story, any story, but it's almost impossible if it's your own. You always start at the wrong end, always say too much or too little, always miss the most important parts.

That last part, about Joar and the blood, just tumbles out of Ted. He realizes at once that it's a mistake, of course, Louisa is sitting beside him on the rocks looking like she can't decide if she is moved or scared or angry. Mostly angry, from the sound of it.

"You said it was a love story! And it ends like THAT? What HAPPENED?" she snaps.

Stories are complicated, memories are merciless, our brains only store a few moments from the best days of our lives, but we remember every second of the worst.

"It's . . . twenty-five years ago," Ted says, as if he's trying to convince himself that it's nothing to cry over.

Louisa sobs furiously:

"Not for me! I wasn't there! For me, it's happening NOW!"

"I'm sorry," he whispers, and then it's as if everything happens again for him too.

The sun has come up, the world is waking, the day is starting. He pulls the towel more tightly around his shoulders, then he tells her everything. He tells her about the knife. That it was Ali who gave it to Joar that last winter, because she was the first to understand how everything would end. She couldn't imagine any other story except one where Joar's old man killed him, or the other way around. By the time summer came, no one else could either.

Ted tells how Joar hid the knife in the soil beneath the flowers in the tin box outside his window, but how he had to move it when his mom got suspicious. After that Joar kept the knife in his backpack, which was lying on the floor of his room the day his old man came in and saw the bird.

"A violent man is a sickness for all around him. Violence is a plague that spreads through everybody it comes into contact with . . . ," Ted says, as if he's trying to balance his feelings by talking formally, like a teacher, but it doesn't work. When he goes on, his voice is just fourteen years old again.

"Joar thought he was going to turn out like his old man. That violence is something you inherit. But that's wrong. Violence isn't a genetic illness, violence is a contagion, it passes from skin to skin. The heart gets infected. It's exhausting to always be angry when you're a child, constantly having to tense your body not to cry, because you know that if you start, you'll never be able to stop. In the end Joar just couldn't bear it. In the end he was prepared to do anything just so he could stop feeling everything all the time. And I remember thinking: when it happens, no one will be able to say it came as a surprise. Because everyone had always known: one day he would kill him."

Louisa can't breathe as Ted's face cracks, a broken, hesitant little smile that makes his gaze lose its focus, because he suddenly realizes how angry Joar would have been if he heard that.

"Joar would never have liked anyone to talk about him," Ted says quietly.

The only story Joar would ever have wanted to hear was of course the one about the artist and the painting, about a happy life and dreams coming true, because the only dreams Joar had were for someone else.

"But if you want to understand the painting, you have to understand Joar," Ted explains. "And if you want to understand him, you have to understand his mom. Because her story is his. But . . . Joar's old man? I intend to say as little as possible about that bastard."

He remembers how much blood there was on Joar's hands, as if he had dipped them in a barrel. He remembers his friend's eyes: desperate, terrified. He was sitting huddled up outside the window of Ted's basement room, holding out the crushed little box. He could hardly lift one arm, half his face was so red and so badly hurt that he couldn't open the eye on that side. He was shaking, so Ted was forced to climb halfway out through the window with his ear close, close to Joar's lips to hear.

Joar whispered that the bird had been lying in the box in his arms, defenseless, when his old man came into his room the first time. His mom had tried to stand between the man and the boy, as usual, but it was too late. His old man had already heard them laughing. He hadn't said anything, just took a couple of swigs of whiskey straight from the bottle and disappeared back into the kitchen. Then there was nothing but waiting.

"Anyone who hasn't seen real violence probably won't understand that, but the minutes between the beatings are the worst," Ted says, there on the rocks.

"Because you never know how many punches you're going to get," Louisa concludes, pulling the towel tighter around her shoulders.

Ted feels ashamed at that, because she probably knows more about violence than he does. But she nods for him to go on, so he tells her that the most evil thing about men like Joar's old man is that he wasn't evil all the time. Sometimes he was sober for weeks, then he and Joar's mom would go for long walks and talk about getting a dog, once he bought a tent so he and Joar could go on a fishing trip. Sometimes Joar got to hold the tools when his old man fixed the car, that was how the boy learned about engines. Some evenings the three of them all ate dinner like a normal family, and his old man would be attentive and charming, even funny. That was the worst thing Joar knew, when he heard one of the man's jokes and thought that that was where he had inherited his quick-wittedness from, because then he feared that he would get everything else too.

The good days were never good, they were a lie, they never lasted. There were just enough of them for his mom to believe that the bad ones were somehow her fault. When Joar was small he often used to sit on the toilet seat watching as she put her makeup on. He would sniff her perfume and ask, over and over again, how he smelled, terrified that he would smell like his old man. He wanted to smell like her.

"You smell like the best thing in the world, and the best thing in the world smells like you," his mom used to reply, but that didn't help the boy much.

His mom always used to get dressed up, even if she was only going to the supermarket.

"If you wear nice clothes, people forget what your face looks like," she used to say in front of the bathroom mirror.

"Your face is really nice," he would reply.

"Your face is really nice too," she replied, and then he replied sullenly:

"Mom, you once said I had a good singing voice, so you obviously can't be trusted!"

Then she laughed so hard that he had to run out, because there was no window in the bathroom.

When it was Joar's birthday he asked for aftershave, and her heart must have broken, because she probably thought children his age ought to be asking for a bicycle. Some mornings her arms hurt so badly that he had to help her put makeup over the last of her bruises. He did it so carefully and thoroughly, became almost as good at it as he was at skating, and that was something she could probably never forgive herself for. The amount of violence her boy had seen.

Of course, Joar's old man always promised not to do it again, but that only meant he always hit her as if it was his last chance. Sometimes he would cry and whisper that if she left him, he'd kill himself, but more often he yelled that he would kill her and the boy first. Most mornings he couldn't even remember who he had hit at all.

Joar got bigger and started to step between them, somewhere in the mathematics of cruelty, presumably, the boy hoped that his mom would get hit less then, but it just got worse. All they did was to try to protect each other, but neither of them could. They had nowhere to go, they were too small and the planet wasn't big enough for them to run from that man. The mornings after the worst days, Joar's mom would get up and put on her most beautiful clothes and Joar would play soccer during every break at school, so no one would ask where his injuries came from. Even so, the good days were worst of all, because there were always just enough of them for you to forget they were merely a countdown.

Joar had been sitting on the floor of his room with the bird and his mom, he had heard his old man laughing drunkenly at something on television. What made his old man's eyes turn black after that and sent him charging up into his son's room isn't important, it could have been anything at all. He had no damn fuse, that man, no rhyme nor reason. No logic. The only thing cruelty like his wants is to cause as much damage as possible. Why? No one knows. Sometimes it was enough that someone else looked happy, just for a single moment.

When Joar sat there outside Ted's window with bloody hands and told him everything, he couldn't stop the tears running down his face, and that made him shake with fury. Because that was precisely what his old man wanted that night, to see his power over the boy. The man hadn't even looked at the box when he tore it out of his son's hands. Joar's mother's scream must have been heard across the whole block, but what difference did that make? How many screams must the neighbors have learned to ignore over the years?

Joar's old man had just stared at him, his foot crushing the box and the remains of the twigs and leaves and life inside it without breaking eye contact with his son for a second. Such is cruelty.

Ted never found out exactly what happened in the room after that, and what little he did know he didn't want to tell Louisa, because as little as possible should be said about that bastard. But there was a knife in a backpack, there was a boy on the floor, there was a mother with her arms around the neck of a man who wouldn't stop hitting.

When Joar stood outside Ted's window later that night and held out the box, Ted's hands ended up covered in blood too.

"Hide it," Joar whispered.

"Come inside," Ted pleaded, but Joar shook his head and looked down at his hands in astonishment, as if he was wondering who they belonged to.

"I have to get home before he notices I'm gone," he whispered.

Then he turned around quickly and went out into the darkness. Ted called out without thinking:

"I love you!"

Joar stopped, just for a moment, without replying and without turning around. Then he ran.

Ted's voice is barely audible there on the rocks now, Louisa has to move closer to hear about Joar sneaking back into his home. His old man was snoring on the sofa in the living room, passed out drunk with his son's blood on his shirt. In Joar's room his mother was on her knees, scrubbing the floor. It smelled so good in there that Joar felt dizzy. He had had two small bars of soap on his bookcase, Ali had given them to him as a Christmas present, she had stolen them from a shop specially for him. Obviously they were far too nice for Joar to wash himself with, so he used to just sit in bed smelling them when he was unhappy. They hardly weighed anything, barely as much as a bird.

After his old man had come into his room the first time that evening, then gone out again, Joar and his mother had quickly wrapped the soaps in a sock and placed them among the twigs and leaves in the box. When his old man had drunk himself angry enough and stormed through the door the second time, full of whiskey and bitterness, he had torn the box out of his son's hands and Joar and his mother had screamed. His old man had just laughed, that's how predictable his hatred was. He hadn't even looked in the box before he threw it to the floor and stomped on it, he had been too preoccupied looking at Joar, too eager to see him broken at the bird's death. And the boy had cried, just as the man wanted, but not about the bird, but about the cruelty. His old man couldn't tell the difference in his tears, too stupid to realize that there could be one.

When the man was finished stomping on the box he proceeded to hit his son and his wife all around the room. When he had finally exhausted himself and staggered back out to the sofa, Joar had crawled up from the floor and opened the window. The tin edges of the window boxes were razor-sharp, and he had been shaking so much he cut his hands. When he picked up the bird he'd hidden in the loose soil beneath the plants, he got blood on its wings, and when he put it back in the crushed remains of the box, he got blood on that too. But the bird was breathing. He had carried it to Ted and hurried back. And a life was saved.

He helped his mom scrub the floor, their faces bruised and their hearts broken. Even so, they were both smiling, because a small bird was a big victory over an eternal tyrant. Joar took deep breaths of the smell of the soap and whispered into his mom's hair: "I love you."

"How can I be so lucky?" she whispered.

That night they slept next to each other in Joar's bed, she with the boy in her arms, the boy with the backpack in his. His old man was passed out on the sofa. The next morning when Joar woke up everything smelled burnt.

His old man had been picked up by a workmate at dawn, still too drunk to make his own way to work, leaving just silence and smoke behind. Joar rubbed his eyes hard and stumbled out into the kitchen, confused. There stood his mother, in fresh makeup and with a look of embarrassment in her eyes: "I tried to bake muffins. I think they got a bit burnt . . ."

Burnt? They were cremated, Joar thought, but of course he didn't say that.

Early one morning at the end of July they set the bird free down at the pier. It had stayed at Ted's for a week or so, but Joar had been there every day to feed it seeds and worms.

There were five of them. That had been Ali's idea. Of course at first Joar's mother thought they were joking when they rang the doorbell, but then she had run and put her makeup on, and her prettiest high-heeled shoes. Even though Joar had explained again and again: "We're going to a PIER, Mom! By the SEA! We're not going to set the bird free in a NIGHTCLUB!"

She had taken her shoes off and walked the last bit down to the water barefoot, almost ceremoniously, and said proudly to her son: "Am I the first grown-up who's been allowed to come here with you?"

And Joar had replied tenderly: "You're not a grown-up, Mom."

She hadn't met his friends many times, yet she still knew all about them. When Joar was out of earshot, she had whispered to Ted: "He brags about all of you all the time!"

Ali heard that, unfortunately, and then she felt obliged to run and hit Joar really hard on the arm so he would hit her back. So that everyone would think that the tears in her eyes were because of that.

"Are you crying? I didn't hit you that damn hard!" Joar muttered.

"Shut up," Ali sobbed, she loved birds almost as much as she loved boys who loved birds.

"Can I ask something?" Joar's mother asked once they were standing on the pier.

"Not now, Mom," Joar said, but his mom asked anyway:

"Why doesn't anyone adopt birds? I mean . . . you can buy birds and dogs, and you can adopt dogs, but you can't adopt birds?"

"Who the hell adopts dogs, Mom?" Joar groaned.

Then Ali, friend of all animals, snapped:

"Anyone who isn't an idiot! You shouldn't buy dogs because there are so many homeless dogs!"

"How do you know they're homeless? Maybe they just don't want to live in a house!" Joar retorted.

"You idiot! Do you think dogs ought to live on the street?"

"Okay, so go to the jungle and adopt a lion, then! Why should lions be homeless?"

"Lions don't even live in *jungles*, you idiot!" she shouted.

"I'm not a fucking idiot, you fucking idiot!" he shouted back.

"LOOK!" Ted cried out.

And that was when the bird took off from the artist's hands. What a moment in life. First it just lay still between the artist's fingers sleepily for a long time, as if it had been told it was time to go to school. But then, without warning, it suddenly raised its head. Spread its wings.

"And then it flew off," Ted says dreamily on the rocks.

"Wow," Louisa says, entirely without sarcasm, which is pretty remarkable for her.

"It looped around the pier, hovered above the sea, looked over its wing for a second as if . . . this sounds stupid . . . but it felt like it was looking at Joar and his mom."

What a second that was, for everyone who saw it. What a damn second. The artist did something wonderful, which no one had ever heard before: he cheered. He jumped up and down on the pier and just screamed out loud with joy. How many reasons do you get to do that in an entire life? The sun broke through the clouds, it was a perfect moment, so obviously the stupid bird had to spoil everything.

It had gone about two hundred feet out over the water when it turned in a big semicircle and flew back. It flew over them toward the town and the apartment blocks.

"WRONG DIRECTION!" Ali yelled, as if it might come back and apologize.

"Maybe it isn't the wrong direction for him," Joar's mom said tentatively.

"How do you know it's a boy?" Ali asked.

"Because it's flying in the wrong direction," Joar's mom smiled.

"Typical boy," the artist said.

Oh, how they all laughed then. Apart from Joar, of course, who just spun around with his eyes looking up at the sky and sighed:

"It can fly anywhere it wants in the whole world, and it chooses to fly back to this fucking town?"

His mother stood beside him and thought for a long time before she murmured: "I think perhaps it flew back to its friends, darling. You would have done the same."

They stood in silence for several heartbeats and considered this. Then Ali got restless and yelled:

"Come on! Let's go swimming!"

Twenty-five years later, on the rocks by the sea, Ted lets the towel slide off his shoulders. He folds it neatly and puts it carefully in his suitcase, sitting next to the box containing the painting. Then he says to Louisa:

"We all jumped off the pier. That was the last time I swam in the sea with my friends."

FORTY-FIVE

Ted's head rocks slowly back and forth. Louisa thinks he looks like that author he had told her about, the woman who was overwhelmed with grief. He clears his throat in embarrassment when he notices that she's staring, then he reaches for his pants, takes something out of the pocket, and holds it out to Louisa. It's the drawing of the artist that she had left on the train.

"No, don't give me that, it was a present for you," she says, wounded.

He nods.

"I know. I want it back, but not until we get where we're going."

She hesitates, then reluctantly puts the drawing in her backpack.

"Okay. Until we get there."

"I'm serious! I want it back. One day it'll be worth millions!" he insists.

"Sure!" she laughs, as if it were a joke.

Ted looks at his wrist, where his watch should have been, then he looks at the sun instead.

"I think we'll be in time to catch the next train."

"How do you know that?" she wonders.

"You can tell from the sun roughly what time it is."

"No, I mean: How do you know when the next train leaves? Have you learnt the timetable by heart, or what?"

"Yes," he says, as if this were normal behavior.

"You're really weird."

"Thanks. Same to you."

She snorts and stands up, and he does the same. They go off in different directions and each finds a large tree to get changed behind. When the first drop lands on Ted's hair, he doesn't realize what it is because his skin is already so damp, but then he hears the patter on the treetops and Louisa crying out:

"TED! IT'S RAINING! THE PAINTING . . ."

Ted looks at the box and watches with growing panic as drop after drop falls from the sky, leaving small black marks. For a moment he seeks shelter under the tree, like people do in movies, but that doesn't help at all. Trees are far less loyal in real life. So he runs, with his suitcase and the box in his arms, slipping and stumbling like a greedy pigeon with a sandwich that's far too big. Louisa rushes up to his side, throwing her backpack on as she runs, then takes the box from him. By the time they reach the shopping street where they broke into the sporting good shop, their feet are splashing on the ground, soon their breathing is coming in gasps and their rib cages are blast furnaces, but they don't stop until they reach the train station and have a roof over them.

"Is . . . it . . . okay?" Louisa gasps as Ted peers down inside the box.

He nods, exhausted, and slumps down onto a bench.

"I'm really . . . really . . . sick of running."

"It's crazy . . . that you're so bad at it . . . even though you do it so often," she gasps back.

They don't have time to say more before the train arrives. They struggle on board, earning unhappy looks from the other passengers, even though the rain has actually washed the worst of the dirt from their clothes. Ted sinks into the seat and closes his eyes, falls asleep almost at once. When he wakes up, Louisa is asleep on his shoulder. He looks out the window and exclaims:

"Wake up! Louisa, wake up! We're getting off here!"

She sits up in panic and shouts out loud:

"I WASN'T ASLEEP! I'M READY! WHAT? WHAT THE HELL DO YOU WANT?"

She waves her fists at Ted before her brain remembers who he is.

"OW!" Ted hisses when she accidentally pokes him hard in the cheek.

"Sorry, I . . . What's happening? Where are we?" she asks in alarm.

He nods at the platform outside the window and suddenly smiles secretively.

"Come on. I'm going to show you something I think you'll like."

They get off the train, and she sits on a bench with the painting and their bags while he goes and buys tickets. It takes ages, when he finally comes back it's already afternoon.

"You've been gone forever. Did you have to travel back in time and invent the train or something?" she asks.

Ted lowers his voice, sudden terror in his eyes.

"There are policemen here, checking the identity of all the passengers. I heard them saying that two men were attacked a few stations from here, that they were beaten with an iron pipe so that one of the men had his arm broken . . ."

"ATTACKED? They were the ones who attacked US!" Louisa shouts.

"Shhhhh!" Ted begs her.

"What are we going to do?" she whispers, panicking when she sees men in uniform approaching.

All her life she's been taught to run from those men, but now it's too late, and she should have known better. She's relaxed too much, tricked herself into thinking she belongs in Ted's world. She doesn't, she never will.

"Just act normal! Or, you know, don't act normal for you. Act normal for normal people," Ted hisses.

"Sure! It's not like I'm on the run from a foster home, and carrying a world-famous painting worth a fortune, and traveling with a strange man whose last name I don't even know, or anything like that! Just act normal!" Louisa hisses back.

"Just be quiet and smile," he says sternly.

So she does, which is probably the first time in their entire relationship that she has followed instructions, and of course that's a mistake too. They make it to the train, they're just on the steps, for a moment they both think they're safe. But Louisa should have known better.

"YOU THERE! STOP!" a voice behind them yells.

They turn around to meet the eyes of an angry man in uniform.

"Tickets and identification," he says, like an order, not like a question.

Louisa kneels down and quickly searches her backpack for her passport, panic rushing through her body when she can't find it.

"It was right here, right here . . . ," she whispers anxiously on the ground.

She hears the man talking angrily over her head. She can't even register the words, but she's heard voices like that thousands of times before, full of promises of violence. She knows he can see the guilt in her darting eyes and trembling fingers. Where IS that damn passport? Her stupid brain should know, but it starts thinking about Fish instead, how she always told Louisa that a passport is proof that you exist, that you're a somebody. But the backpack is empty now, and Louisa's face is burning, and Fish was wrong, her brain screams. Louisa has always been a nobody. She will always mess everything up. So she acts on instinct, it's too late to save herself now, but maybe she can draw the policeman's attention and give Ted time to get away from here? It's stupid, instincts often are, society is not built for teenage brains full of fight-or-flight responses. She closes her backpack and clenches her fists and gets herself ready to run.

"Going north? You live there?" she hears the policeman ask just then, and it confuses her, because he sounds like he's in the middle of a conversation.

"Yes," she hears Ted answer, with surprising calm.

"Are you and the girl traveling together?" the policeman asks.

"Yes. She's my daughter."

It's the best lie Ted has ever told.

"What happened to your face?" the policeman wants to know.

"I fell down some stairs," Ted answers.

It would have made Louisa laugh if she weren't so terrified. But it's only as she looks up that she realizes the policeman isn't even looking at her, he's only looking at Ted. Louisa can't even hear the rest of the questions over the loudness of her own breathing, but eventually the policeman hands Ted his passport back with a short nod, and leaves. Just like that. Louisa stares at Ted like he's just performed black magic. He looks scared, but also insulted.

"What happened? What did he say?" Louisa whispers in shock.

"He said the police stopped a drunk driver and his friend a few stations from here. And to get out of being arrested, apparently the drunk driver told them he was driving to the hospital because he and his friend had been attacked and beaten with iron pipes by a . . . gang."

"Gang?" Louisa repeats.

"Yes. Because apparently, those men didn't want to admit even to the police that they'd been beaten by a girl," Ted sighs.

"So then why did the police stop us?"

"They didn't. They stopped me. The men claimed that the gang fled on a train going in this direction. So the police are talking to everyone around here who looks . . . suspicious."

Louisa's face lights up like that's the nicest compliment she's ever gotten, to not look suspicious.

"So the policeman thought *you* looked like you could be a gang member, but as soon as he heard your obnoxious way of talking, he understood that you weren't?" she smiles.

"It's not funny, Louisa, we could have been arrested," he insists.

"Maybe you joined a gang while you were in prison?" she laughs.

"Stop it," he mutters.

"Maybe it was a library gang? Maybe you beat the other gangs with the power of knowledge?"

Ted leans down on the ground and picks up her passport. It had just fallen out of her bag.

"You need to keep hold of this," he says, like an annoyed dad would, to change the subject.

"I know," she says, still grinning.

"I mean it! You need to take things seriously!" he snaps.

She falls silent, ashamed.

"I'm sorry. I know. I need to keep hold of the passport. It's the only proof that I exist," she hears herself answer, voice suddenly trembling.

He stops and looks at her then, with softer eyes, and shakes his head slowly.

"Is that what you think?"

"Fish always said so."

He shakes his head again, with greater determination.

"You're proof enough, Louisa. Every time you draw or paint something, you're proof enough. Now come on, I've got something to show you."

There's another train standing at the platform opposite, and when he leads her on board she looks like someone who has just tasted chocolate for the first time.

"Beds? On a train?" she whispers in astonishment.

"It's a sleeper train," Ted nods.

But that isn't the best thing. He shows her their compartment, with a bed for each of them and little curtains to draw, and something absolutely fantastic: a lock on the door.

As soon as Louisa's head hits the pillow she's asleep, she hasn't slept so soundly since she was sleeping next to Fish. Ted falls asleep too, even though Louisa snores. When they wake up again it's dark, the train is moving, they've slept the day away.

"Are you awake?" Louisa wonders in the gloom when she hears his breathing change.

"Yes," he says, thinking that you never have to wonder if Louisa is awake, because if she isn't asking questions, she's asleep.

"Can I ask you something?"

"Can I stop you?"

"It's been a really long time since you went to the toilet," she says.

"That isn't a question," Ted mutters.

"You peed in the sea, didn't you?"

"No," he lies.

She laughs so hard that the bunk creaks.

"Can I ask something else?"

"Preferably not," he says, but of course that doesn't make any difference.

"What happened to Joar's knife?"

Ted is glad the light isn't on then. The world stands still outside the window, the train thunders through the night as if everyone on board is on the run, his lips chase each other in an effort to stop trembling. Then he replies:

"The knife was in his backpack. Joar had come up with a plan. He was going to wait until his mom wasn't home, because he knew that she'd try to stop him if she . . ."

"Wait! Wait!" Louisa suddenly pleads, and changes her mind, muttering: "I shouldn't have asked. I should have just let you finish the story with you going swimming at the pier and setting the bird free. That was a perfect ending. When you were all still happy."

"Yes," she hears Ted reply.

She thinks for a whole minute before she decides:

"Okay . . . but before you tell the ending, tell me this first: How did you get the money for paint and brushes and everything for the painting?"

The train passes an illuminated platform, and in the cones of light she sees Ted's teeth glint as he smiles.

"Well, we most certainly didn't sell any stolen bicycles."

FORTY-SIX

Of course it had been Ali's idea, Ted explains on the sleeper train, that they should steal bicycles and sell them. Joar was already something of an expert at that, he had sold his first stolen bikes in the schoolyard when he was just eleven years old. Unfortunately, the police had appeared and really didn't think that was a suitable business idea, because the police were really bad at encouraging young enterprise, if you asked Joar. The only reason he'd gotten away with it was that he was so small they didn't think he was capable of a crime like that, which had annoyed him so much that he had almost confessed just for the sake of it. The artist had stopped him, of course, and after that he let Joar steal the occasional bicycle, but never let him sell them again. It was too dangerous.

But that summer before they turned fifteen, Ali thought it was definitely worth another attempt.

"What are they going to do? Throw us in prison? We're like . . . still kids!" she groaned.

That was the day after they set the bird free.

"I think they have prisons for young people," Ted said.

"Ha! How would they even keep Joar locked up? He could squeeze out between the bars!" Ali grinned.

Under normal circumstances they would have had a fight after that, the pair of them, but Joar was so covered in bruises and swelling that Ali didn't want to make it worse. So she just stuck her tongue out and he gave her the finger and she laughed. Then the artist said shyly:

"No. Please. If you steal bicycles to buy paint, then it will sort of . . . be felt in the painting. I don't want you to become thieves for my sake."

So that was the end of the discussion. They spent the rest of the day watching superhero movies in Ted's room, it was raining outside and they didn't have any more ideas. Ted and the artist glanced at Ali's backpack from time to time, but she just mimed "wait" to them. They had to wait several hours until Joar went to the bathroom before they could bring out what they had been hiding. When he came back down the basement stairs, Ali sang "Happy Birthday" at the top of her lungs, and when he covered his ears she threatened to do it again. He tried to look like he was bothered, even a little irritated, but the truth was that he had never believed they would remember his birthday. So he didn't tell them that it was actually tomorrow.

Ted held out a bottle of aftershave. It had belonged to his dad, but had been sitting in a cupboard unopened. Ted had carefully wiped the dust off and tied a little ribbon around it, and the artist had written a card.

"Hope you think it smells good," Ted said.

"Yeah, really, because you smell like a pile of garbage," Ali said, but in a way that if you had heard the words in a language you didn't understand, you would have sworn she was saying "I love you."

Joar held the bottle as if it were a bird. The artist reached down into his backpack and took out a small bunch of flowers he had stolen from an old lady's garden.

"They're not stolen," he said. "They're adopted."

Ali and Ted laughed. Joar smelled the flowers and muttered: "You're all garbage."

He wiped his eyes angrily with the back of his hand. He couldn't use the aftershave yet, because he had so many cuts on his body that it stung too much, but he would sleep with the bottle in his arms that night.

The next morning his friends would wait for him at the crossroads until the sun was high in the sky, but he wouldn't come.

It was a dazzlingly beautiful day, cloud-free and windless, all the colors of the sky and earth seemed sharper than the day before. Unless that was just how the friends would remember it. Sometimes we remember the last moments before a great catastrophe as more beautiful than they actually were.

Ali got worried and walked toward Joar's house. She saw his parents set off to work, his old man stumbling out to a workmate's car to go to the harbor, his mom hurrying off in the other direction in full makeup. She looked so happy, Ali thought, she looked like she had a real bounce in her step. That was the last time any of the friends saw Joar's mom like that. When Ali rang the doorbell to their apartment, no one answered. Joar was gone.

So Ali went back to the crossroads, lay down on the grass beside Ted and the artist, and they did the only thing they could do: wait. They lay on the grass until they ran out of both cookies and jokes, but he still didn't appear. Half the morning disappeared. To pass the time, Ali eventually asked, in that perfectly unconcerned way that only she had mastered, why boys had two testicles. She had evidently been thinking about this for a long time, but neither the artist nor Ted had a particularly good answer. Ted said instead that once when he was little, his big brother had tricked him into believing that men should really have three. Several anxious months followed for Ted before he found out the truth.

"But why *do* you have two, then?" Ali repeated.

"Typically smart of men to have their own spare parts," Ted smiled.

"Typical of men to need spare parts," Ali pointed out.

"COME ON!" a voice behind them called out.

They spun around on the grass and caught sight of Joar. He was coming from the wrong direction, not from his house but from town. His bruises were glinting in the sunlight, but he looked so proud that you hardly noticed them. It looked like he was a foot taller than yesterday.

"Come on!" he repeated, and set off ahead of them.

"Where to?" the others wondered, but he didn't answer, so they just hurried after him.

Ali talked all the way, about things no one would remember

afterward but which were very funny at the time. Ted would remember that everything smelled of sun, and that he didn't know if there was a special word for that.

"What . . . what are we doing here?" the artist eventually said, anxiously.

Only then did Ted and Ali look up and realize where Joar had led them. They were standing outside the little shop in town that sold art supplies. Joar never explained his plan to any of them, it hadn't occurred to him that it might be a problem, so of course it immediately became a pretty big problem. If anyone had asked Ali, she would probably have said that it was typical of a boy to believe that everyone could read his thoughts simply because he had so few, but in Joar's defense, she probably wouldn't have listened if he had explained what he was thinking in advance anyway.

He took the artist into the shop while Ted and Ali stood guard, somewhat confused, outside, not that Joar had asked them to, but because they realized it might be needed. Once the artist realized what Joar was actually planning to do in there, he panicked and tried to persuade him not to, because he refused to let Joar become a thief for his sake, but Joar had had enough of discussion by then.

"Just show me what you need! The summer's almost over, damn it! That picture needs to get painted!" he demanded impatiently.

So the artist nervously looked around the shop and pointed. His face got redder and redder as Joar picked up more and more things, and when they approached the shop assistant behind the counter, the artist's whole body was shaking so badly that if he had been holding milk, it would have been butter. Ali and Ted were standing outside, feeling more and more nervous, knowing damn well from experience that a security guard or police officer would show up at any moment. So when Joar and the artist finally came out the door with their arms full of paints, brushes, and canvases, their friends quickly grabbed everything from their hands and ran.

Seeing as they were geniuses, of course they both ran off in different directions, but unfortunately, the geniuses chose the opposite directions and ran into each other. Ali leapt to her feet, so panic-stricken that she didn't look where she was going, and ran straight into a lamp-post. Ted staggered to his feet, still dizzy from colliding with Ali, and managed to get halfway down the street before he realized no one was chasing him. Then he stopped so abruptly that his body was caught by surprise and he fell over again.

Joar was still standing calmly outside the shop, yelling: "What the hell are you idiots doing?"

It had been a good day. Early, early that morning Joar had been woken up by his mom, one hand gently on his shoulder and the other holding a finger to her lips.

"Shhh," she had whispered, and nodded for him to follow her.

They had snuck out of the apartment while Joar's old man lay snoring, hungover, on the sofa. Joar and his mom hurried down to the basement and over to a small storage compartment. Right at the back, where his old man never went, his mom had hidden her birthday present for Joar. She didn't own anything of any value except her ice skates, which she had been given by her own mother. So she had sold them to buy a bicycle.

Joar had had many bicycles in his life, but that morning was the first time he had one of his own. In the light of dawn he had ridden it around, around, around the whole block. He had never felt so free, so big, so full of possibilities. That was why he hadn't shown up at the crossroads to meet his friends all morning. He had cycled so fast that the wind tugged at his hair, he had let go of the handlebars and ridden with his arms outstretched toward the horizon, he had pedaled all the way into town before stopping. There he had sat on a bench and waited until the sporting goods store opened, and then he lifted the bike onto his shoulder and carried it inside, because if you left a bicycle out in the street in this town, any old thief might steal it. Joar argued with the man in the shop for a long time before they came to an agreement, then Joar had run all the way home to the crossroads, calling breathlessly to his friends: “COME ON!”

Some time later he was standing outside the art supplies shop and shaking his head in disbelief. Only when Ted and Ali got up from the ground and realized that no one was chasing them did they see that the artist was standing next to Joar holding something in his hand: a store receipt.

Joar grinned and exclaimed:

“What do you think I am? A THIEF or something?”

Joar had sold many bicycles in his life, but that day was the first time he had sold his own. And that was the money they used to buy the canvas and paint that would change the world.

“Good ending, that, too,” Louisa whispers in the darkness of the train carriage.

“Yes,” Ted says.

She doesn’t ask him to tell her anything more, so he doesn’t. They just lie in their bunks, one of them on his way home, the other on her way farther away than she has ever been.

“Good night, ghosts,” Louisa whispers.

“Good night, good night,” Ted replies.

FORTY-SEVEN

It's hard to tell a story, particularly when it doesn't end happily for everyone. Ted dreams of the sound of a human head being struck with terrifying force, so loud that it must have been heard through the walls. In the dream all the hard men from the harbor stand in silence outside Joar's house, with shock and shame in their eyes, and at the crossroads where Ted and his friends always promised "tomorrow" to each other, the sound of sirens echoes.

He wakes up with a slight jolt, sweaty and scared. He blinks against the light. Louisa is sitting on her bunk, wide-eyed as she gazes happily out through the train window, because now they're close to the sea. She turns and notes that he's awake, and asks at once:

"Are we there yet?"

"Soon."

"How soon is soon?"

"Fairly soon."

"You'd have been a really annoying dad," she snorts.

"Thanks," he smiles.

She hesitates before asking:

"Do you want to tell the end of the story now?"

He thinks for a long time before shaking his head.

"No. Not yet. But I can tell you a story about the time we stole a car, if you like?"

If she likes?

So as the train approaches the town that took his entire childhood, Ted tells her about the days when the artist painted the picture. How his friends sat beside him in Ted's basement until they felt dizzy from the smells of the paint and turpentine and mineral spirits, or whatever all the jars and bottles contained. The artist tested different types of paint, different techniques, most of them in ways he had probably only guessed, because he had no teachers. One day he would go to a fancy art school and realize that he had already made up everything they taught there, only backward. His brain wasn't normal, one day the world would be grateful for that.

Ted often went up and down the stairs in those days, fetching food from the kitchen, and one evening when he was warming up some lasagna for Ali he heard his big brother playing the piano. Then Ted fetched one of their dad's beers for him, and realized that it was the very last one. When his big brother took it, and realized the same thing, he went and got two glasses. They drank a silent toast at the piano.

"Do you know what Dad's favorite meal was?" Ted's big brother asked when he smelled the lasagna.

"Lasagna?" Ted guessed.

"No, no, cold grilled cheese sandwiches. Like, grilled cheese sandwiches, but after they've been in the fridge overnight. That was the only thing Dad knew how to make when he met Mom. Cold grilled cheese sandwiches, and cheese puffs that have been in an open bag for three days and gone a little stale, and flat Coca-Cola . . . he loved that. I mean, can you believe what a waste it was that Mom got so good at cooking for *that* guy's sake?"

Ted laughed.

"Tell me something else," he asked.

His big brother grinned. He wasn't even particularly drunk, but he still went on:

"When I was little, Dad and I used to hide behind the piano here and jump out and scare Mom."

"Did she get angry?" Ted smiled.

"Are you kidding? She hated it when Dad scared her, so he did it all the time, the moron. One time he jumped out of the hall closet when she was holding a shoehorn, and she got so scared she smashed it into a mirror. She was furious, because now she was going to have seven years' bad luck, she said, and Dad just went: 'If I hadn't ducked, you'd have knocked my TEETH out!' and Mom went: 'Well, that would only have been bad luck for YOU!'"

When his big brother finished the story, Ted asked tentatively if he could hear it again. He giggled just as much the second time. That probably wasn't a bad feeling at all, if you were a big brother who hadn't felt like a good big brother for a very long time.

"Do you want to have kids?" Ted asked out of nowhere.

"Kids? Hell. I don't know. I probably wouldn't be a very good dad," his big brother mumbled.

"Yes, you would," Ted said confidently, and then his brother played a whole song because he had such a lump in his throat.

"You'd be a better dad, Ted. Dad always said you were the smart one in the family. No one knows where you get it from," he said after a while.

"No, I'm an idiot," Ted whispered.

"Don't say that!" his brother retorted in a flash, suddenly upset in a way that was a big compliment.

"Sorry," Ted said, without really knowing what he was apologizing for.

"When you were at preschool, one of the teachers said you were the smartest in the whole group. On the way home that day, Dad said you'd be the first person in the family to go to university," his big brother said, unable to hide either his envy or his pride.

"I don't even know how you go about going to university. That isn't for people like us. It costs money! I'm not—" Ted protested, but he was interrupted by feet padding into the kitchen.

It was Ali, she had been sitting in the basement waiting for lasagna, and in the end hunger had got the better of caution. She looked horrified when she saw Ted's big brother, and just snatched the lasagna out of the microwave and hurried back downstairs, like a mouse with a piece of cheese. Ted's big brother looked at her, then at Ted, and said:

"I'm glad you've got good friends."

"Me too," Ted nodded.

"Are you going out with any of them?" his big brother asked, and Ted almost fell off the stool.

No one else would probably ever understand that this was the most loving and accepting thing his brother had ever said to Ted. That he didn't just ask if Ted was going out with Ali, but if he was going out with any of them.

Ted shook his head. His brother played another song before asking:

"What do your friends think you should be when you get older?"

Ted rolled his beer glass carefully between his hands, making waves in the foam.

"Teacher," he admitted.

His big brother nodded and said:

"If you go to university and become a teacher, I could imagine having kids. Because then my kids would have someone to look up to."

Ted drank his beer and replied:

"You're enough to look up to."

That was the first time his big brother had ever been told that. That he was enough.

Life is long, but it moves at high speed, a single step here or there can be enough to ruin everything. A few months after that evening, Ted's big brother would be on his way to a party with the Ox. He would never get there. Perhaps it was fate, perhaps coincidence, perhaps the big brother would just remember what his little brother had said, the bit about picking friends that are better than you. Perhaps knowing that you are enough for one person goes a long way. So, suddenly, he would ask the Ox to stop the car, get out and walk home again. The Ox would be furious, and would stand in the road yelling at him, but the big brother would never turn around. Later that night there would be trouble at the party, the Ox and a few of his other friends would assault another guy so badly that he almost died. They would all end up in prison. Not long after that, Ted's big brother would meet a girl and fall in love. It's a long life, but fast, one single step in the right direction can be enough.

Ted left his brother at the piano that evening after they had drunk the last of their dad's beer, he went back down to the basement, stumbling over that one step that was just a bit higher than all the others. He didn't lift his feet up when he walked either, that was something he had inherited. It made him proud.

His room was totally silent when he walked in. His heart sank straight down into his stomach then, because something must have happened, something must be terribly wrong. He stared at Ali and Joar, but they were staring at something else.

"What's ha—" Ted gasped anxiously, but Joar interrupted him.

"He's finished. He's finished the painting."

And there they were. Three teenagers on a pier by the sea, almost hidden in all the blue, so if the picture had been hanging on a white wall in an exclusive art auction, rich adults would have been able to walk right past without seeing them. But now they were alive forever: Joar, Ali, Ted.

"You have to sign the painting," Ali whispered.

The artist hesitated. Then he painted small skulls and wrote a name that wasn't his own in the bottom corner.

"What are you doing? You have to write your *own* name!" Ali insisted, but he shook his head shyly.

"If anyone sees the painting, I don't want them to know who I am. I only want to be who I really am . . . with you."

So right then, at the age of fourteen, he came up with his artist name: *C. Jat*. The initials of Christian, Joar, Ali, and Ted. They probably should have known then that he was much too fragile to become famous. But it was too late, the picture was far too beautiful not to carry him around the world.

"Why didn't you paint yourself on there?" Ali asked.

"I did. I'm sort of like all this . . . everything around you," the artist whispered.

"Damn alien," Joar said, and then he said something altogether incredible: "I love you."

"I love you and I believe in you," the artist replied.

"I believe in you and I . . . I . . . the other stuff too," Ali mumbled.

But Ted said nothing, because when he looked at that painting he couldn't breathe. Twenty-five years later, he still can't.

"It was Joar's idea that we should steal a car," he tells Louisa on the train now.

"What for?" she smiles expectantly.

"Because he was in a hurry to show us something before the summer came to an end," Ted says, and his voice is both exultant and sad. Both happy and unhappy. Because it's that sort of story, with that sort of ending.

So they stole the car. It wasn't a great idea, it really wasn't. Admittedly, it was Joar's old man's car that they stole, so it probably wasn't exactly a real "theft," because Joar had sat in that car thousands of times with his mom. In fact, the only thing missing on this particular occasion was her. Sure, Joar shouldn't have been driving the car that day, because he was fifteen years old and had no driver's license, but if we're being strictly honest here, his mom didn't have a driver's license either, and she drove all the time.

The apartment was empty when Joar ran home, his mom had taken the bus to work and his old man had gotten a lift to the harbor with a workmate. It was almost his summer vacation now, so the old man was drunk every day, as if alcoholism was a sport and he was warming up for a big competition, and even he realized he couldn't drive his car under those circumstances. Even so, Joar's mom didn't dare take the car, she was too scared of getting in an accident, not that she was worried about getting hurt, but she was worried about the car getting hurt. This close to her husband's summer vacation, she couldn't afford a single risk that would make him angry, the man could explode from the slightest cross-draft.

The car keys were always kept in a jar on the counter. Not that his old man ever put them there, but his mom always found where he'd left them and returned them to the jar, so that he wouldn't be furious the following day when they weren't there. Sometimes she had to look for hours, in his jackets and pants and under the bed, some nights she and Joar would walk around the lawn outside the house with flashlights. It was always his mom who found them, Joar never understood how, but she would just smile proudly and say: "Moms find everything, darling."

So Joar took the keys and packed his best friends into the car and drove off without saying where they were going.

"Joar, I don't think this is a good idea," the artist felt obliged to point out from the back seat.

"Definitely not one of your best!" Ali agreed, looking anxiously at Joar, who could hardly reach the pedals as they reversed in the parking lot.

"You don't even know what the idea *is*!" Joar said defensively.

"Does the idea involve you driving this car?" Ali asked.

"Yes, but—" Joar began.

"Then it's a bad idea."

Joar turned to Ted and the artist in the back seat as if they ought to be backing him up. Neither of them dared look him in the eye, but Ted plucked up the courage to mumble:

"I . . . think . . . maybe it's better if we . . . don't . . ."

"That's what I'm saying! Maybe your worst idea ever, and you've had some *really* bad ideas!" Ali said.

She said this with a trace of fear in her voice, hearing that from her was like snow in August, wrong thing in the wrong place. It would be many years before Ted realized this wasn't because she was scared for her own sake, or for Joar's, she wasn't worried about their future because she always thought what Joar did: that they didn't have one. She was just worried because he was taking the artist and Ted with them.

"I've never had a bad fucking idea in my life," Joar muttered, and in his defense he was saying this to Ali, the queen of bad ideas.

"YOU haven't?" Ali howled.

"Name one!"

"That time you tried to have a barbecue indoors," Ali replied instantly.

"And when we were at my neighbor's birthday party when we were eight and you ate three helpings of spaghetti before you went on the trampoline," the artist smiled from the back seat.

Joar looked annoyed, but maintained sulkily:

"Okay, maybe those weren't exactly fucking perfect ideas."

Then Ted dared to add:

"And do you remember that time I fell asleep in the cafeteria at school, and you tied the laces of my shoes together, and then you pinched my nose really hard to wake me up, but when you started to run away it turned out that you'd actually tied one of your shoes to one of mine!"

Then the artist laughed so hard that Joar turned around and roared:

"Quiet in the back! Or you'll have to walk home!"

He would have been a good dad, Ted thought then. The artist stuck his tongue out. Joar reached back and tried to tickle him.

"Watch out!" Ali yelled.

"Watch out for what?" Joar shouted back.

"The road!"

"I'm supposed to be on the damn road!"

"But you have to LOOK at the road when you're driving!"

"Make up your damn mind," Joar sulked.

Ted looked at the cars passing them, cleared his throat nervously and asked:

"What do we do if we get stopped by the police?"

"We run," Joar said, as if that were entirely obvious.

"From the police? They've got dogs," Ali pointed out instructively.

There really aren't letters big enough to convey the size of the letters Ted used at that point to exclaim: "DOGS???"

Joar rolled his eyes so hard that Ali had to grab the steering wheel to stop them from ending up in a ditch.

"Okay, okay, we don't run. If the police turn up, we say you've got an inflamed appendix, Ted!" Joar said, pointing at a place on his stomach where his appendix definitely wasn't.

"The appendix is . . . here," Ted whispered, pointing to his own stomach, still upset about the imaginary dogs.

"I told you, you should be a teacher," Ali smiled.

Then the car started to smell a little like someone had farted, and Ali said it definitely wasn't her, which of course is something you say when it definitely was. They drove the rest of the way with the windows down and their heads sticking out of the windows like Labradors. Apart from Ted, who imagined he had his head sticking out of the window like, for instance, a small and entirely harmless cat.

"There!" Joar said suddenly, and stopped the car.

"What?" the others all wondered at the same time.

Joar pointed to a large white building.

"There!"

It was a museum. The friends didn't get out of the car, but the artist moved to Ted's side and looked out his window, so close to each other that Ted could hear his heartbeat. Joar's voice became serious as he pointed and promised:

"Inside there is where your painting is going to hang when you win the competition. Everyone will admire it. Waiters will go round serving Champagne and those tiny sandwiches that rich people eat. And you'll walk in and everyone will applaud."

The artist whispered back:

"You'll be there too, Joar."

And Joar replied:

"Sure, sure, I'll be there too."

Ted falls silent on the train. He looks out the window and recognizes where they are. The outlines of the town, and of himself, are growing clearer and clearer. It is probably never easy for anyone to return to the place where they grew up, there's no way to forget who you are there, no matter how hard you've tried to become someone else. But for Ted it's impossible to come home now, he realizes, because home was the people.

He doesn't tell Louisa that everyone inside the car that day knew deep down that Joar was lying when he promised that he would be in the museum when the artist won the competition. Joar was in a hurry to love, because he knew he wouldn't have the chance much longer. July was over, the next day was August, and that was the start of his old man's vacation. Ted doesn't tell Louisa that on the day Joar stole the car, his friends had seen him shake his backpack from time to time, out of the corner of their eyes, to feel the weight of the knife at the bottom of it, checking that it was still there.

Instead Ted says:

"As we sat there looking at the museum, Ali said: 'Okay. This wasn't your worst idea.' And then she held Joar's hand, in that way people do when they belong to each other, as if it's more natural to touch each other than not to. And Joar didn't pull his hand away, he wasn't embarrassed, and that was the first time I realized that they had kissed each other. And I remember sitting there in the back seat hoping that those two would get to grow old together."

The train stops. Ted closes his eyes, fills his lungs, gets to his feet, and picks up his suitcase and the box containing the painting. Louisa follows him out onto the platform. They've arrived.

FORTY-EIGHT

Nothing about the train station feels like home. The town where Ted grew up no longer exists, it doesn't even look the same as it had two years ago, the last time he'd seen it. Excavators are clawing at the earth, all the buildings are covered with scaffolding, orange tape shows where you aren't allowed to walk. This town is shedding its skin, all the time, it's excellent at reminding men like Ted that they belong to the past.

His body tenses, he shrinks a little, almost as if he's expecting to be hit. Louisa follows him in a silence that's unlike her. At the end of the platform there's a view of the sea, and Ted stops there for a moment. If the town hadn't recently built luxury apartments down in the old harbor district, you would have been able to see all the way to the pier from there.

Two workmen begin hammering a plank into the ground a short distance away, and Ted jumps at the sound as if it were a pistol shot.

"Are you okay?" Louisa asks anxiously.

He nods. It's a lie. He stands there thinking about Joar and that last day in July, the hours after they had been to the museum, and all he can remember is the sound of a human head being struck. It must have been terrible, twenty-five years later he still dreams about it sometimes, even though he didn't even hear it. He is scared of a sound he didn't even experience. That's the worst thing about having a vivid imagination: it works in all directions.

He has thought about that day so often since then, has thought that the force of the blow must have been so immense that it was a miracle the whole head wasn't ripped off. Because the human body is so tough but so soft, we're a lethal animal yet completely unprotected. Fists and elbows can break ribs and crush jaws, one blow to the temple can mean the end, one single unguarded moment can extinguish a brain. One single really hard blow is enough. We think we're so big, but we're small, fragile, pathetic.

That last summer as children only lasted a few weeks, but it will carry on inside Ted for his entire life. Time weighs more when you're little. In hindsight he never remembers Joar saying, "I have to kill my old man," it was just something that Ted suddenly saw in his eyes. There was no anger in them, oddly enough, no blind fury. Everything had already burned out, inside Joar there were just ashes left, together with the cold calculation of a fifteen-year-old who had weighed all the options and concluded that this was the only one that remained.

He never stood a chance. Joar was dangerous, but the world was more dangerous. The world is undefeated.

"Come on, we're going this way," Ted whispers.

He carries his suitcase and the box containing the painting down the steps toward the street. Louisa follows him with her hands nervously clutching the straps of her backpack, her eyes darting in all directions, as if she's trying to recognize places from his story.

They take a bus the last bit of the way, but don't get off by the crossroads where all the friends grew up. They head in a different direction, toward the churchyard. Louisa stops at the gate, not because Ted asks her to, but because she feels it would be an intrusion to go with him. She wouldn't have wanted any company visiting Fish's grave.

Ted bends down next to a flower bed by the church, looks over his shoulder to check that no one is looking, then picks three small flowers. He stops at one of the graves, crouches down, and whispers:

"I didn't steal these. They're adopted."

Then he apologizes for not having the artist's ashes with him. As if that were necessary. As if those four teenagers twenty-five years ago weren't a love story, belonging to each other forever, impossible to separate. Ashes or not.

"I love you and I believe in you," he smiles, and pats the stone.

Then he walks back to the gate, picks up his suitcase and the box containing the painting, and nods to Louisa:

"Come on. Not far to go now."

"To what?"

"The end of the story," he says.

They pass some big, beautiful houses where rich people live. Then some smaller ones, for less rich people, and soon some even smaller ones. The cars get rustier, the lawns browner, until eventually they walk up a hill along a narrow cul-de-sac full of ramshackle little houses. Ted stops in front of the last one, steps up onto the narrow veranda, and knocks on the door. When it opens, twenty-five years have passed since that summer, but the eyes are still exactly the same. All the air goes out of Louisa. She's never even seen him, but of course she knows instantly who the man in the doorway is.

Joar.

FORTY-NINE

There is a particular way of missing someone, the way you can only miss your best humans when you're fourteen years old, when you go your separate ways outside your houses and your skin feels cold when they turn away. Ted remembers how he had felt it already as they sat there together in the car outside the museum. He remembers feeling frozen, even though the sun was shining.

"I'm not going to win the competition, you're just going to be disappointed . . . ," the artist whispered.

He was probably expecting Joar to get angry, but instead his friend just leaned over the steering wheel and pointed calmly to the large white building.

"You're going to fucking win. But that isn't the important thing."

"Then what is?" the artist asked.

"The important thing is that you understand that you belong there," Joar answered.

The world is full of miracles, but none greater than how far a young person can be carried by someone else's belief in them.

They sat there together, in the roar of the car's air-conditioning, with their eyes closed and their chests rocking. And that was their whole childhood. They sat there until Joar muttered:

"Seriously, Ali . . ."

"It WASN'T me!" she immediately yelled.

"No, no," the artist giggled then, "because it was me!"

They threw the car doors open and tumbled out, lying on the grass and coughing as if they'd been poisoned. It had started to get really windy, there was a storm brewing, but not even that helped disperse the stench.

"What have you been eating? A corpse?" Joar groaned.

"It's those cookies Ted always brings with him," the artist said defensively.

They lay there gasping on the ground next to each other, and it was Ali who turned her head and caught sight of something utterly wonderful: on the lawn outside the museum was a sprinkler. Ten seconds later, they were all soaked.

Those were their last breaths before August, summer no longer felt endless, soon they would be adults. Telling stories is hard, but if someone really wanted to tell the story of those four friends, they could have stopped there by the car outside the museum that day. Because then it would have been a happy ending.

But then Joar reached for his backpack, shaking it to feel the comforting weight of the knife, and to his surprise, he noticed a smell. At first he couldn't place it, but it smelled good, it smelled . . . clean. The panic struck him all at once, he tore open the zipper of his backpack, peered down to where the knife should have been, but all he found there was soap.

FIFTY

Louisa just gawps. Joar's eyes keep darting around the doorframe, full of restlessness and anticipation, as if they still belong to a rowdy little brat who has just put fireworks in someone's mailbox. But apart from his eyes? His face is twenty-five years older, his body a few pounds heavier, his skin many wrinkles richer. Beneath his eyes he has blue circles with a depth that requires dedication, you don't get those from just a few nights' poor sleep, they demand years of devotion in dark rooms with bottles you don't leave half full.

"Hello, Joar," Ted says warily, as if he isn't entirely sure which version of his friend he's going to encounter.

Joar looks him up and down with a degree of surprise, as if he has woken up in the future.

"You're losing your hair," he notes, without saying hello and without so much as glancing at Louisa.

"You've got a bit of a beer belly," Ted smiles back tentatively.

"I'm fat, you're ugly, at least I can go on a diet," Joar retorts, quick as a flash.

Ted's hand sticks out a few inches, but stops in midair, as if it doesn't know if the rest of him is ready to touch anyone yet.

"You're . . . not fat," he whispers, instead of saying what he wants to say: *I've missed you so much.*

"You've gotten old," Joar says, instead of saying what he probably feels: *My skin has felt cold, all alone here.*

"*I've* gotten old? We're exactly the same age!" Ted protests.

Joar snorts.

"We are NOT the same age. We might have lived the same number of years, but we sure as hell aren't the same age. You've been eighty years old since we were twelve."

Then Ted suddenly laughs so loudly that Louisa jumps and wonders where he has been hiding all that noise. As if all this time there has been an extra roar of laughter, just for Joar, unused for years. Then the man in the doorway turns to her.

"So you're Louisa?"

The question is so direct and the eye contact suddenly so intense that Louisa starts to stammer:

"How . . . how do you know that?"

Joar nods to his old friend.

"Ted called from the train station."

"When I went off to get the tickets for the sleeper train," Ted confesses, as if he wants to apologize for doing it in secret.

With a degree of reluctance, Joar defends him:

"Ted probably didn't want to say you'd be meeting me because he didn't know if I'd have drunk myself to death before you arrived. But there's no need to worry, I'm sober, I may look hungover, but that's just my natural damn look these days."

Louisa shifts her weight from one foot to the other. Ted glances at her and adds:

"I've told her about you, Joar. About us. But I think maybe that Louisa would have hoped to meet you when you were . . . a teenager."

With her ears turning red, Louisa snaps:

"Stop it!"

"I'm just trying to explain!" Ted snaps back.

"You're embarrassing me!" she hisses.

Joar looks from one to the other. For two people who have only known each other a couple of days, they really have found an impressive number of ways to get on each other's nerves. Then he squints at Ted and asks:

"What the hell have you done to your face?"

Ted feels his bumps and bruises, and realizes that the tape on his glasses is coming loose again.

"It's a long story," he says tiredly.

Louisa groans.

"Stop saying that! It isn't! You got mugged and beaten up! It's a really short story!" She points toward the metal construction that leads up to the narrow veranda. "Can I ask something? Is that ramp for a wheelchair? Does someone in a wheelchair live here?"

Joar smiles weakly, then he grunts:

"Do you know what that is? It's a fucking long story."

"Everything is with you two, clearly!" Louisa says sullenly.

Joar looks hesitantly at the box by Ted's side.

"Is that . . . the painting?"

His voice falls off a cliff at the end of the sentence.

"Yes! Do you want to see it?" Ted offers enthusiastically, but Joar shakes his head firmly.

He isn't ready for that yet, so he blinks angrily and looks around as if some dust has just blown into his eye and the wind is about to get yelled at.

"Do you want coffee?" he grunts.

"Yes, please," Ted says.

"Have you got any Coca-Cola?" Louisa says hopefully.

"Do I look like some sort of goddamn Mescaline-starred restaurant?" Joar complains.

Ted really is a good friend to him for not pointing out that it should be "Michelin."

"Are you always this nice to guests?" Louisa asks, rolling her eyes.

Ted can't help smiling at that.

"We haven't seen each other for a few years, but he used to be even worse . . ."

Joar snorts indignantly:

"Ted's the only one who's changed! He was much quieter when we were little, he didn't used to fucking argue as much as he does now!"

When he turns to go into the house Louisa sees something on his leg.

"Is that an . . . ankle monitor?" she asks.

"Well, it's not a damn piece of jewelry," comes the reply.

"Why do you have it?"

"Because they didn't have room for me in prison anymore."

"You've been in prison?"

"Do bears shit in the woods? Do one-legged ducks swim in circles?" Joar replies.

She groans impatiently. "Were you in prison for having a terrible sense of humor?"

"I've got a GREAT sense of humor!"

"So what *were* you in prison for, then?"

"It's a long story," Joar mutters.

Louisa takes a deep, deep breath, then glares at Joar, then glares at Ted, then glares at Joar again, and asks:

"Do you have a pillow?"

"What?"

"Do you have a pillow?"

"Of course I have a damn pill—"

"Can I borrow it?"

Joar looks at Ted, who shrugs his shoulder uncomprehendingly, and Louisa looks so adamant that not even Joar protests. So he disappears into the house and comes back with a pillow, and Louisa takes it with one hand and then spends thirty seconds punching the pillow over and over again as hard as she can with her other hand. When she's finished, she holds the pillow up, first toward Ted and then toward Joar, and roars:

"If I have to hear 'It's a long story' one more time, I'm going to hit both of you in—"

"Okay, okay, okay!" Ted says, carefully backing out of range of her swinging fists, but Joar just laughs.

"I can see why Kimkim liked her," he says.

"Who the hell is KIMKIM?" Louisa shouts, by now thoroughly tired of no one telling a story from the goddamn beginning in this goddamn house.

Joar's gaze wavers for a moment and his shoulders sink as the air goes out of him. Then he touches the box containing the painting for the first time, as if he were gently touching the cheek of someone asleep.

"His name was Kimkim. That other name, C. Jat, that was just what he put on his paintings. That was what he used when he became famous. Because then he probably felt like . . . someone else. But when he was with us, when we were his, then he was just Kimkim."

"Kimkim?" Louisa repeats skeptically.

She feels a little betrayed that someone she has always known as "C. Jat" wasn't actually called anything even remotely close to that.

"Kimkim," Joar nods affectionately.

Ted touches the box then as well, at the other end, that's the closest he and Joar get to touching each other.

"The first time we met, when Joar almost ran me over on his bike and drowned me—" Ted begins.

"You should have watched out!" Joar grunts.

Ted rolls his eyes so hard that his pupils scratch him on the back on their way home.

"Sure, sure, when I didn't watch out. And almost drowned! When I got up on the pier and saw him and Joar for the first time, he said: 'This is Joar. And my name's Kim.' But I had water in my ears, so I said: 'Kim?' And he said: 'Kim!' And I said: 'Kim? Kim?' And Joar thought that was so funny that from then on, he always called him Kimkim."

"But Ali usually just called him Kim. Because she always had to be special," Joar snorts.

Louisa peers at Ted:

"What did you call him?"

"I hardly ever said his name," Ted says quietly.

It's a funny thing. The person we fall in love with, we hardly ever call by their name. Because it's somehow just so obvious that it's you I'm talking to, that it's you I'm always thinking of. Who else?

"Kimkim. Yes, that suited him," Louisa nods, as if she were holding the name up in front of a mirror in a dressing room. "Can I ask something?" she says, then immediately asks: "Is it uncomfortable?"

She points to the ankle monitor.

"Yeah," Joar grunts.

"And you're not allowed to go outside the house?"

"No."

"What happens if you do?"

"I blow up. There's dynamite inside it."

Louisa's eyes open wide.

"Seriously?"

"No, you idiot, are you always this dim?"

Louisa throws up her arms.

"Oh, sorry, because all *geniuses* wear ankle monitors? Is it so your brain cells won't escape, or what?"

At first Joar looks insulted, then rather amused. He grins at Ted.

"This must have been the longest train trip of your life."

Ted nods his strong, strong agreement and Louisa looks affronted. Then they go inside the house and she brightens up, because Joar finds a can of orange soda at the back of his fridge. Louisa drinks it like it's the last can of orange soda on the planet. Ted goes and pees twice during the course of one cup of coffee. Then he asks her:

"Have you decided yet?"

"Decided what?" she wonders.

"If you want to hear the rest of the story or not?"

She nods, after some hesitation.

"What story?" Joar asks.

"About us. About the summer when Kimkim painted the picture."

Joar's eyes narrow suspiciously.

"How much have you told her?"

"Up until you turned fifteen. And we went to the museum for the first time. And sat outside it in the car. And Kimkim farted. And you discovered that . . . that the knife wasn't in your backpack."

Joar drinks his coffee and looks like he has never wanted a shot of whiskey more in his entire life.

"You're the one who's good at telling stories, damn it."

"This part belongs to you," Ted says quietly.

So Joar tells her. With slightly fewer adjectives than Ted usually uses, and rather more swearing.

FIFTY-ONE

Joar stood outside that damn museum, digging through his damn backpack, but he couldn't fucking find it. All he could find at the bottom were two damn soaps, taped together so they weighed roughly the same as a knife. Of course Joar should have known better than to try to hide anything from her, she who had already told him that moms find everything.

"She took it . . . I have to . . . fuck fuck fuck . . . I have to go home!" was all Joar managed to say.

He drove the car at full speed with trembling hands back through the town. The storm had come in over them now, the wind was rattling the windows, so they saw the flashing lights ahead long before they actually heard the sirens. When they were near the harbor, the ambulance rushed past them. As they turned toward the houses at the crossroads where they always called out "tomorrow" to each other, they saw the parking area outside Joar's building. In the spot where Joar's old man's car had stood when they stole it, there was now a police car. Outside the door to the stairwell stood a group of serious men with hard bodies, bowed heads, and broken glances. They were Joar's old man's workmates from the harbor. One of them was Kimkim's father.

Joar stopped the car and leapt out, he was running before his friends had even opened their doors, he was screaming desperately through the wind. He didn't slow down when the men from the harbor held out their hands, he forced his way through the crowd so wildly that even the heaviest men backed off. When one of them tried to grab his backpack, he just slithered out of it and rushed on into the stairwell.

There was a body lying on the floor of Joar's room. The window was ajar, dirt from the tin flower box had blown in across the floor.

Joar glances at Louisa. The kitchen was already small to begin with, but now it feels like a matchbox, ready to ignite at any moment. Joar whispers:

"It must have been one hell of a . . . one hell of a blow to the head. It must have been heard through the fucking walls. People think we're so damn hard, so damn tough and dangerous. But we're fragile. We're defenseless little creatures. One single really hard blow to the temple is enough. One single second when you're not prepared, it can shut down your brain. That was . . . I had a plan . . . my mom was going to work the night shift that night. She wasn't supposed to be at home! That was why I kept checking if I had the knife all the time. I was planning to wait until my old man came home drunk and . . . but . . . I didn't have time."

In a voice so fragile that Louisa has to lean across the table to hear, Joar explains that he had prepared a small box. He was going to pretend he'd found another bird, and look extra happy so his old man would hate him more than ever. He would leave the knife under the flowers outside the window again, then he would wait until his old man stumbled into his room, and when the bastard grabbed the box Joar would reach through the window for the knife and stab his old man before he had time to react. It was a good plan. It would have worked if he had gotten the chance.

"I just remember screaming 'MOM,' over and over again. And I remember hearing someone yell my name, outside the house . . . ," Joar whispers.

Ted clears his throat gently.

"It was Kimkim who yelled."

Because Kimkim had run after him from the car, but had been stopped by the men outside the building. He wasn't strong enough to fight his way through. One day perhaps they would brag about that, those men, that they had once been so close to one of the world's most famous artists. But that day they didn't say a word, they just stood there, cowardly and silent, weak and pathetic, despite all their muscle.

Then a howl was heard from inside the apartment. Then all Ted remembers is the longest, most unbearable silence he has ever experienced.

He has often wondered what went through the minds of the men from the harbor outside the building then. He's spent so much time wondering what Kimkim's dad, the biggest and strongest of them all, might have been thinking. Ted saw the father meet his son's gaze, and that was the first time Ted could ever remember Kimkim not breaking eye contact. He stared so accusingly that his father shrank. Those men from the harbor would have to bear an eternal shame, all friends of men like Joar's old man have to do that. Because that silence after the howl from inside the apartment was nothing compared to the silence the men themselves had all been walking around in, day after day, year after year.

"The biggest threat to men's health, statistically, is heart disease," Ted says thoughtfully at the kitchen table. "Do you know what the biggest threat to women's health is?"

"Men," Louisa says, because all women know that.

Joar spins his coffee cup, leaving marks on the old kitchen table. Then he tells Louisa how he saw his mom's body lying there on the floor of his room. How he yelled "MOM" over and over again. Then his voice sinks:

"Everyone . . . knew. They all knew what he was doing to us. Kimkim's old man and my old man worked together for years. Some of the men from the harbor grew up on the same street as him. You know . . . you didn't choose your friends in this town in their day. You became friends with the kids you lived next to, then you had fights with the kids from the next block . . . that's how they ended up so loyal to each other. When they got jobs for each other in the harbor, they always said 'the right sort of guy,' and by that they meant that he could punch someone in the mouth and keep his own mouth shut. Because in the harbor, you have to be able to trust each other, it's dangerous as hell down there, trucks driving at full speed, cranes lifting containers that weigh several tons on cables that look like shoelaces . . . you have to have each other's backs. You have to be able to trust that the guy behind you will yell 'WATCH OUT!' if something's about to hit you in the head. You understand? Kimkim's old man was missing two fingers on one hand, because one time when they were young, he got his hand caught in a machine, it hurt so much that he passed out. It was my old man who saw and managed to pull him free. Otherwise he might have lost his whole damn arm. You know . . . Kimkim's old man would have done anything for mine after that. Anything at all. Because those men have to be able to trust each other, right? You have to know that someone is going to yell 'WATCH OUT!' when you're in danger? So they convince themselves that they have to be able to trust each other with . . . everything. So if someone talks shit about the boss in the locker room, you keep your mouth shut. If he cheats on his girlfriend, you keep your mouth shut. And if he . . . if he smells of alcohol when you pick him up in the morning? If he has stains on his knuckles that look like . . . like his wife's makeup? Because he didn't even wash his hands after he hit her? If he has stains on his shirt that he says are paint but which look a hell of a lot like blood? Then you keep your mouth shut. Maybe you ask his wife one single time, you know, if everything's okay with her and the kid . . . but of course she just laughs and says everything's great. Because what's she going to say? *Help us? He's going to kill us?* It's obvious as hell that she won't dare do that. And that's absolutely fucking perfect for all those right sort of guys in the harbor, all those big strong men, because then they don't have to ask again. They can just let it happen. Because obviously they haven't seen anything, they haven't heard anything, they just *had a feeling*. And you don't call the damn police for that, because what the hell are the police going to do about your *feeling*? So when I came home that day, and I saw Mom lying on the floor of my room and realized what had happened, I just remember that I . . . I lay down on the floor beside her and held her hands. And I had never felt like that before . . ."

The coffee cup spins around, around on the kitchen table, leaving wounds in the wood. Louisa thinks about the men who stood there outside Joar's apartment building, and she thinks about Fish telling her what evil among men is like: It's like water being heated up a little at a time. It gets worse and worse, but so slowly it's hardly noticeable, so everyone can convince themselves that it's probably normal, until we're all boiling.

"He was funny, my old man," Joar suddenly says with a sad grin. "That's probably what caused the blow. He'd told a joke down at the harbor, and everyone laughed, and he was probably so pleased with himself that he didn't look. And it was windy as all hell that day, there was a storm coming in. But I guess no one dared complain, no one said that maybe it was too dangerous to loosen those damn steel beams then, because, you know . . . real men, the right sort of guys, they don't complain. My old man walked right in front of a crane, and the guy driving it turned too fast, he didn't account for the wind. That's all it takes, you know, just a few grams wrong in the weight distribution this way or that, and the beam starts to swing. My old man didn't have a chance of seeing it. And you know what? I've wondered every day since then how many of his workmates saw it, and how many shouted 'WATCH OUT!'"

Ted sits there stirring his coffee, he can still remember the look on Kimkim's dad's face outside Joar's apartment building, and how he crumbled and gazed down at the ground when Kimkim stared at him. It wasn't shock on the man's face then, it wasn't grief, just shame. Joar's cup spins, spins, spins on the kitchen table. It takes so little to crush a person, one small step this way or that. He says:

"Mom looked so horribly small as she lay there. Like a child who'd fallen out of a tree. I remember, the window was open, I could smell the flowers, I remember there was dirt on the floor. I know I looked for blood. I ran over and touched her shoulder, because my heart was beating so hard that I couldn't even hear if she was breathing. Then I just heard her whisper my name and start to cry."

Ted sits on the other side of the kitchen table but feels miles away. He's thinking about what it was like standing outside in the silence. He remembers Kimkim telling him afterward that it was the first time he had seen his dad cry, with his face hidden behind his eight fingers. Ted remembers that too, and he remembers wondering who the man was crying for: Joar's old man, Joar's mother, or himself?

Joar clears his throat and gathers his strength before he goes on:

"Right after the accident, the men from the harbor and the police went to see my mom and tell her what had happened. They didn't want her to find out over the telephone. And do you know what she did then? She ran straight into my room, because she was so scared that that was her first instinct: to protect her child. But of course I wasn't there, I was at the museum, so she just lay on the floor crying and crying until I came home. And when she heard me in the doorway all she managed to whisper was: 'Joar, Joar . . . your dad's been in an accident. He's in the hospital. They say he's going to . . . die.' And I tried to comfort her, but she sobbed: 'You don't understand, darling! I took your knife. I was . . . I was going to kill him. If he'd come home I would have . . . killed him.' And then she just screamed. Like she'd been holding it in for years. I don't know if it came from grief or relief. But I remember lying beside her and that I had never, ever felt anything like that. I felt . . . free."

Ted thinks that it takes so little for a life to take a different direction. Change weighs nothing. Like a knife, like a bar of soap, like a tiny animal.

Joar smiles weakly at Louisa:

"Do you know what my mom asked? When we were lying there on the floor? She asked why I was so wet. I said I'd had a water fight with my friends. And then she worried I was going to catch a cold. Even then, she was . . . worried about . . . me."

Ted says nothing, but he remembers standing beside Ali and Kimkim and looking up at the flowers outside Joar's room, and he could have sworn that at that moment a bird landed by the window. It sat there for a couple of moments, peering in, then in a blink it was gone, spreading its little black wings and flying away. And Ted thought about how life is so fragile, coincidence decides so much, it takes so little to change everything.

Down in the harbor, when the heavy construction crane turned just a fraction of a second too quickly in the wind, it probably wouldn't have taken more than a few extra grams to change the weight distribution so that the steel beam started to sway. It would probably have been enough for a small bird to land and take off again.

FIFTY-TWO

Joar's old man didn't die. Of all the strange things that happened that summer, perhaps that was the strangest of all, Joar tells Louisa.

"Time's such a damn thief, you don't notice what it's stealing from you," he says, the skin hanging heavy under his eyes.

The mornings after his old man's accident blurred together, the days ran away, one week became another. The doctors at the hospital told Joar and his mother that his old man had suffered terrible brain damage, they said that when he woke up, everything would be different. He wouldn't be able to walk, he'd hardly be able to speak, he'd need help with everything. The doctors looked so upset when they said, "He'll never be himself again," because presumably they thought that was why the man's wife and son had tears in their eyes.

Of all the strange things.

His mother would stay with his old man, Joar knew that at once, not because his old man deserved it, but because the bastard needed her. Joar realized that no one else would understand that, because how could they? There was no one like his mother to compare her to. She smiled and people saw superficiality, she was kind and people saw weakness, no matter what she did they would always talk crap about her in the supermarket. Women like her can never do the right thing, their men's guilt is always theirs. Even Joar underestimated her, he realized, and felt ashamed. He had always assumed that her goodness made her light, and the world isn't built for light people, the planet spins and they keep getting thrown into walls and fists. But now he and everyone else could see the truth: it was his old man who was tiny, his mother was the giant.

Her son thought that the woman had a thousand lives inside her that she could have lived, but she would never wish for any but this one, because this was the only one where she had this particular son. He left the hospital room to go and get coffee for her, when he came back she was asleep in a chair beside his old man's bed. He looked harmless now, that bastard would never be able to raise his fists against her again, Joar tried to think that perhaps that would have to be enough.

The men from the harbor sat in the waiting room, they stood up when Joar arrived, he went from man to man and shook hands with them all. He still had all the bruises and cuts left from his old man's most recent assault, and when he looked all these right sort of guys in the eye, many of them looked away. They had seen that his mother had a black eye as well, it was impossible to pretend not to know what had happened then, yet still they tried. Men always have excuses, but deep down they knew the truth now. They had minded their own business, never asking questions they didn't want the answers to, making do with only one side of a man. As if that was all a man has. That guilt was theirs to carry forever.

Kimkim's dad was last in line. He was the only one who didn't try to wipe his wet cheeks, and when Joar saw that, he struggled to keep his own dry. When they shook hands, the man didn't look away from the bruises. Instead he leaned over and whispered, with a sob in his voice:

"I'm sorry I stayed silent. I'm sorry I was a coward."

Joar looked at him and wondered if he meant his silence all the times he had picked up Joar's old man in the mornings, or if he meant his silence in the harbor. He wondered if any of the men had yelled "WATCH OUT!" when the beam was swinging, or if they had just let it happen. He never asked. He just said:

"You should say the same thing to Kimkim. Before it's too late. Soon he'll go far away from here, and I hope to Hell that he never comes back . . ."

Kimkim's father's eyebrows jumped for a moment at that, then he blushed, he knew his own son so little that he didn't even know his friends called him "Kimkim." Joar walked away, his back straight, leaving the man standing there, bent double.

Joar fetches more coffee in the kitchen in his little house. It is clean, Louisa notes, it's old and worn but everything smells good. The lawn is the prettiest on the whole street. Joar clears his throat again and says:

"On the way back through the hospital I walked past one of those God rooms, or whatever the hell they're called?"

"Chapel," Ted says.

"Chapel!" Joar nods and smiles at Louisa. "I went past and looked in, and which three idiots do you think were lying asleep on the benches in there?"

"Your idiots," Louisa grins.

Joar grins too. He says he didn't know how long they had been there waiting for him, but it was just so obvious to them that none of them were going home until they were all going home. Who has friends like that?

Ali woke up sleepily and leaned her head against Joar's shoulder when he crept down by her side. Ted was snoring. Beside Kimkim lay a drawing, he had drawn the chapel, but he had drawn a light through the window that wasn't there in reality. And who the hell can do that? Draw *light*?

"Do you think God exists?" Ali asked her friends.

"Yes," Kimkim replied, running his pencil across the drawing so gently that it was impossible to know if it made a difference on the paper or just inside him.

Joar was breathing hard.

"Damned if I know . . . I don't even think all the people who go to church every Sunday believe in God. I think they just need company. To feel that they belong to a group."

Kimkim nodded gently and replied:

"But I don't think that means that God doesn't exist, Joar. I think maybe that's what God is."

They woke Ted, and walked close, so close to each other as they left the chapel. Joar found a vending machine and managed to sway and shake it so a can of soda came loose and fell out for free. One small victory against the universe, things like that shouldn't be underestimated. The four friends shared the can and just as they drained the last drops, Joar opened his eyes wide.

"Where's the drawing? Did you leave it in the chapel?"

"Think so . . . ," Kimkim said.

"Are you crazy?" Joar exploded. "That's worth millions!"

They ran back, but the drawing was already gone.

"It doesn't matter, I'll do another one," Kimkim promised.

"You should just draw money, it would save time!" Joar said.

Kimkim laughed, then Joar laughed, and then Ted and Ali laughed too, and perhaps that was the last time they all did that out loud, in such a liberating way, together.

They didn't see the man standing behind a corner, eight trembling fingers carefully holding Kimkim's drawing.

FIFTY-THREE

Louisa has finished her orange soda. She leans back in the kitchen chair and stretches her arms sleepily in the air.

"So all that happened . . . and then Kimkim won the art competition? That's a good ending, that is. A sad story, but a good ending."

Ted and Joar glance at each other, clear their throats uncomfortably, then Ted mutters:

"Absolutely. It's a . . . good ending."

Louisa groans in despair.

"What? Is there more? I don't know if I can bear to hear more!" she snaps, but then her anxiety creeps out as she asks: "I don't know if I want to know that not everyone got a happy ending . . ."

Ted nods and quickly wipes his eyes, looks at the time and stands up.

"I think it's time for me to go now."

"Where are you going?" Louisa shouts, as if he had thrown her down a well.

Ted nods calmly toward the box containing the painting.

"I'm going to do what I promised. What we came here for. I'm going to help you sell that."

Louisa starts to get to her feet to protest, but by then he is already out in the hall and closing the door behind him. He really is surprisingly quick for someone with a limp, Louisa thinks sullenly, slumping back down in her chair.

"Would you like more orange soda?" Joar asks.

"No thanks," she says.

"Good. Because I don't have any."

He grins, but she can't bring herself to smile, even a little bit. The silence becomes oppressive.

"Well," Joar says.

"Well?" she grunts back.

He frowns. Hides his curiosity behind irritation.

"Well? What are you going to do with all the money? From the painting?"

"I don't know," she mumbles.

"What do you mean, you don't know? You're rich! You can do whatever you want in life now!"

"I'm sure that would be perfect, if I knew *what* I wanted to do," she replies, looking down at the table.

"How old are you?"

"Eighteen."

He snorts.

"And you don't know what to do with shitloads of money? Damn, you're a bad teenager. Buy a sports car! And drugs! Start a zoo! I would have bought a bunch of monkeys. You can't be in a bad mood if you've got a bunch of monkeys. Especially not if you've also got drugs."

He thinks she's going to smile, but he can forget that.

She just whispers:

"I didn't even want the painting to start with. You should keep it, you and Ted. You were his best friends, I'm just . . . I'm just a stupid kid he met in an alleyway. I tried to leave both Ted and the painting on the train, but things just kept happening, and I . . . I just wanted to hear the end of all the stories about you. But now I don't even know if I want that!"

"Why not?" Joar says, even though he probably understands all too well.

"Because it doesn't feel like there are going to be any happy endings at all!"

Joar spins his coffee cup for a long time before he replies:

"You're the happy ending."

"What?"

"Kimkim gave you the painting because he saw you paint. You're the happy ending to his story. The life you live from now on. Everything you paint."

"I need to go to the bathroom," Louisa whispers.

She doesn't. She just needs to be able to fall apart in peace. Surely there should be some boundaries for the sort of thing people are allowed to blurt out when you've only just met them? When she finally goes back into the kitchen, she takes her drawing of Kimkim out of her backpack and gives it to Joar.

"I drew this of Kimkim. The way I imagine he looked when he was young. I gave it to Ted, but he gave it back, so you can have it."

Joar has to lean on the table to stop himself from falling off his chair.

"It looks . . . exactly like him."

Then he grunts that he needs to go to the bathroom too, but really he just sits on the other side of the wall taking deep breaths for a long time. When he comes back, he nods to Louisa and says:

"Come with me. I want to show you something."

He carefully fixes the drawing to the fridge, then leads her through the little house, up some stairs, then opens a window and climbs out onto the roof. Louisa peers out after him and asks suspiciously:

"Is this roof going to hold me? It looks like it's made from milk cartons."

"It can hold me!" Joar snorts.

"Sure, but what do you weigh? I'm a normal-sized human!"

"You're not fucking normal in any fucking way. Stop making a fuss and come on!" he insists.

So she clambers out hesitantly after him. He tells her she doesn't need to take her backpack, and she looks like that's the most insane thing she's ever heard. Then he chuckles and mutters, "The world is full of thieves," and she mutters back, "Exactly!" Then they sit next to each other with their feet dangling over the edge, and only then does Louisa realize that the reason she and Ted had walked uphill on the way there was because the house is on a . . . hill. With a stunning view of half the town. Joar points toward some houses and says:

"Ali used to have a game. She would point at houses and say, 'If we lived there,' and then you had to imagine things about that life. But her favorites weren't the most expensive houses, but the most normal ones. The boring ones. She would point at them and say: 'In that house I live a normal life. I'm married to someone ordinary. We have boring jobs and boring friends. I put little stickers on plastic containers in the freezer, like Ted's mom does, and they say things like *chicken soup* and *vegetable pie* and *lasagna*. You know, I have to do that because I have so much food in the freezer that I'd forget what's in them otherwise! And I always have spare lightbulbs in the house, and I have two boring little kids who lie in their beds asking strange questions, like why polar bears don't eat penguins, just so they don't have to sleep. But they won't be *scared* of sleeping, Joar! They'll never be scared at all. They'll just get to be ordinary, boring children with ordinary, boring parents all the time. I'd be good at that, don't you think, Joar? I'd be awesome at being boring!' That's what she would say. That was her game."

Joar falls silent there on the roof. Smiles. Shakes his head. It was a lie, of course, Ali would have been good at a lot of things, but being boring? She couldn't have managed that for a second, the lunatic.

"Can I ask something?" Louisa says.

"Yes."

"Why . . . don't polar bears eat penguins?"

"Polar bears only live at the North Pole. Penguins only live at the South Pole."

"Was it Ted who told Ali that?"

"Yes."

Louisa smiles at that. Then she points to a house with lights on in all the windows and says:

"If you lived there, then?"

Joar thinks for a while.

"If I lived there, I probably wouldn't have an ankle monitor, I'd have a normal, boring job."

"Like a high school teacher? Like Ted?"

"Not *that* boring, calm down," he snaps.

She laughs.

"Would you be married to someone ordinary? Like Ali would have been?"

"No."

"Why not?"

"Because that was . . . her thing. She said people like her and me couldn't be with each other, because you can't both be broken and crazy. You need to have one of you who's ordinary."

"But you never found anyone?"

"I never looked."

"Was Ali your first love?"

"My last."

Louisa blinks out across the town. She points at a huge house with an array of illuminated windows and whispers:

"There. That's the house I live in when I've sold the painting and got all the money. With my friend Fish."

"Fish?"

Louisa nods, but then she looks embarrassed.

"Yes. Only she's dead. Can you live with dead people in this game?"

Joar nods.

"In this game you can live with whoever you want to. Has it been long since she died?"

Louisa shakes her head.

"It was . . . very recent. She liked games. She loved fairy tales! That's why it's so wrong that she died and not me, because she was kind of the hero in our story. Do you understand? The main character! You're not supposed to die first then!"

"That isn't the same thing," Joar says.

"What?"

"The main character and the hero. They aren't the same thing."

Louisa glares at him as if he's talking complete nonsense, but she will never forget that. Something very, very small but very important changes inside her then.

Joar points:

"Do you mean that pink house? With the big tree in the garden? Is that where you're going to live, you and Fish?"

"Yes."

"Good. Then I can live in the house next door," he smiles.

She looks at him apologetically.

"Forget it. You'll never be able to afford to live next door to me when I've sold the painting. I'm, like, really, really rich!" she informs him. "But maybe you can come and clean my pool, if you need a job?"

He bursts out laughing so hard that it echoes across the town. So does she. Then Joar says, out of nowhere:

"Ted isn't going to leave you. If that's why you don't want to sell the painting, because you think he'll leave you and you'll be alone again . . . he won't do that. Ted is really, really fucking bad at leaving people."

Louisa pretends to be very interested in a house in the other direction so he won't see her wiping her whole face with her shirt. Then she says:

"You're bad at that too. I saw the wheelchair ramp down there. You lived here with your dad after the accident, didn't you?"

Joar lies on his back on the roof.

"Yes."

"You took care of him? Despite everything he had done to you?"

"He became a different man. It's hard to explain. He could hardly talk, he needed help eating, washing, going to the bathroom . . . but that isn't what made the difference. The real difference was in his eyes. There was no hatred in them anymore. Hell, in the end even I didn't hate him anymore. In those last years I called him 'Dad' when I fed him. I'd never called him that in my entire life."

Louisa replies through gritted teeth:

"I haven't had twenty-five years to stop doing that. So I still hate him. I've only just started."

"That's kind of you, but there's no need," Joar says.

"Yes, there is! Because you just stayed here with him, your whole life, instead of—"

Joar's laughter interrupts her.

"Instead of what? Becoming a professional soccer player? An astronaut? What the hell would I have become? I didn't have a future anyway, all the damn adults I met believed I was going to die young. All this is a bonus for me. Besides, I didn't stay for my old man. I stayed for Mom. They moved here, because staying in the apartment was impossible with the wheelchair, so I had to move with them to look after the house. Mom is . . . hell, she doesn't even have a driver's license. And she cuts the grass in high heels, for goodness' sake."

Then Louisa thinks that perhaps life is long, but when that steel beam swung through the air in the harbor that day, it slowed Joar's time down. Now it is creeping forward. Before the steel beam, he had been in a hurry to get to the summer, in a hurry for tomorrow, in a hurry to love his friends. But during the twenty-five years since then, he hasn't been in a hurry to do anything.

"Is your dad dead now?"

"Yeah. He passed away a few years ago. There was only me and Mom and a few old guys from the harbor at his funeral. The guys who were left. Men don't live long in this town, people usually say, they all kill themselves, fast or slowly. With either a shotgun or the bottle."

"What happened to your mom?"

Joar's breathing grows more shallow, as if it is sliding about in his throat. It takes a while before Louisa realizes this isn't because he feels despair, but the opposite.

"Mom met a man. A kind man. Not a mean old bastard and not a fucking monster. Just a nice, boring, sober man. He doesn't fight, he doesn't even raise his voice, she always gets to choose what TV shows they watch. He buys her flowers every Friday. They live a couple of hours away from here now. She called me the other day and said they've started playing tennis. Who the hell plays *tennis*?"

He laughs so hard that summer arrives on the roof, even though it isn't even May yet.

"A happy ending," Louisa whispers.

"Yeah. Mom got a happy ending. No damn woman has ever deserved one more."

"But you still live here in this house?"

"Yeah, what the hell, I could have moved, but . . . well, I was otherwise occupied."

He waves the leg with the ankle monitor.

"What did you do?"

"I knocked someone out."

"Who?"

Joar sighs.

"On the way home from Dad's funeral, I saw a man hit a woman, next to their car, and inside the car a little girl was screaming."

He doesn't have to say more. Louisa understands. One day she will go find the old newspaper article about the assault, and will read that the man was beaten so badly that when he woke up in the hospital, he told the police he'd been attacked by at least five people. If Joar hadn't gone to the police station to hand himself in, everyone would probably have believed that.

"Was it horrible? Being in prison?"

Joar shrugs his shoulders.

"It was okay. Ted sent books. Really, really *boring* books, but still . . . there was enough time to be bored. After a while I got a letter from an old man, he was that woman's father, the child's grandfather. He wrote to tell me that they had left that damn man, he hoped that would mean something to me. It did. Not even Ted's books felt so boring after that. At the end of my sentence there weren't enough cells, there are so many men like me these days that we have to wait in line just to go to prison, so they let me out with this." He waves his ankle again.

"Were you in prison when Ted got stabbed by that kid at his school?" Louisa asks, and regrets it at once, because Joar looks so ashamed that she's afraid he's going to jump off the roof.

"Yeah," he whispers, because all the people he loves are still his responsibility, all the time.

"And you were in prison when . . . Kimkim got sick?"

"Yeah."

"Did you see much of each other before then?"

"No. We only met one single time after that summer when we turned fifteen."

"What? Why?"

His grin wanders sadly from one ear to the other.

"It's a long story."

Then Louisa makes herself comfortable on her back, takes a deep breath of the town, and whispers:

"Okay. You can tell me the rest of it now."

"The rest of what?"

"The rest of the whole long story! About everything! About the competition and the painting and . . . everything. But it mustn't only be unhappy! It must also be a bit . . . you know . . . ordinary too."

So Joar takes a deep breath as well, and then he begins telling her the end.

FIFTY-FOUR

After his dad's accident, the evening after the friends had sat in the chapel in the hospital, Joar almost killed himself in the car. Well, it was actually Ali who did it, the goddamn lunatic. That was the evening she told them her dad had gotten a new job, in another town, far away. Her dad owed money to the people around there, he always did, and now they were rude enough to want it back.

Joar blinks up at the sky there on the roof.

"I didn't cry after my dad's accident. And I didn't cry that night with Ali either. I don't know if that hurt her. I should have said something smart, but all I could say was that it was . . . good. Because she could never live in this town, not as her full self, she couldn't be . . . everything she could be, not here."

"What did she say?"

"That I could fucking go to Hell if I wasn't going to fucking miss her. So then I told her the truth: that I would never fall in love with anyone again. And then she kissed me. She had only done that once before. Afterward of course she said it was me who kissed her, but she was out of her damn mind . . ."

Louisa is lying down, so she has to wipe the tears out of her ears.

"So the two of you were a love story."

"She'd have punched you in the face if she heard that," he laughs.

"Why couldn't she stay with you?"

"Her dad needed her," Joar says, as if it were obvious.

"You're all the same, all of you. You can't abandon people who need you," Louisa says.

"You're one of us," Joar replies, and that sets a new record for the kindest thing he's said to her.

"What happened with the art competition?" she asks.

So he tells her: About how he and Ali were out driving all evening. How they stopped the car on a hill not far from the house where Joar and Louisa are sitting now, and fell asleep there in each other's arms. They spent one entire night together, some people might think that doesn't sound like much, but they can never have been properly in damn love. Most people have never had a hint of how that feels.

Ali drove on the way back, Joar taught her. She drove roughly as well as she had been able to swim the first time he met her, so they almost crashed, heading at full speed straight toward a brick wall. She stopped abruptly just at the last moment, Joar screamed out loud and she stared at him, sweaty and happy, with her big, wild eyes, and yelled:

"Now you know!"

"What the hell are you talking about, you psychopath?" he yelled back.

Then she leaned against his neck so that he disappeared in all her hair, and she said:

"Now you know that you don't want to die either. You're not allowed to, okay? If you die before I come back here, I'll beat you to death!"

"Come back here?" he teased. "Why would you come back here? Aren't you going to live in a big house with someone ordinary?"

"One day maybe we can be ordinary enough, you and me," she whispered.

They stopped by the sea, Joar collected driftwood, that was how he made the frame for Kimkim's painting. Even when it was hanging in an exclusive art auction twenty-five years later, it still smelled a little of the sea.

When they got back home they met Ted and Kimkim at the crossroads and went back to Joar's. They cleaned the apartment, because Joar wanted it to look nice when his mom came home from the hospital. Ali wasn't all that great at cleaning, so she sorted a box of old toys, although she mostly just played with them. She held up a Superman figure and asked: "Why does he wear a cape, actually? It doesn't have any powers, he can fly without it, can't he?"

It was Kimkim who replied:

"I think it's because it's hard to draw movement. So when the people who made him up had to draw that in the comic, they needed the cape to show that he was . . . moving."

"Oh!" Ali said, the way you do if you understand absolutely nothing.

So Kimkim tried to demonstrate by taking his shirt off and running around the room with it behind him, but he wasn't looking and ran into a wall. It was actually very dangerous, because Ali almost suffocated with laughter. Then Ted said he'd read that Superman's cape was actually a blanket. It was the one his mom had wrapped him in when he was little and his parents had sent him away in the rocket to Earth. That was such a heavy thought that they all just lay on the floor staring up at the ceiling.

"Will you forget me if I move?" Ali eventually asked.

"Definitely!" all her boys replied.

"You're so damn mean," she laughed.

"Forget you?" Ted mumbled. "We can't even remember a life before you turned up. How could we forget you?"

She lay there for a long time before she promised:

"I believe in you. I trust you. I'll never trust anyone again the way I trust the three of you."

"Me neither," Ted said.

"Me neither," Kimkim said.

"Nerds," Joar said.

"You're a nerd," Ali said, and held his hand.

They lay there like that for several hours, next to each other on the floor of Joar's room. Then they framed Kimkim's painting.

Joar clears his throat on the roof.

"That's probably . . . damn . . . I don't know how to say it. That's, like, one of my strongest memories. I thought about it every night in prison when I was trying to sleep."

Louisa is silent for at least twice as long as she usually manages, then she says:

"Fish read in a book that in Heaven, you get to choose one moment from your life. Your best moment. And then you get to feel like that forever. She said it doesn't matter if we live till we're eighty then, because that's just lots and lots and lots of nows. And one single really good now is enough."

"I had a lot of nows. Millions," Joar says gratefully.

Then he tells her how Ali asked:

"Do you think there'll be good food at the party when your painting wins the competition?"

"Of course there'll be good food. Rich people fucking love food," Joar said.

"Hope there's Champagne, then I can get as drunk as a skunk," Ali giggled.

"What date is it?" Ted asked.

"What?" Joar said.

"I mean . . . what date is the competition? When we have to hand the painting in?"

They hadn't even thought of that. Joar flew up and started hunting through drawers and bookshelves. He had hidden the newspaper containing the announcement, so he wouldn't accidentally wipe himself with it the next time the toilet paper ran out, but he had hidden it too well. So he went around and around the room in a rage over how damn smart he'd been. When he eventually looked under the last thing in the last drawer, and there it was, he leafed through it so fast that he tore the pages. Then he saw the date and breathed out so heavily that he almost fainted.

"A week from now," he gasped.

His three friends looked over his shoulder. It was the first time any of them had actually seen the announcement, and they would remember that moment as if the floor had vanished beneath them. Joar thought he had read it so many times that he had memorized every word, but even so, he had missed the most important thing. None of the others dared say anything, so in the end it was Ali who said, in slow despair:

"But it says . . . maximum age thirteen, Joar."

"What the hell are you talking about?"

"It says you have to be . . . thirteen or under," Ted repeated.

"What the hell does that mean?" Joar wondered furiously, as if his brain couldn't even comprehend the meaning of the numbers.

"It's a competition for children," Ted said.

"We aren't children anymore," Ali said.

"I cried then," Joar says quietly up on the roof.

FIFTY-FIVE

Disappointment is a powerful thing. Used correctly, it is stronger than fear, more terrible than physical pain, if you see it in the eyes of the one you love, you'll do almost anything to make it stop.

"The army ought to find a way to use disappointment as a weapon," Joar says up on the roof.

He bites his lip and digs in his pockets.

"Damn, I don't have any cigarettes . . . ," he mumbles.

"I do!" Louisa says, and reaches for her backpack.

"No, no, don't worry. I've stopped smoking, I just forget that sometimes," he says.

"You're very strange," Louisa informs him.

"I've heard that once or twice," he answers.

She dangles her feet over the edge of the roof and looks at all the houses she can live in now that she's going to be rich. She'd imagined it would feel different, because her dream was always to be rich with Fish. Now it's just frightening to own anything, because everything she's ever had, she's lost.

"It wasn't your fault, that thing with the competition . . . ," she tries to say encouragingly.

But of course she can see in Joar's eyes that everything is his fault. Everyone was his responsibility. He sighs:

"Do you know what the worst thing was? That when Kimkim realized there wasn't a competition, he didn't look disappointed at all. Not even sad. Just relieved. That's when I realized that I had to drive him away from this fucking town, any way that I could. Because if he had been given a single chance to stay here, he would have stayed forever."

The night comes padding in from all directions, dusk stuffs the town in a sack, lights go on in the houses down the hill like bullet holes in the darkness.

"So what did you do?" Louisa asks.

"I stole my dad's car again," Joar smiles.

Then he tells her about their very last adventure. Their last really big act of stupidity. He waited until it was dark, then he gathered all his friends and told them to come with him. He forced them to wait in the car while he climbed into Ted's basement to fetch something, then put it in the trunk and drove off. It was the middle of the night, so the friends couldn't see where they were going, didn't realize where they were until they were standing outside the museum again.

Joar took a large package out of the trunk of the car, balanced it above his head, and ran around to the back of the building, by the time his friends caught up to him he had already broken a window and slithered inside. The others slithered in after him, but a little too quickly, and landed in a shrieking heap on the floor with someone's feet in someone's hair and someone's knee in someone's stomach and someone's backside in someone's face.

"Iiidiiiooots," Joar groaned. "Are you trying to set the alarm off or what?"

"*You* were the one who broke in!" Ted said, before looking around and realizing that unfortunately he was definitely an accomplice now.

Ali muttered that it smelled funny, and Joar muttered back that maybe *she* smelled funny, and she hit him on the arm and he yelped and Ted hushed them both.

The only one standing completely silently was Kimkim. He was just staring at the white walls that seemed to reach hundreds of miles up to the ceiling, his head leaned back, gasping for air. When his eyes wandered from painting to painting, he looked like someone feeling sand between their toes for the first time, or making their first snow angel.

Then Joar carefully unwrapped the package he had collected from Ted's basement and took out Kimkim's own painting, with its driftwood frame. Only then did Ali and Ted understand what Joar's plan had been the whole time, so they helped him to carefully take another painting down from the wall and hang Kimkim's painting there instead. Then all four friends just stood there in the middle of the big room, lightheaded with happiness, and perhaps that was the first time Kimkim saw what the others had always known.

"Screw that competition. I just want you to get it into your head that your art belongs in a place like this. And that you belong here . . . too," Joar said.

Kimkim cried then. Ali stood next to Joar and held his hand and mumbled:

"This is actually your best idea ever. You idiot."

Up on the roof, Joar coughs, as if his body refuses to forget that it actually belongs to a smoker.

"It was a good plan. Really was. I just hadn't really thought through what we would do if a security guard showed up."

"What happened?" Louisa wonders.

"Well, a security guard showed up," Joar informs her.

"I get that! I'm not stupid! But what *happened*?"

Joar sighs.

"Well, we ran. And we were seriously damn good at running. We were damn bad at a lot of damn things, but running? We could do that. So when the alarm in the museum went off and that security guard arrived, we could have run away from him without any trouble. He was slow and really old. Well . . . yeah . . . now in hindsight, maybe he was like thirty-seven or something. But that was old to us at the time! Either way: he would never have caught us. No chance! The problem was just, well, that he didn't *have* to catch up with any of us, he just needed to catch up with the painting. We were really good at running, but we were pretty bad at carrying . . ."

Then he tells her that the alarm went off when Ali was looking for a light switch. So she would always tell everyone afterward that it was all her fault. All they heard was a low beeping sound from a different room of the gallery, they didn't even understand that they had triggered an alarm until they saw bright lights through a window and realized they were the headlights of a car. The security guard came running in, insanely old, but that didn't matter at all.

Joar and Ali tried to run with the painting between them, but Ali was taller than Joar, just tall enough for him to have to stand on tiptoe to kiss her. Highly impractical if you had to carry something together. So they stumbled and lost their grip, the stone floor was like ice, so the teenagers slid in one direction and the painting in the other. Ted and Kimkim tried to run in different directions, but of course they picked the wrong directions and collided.

The guard came rushing after them, or maybe "rushing" is a bit of an exaggeration, but he arrived with some degree of speed. He was doing his best. As he stopped breathlessly beside the painting, obviously he jumped to the only logical conclusion: the teenagers had broken in to steal it.

"And then everything got seriously confused," Joar explains to Louisa. "Because when the guard picked up the painting, we all came running back, and he couldn't understand what was going on, because, you know, thieves usually run in the other direction. So Ted stepped forward and said: 'Sorry we broke in! You don't have to call the police! We'll go now, we'll just take that with us . . .' and then we all pointed at the painting the guard was holding. And then of course the guard looked at us and said: 'Are you completely out of your minds? I can't give you the painting you were trying to steal!' And then I said: 'We weren't fucking trying to steal the damn thing, it's ours!' And then the guard started rolling his eyes and said: 'Yeah, that's really logical! You brought your own painting with you when you broke into a museum?'

And then I said: 'YOU can be logical, you asshole!' And then Kimkim said . . ."

Joar falls silent for a moment. Coughs again, like he's looking for his voice.

"Then Kimkim said what?" Louisa asks impatiently.

Joar collects himself.

"Then he said to the guard: 'You must see that that painting doesn't belong here. It's not nearly as good as all the others.' And the guard hesitated and said: 'I think it's . . . nice. But I don't know anything about art.' And then I said: 'So give it here, then! It's worth millions!' And sure, that really wasn't super smart, because that's when the guard said he was going to call the police. So then Ali cried out that surely he could see that it was *us* in the painting? But the guard looked at the painting and at first he didn't see anyone at all. He could only see the sea. So we had to show him, and then he brightened up and thought it was wonderful. He had tears in his eyes, I swear to God. But then he said that the kids there on the pier, they could be any kids at all. And then Ali said: 'We aren't kids anymore.' And then . . . hell . . . it was as if all the air went out of us all. And we probably looked so sad that the guard said: 'Okay. If you get out of here now, I won't call the police.' But obviously we couldn't leave without the painting. So it ended up becoming the world's weirdest hostage situation. So then the guard sighed: 'All right. Can you maybe call an adult who can come and confirm that the painting is yours?'"

The four friends had stood there thinking that that was nice of the guard, to give them that chance, but above all to think that they had an adult they could call. Joar's mom was at the hospital, Ted's mom was at work, Ali's dad was at a party, Kimkim's mom was passed out in her apartment on sleeping pills, and his dad was sitting in the darkness drinking whiskey in his. But that was when the artist who would one day be known as C. Jat suddenly raised his head and ran off a series of numbers from memory. The others didn't understand a thing until he blurted out: "I've got one! I've got an adult we can call!"

Joar peers over the edge of the roof. There's a car driving slowly up the hill, along the winding road between the run-down houses.

"Who was it? Who did you call?" Louisa asks impatiently.

"Here she comes now," Joar answers.

FIFTY-SIX

Ted gets out of the passenger side of the car and looks up at the roof anxiously.

"Why are you sitting up there? You might fall!" he calls to Louisa.

"What about me? I might fall too," Joar shouts back, insulted.

"You're old, you don't have so much to live for," Ted replies.

The driver's door opens and a woman in her seventies gets out. She's short and stern-looking, she looks a lot like the sort of woman who might well end up in prison if a young person asked if she needed help crossing the street. Ted calls to Joar to come down to the kitchen, but of course Joar calls back defiantly that no, they'll have to come up to the roof! Ted asks if Joar is insane, and Joar replies that Ted should stop being such a little coward. Then Ted looks a little like he might be thinking of saying that the woman next to him is far too old to sit on a roof. And the woman notices, and then she decides that she's *definitely* going to sit on the roof. So a few minutes later she's up there dangling her legs, and that's how Louisa meets Christian's mother.

"So, my dear, you're the one who's been given the most beautiful painting in the world?" she smiles.

"Yes," Louisa replies, heavy with guilt.

Then Christian's mother pats her on the knee, and Louisa doesn't actually hate it at all.

"Kim must have liked you an awful, awful lot, my dear. I'm sorry you lost him."

"I'm sorry you lost him too," Louisa says, and then she adds: "And I'm sorry you lost Christian. Ted told me about him."

"Thank you, my dear. Ted told me that you lost someone you loved too."

She holds out her finger and catches a tear as it rolls down Louisa's cheek, no adult has ever done that for her, so the question just tumbles out of Louisa:

"Did you get over it? Christian dying?"

The woman shakes her head sadly.

"No, no, my dear. You never get over death. Not if you're someone who loves. But it's easier if you're a parent. Then you don't have a choice. I have another child, Christian's younger sister, I have grandchildren now. People always say that you should live as if every day was your last, but when you have children you realize that you have to live as if every day was their first. That's hard for you to understand, you're only a child yourself—"

"I'm eighteen!" Louisa protests, as if the woman ought to be impressed.

"I'm sorry, you have so much life ahead of you, so many losses," the woman replies, and then she asks: "Do you see her everywhere? The person you lost?"

"Yes! It's like I see her out of the corner of my eye, all the time, in crowds . . . ," Louisa nods.

Then the woman holds Louisa's hand, and to her own surprise, Louisa lets her.

"The first years, I was angry every time that happened," the woman says. "I thought I heard Christian's voice in the supermarket, or saw his favorite sweater disappear around a corner, but when I ran after him it was someone else. Oh, I hated it! I was furious! Until one day I realized that it wasn't a curse, it was a blessing. Those were little winks from Heaven. It was Christian playing hide-and-seek with me, the way we did when he was little. So every time it happens now, every time I see him out of the corner of my eye, I whisper: 'Peekaboo.'"

They are interrupted by a curse. It's Ted, trying to climb out onto the roof without losing his footing, and of course losing his footing at once. He almost slides over the edge, Joar catches him at the very last second.

"How the hell are you still alive? Everyone else dies, but you're still here . . . ," Joar mutters when Ted finally sits down.

"I seem to be more difficult to kill than one might imagine," Ted admits.

The sun has gone down and the streetlamps have come on, the shadows dance around them. Louisa looks over her shoulder and whispers out into the darkness:

"Peekaboo."

They sit there in silence for a while. Then Christian's mother clears her throat authoritatively and announces:

"I'll make some calls tomorrow, my dear. It won't be hard to sell the painting, you just need to decide if you have any preferences."

"What does that mean?" Louisa asks.

"If you want to sell it directly to a collector, or if you want to sell it at auction. There'll probably be more media attention with an auction, and you might get more money for it."

Louisa shakes her head.

"No, no. No attention. Please."

"Well, then," the woman says, as if discussion of the matter is concluded.

"Can we go down to the kitchen now?" Ted wonders hopefully.

"No! I haven't finished the story of that night when we broke into the museum yet!" Joar says. "You think you're the only one allowed to tell stories here?"

But he lets Christian's mother tell the rest of it, because this part belongs to her. How her phone rang in the middle of the night and she was terrified, because she could never hear that sound without thinking something terrible had happened. And how a scared boy at the other end stammered that he had been given her number by Christian.

She mumbled back drowsily: "It's . . . you?"

Kimkim, more than a little confused, whispered back: "What? Who am . . . I?"

Then she gasped: "You're the boy my son called me about, that last time, when he said he had found one of us."

Kimkim got so nervous he slurred his words as he tried to explain, but she didn't even let him finish. She just asked for the address, getting dressed as she did so, then took a taxi to the museum and threw money at the driver before running inside. There she collided with the security guard. Unfortunately the guard immediately asked if she was all right, but in a tone that suggested she was extremely fragile, and isn't that typical of men? So the atmosphere wasn't great to begin with.

Then the guard explained that she had to identify a painting and confirm that it was painted by one of the children, and then she saw it. Dear Lord and all the angels in Heaven, she saw it and almost fell over. How did her heart not burst every button on her blouse? Incomprehensible.

"That's the one," Joar said, pointing.

"Yes, I can see perfectly well that it's *that* one!" she snapped so sharply that even Joar was lost for words.

"I . . . was just trying to help," he muttered, so Christian's mother softened a little and said:

"I'm sorry for my tone, but I teach art history! So of course I understand that *this* is the painting. Anyone can see that it doesn't belong here!"

Then Kimkim said disconsolately behind her:

"I know, I know, it doesn't belong here, it was stupid, all of this. Can we just be allowed to go now? We won't cause any more problems, I promise . . ."

But Christian's mother swept her hand excitedly around at all the other art on the walls, then pointed at his painting:

"Of course it doesn't belong here! None of the artists who painted those could paint like *this*!"

Kimkim was almost crying now:

"No . . . no, I can't paint like real artists, I get it! I haven't been to art school or anything, I—"

Then Christian's mother clapped her hands together in a mildly frustrated prayer and exclaimed:

"No, thank goodness, you haven't had any training! No one who's had any training paints like that! Art doesn't require training, dear child, art just needs friends."

Then she crouched down in front of his painting, and when she saw the skulls next to his name she sobbed so hard that no one really knew what to do. The guard cleared his throat.

"So . . . you can confirm that this painting belongs to the kids?"

"Yes, yes, yes!" she sobbed.

"And . . . can you drive the kids home too? They have a car parked outside, but I think the shortest one drove them here, because he's holding the keys, and how old can he be? Eleven?"

"FIFTEEN! And I drive a hell of a lot better than you! How old are you? Sixty?" Joar snapped.

"I'm thirty-seven," the guard said, a little hurt.

"You look ten years younger," Ali said quickly, and the guard brightened up.

"Like hell he—" Joar began, before being fully preoccupied with getting kicked in the shin really hard.

"Let's go, before he calls the police!" Ali hissed, and Ted and Kimkim nodded eagerly.

So Joar stepped forward to pick up the painting, but Christian's mother asked:

"May I . . . carry it?"

They let her. She carried it as if it were alive.

FIFTY-SEVEN

It's hard to listen to the end of a long story. Especially if you have a really important question that you don't dare ask.

It's a beautiful night, the air is light and clear and full of promise. Soon it will be warm, soon summer will be here, soon everything will be better. Joar and Ted and Christian's mother sit there on the roof under the stars and take turns telling Louisa everything.

They tell her about the car ride home from the museum. How Christian's mother asked if Kimkim had done any other paintings, and when he shook his head she whispered in astonishment:

"This was the first? What a gift to the planet, all the things you're going to create . . ."

Honestly, no one in the car understood what the hell that meant, but then she asked: "Have you done any drawings?" and then all four teenagers looked at her as if she were completely crazy.

Had he done any drawings?

When Ted's mom got home that evening she found to her horror that there was a strange lady in her basement. Ted's room was full of Kimkim's drawings, hundreds of them, carefully spread out across the whole floor, like a map of a boy's heart.

Ted's mother stood in the doorway, uncomprehending, and Christian's mother turned around and smiled: "One day you'll brag to everyone you meet that this young man once sat in your basement, drawing."

In Ted's mom's defense, she never did. Not even when Kimkim became world-famous. She just left the room, and saw that Ted, Joar, and Ali were sitting on the stairs so as not to be in the way, so she asked if they were hungry. Ali couldn't help herself from blurting out: "Is there any lasagna?"

Then Ted's mom did something incredibly unusual: she smiled.

"Are you the one who's been eating all my lasagna? I wondered where it was going. Neither of my boys have ever been that fond of it."

"It's my favorite food in the whole world," Ali said shyly.

"Lasagna?" Ted's mom repeated, surprised, because she had never heard a teenage girl say that.

But the teenage girl shook her head and corrected her:

"Your lasagna."

Then Ted's mom wrung her hands and didn't know where to look. That happens if you're not used to compliments.

"I can teach you," she said.

Ali stared at her as if Ted's mom had just promised to teach her how to conjure up kittens out of thin air.

"Teach me? To make . . . lasagna?"

"It isn't difficult," Ted's mom smiled, and that was the first time in years Ted could remember two smiles from her in the same evening.

Then she went up to the kitchen, followed by Ali, and a better lasagna has never been made, in that house or any other. Ted and Joar sat on the stairs listening to their laughter, then they heard Ali talk about her mother's death, and Ted's mother talk about Ted's dad's death. Ted hadn't heard his mom talk so much since long before the funeral.

"Did you love him a lot?" Ali asked.

"Still. I love him a lot still," Ted's mom replied.

"Is it horrible being an adult?" the girl asked.

"Unbearable," the mother replied. "You fail with almost everything, all the time."

"Not with lasagna," the girl pointed out.

"No, maybe not with lasagna, perhaps that's why I make it. One single thing I'm not bad at," the mother admitted.

Then Ali said, as if it were an altogether objective observation:

"You're not bad at being a mom. Everything works in your house.

The lights all come on when you click the switch, the toilet's clean, and there's always food in the freezer."

Ted and Joar sat on the stairs and heard Ted's mom answer:

"You only know me through my son. So of course you think I'm a good mom. But Ted isn't my doing, he's . . . a small miracle. The truth is, he's given me far more love than I've given him."

Ali thought for a long, long time before she said:

"Ted gives everyone more love. But I think you've both given each other the same amount: everything you had."

Then they ate lasagna.

Christian's mother gathered together all of Kimkim's drawings from the floor of the basement and carried them carefully out into the morning light, out into the world, and so the next adventure began.

A week or so later Kimkim was sitting with his friends at the crossroads, promising "tomorrow." It was Ted's idea to write their names on four rocks and bury them in the grass there between the houses where they had grown up, and when they all met again, they would dig them up. They sat beside each other with dirt on their fingers and Ali whispered:

"It wasn't me."

But of course it was. So then they all farted. They put the rocks in the ground and that was the last burial that year. And summer was over.

Ted sits on the roof and says to Louisa:

"It might sound like an unhappy ending, but only if you forget how many times during this story we've told you that someone laughed. How many really good *nows* is that? How many people ever have more?"

When autumn came, the Owl taught art at the high school again, but Kimkim never went back to his classroom. Christian's mother visited her son's grave every day, but suddenly one morning she wasn't there. She was standing in a schoolyard in a town many hours away, waiting for Kimkim. It was an art school, the principal there had done her a big favor, but she had insisted that she was doing the school one. The principal laughed then, but one day he would thank her. He would brag about that student every day for the rest of his career.

Kimkim said good-bye to his mom with a handshake, but she did something miraculous: she hugged him.

"I'm so sorry I didn't understand," she whispered in his ear. "Don't be like all the other children! Don't be normal!"

Kimkim didn't want to let go of her then, she had to force him to by wriggling out of his grasp. Children aren't responsible for their parents' happiness, but they still try. Inside her apartment lay a heap of his drawings, Christian's mother had been there and dropped them off, because she wanted the woman to understand. The woman did, eventually, and even the demons in her head probably got it then. They almost made their peace with her after that.

Kimkim's dad drove him to art school in his rusty old car. They didn't say much, but just as they were driving into the schoolyard, his dad mumbled:

"I hope you know I was never ashamed of you. I'm ashamed of myself."

Kimkim wanted to explain everything he felt then, but he didn't have enough words, so he said the biggest ones he knew:

"I love you and I believe in you, Dad."

His dad would no doubt have said the same thing back if he knew how. He had to take the bus home. He still had his son's drawing from the hospital chapel, it hung on his kitchen wall as a great treasure, but the rest of the apartment was almost empty. It wasn't until much later that Kimkim found out that his mom and dad had sold just about everything they owned, including his dad's car, to be able to buy everything he needed for art school. Christian's mother helped a lot too. When the men in the harbor found out, they organized a collection of their own, his dad would never brag about his son, but all his workmates down there would do it for him. One single good deed can't outweigh a lifetime of bad ones, but those men were prepared to give it a try. They were hard people who had lived hard lives, but one damn Saturday they would go to a damn museum and see a damn painting, and that feeling would be like a damn sunrise in their chests: that they had been part of something beautiful.

Kimkim's mom would never be entirely whole, some people never are, she got lost on her way home from the supermarket more and more often. She spent her last year living in a nursing home. Kimkim sent drawings every week, and she papered the walls with them. He was there when she died, he had just graduated from art school then, and sat by her bed for a long time afterward, holding her hand. As if the demons fell asleep on his lap.

A week later he went for a walk with his dad. They didn't say much, but there were little smiles here and there. They parted with a hug. When his dad went home that evening, he sat in the chair in his kitchen, surrounded by his son's drawings, and fell asleep calmly and gently. Kimkim buried both his parents on the same day. Then he left the town and never came back. The world was waiting.

The starry sky above the houses is making Louisa dizzy, after a while her eyes don't know if they're staring up at the universe or down into it. So she closes them and breathes slowly and then, at last, she asks the question she really doesn't dare ask:

"What happened to Ali?"

Joar and Ted lie there in silence, as if they are both hoping the other will say it, then they both start talking at the same time, the idiots. Ali would have liked that.

When she and Joar parted for the last time, they were sitting on the steps outside her house. Ali explained that her dad had found a job in another country, also by the sea, but not like here. By that sea there were long, chalk-white beaches. Summer never ended there.

"I'm going to learn to surf!" Ali said.

"You're probably going to be the fucking best at it," Joar nodded.

She grinned, wild and happy.

"You think?"

"When we met, you could hardly swim, now you swim better than any of us. You can learn to do any damn thing you want."

Then she kissed him so hard he fell off the step. When she left he gave her a red blanket, like Superman's cape. Then she flew.

They wrote letters to each other every week for several years. Not to brag, but Joar was right, she did end up being the best at surfing. She wrote to him that she had never felt so happy as when she was paddling out to sea, straight into the sunrise. Then she felt like she knew what she was doing on Earth, she wrote. How many people find something that makes them feel like that? How lucky was she?

Early one morning, not long after her eighteenth birthday, she went out into the water and never came back.

When Louisa hears that she cries so hard that the whole roof sways. She bitterly regrets asking. Because who can make someone grieve for a person they never even knew, so that it hurts this much? She cries so it feels like her ribs are breaking. Joar gets so unnerved by her tears that he eventually mumbles:

"It was . . . it was over twenty years ago."

"Not for ME! For me she died NOW!" Louisa snaps.

That's the worst thing with stories.

"For me too," Ted whispers.

And then Joar sits there under the stars and he too loses Ali all over again. That's the worst thing about death, that it happens over and over again. That the human body can cry forever.

"What is that thing you always say? About people living quietly . . . ?" Joar whispers.

"That's Henry David Thoreau," Ted whispers back through the darkness. "Most men lead lives of quiet desperation."

Joar nods slowly.

"Well, you can say a lot of things about Ali, but that's one damn thing she definitely didn't do. She wasn't quiet for one single damn day of her life."

They laugh. You've lived a pretty remarkable life if you can still make your humans do that, more than twenty years later.

"Hope she and Fish find each other in Heaven," Louisa says.

"Hope not! Or there won't be any Heaven left by the time we get there . . . ," Ted answers.

"Can I ask something?" Louisa asks, then asks immediately: "How do you cope with death?"

It's Christian's mother who answers:

"It's art that helps me cope. Because art is a fragile magic, just like love, and that's humanity's only defense against death. That we create and paint and dance and fall in love, that's our rebellion against eternity. Everything beautiful is a shield. Vincent van Gogh wrote: 'I always think that the best way to know God is to love many things.'"

"It's cool that we happened at all," Louisa whispers.

"Something like that," the mother smiles.

Then Ted tells Louisa the story of how Kimkim came home to bury his parents, not long after he left art school. And how he and Joar and Ted made a grave for Ali too, so they had somewhere to leave adopted flowers. They picked out a large rock and snuck into the churchyard at night and found an empty spot. Kimkim painted her name on the rock and surrounded it with small wings. Then they stole a shopping cart outside the supermarket and rode down the steepest hill in town, almost killing themselves in the process, and then Ali was with them. She was with them forever.

It was when they were sitting on the pier in the darkness that night and Kimkim whispered, “I think I’ll stay here now,” that everything changed.

“And do . . . what?” Ted asked in surprise.

“I don’t know. Work in the harbor, maybe?” Kimkim said, shrugging his shoulders.

That’s when Joar exploded in a rage like they’d never seen. He yelled at Kimkim for so long and so angrily that even Ted got upset. There was a terrible argument among all three of them, and in the end Kimkim and Ted stormed off, leaving Joar sitting alone on the pier.

Joar sits curled up on the edge of the roof now. Mumbles:

“If I’d asked him to stay, he would have stayed forever. Hell, I *wanted* him to stay. That’s why I had to . . . yell terrible things at him. I shouted that I’d had to fucking look after him since preschool, but that I couldn’t do it anymore, because I can’t look after an infinite damn number of people! Now he had to damn well look after himself! I was as cruel as I could possibly be . . .”

Ted leans his head as close to his friend’s shoulder as he can without touching him, and admits:

“It took me a long time to realize why you did that. But you knew that the only thing keeping Kimkim in this town was the fact that he didn’t want to leave you. So you drove him away. He cried that night, but I know you cried more. And I told him that he ought to go traveling, see the world, and in the end he agreed. So he went. And I saw you, you’d climbed into a tree and sat there watching the taxi as it drove away.”

Joar’s voice swings between two different ages, fifteen and now:

“And then he called me, months later, from somewhere in Asia. In the middle of the night! He didn’t understand that there was a time difference, the moron. He’d found a mural, or whatever the hell it’s called. He sounded like he was in love, he said that the first person he wanted to tell about it was me. And then apparently he forgot that I was an asshole. And I remember him talking, and I just thought that he sounded so . . . happy. He *could* be happy. Just not here.”

"Did you ever meet again?" Louisa asks, and Joar smiles a broken little smile.

"I had problems for a few years. I was a damn idiot. I was drinking a lot. I stood at the airport a couple of times, but I never dared get on the plane. I didn't want him to see me so messed up. I wanted him to remember me young. Remember me . . . beautiful."

"It's hard to be an adult," Ted says.

"It's hard to be a child too," Louisa points out.

"Speak for yourself, I was awesome at being a child!" Joar says.

"Yes. Yes, I can imagine," Louisa admits.

Then Joar glances at Ted and says:

"I thought I'd managed to scare Ted here away too. But he kept coming to visit me, the whole damn time, even though I was drunk and told him to go to Hell. He's bad at that, Ted is, he really can't go to Hell . . ."

"He doesn't like traveling," Louisa says.

Joar laughs so hard he's shaking, and part of the roof comes loose. Now the rain will get in. He's bound to blame it on Ted.

"And Kimkim never came home again?" Louisa asks, and Ted answers:

"No. He stood at the airport a few times too. But it's scary to go back to a place where you hurt so badly and felt so small as he did here, you think you're going to become the same person again. Maybe you'll understand that when you get older."

"I understand it now," Louisa says, and Ted feels ashamed.

"Yes, you probably do. I'm sorry about that."

"What about at the end, then? When he got sick?" she wonders.

Joar waves the leg with the ankle monitor.

"I couldn't travel then. Good excuse for a coward."

"Did you talk on the phone?"

"Yeah. The last time was just a few weeks before he died."

"What did you say?"

"We talked about Ali. We told stupid jokes. I told him I loved him."

"What did he say?"

Joar glances at Christian's mother and replies:

"He said that thing that you always said, the thing that painter said. That you should paint like the birds sing. But Kimkim said it was never like that for him. He said he painted the way we laughed."

In a few hours the sun will rise, the air will be a degree or two warmer, summer will be on its way. It's probably just her imagination, but Louisa could swear she can hear a cat meowing out there in the darkness, sleepy and happy and on its way home. It's probably Ted's imagination too, but he can hear both the cat and the sound of birds taking flight, the gentle rustle of wings. Then he suddenly hopes that the cat doesn't sound so happy because there's one bird missing. That ruins the romanticism of the moment, it really does.

Soon the world will smell of rain. As the first drops land on the roof from the sky, the four people get up and crawl back into the house.

Ted is obviously a little taken aback when he sees Louisa's drawing of Kimkim on Joar's fridge.

"You gave that to me!"

"You gave it back, you had your chance!" Louisa flashes back.

"You can't just do that!" Ted snaps, as if he's considering contacting a lawyer.

"No? It was super easy! I just *did* it!" she points out, like a five-year-old inventing her own rules in a game.

They carry on like that for a while, and will carry on carrying on, because Joar is right. Ted will never abandon her.

"Little brat," Ted mutters.

"Miserable old bastard," she grins.

Joar carefully lifts the painting out of the box while this is going on, just as Christian's mother walks into the kitchen. She has to lean against the wall then, the old art history teacher.

"Dear God . . . it's incredible . . . completely incredible," she exclaims in delight.

Louisa doesn't understand her reaction at first, because it looks like Christian's mother is seeing the painting for the very first time. It takes a handful of seconds before Louisa realizes that the woman isn't looking at the painting at all. She's looking at Louisa's drawing.

FIFTY-EIGHT

Louisa finds one last way to make Ted really, really nervous before the night is over. She's pretty creative when it comes to annoying him, you have to give her that.

"This is a really, really bad idea," he repeats time after time in the car.

Christian's mother is driving, Louisa is sitting in the front, Ted is sitting in the back hissing "Watch out!" through his teeth every time a medium-sized leaf drifts across the road.

"Ted doesn't like being in a car much," Christian's mother says apologetically.

"Ted doesn't like anything very much," Louisa sighs.

"I like lots of things! Just not things that move!" Ted sulks.

Christian's mother smiles at Louisa.

"He only likes books. When all his friends moved away, Kimkim to art school and Ali abroad and Joar to the other side of town, I told Ted he could come and see me and read books whenever he wanted. From then on I couldn't get rid of him."

"You've got an awful lot of books," Ted says in his own defense from the back seat.

Then Christian's mother explains about the large room in her house that she turned into a library after Christian died. Ted came there every day. There was a comfortable chair, a safe place, and shelves filled with imaginary friends. That was why he became a teacher. Because he wanted to give that security to other children, teach them how to have adventures without moving.

"So you became a history teacher. The most booooring subject possible," Louisa informs them.

"You're boring!" Ted retorts.

Then Christian's mother looks sternly in the rearview mirror.

"Ted! Stop being so immature!"

Ted glares sullenly out the window.

"She started it."

Then, unfortunately, Christian's mother sees something else in the mirror and exclaims anxiously:

"Uh-oh. Police."

Louisa raises her eyebrows.

"Don't tell me you don't have a driver's license either, like Joar's mom?"

"Of course I've got a driver's license, my dear!" Christian's mother snorts, before adding: "Just not . . . at the moment. It's on hold for a while."

Then it's Ted's turn to sound anxious:

"How can a driver's license be on hold?"

Christian's mother groans.

"I was driving a tiny bit too fast. So the court took it away from me. But if you think about it, that's only because I'm too good at driving. So I know how to drive fast."

"So you're saying the court took your license away because they were jealous?" Ted asks.

"Absolutely. That sounds good. We'll use that excuse," she nods.

"If the police have dogs, I'll never forgive you," Ted gasps, and Louisa sighs:

"For goodness' sake, Ted, can you just try not to be yourself for a little while?"

He defends himself by saying:

"This was *your* idea! Even Ali and Joar never had ideas this bad!"

Louisa whispers to Christian's mother:

"If the police stop us, I'll say he kidnapped me."

"Louisa! That isn't funny!" Ted shouts.

But Christian's mother thinks it's so funny that she giggles so hard that she accidentally puts her foot on the brake pedal really hard. Meaning that the police car almost drives into the back of them. One of the police officers gets out and walks over, and asks if everything's okay.

"Well, apparently I'm either driving too fast or I'm driving too slow, you're never happy . . . ," Christian's mother snaps.

The police officer looks a little hesitant.

"Where are you going?"

"He's kidnapped us," Louisa says immediately, nodding toward the back seat.

The police officer looks at Ted, the world's unhappiest man, with his dirty suit jacket and taped glasses and his whole face covered in bruises. Then the police officer laughs.

"A kidnapper. Sure, sure . . ."

Then he wishes them a pleasant evening and drives off. Ted has never felt so insulted in his entire life. The women, old and young alike, laugh so hard that the car rocks. It isn't a bad night, not a bad night at all.

They stop outside the museum. Louisa breaks in through one of the bathroom windows. Ted hits his head when he crawls in, and has to tape his glasses again. Christian's mother finds a spare place on one of the walls. That's where they hang Kimkim's painting. They sit side by side on the floor and look at it.

"Do you still think this is a bad idea?" Louisa asks.

"Yes! You should sell it and take the money and have a fantastic life," Ted answers.

She shakes her head sadly.

"That won't work. If I see this painting as money, then I'll see all paintings as money. Then I'll never be able to paint anything."

Christian's mother is sitting beside her, and there is such a long silence that she feels that perhaps they're expecting her to say something, so she does what she usually does and quotes a poet: Tomas Transtromer:

"*Don't be ashamed to be a human being—be proud! Inside you one vault after another opens endlessly. You'll never be complete, and that's as it should be.*"

Louisa hugs herself then. Ted carefully cleans his glasses and says:

"Kimkim used to sit in a window looking down at the street and ask how everyone else could bear to be human."

"What did you tell him?" Louisa asks.

"I said that maybe we could learn how."

"Have you figured it out yet?"

"Maybe I'm on my way. That's all anyone can be."

Then Louisa's face lights up.

"On your way? So . . . more traveling?"

"Shut up," he smiles.

She doesn't, of course.

"It belongs in a museum," she says to the painting.

"So do you," Ted tells her.

He's said some nice things, but that could be a record.

"What are we going to do now?" she asks.

"You're asking me? This was *your* idea!" he snaps.

"So? Am I suddenly supposed to have another plan? You're the grown-up here!"

"So I'm supposed to have a plan? I can't even fall asleep on a train without you leaving me!"

"I left you one time. ONE TIME! Can you just stop going on about it?"

"NO!"

Louisa hides her gaze in the painting for a long time before she mumbles:

"Okay. I won't do it again."

"Okay," Ted mutters.

"Okay!" she repeats.

"We'll figure out a plan," he mutters, annoyed.

Like a dad would.

Then Christian's mother clears her throat, puts her hand tenderly on Louisa's shoulder, and says:

"My dear, I have a suggestion for what you can do next . . ."

That's the happy ending.

FIFTY-NINE

The alarm goes off when they're about to climb back out through the window. It's mostly Ted's fault, Louisa will explain to everyone. They crawl out onto the grass and run to the car, arguing. Christian's mother drives away like someone who really, really shouldn't have a driver's license. The following day the local newspaper writes about the break-in, but it takes several days before anyone discovers that the thieves didn't actually steal anything, but left something behind instead.

When the story eventually spreads, it gets told on news broadcasts all across the globe, about how the world-famous painting, which was bought at auction by an anonymous buyer just before the artist's death, has now suddenly appeared in a museum in his hometown. Tourists come from near and far to see it. Journalists try to uncover the true story behind the mystery, they call it "the reverse heist," and several of them phone the man who owns the auction house that sold Ted the painting.

So one day the man from the auction house calls Ted and says that unfortunately he's lost Ted's phone number. Ted doesn't understand what he means at first, so the man kindly explains that he loves art, he loves it so much that sometimes he loses his mind.

"You tend to forget these things, when you've been selling paintings for millions for long enough, that it all started with falling in love. But when I read about *The One of the Sea*, I was reminded of how much I liked it. I stood for hours just looking at it before we sold it. Not because it's perfect, but because it isn't. It's one of the most human works of art I've ever seen. I was pleased to hear that it's hanging in a museum now. Some works of art shouldn't be owned by anyone. They should belong to everyone."

"I agree," Ted says, whereupon the man repeats:

"So I'm afraid I can't find your phone number. And I'm afraid all the documents about the sale with your name on them have disappeared. So when reporters call me and ask, I won't be able to help them."

Then he hangs up. The painting remains in the museum, and no one ever finds out how it got there. That too becomes a pretty good story.

Ted gets another call as well. It's the conductor from the train. He still has the box containing the artist's ashes, he's been trying to get ahold of Ted since that night when Ted ran off the train. Eventually he got ahold of the mother who had taken Ted's suitcase and the painting, and she still had Ted's number on the scrap of paper he had given her on the platform. It's . . . a long story.

The conductor promises to send the ashes to Ted, but not by mail, of course, because you can't rely on the post office. He sends it via conductors. From one train to the next, all the way home.

"Call me sometime, if you like," the conductor says.

"Yes, of course, I'll call to let you know it's arrived!" Ted says, misunderstanding.

The conductor laughs.

"No, I mean . . . you can call me sometime. If you like."

Then Ted blushes. He probably isn't ready to fall in love again yet, but it's nice to be asked.

"I might even take another trip by train," he says shyly.

"I'll keep an eye out for new passengers," the conductor promises.

Kimkim is buried on a day that feels like the start of summer. The minister reads from the Bible, Christian's mother reads poetry, Louisa paints small wings on the gravestone. Once the minister has gone, Louisa and Joar slip away and pick up Ali's stone and move it next to Kimkim's. Joar has been given permission to attend, even though he's wearing the ankle monitor, because Ted found out that they make exceptions for funerals. As they stand there covering the graves with adopted flowers, Joar asks very seriously if they could pretend that Ted has died and is getting buried tomorrow? Because Joar would really like to go to the movies.

On their way back from the churchyard they come across some children drawing on the road outside their houses with chalk. Louisa stops and asks if she can join in, then she draws skulls and cockroaches that look so alive that the children's eyes almost pop out of their heads. When the children's parents call them home for dinner, one little girl turns around and says: "You can keep the chalk! I've got more!"

Louisa takes it and draws on every single wall between the church and the sea. She finally gets to see the pier. The old harbor district is different now, the town has built luxury apartments there, and there are restaurants with complicated names and shops no one can understand what they're selling, and there are angry people with little dogs everywhere. But when they walk to the end of the pier and sit there dangling their legs over the edge, Louisa sees exactly what the four friends saw twenty-five years ago: an endless sea, a great friendship, a true love story. She hears them giggle. Detects the smell of a fart. All of it.

"Do you think you can learn how to live without Ali and Kimkim?" she asks as they're slowly walking back to Joar's place.

Joar just grins and points to a large house.

"We aren't without them. Kimkim lives over there. And sometimes he lives there. And Ali lives there, I see her every day when she's taking the trash out."

Ted points at other houses and tells stories and fantasies. Their humans arc playing hidc-and-scck.

"I think Fish lives there today," Louisa eventually decides.

"Yeah, that's a good house. One of my favorites," Joar nods happily.

They walk close to each other and see their friends everywhere all day long. Winks from Heaven.

"Have you decided yet?" Louisa asks, looking at Ted.

"About what?"

"About what you're going to do with your life."

The corners of his mouth twitch nervously. He starts hesitantly, but then the words just pour out of him:

"I found out what happened to the boy who attacked me. He's in prison. They have schools, in prison. They have . . . teachers. I thought I might be good at that. It's a stupid idea."

Louisa shakes her head.

"It isn't stupid."

"It's a bit stupid," Joar interjects, nodding to the leg where Ted got stabbed.

But as they walk they notice that Ted is actually moving better and better, less and less uncomfortably. Getting stabbed with a knife is a trauma for the whole body, his leg was probably the part that healed quickest, it was other parts of Ted that were limping. Slowly, slowly he's daring to be a person again. One day, not long from now, Joar will even take him out for a bicycle ride again. Dear God, how they will argue then.

"You'll be a really good teacher in a prison," Louisa says encouragingly, and adds: "Plus, it's a bonus that there are armed guards to protect you, because obviously you need that."

Joar roars with laughter, and then Louisa turns around and asks quickly:

"So what are *you* going to do, then?"

"What the hell do you mean?" Joar snaps back.

"With the rest of your life?"

"What the hell kind of question is that?"

"Look, I know you're old, but you're not *that* old. You can still do something."

Joar looks like he's never thought about that. After a long while he says sullenly:

"I might try to set up a damn business repairing engines. I might start a damn workshop in my fucking backyard."

"I can paint you a sign," she smiles.

Joar thinks for a long time. Then he grunts, with the most irritating declaration of love a person like him can give:

"As long as you don't stay."

She promises.

The next day Christian's mother calls a certain principal she knows. He sighs that he's only doing this as a favor to her, but she insists that she's the one doing the school a favor. One day she is proved right, again. Ted and Joar empty their bank accounts to make sure Louisa has everything she needs when she goes. Well, it's mostly Ted who funds it. But Joar makes coffee while Ted goes to the bank, and that counts too, if you were to ask Joar.

So Louisa gets to go to art school. She almost completely manages to avoid learning anything at all from the teachers, it has to be said, but she makes friends. Some are classmates, but most of them are men and women who have been dead for hundreds of years. She goes to art galleries, she cries, she finds out how hard her heart can beat. She grows up, she paints every day, she tries to learn to be a human being. One morning she packs a bag and sets off, traveling by train and boat and even airplane, all the things she has only seen in movies. She sees the world, then the world sees her. Her art becomes famous. She becomes someone else's postcard.

One day she will be riding in a big black car in a bustling city far away, and suddenly she will yell at the chauffeur to stop. At the far end of an alleyway a teenager wearing a hoodie will be painting the wall of a building. Louisa will approach cautiously with her hands raised, with paint stains all over her fingertips, to show what she is. The teenager will back away warily, but won't run. Louisa will stand close to the wall, breathing in the painting, in the middle of an explosion of storm and longing, and then she will know.

Ted stays in the town by the sea. He becomes a teacher again. He lives an ordinary life, it goes slowly, but perhaps he's getting ready to fall in love again. He rents a small house on the same street where he grew up, from his bedroom window he can see the crossroads where he always called out "tomorrow" to his best humans. The four rocks that they wrote their names on are still buried in the grass there. On weekends he goes by train to a town an hour away, his big brother has a job there and their mom has moved into his basement. Ted sits in the kitchen and plays cards with her. Before he leaves, he says good night, first to her, then to all the ghosts.

He has a good relationship with his brother, apart from the fact that his brother keeps dogs, they don't like Ted and the feeling is definitely mutual. But his brother's wife is a loud, funny woman who likes cold grilled cheese sandwiches, flat Coca-Cola, and stale cheese puffs. They never have children, but there are kids in the next house, and one afternoon one of them knocks on the door and asks if Ted's brother perhaps gives piano lessons. Because they have all heard him playing through the walls. That's a really good day.

From time to time Ted goes to see Christian's mother and talks about poetry, sometimes they read fairy tales, but usually they just sit in silence together in the same room.

The minister at the church eventually realizes that there is one gravestone too many in the churchyard, but he never says anything. Who would it be disturbing? The dead? They're all busy anyway, playing peekaboo. When the townspeople find out where Kimkim is buried, there's a line out through the gates to lay flowers there. In the evening Christian's mother comes and helps the minister pick up the flowers and put them on graves that no one visits.

One damn Saturday Ted knocks on Joar's damn door. It's early as hell, Joar points out, but Ted just tells him to hurry up. They need to be there when it opens, before it gets crowded, and on the way out Joar yawns that perhaps being in prison or wearing an ankle monitor wasn't so bad after all. They take Joar's dad's old car, nobody knows how he's managed to keep the old wreck running, but he's good at keeping things alive. He gets that from his mom.

He and Ted drink a damn cup of coffee and drive to a damn museum, arriving before it gets damn crowded. They pay for their damn tickets and walk to the very far end, where there's a damn painting hanging. They stand there looking at it for an hour, but really for a whole summer. Then Ted feels something touch his fingertips, and it takes him several seconds to realize that it's Joar, holding his hand.

One evening, Ted wakes up in the middle of the night because the phone is ringing. He answers, half asleep, and the voice at the other end starts babbling immediately.

"Louisa?" he mumbles, confused.

"Yes! Of course it's me!" she yells.

She never says hello when she calls, she always just starts talking, because she knows Ted has two seconds every time where his heart is in free fall otherwise, because he always thinks something terrible must have happened. It's actually incomprehensible that a man who worries as much as he does hasn't had a heart attack. Especially considering that he's so very, very, very old.

"Is everything okay?" he grunts.

"Why do you sound so weird?" she asks.

"It's the middle of the night," he informs her.

"Oh! Right, yes, the time difference. It's evening here!" she replies.

"How nice for you."

"Were you asleep?"

"In the middle of the night? Yes, most normal people usually are."

"You're not normal in any way," she laughs, making the phone rattle.

"Can we talk tomorrow?" he asks, and closes his eyes.

"No, no, wait! I just want to tell you something!"

"What?"

"I've found one."

"One what?" he mumbles.

"One of us!" she replies confidently.

First she hears a bang, when Ted drops the phone on the floor. Then she hears his voice again, wide awake now.

"Tell me," he whispers.

So Louisa tells him everything: about a teenager in an alleyway and a painting on the wall of a building. She tells him about the speed a heart can beat at, which no one who's stopped being young can remember. She talks on and on, and Ted listens, and Heaven leans closer to the roof of the house to hear. Louisa tells him about art so beautiful that just seeing it makes you too big for your body, a sort of happiness so overwhelming that it's almost unbearable.

"When I was standing in front of that painting, I forgot to be alone, I forgot to be afraid, do you understand?" she says.

Of course Ted understands. If you've experienced it once, you never forget it. If not, there probably isn't any way to explain.

"If that artist is one of us, really one of us, you have to do whatever you can to help," he says.

"I know," she says proudly.

And so the next adventure begins.

"You sound happy," he smiles.

"I am. You sound happy too."

"Maybe I'm on my way."

"That's all anyone can be, Ted. On our way!"

"You sound grown-up."

"You sound old."

"I've always been old."

More rattling on the line. Then she asks:

"Can I ask something?"

"Preferably not," he yawns.

"Well, it isn't really a question, it's more of a suggestion."

He replies with a sigh, and she of course interprets that as enthusiasm, so she goes on:

"I know what you ought to do, Ted, with the rest of your life! You ought to write a book!"

Ted is sitting on the edge of his bed. The sun is on its way up outside the window. He presses his feet gently against the floor, making one of the floorboards creak. Then he laughs quietly.

"What would someone like me write a book about?"

ACKNOWLEDGMENTS

Neda. Eighteen years together and you can still knock me over with a single look from across a crowded room. I know I'm an annoying idiot, but if I can be any man, I want to be yours. I promise you half of the french fries, forever.

My children. I'm sorry I'm so weird, I'm sorry I forget where I parked the car so often, I'm sorry I ate all your candy last night. I hope you know I'm doing my very best, being your dad. It's my greatest adventure. I'm so proud of you.

Donkey, our German shepherd, who drives me absolutely crazy, which probably saves me from actually going crazy.

Peter Borland, my editor, for sticking with me through this entire project. Thanks for not giving up on me. **Libby McGuire,** for the continuous support and encouragement. **Niklas Natt och Dag,** who's shared an office with me for sixteen years without changing the locks. I believe in you.

Vanja Vinter and **Christine Edhäll,** for reading this book over and over (and over) when I was struggling, and helping me find my way. I'll never forget it.

My mother and **my father,** who always made sure I had books in my hands and food on my table.

My sister and **Paul** and **E** and **J.** Build all the Lego. All of it.

Riad Haddouche, Junes Jaddid, Erik Edlund, and all my other friends from the town by the sea. **David Magee,** for all the emails. **Rita Wilson,** for all the texts, all the thoughts, all the support. **Carl Stanley,** for the long walks and talks. **Johan Jureskog** and **Polly Jureskog,** for marvelous dinners in times when we really, really needed them the most. **Philip de Giorgio,** for constantly reminding me of how fucking old I am. **Alex Schulman,** for reading a very early draft of this story and giving invaluable advice.

Kim Schefler and **Michelle Elsner,** for being much more than our attorneys. If you hadn't stepped in when you did, I would have retired. **Håkan Rudels** at Bonnier, for being fair and honest, even in strange times. **Tor Jonasson,** without whom my career wouldn't have been what it is. **Ariele Fredman Stewart,** who in many, many ways built the American part of it.

Everyone at Atria and Simon & Schuster, for giving me a home away from home. **Adam Dahlin** and **Håkan Bravinger** at Norstedts, for giving me a new one here at home. **Byrd Leavell, Sophie Baker,** and everyone else at United Talent Agency, for getting everything together.

Sandra Pettersson, Christoffer Carlsson, Amad Osman, Miguel Guerrero, Marcus Leifby, Jakob Kakembo Andersson, and **Petter Eneman.**

But most of all: Anyone who has read this, or any other of the stupid little detours the voices in my head have taken me on in the last ten years or so. Telling stories is the only time I really feel like myself. Thanks for following along.